ANOTHER
PAN

THE SECOND OF
ANOTHER SERIES

ANOTHER PAN

DANIEL & DINA NAYERI

CANDLEWICK PRESS

Copyright © 2010 by Daniel Nayeri and Dina Nayeri

First edition 2010

Library of Congress Cataloging-in-Publication Data

Nayeri, Daniel.
Another Pan / Daniel and Dina Nayeri. — 1st U.S. ed.
p. cm.
Summary: While attending an elite prep school where their father is a professor, Wendy and John Darling discover a book which opens the door to other worlds, to Egyptian myths long thought impossible, and to the home of an age-old darkness.
ISBN 978-0-7636-3712-5
[1. Characters in literature — Fiction. 2. Mythology, Egyptian — Fiction. 3. Fantasy.]
I. Nayeri, Dina. II. Title.
PZ7.N225An 2010
[Fic] — dc22   2010006606

10 11 12 13 14 15 BVG 10 9 8 7 6 5 4 3 2 1

Printed in Berryville, VA, U.S.A.

This book was typeset in Slimbach.

Candlewick Press
99 Dover Street
Somerville, Massachusetts 02144

visit us at www.candlewick.com

"Hello?"

"Hey. All set for tomorrow?"

"D&D's writing session? Sure, I have things covered on my end."

"Let's go over it again, just in case."

"OK, for a level-one spat, I distract her with background music."

"For level two, I have a purse full of Snickers bars ready."

"For level three, I turn off the Internet access, and they lose Skype connection for fifteen minutes . . ."

"At which point, I step in with the Snickers."

"And for a level-four fight . . . Um, what do we do for level four?"

"Let's go with pastries; pray we never see a four. See you at Christmas."

"OK. Good night."

This book is dedicated to our friends and family.
For giving us the happy thoughts.

THE DARKNESS BREAKS IN

New York (spring)

All nights come to an end—that is to say, all nights see the break of day. For those of us who are afraid of the dark, or at least not very fond of vampires or impending alarm clocks, thankfully, all nights do end. As the sun comes crashing up over the horizon, flooding the world with flashes and revelation, the night and all its creatures retreat, crawling back into their caves. For most of us, that's great news. Sure, there are plenty of wonderful uses for night—sound sleep, for one; stargazing and fireworks, for two more—but it is a documented fact that evil is a nocturnal animal. There are no *day*mares, for example. No one has ever brought a car to a screeching stop to let a werewolf cross the road at noontime. It's not how things work. The only monsters that prowl in the daytime are orthodontists.

When it comes to death and destruction and all that, night is right. Under its downhearted blanket, all sorts of things can go wrong. For instance, you could take a tumble down a flight of stairs. Or you might fail to see a hundred reptilian tongues salivating on your pillow, just waiting for that nest you call hair. *Or* you could scream out when the snakes get you, and *someone you love* could take the tumble down the stairs. And now you've done it. You and the dark night and all its nighttime creatures. It's easy to suppose that that's why daytime was invented. One might even take solace in the fact that all nights come to an eventual end. All nights, that is, except for one.

You probably don't remember.

The dawn froze in New York City so that the day was long overdue, but no one seemed to notice it. The gridlock on Fifth Avenue was wound tighter than a mummy with a mortgage, but the drivers sat politely in their cars, not making a single noise. A flock of pigeons was kind enough to preserve the silence by pausing in mid-flutter, twelve feet off the ground, in a static explosion of fungal breadcrumbs and greasy feathers. Even the motionless wave of rainwater almost splashing a passing woman, the bicyclist whistling at the oblivious tourist, the foulmouthed businessman holding a cappuccino to his mouth and a cell phone to his ear—all were frozen in mid-step, stride, or syllable.

The only thing moving in the still city was the lady with silky clothes and ivory skin and blond hair. The governess Vileroy. Her body was broken, her hair singed, her elegant clothes in tatters. As she stumbled through the bedroom of her Manhattan apartment, she clutched her throat and gagged in short spasmodic bursts. Her carefully constructed body was falling apart around her, lifetimes of splendid trappings ripping away like curtains. She seemed to be bending in odd directions, like a tangled marionette. Her hacking was the only noise to be heard.

The lady called Vileroy climbed out of the shattered window, then her still-female form angled down the fire escape and crawled to the street below. Somewhere far off, a street lamp extinguished itself. She lurched along the streets of the Upper East Side, bits of skin and hair flying away, her face contorted in agonizing fits of pain. She crossed a road—half woman, half nebulous haze—moving past a car and then a bicyclist, who was pursing his lips to whistle at an oblivious tourist. She whistled her own tune. It was the wheezing sound of trapped air escaping a dead body. Another fit of coughing consumed her, and a black mist escaped her mouth. She was crawling now, on what little remained of her four limbs.

The lady continued to inch forward, pulled onward by a beckoning force. Soon, she no longer inched or lurched, but seeped through the city streets like smog, unseen and undetected. A demon with no purpose, a darkness with no light. A governess with no children. She paused to listen, and the voice called to her again, taunting her. It was the voice of a new darkness. A voice that she knew she needed in order to survive. It was not temporary, like her crumbling body. It was something more precisely measured on the eternal scale. *The voice of a black divinity bigger than this individual demon.* The voice pierced the billowing black fog that was slowly leaking out of the dark lady, leaving behind silky clothes and ivory skin and blond hair. Soon, the lady was engulfed in a sea of reeking black fog—the stench of all the world's malice, hatred, and merciless intentions.

Her one devilish eye, a crucifix branded in its blue core, did not abandon her as she lost her last vestiges of humanity. It was her most true part—the only part of her that could never die and fall away. When the hindrance of the broken body was gone, the black fog billowed on . . . until it reached the Marlowe School.

In the tranquil night, Marlowe looked like an ancient monument, grand and imposing. No one saw the thick, polluted cloud overtake the school and disappear into the basement. No one was there to see the broken eye rush hungrily for whatever lay under Marlowe.

Damaged and starving for deliverance, the darkness was drawn deeper inside. Past the marble hallways and satellite classrooms and lockers stuffed with hoodies, Harvard applications, and half-eaten snack cakes, it crept toward its purpose. The basement was dusty, full of old, forgotten exhibits and books with the edges curled shut. In the corner was a computer graveyard overrun with cracked keyboards and monitors the size of headstones. But recently, a section had been taped off for a new shipment. Statues, boxes, and aging artifacts were piled together around a sarcophagus. A yellow sign rested against the wall:

Marlowe Egyptian Exhibit
Courtesy of the British Museum
Location: Barrie Auditorium
Curator: Professor George Darling

Among the chaos of the unassembled exhibit, the demon eye of the former governess devoured the scene until it found a small statue in a far corner. *Neferat.* A plaque rested at the feet of the oddly female statuette, its body curved, its head worn by time but clearly elongated, like a wolf or a jackal. The darkness did not linger long. This was the source of the calling. This was the timeless task. This was the place where she would rest, alone and undisturbed, until she had regained her strength.

The statue shook.

Then the eye was gone, the last wisps of fog snaking their way into the long but featureless head. For a brief moment, stone became flesh and the statue's head turned. An alabaster ball that had been its left eye fell out and rolled across the floor. A new eye flashed blue in its place and broke into four parts.

Out in the streets, the morning came alive again.

A woman felt a chill and blamed it on a splash of rainwater.

A bicyclist reeled at a stench and turned his nose at a tourist.

A businessman spit out a mouthful of sour cappuccino.

The governess Vileroy was gone. But not truly gone. The night began to end, but the darkness was only just starting, preparing once again to haunt the Marlowe School.

For the three months of summer vacation, when the school was empty and no teachers or parents were watching for signs of excess dirt, unexplained toxins, or any kind of danger to their children's health or comfort, the darkness lurked, rebuilding a lost strength, polluting Marlowe from below, slowly blackening the air, so that in the fall, when the administration came back from their European travels to open the doors onto a new academic year, they couldn't really tell what was different. Something was different, though. . . .

❖❖❖

No one had seen the bland, plain-looking woman with poor posture crawling out of a closet in the basement—clearly sick, she coughed into a white lace handkerchief and wiped the sweat from her pale face. She hadn't wanted to be summoned into the world so soon. Three months is nothing on the eternal scale, and the once-beautiful governess had not yet gained back all that she had lost. She was desperate to creep back into the dark, past the ancient statue, and into the unseen places where injured demons recover and lick their wounds. But an old child had come looking for her, and so she was back in the world of the living in this frail human body—not fully healed. She was no longer beautiful. No longer tall or regal. Her face was scrunched together, her nose too fat, her eyes (even the unchanging branded eye) too small. Her blue sweater was moth-eaten and smelled like disease. And so no one noticed the new school nurse as she staggered into her office.

The Year of John

New York (summer)

The summer between middle school and high school is an irreversibly, undeniably crucial time for an image makeover—in fact, if you're looking to reinvent yourself, it's a once-in-a-lifetime opportunity. Particularly if you happen to be a thirteen-year-old, skinny *ex*-nerdling who is starting high school a year early. It won't help if you're a teacher's kid, that's for sure. And it won't help if you have an older sister already going to your super-exclusive, socially impossible high school (in this case Marlowe)—unless, of course, you've spent a whole summer with a killer game plan.

John Darling happened to be a grand master of game plans. And in his entire thirteen years of life, he had never wanted a plan to work as much as this. Sure, John was shorter than the other kids at school. He was thinner, weaker, and less . . . well, just less, as far as he could tell. Less of everything. But in high school, he would eradicate all vestiges of his previous self. No more John the Loser. No more John the Gaming Nerd. No more John the Joke.

"This is the *Year of John,*" he said to himself, and sometimes to his sister, Wendy, who told him to just relax, because everybody liked him the way he was. But John didn't want to hear that. What did Wendy know about not being cool? And about starting at a new school a year too young? She was hot (strawberry blond hair, cute little freckles, and a tennis-team build) and popular (but definitely still in the three digits if you're counting Facebook friends, which John did). And now Connor Wirth, aka Captain Marlowe, was hitting on her. Wendy couldn't possibly know anything about John's problems—about being alone at lunch, worrying if anyone will come to your birthday, wondering if you'll have to spend your free period in the science lab instead of out on the front lawn with the popular kids. But John wasn't one to give up. He was a man of action. "This is the year I'm gonna be a badass . . . get some respect."

Last spring, John had gotten in to Finnegan High, the city's toughest school in terms of pure academics and a place where he would have fit in perfectly. It was just as selective as Marlowe, but it was no rich-kid haven. Its admissions were based only on test results. If you got in, they'd pay your way, whatever your family's needs. But John had turned it down in favor of Marlowe (which was also free of charge for him and Wendy, since their father taught ancient civilizations there). He knew that he *could* make it there. Even though his father had resisted, urged him to take the Finnegan offer, John knew that if he tried hard enough, he could be one of them—not just part of the intellectual elite, but the social elite too. He could graduate from Marlowe a part of something so much better, so much bigger, than just the clique of supersmart New Yorkers headed to MIT. He could come out of it with an acceptance to a top college *and* the friendship of the people who would *really* run the world. Those Finnegan guys, sure, they'd be successful, but they would probably all be crunching numbers for the overprivileged party boys from Marlowe. That's the way the world worked, and John knew that.

He had spent the last three months lifting weights, cultivating the slightest Hamptons tan in his backyard, scoping online discount stores for all the designer duds he could afford on his meager allowance, and trying to hang out with Connor Wirth, who had invited Wendy (and therefore John) to his family's Fourth of July party. Usually, John hated having Wendy involved in his life, but this Connor thing, whatever it was, could be his ticket. After the party, John started methodically changing his Facebook image.

The thing about Facebook is that you can't just change yourself all at once. People will know and then they'll fire back, calling you out on your wall, tagging you in all sorts of embarrassing old pictures (and John had been to enough Cosplay conventions to be worried). So, since leaving middle school in June, and especially after the party, John had uploaded cool new pictures of himself with all the right people, joined less embarrassing groups and fan pages, and started tailoring his status updates. He kept ignoring or deleting any mocking comments from his old gaming buddies until they finally shut up about it.

John Darling is psyched to have his bud Massimo visiting from Torino. . . . We couldn't go out, though, 'cause I'm trying not to get back into that lifestyle . . . spent too much of last year toasted. . . .

John Darling had a great time last night . . . but don't ask for details, 'cause she knows who she is and that's all I'm gonna say about that.

John Darling *Connor Wirth: Hey, bro! Are you lifting weights tomorrow? I'm gonna lift anyway, so you can come if you want. Whatever . . .*

Connor Wirth *John Darling: Hi, little buddy. Sure, you can lift with us again. Say hi to your sister.*

❖❖❖

Poor John, Wendy thought as another one of her brother's transparent Facebook updates dropped onto her mini-feed. *What? He's telling people he used to have a drug problem?* Wendy had tried to be understanding the previous week when he started talking about his supposed sex life and his summer fling with a Bulgarian girl who was too Bohemian to have a Facebook profile, but this was too much. He could actually get himself into trouble for this. She couldn't say anything to John, of course, because he was so sensitive about his summer reinvention campaign that he would have a fit if Wendy even suggested that people weren't buying his act. But to Wendy, it was obvious what was really going on. John was lonely. Maybe he needed an older brother. He wanted to be someone else—to prove to everyone that he was big and important and deserved respect. And if this was the way he chose to get it, then . . . fine . . . She couldn't be his older brother, but maybe she could look the other way.

Tomorrow, on her date with Connor, she would ask him to invite John to something low-key. Maybe they could play soccer together. That would help. Wendy had been quietly dating Connor Wirth since early July, but she hadn't said anything to her family—even though Connor had introduced her as his girlfriend to his three best friends, even though he had called every day for a month. *Why take the risk?* she thought. *Who knows what will happen once school starts?* Wendy was a pragmatic girl. She knew that boys her age were fickle and couldn't be trusted. And who knew if Connor would suddenly forget all his fawning speeches when he was faced with his shallow, social-climbing friends and their judgmental attitudes? Maybe he would pretend she didn't even exist.

Just then, her cell rang with Connor's ringtone. OK, so she had given him his own ringtone. It wasn't even that good a song . . . hardly a commitment. OK, fine, it was her favorite song, but only from this summer.

"Hey, Connor," she said, and immediately began forgetting about John. "What's up?"

"Wanna come over?" Connor said, then added, "My mom's back from Biarritz."

"You want me to meet your mom?" said Wendy, elated and wondering why she ever doubted Connor.

"Oh . . ." Connor said, and starting to mumble, "um . . . she's not here *now.*"

"Right." Wendy could feel herself turning red. "I mean—"

"I just meant that she brought the cheese I told you about . . . made it through customs and everything," said Connor. "We can watch movies and eat it all before she gets home."

Normally, Wendy would be mortified by such a humiliating mistake. But Connor seemed to rebound quickly enough, going on and on about the cheese (a bit too long, actually, so he was obviously nervous), probably trying to make her feel better with his own awkwardness. "OK," she said, and reached for her purse. "I'll be there in thirty."

A week before the start of the new school year, on yet another "family breakfast" morning, which Professor Darling insisted they do all through the summer, Wendy stood two feet behind her father and watched him cook eggs. He was burning the undersides, and the whites were still runny on top. When he turned to make toast, she lowered the heat, stirred the eggs, and added more butter.

"Honey, can you set the table?" George Darling asked his daughter, his scholarly puff of hair disheveled, his sensible beige slacks pulled up just a bit too high by his twenty-year-old suspenders.

Wendy picked out a piece of blue lint from her father's snow-white head and said, "Sure, Daddy." At sixteen, Wendy was already running the house.

Their mother had disappeared only a year before, when John and Wendy were twelve and fifteen. She left in the middle of the night, probably thinking the kids would handle it better that way. Like a bad TV mom, she must have thought she did it for *them*, telling herself it would be easier for them to wake up to a whole new life without the bother of saying good-bye or having to listen to made-up reasons. She slipped away with her suitcase as Wendy watched from her bedroom window and thought about her father, who had once been handsome and adventurous. Watching her mother leave was the one event she had felt most acutely in her entire life.

Now, a year later, Wendy was in charge of almost everything around the house. Not because had anyone told her to but just because someone had to fill the void. Her father was way too preoccupied with his work. Besides, he could barely keep himself together. He had spent the better part of the last hour searching for his glasses. He finally located them near the coffeepot. He turned back to the eggs, replacing his glasses on his nose. They were all fogged up. "Ah," he said, giving a satisfied nod to the eggs. "See, honey? Your mom couldn't have done any better than this."

"Nope." Wendy shook her strawberry-blond head. She adjusted the setting of the toaster behind her back, smiling at Professor Darling, who was now rocking on his feet, suspenders in hand, crowing to himself for having made edible eggs. It would be a shame to ruin this proud moment for her aging father. "Mom would've burnt those eggs."

"Daddy, I have news," Wendy said as she arranged the toast on four plates.

Professor Darling glanced at the extra plate and said, "Not again, Wendy. Doesn't that boy get fed back at his house? Last I checked, he had a whole slew of servants."

For the past week, ever since Wendy had revealed her relationship with Connor Wirth to her family, Connor had eaten at least one meal a day at their house.

"Yes, but he likes eating with *us*," said Wendy, putting on her most patient tone. "You never like any of my boyfriends."

"You don't *need* a boyfriend at your age," said Professor Darling. "You need to focus on your grades and on college."

"OK, Daddy, but I have news."

"What?" Professor Darling asked, his lined face breaking into a multitiered fleshy smile, oblivious to the wily ways of teenage girls.

"I got an after-school job," she said, not looking up from the plates. Wendy was a lot shorter than her father. It was easy to hide her motives under wispy bangs and downcast eyes. "At a café near Marlowe . . . I start on the first day of school."

Professor Darling, who had already begun buttering a piece of toast, dropped the bread onto his plate and said, "No, Wendy. We already discussed this. School comes first. Straight As are not optional."

Wendy looked pleadingly at her father. "Daddy, I'm sixteen now, which means it's totally legal, and it pays really well. I spoke to one of the waitresses, and the tips—"

"No. We are not so destitute that my daughter has to waste her exceptional brain on measuring out coffee." Professor Darling's lips had almost disappeared now, and he was obviously trying very hard to keep his voice down.

"I promise my grades won't suffer," said Wendy, "and I can use the cash for John, too."

Professor Darling's perfect volume control now flew away, along with his temper. "*I* will take care of John's needs."

Wendy flinched. She glanced at the door. Connor would be arriving any minute now, and here she was in the middle of a family fight over money. She didn't understand why her father was so rigid on this point. Wendy and John never had enough spending money. Poor John was always making excuses to the few kids who were willing to be his friend (*You go ahead—I went to that concert on opening night . . . Nah, bro, I tore my ACL, so I can't ski ever again . . . Please, MoFo, Cape Cod is so played).* Wendy felt bad for her brother, who had no clue how transparent he was. She had even asked Connor to include John in a few things, and Connor had reported back (shocked) that John had turned down his offer to play paintball.

Quickly, Wendy texted Connor not to come over. **Have2Cancel. XX. Sorry.**

Professor Darling lowered his voice again, and with an apologetic look in his eyes said, "You should be volunteering on the new Egyptian exhibit with me. Last spring I received a whole shipment of things from the British Museum. They gave me almost everything I asked for. It's all been in the basement for the summer, of course, but someone needs to go through it all—" Wendy sighed loudly, but her father ignored her and went on. "Come here. Let me show you what I dug up on the *Book of Gates. . . .*"

"Maybe," Wendy offered listlessly, trying hard not to hurt her father's feelings.

"It would be very educational," said the professor, straightening his glasses. "I think I've got a very early copy. And did I tell you about the Neferat statue? It is exquisite. A dark female deity, previously unknown, that could not only prove the validity of all five legends but could also cast serious doubt on Anubis as the identity of the death god—"

"Hey, John," Wendy interrupted as John came pounding down the stairs.

John filled his plate to overflowing and said through a mouthful of eggs, "What are we talking about?"

"About how great it would be if I got a job."

"Oh, no, no, no," said John. "You can't, Wendy!"

Wendy stared at her brother, confused. "Why not? We could both use the cash."

"'Cause I can't have a sister working at the Shake Shack! Everyone'd know!"

"Oh, John." Professor Darling looked disappointed. "No one at school is concerned with your financial situation."

"You'd be surprised." John looked like a startled animal, his eyes flashing with anxiety.

"We live in a nice house," Professor Darling pointed out, his voice dropping.

Wendy looked around: at the African bust in the corner, the antique wood cupboard, the watercolors in the hallway, all the pretty things that didn't belong to her family. She knew better than to mention it, but John, who was far less tactful, said what they were both thinking: "Everyone knows the house belongs to Marlowe." But it was hardly necessary. Professor Darling already knew. None of his fancy degrees could get his family much respect in this town. Why? Because he didn't own his own coffee table.

After a few minutes of silence, John added, "And everyone's still talking about us."

Professor Darling didn't respond. That part was true. For a year, he had been the teacher with the wife scandal. The faculty lounge was abuzz with it. To everyone even remotely connected to Marlowe, he was the crazy old Egyptologist with a notebook full of unproven theories—no one of them was all that surprised when Mrs. Darling left.

"Give it a rest, John," warned Wendy. The comment about their mother stung more than anything. But she knew that to John the money stuff was far worse. Divorces and scandals were hardly new at Marlowe. And all John wanted was to fit in.

John was perfectly aware (from his many Facebook stalkings) that a nerd at Marlowe could lead a fairly peaceful life provided he had one of three things: money (like Akhbar Husseini, who wore thick Armani glasses and used an inhaler blinged out by Jacob the Jeweler), a famous name (like Emily Vanderbilt-Hearst-Mountbatten, who had criminal acne, bad teeth, and a stable of Photoshop artists for her Page Six close-ups); or a media-worthy talent (like James O'Kelly, who looked like a unwashed rag but spent his lunch hours fending off novice journalists who'd caught the scent of "child genius" all the way from the far reaches of New Jersey). Those kids never got picked on. They may have to throw around some cash to get a prom date or promise face time with their dad for good lunch seats, but they didn't get gang-wedgied in the hall the way John had all through middle school. And as far as Marlowe was concerned, John was coming in with no support system, no trick in his back pocket. If he didn't fix his image fast, he would become Marlowe's official human stress ball.

"Can you at least consider the job?" Wendy begged.

"OK," said Professor Darling. "If you consider working at the exhibit."

"Fine," said Wendy.

"So where's Connor, then?" John asked.

"I texted him not to come," said Wendy, getting up from the table. "I have to run."

John shrugged. He didn't care, anyway. He was perfectly secure that he and Connor were best buds—he didn't need Connor to come here every day to prove it. He shrugged again.

"Everything all right?" Professor Darling asked his son, who was now on his third shrug.

"Whatever, that's all," said John. "Whatever."

Professor Darling sipped his coffee and stared at his son. Thirteen had definitely not been like this for Wendy, and frankly, George Darling thought that maybe he was better at raising girls. *What's wrong with the boy?* For the last three months, he had forsaken everything Professor Darling had taught him—about being an independent thinker, a free mind, a leader of men. Instead, Darling had to watch his teenage son following other boys like a trained pet. If John was craving a role model, if he needed someone to idolize and learn from, then why not choose someone the least bit respectable? "What if you and I do something today?" he said. "You know"—he cleared his throat—"men things."

"Nah," said John. "I'm busy."

"Oh . . ." said Professor Darling. "All right, well . . . later, then."

John started getting up, probably to go back to his summer program of nonstop computer social networking. "John?" Professor Darling called after him. "You know, we're getting a new teaching assistant for the exhibit . . . um . . . Simon Grin."

"So?" John said from the staircase.

"I think you would get along. He's very well read . . . mostly Old Kingdom, I believe. . . ."

"Please," said John. "Sounds like a total noob. Besides, I don't want to make a huge show about that stuff at Marlowe, OK, Dad?"

"OK, son." The professor wiped the coffee from his gray mustache and began picking up the dishes. Then to no one in particular, he said, "Too bad . . . wasting all that knowledge."

OK, so John had done his fair share of nerdery (in his chosen fields of gaming, comics, and ancient Egypt). But those days were over. This was the Year of John. This was the Year of Getting Respect. John knew why his dad was worried. He was probably thinking that John's change of image would mean that he'd let his grades slip or wouldn't work hard anymore. But John wasn't that stupid. He wasn't about to give up on his favorite activities or on the bright academic future he deserved. He'd just play it cool from now on—watch out how he came across. And if this Simon Grin guy knew his stuff, OK, fine, they could hang (because John wasn't the kind of jerk who'd hassle the new teaching assistant)—but it'd have to be somewhere away from campus.

No problem, thought John. He could lead a double life. He had a game plan.

As he settled in front of his computer and typed his Facebook password, John promised himself that this year he would have it all.

John Darling is heading out to swim a mile. Screw swim team and their mandatory follicle testing, man, 'cause they need John Darling, bad . . .

Comment from Rory Latchly: WTF?

Comment from Isaac Chang: Just ignore him. He'll get over it.

Comment from Connor Wirth: Way to go, bud!

JOHN DARLING
A HAPPY THOUGHT

I was at a sleepover for Sanford Marshall's birthday and we crammed Coke and Oreos all night (I ate the most) and had a Smash Bros. tournament, which I won using not even my best characters. Then we played blackjack and I won that easy. And then we played with his Airsoft guns. You can't really win that, but I definitely got shot the least. I hit a plastic figure off his bed and Sanford said, "Good one, bro." So we were totally cool.

WENDY DARLING
A HAPPY THOUGHT

Mom and I went to a lecture Dad was giving to the entire British Museum about his research on an Egyptian book. I couldn't have been older than three, but I remember everything. Dad was nervous, and Mom had stuffed his jacket pockets with handkerchiefs. We knew he hadn't found them, because he kept wiping his sweat on his jacket sleeve while he spoke. There weren't enough seats, so Mom had pulled me onto her lap. She had her arms wrapped around me, and when I'd lean back to look up at her, she'd kiss my forehead. I wasn't worried about anything, not even what the adults thought, when I yelled, "Daddy, look in your pockets!"

Peter's Flight

London (early autumn)

Everywhere Assistant Professor Simon Grin went that day, he had the feeling he was being followed. As he struggled to carry his duffel bag down the narrow stairs of his flat, he imagined there were upside-down faces watching him through the windows, as though kids were leaning over the roof. But every time he glanced over, he managed only to catch a glimpse of something that might have been the last wisp of hair pulling out of view. When he fell down the last few stairs and landed on his bag, which burst like a ketchup packet and sent his toiletries flying, he thought he heard giggling.

He knew it couldn't be hoodlums. After all, he was the assistant professor of Egyptology and second correspondent curator to the British Museum now. He had badgered the dean of faculty housing until he was given a flat in a very up-and-coming part of town. That's how Simon saw himself, up-and-coming. So it made sense to live there with *no* flatmate. This was all very important. Up-and-coming professors (soon to be tenured professor, and then dean of history by thirty-seven) did not share rent.

Simon scowled at himself in the mirror with his sharp, fidgety eyes before heading out. His face was too white, almost pink, and his hair was too red, too carefully brushed, gelled, and parted down the side.

As he was locking up the front door, Simon thought he heard shuffling behind the neighbor's shrubs. Then he thought he heard a "Shhh, you eejit, he'll hear." Simon knew that in lesser neighborhoods it was dangerous to let people know you'd be out of town for a long time. Uneducated thugs would break in and take all your things. Of course, Simon Grin didn't have anything but history books and a fridge full of Vienna sausages. He prided himself on not owning a television, gaming console, or stereo. The only DVDs he had were footage of archeology digs in the lower Nile.

Simon checked his military-grade multifunction watch—with built-in compass, barometer, and gas-filled luminous tracer lamps, capable of withstanding a whole array of activities that Simon would never undertake—and saw that he was running late. When he lugged his bag to the corner, a cab was already waiting for him. *Strange,* he thought. *Cabs don't usually loiter in the up-and-coming parts of London.* Simon jumped in anyway. He couldn't keep the director of the museum waiting.

The cabbie looked like a teenager, olive-skinned and wearing a fisherman's cap. "Where to, sahib?" he said in a mixed-up Bengali accent. Simon squinted behind his spectacles. The driver's tangle of brown wavy hair reminded him of the ancient Greek frescoes depicting playful satyrs and dashing hunters. Simon couldn't quite decide whether this guy was a hunter or a satyr. But he definitely wasn't Bengali. "Tick-tock, sahib," said the cabbie. "Where will it be?"

Simon could have sworn this kid was no more than seventeen. He looked at the ID card behind the driver's seat. *Naamkaran Jarmoosh.* The picture was of a graying Indian man with pocks all over his face, scowling at the camera.

"This isn't you," Simon said in his most accusing tone.

"My old man," said the cabbie.

Simon shrugged. He was in too much of a hurry to get involved in the details of father-son cab-sharing customs—in Bengal or any other place. "The British Museum, *Junior Jarmoosh,* and hurry!"

"You're the boss," said the cabbie in a clearly insubordinate tone that intensified Simon's suspicions.

The cab tore through the narrow London streets with Simon in the backseat, clutching his bag to his chest. A few times, when the car flew over a small hill, the cabbie would shout, "That was some wicked air." And then he'd catch himself and add, "Eh, sahib?"

By the time they reached the museum, Simon was green with nausea. The cabbie swerved in front of the building and parked with two wheels on the curb. Simon paid him and nodded good-bye. He rushed past the guard and through the front door, even though the museum wouldn't open for another hour. When he looked back, he caught a glimpse of the cab, still lingering in front of the museum.

Simon teetered onward toward the director's office. Through the frosted glass, Simon saw the old man bent over his desk, as usual. "Grin, is that you? Get in here."

Simon patted himself down, made sure his tie was straight, and checked his multi-watch. *Six hundred and twelve seconds early, facing due west.* He rushed into his boss's office.

"Sit down, Grin."

"Sir, I'd just like to say thank you for the opportunity to oversee this exhibit to New York. I couldn't be more—"

"You aren't overseeing anything. You're babysitting the bloody things and making sure that nutter, Professor Darling, doesn't shame us with his mummy stories."

Simon paused. "*Professor* Darling? I thought George Darling was the *curator.*"

"They don't have curators at boarding schools, Grin," said the director, without looking up from his papers.

"They don't have professors, either," said Simon under his breath.

The director looked up for only a second, then went back to his papers and said with a snicker, "They do at Marlowe. It's one of those ostentatious American upper-class misnomers—like calling an afternoon party a *soirée.* Really, Grin, did you think that I'd send *you* to the Metropolitan Museum?"

"Well, um, yes," Simon stuttered. "I was told that it was an Upper East Side Egyptian exhibit."

"That's right: you will be *assisting* Professor Darling at the Marlowe High School exhibit."

Simon turned the words *high school* several times in his head. Up-and-coming Egyptologists do *not* waste their careers working with children. He began shaking his leg nervously. "I—are you sure you have the right assignment?" he asked desperately.

"Yes, Grin. I'm quite sure. The items were shipped several months ago, and do you know what kind of strings I had to pull to get just a few worthless pieces to Darling?" Then the director began to mutter, "The man may be a fool, but he has friends in high places." He raised his voice again and looked Simon directly in the eyes. "They're just a few items that were going to storage anyway: a statue of a woman who was a historical and mythical nobody, a few jars and knickknacks, and a badly replicated copy of the *Book of Gates.* Rubbish. Do you think you can handle that?"

"Maybe not," said Simon, his voice going weak. "I mean, if he's such a loony, then why bother . . . I mean, how is a *high school* getting a loan from the Brit—?"

"Look, Grin. Some of our big donors like his insane stories. They wanted to make a gesture on behalf of the museum. And however mad I think he is, the man's said to be an authority on all this. He's read more about the dozen items in this shipment than you've read about any subject in your entire life. Besides, as I said, the items are *worthless.* Nobody else wants them. Free storage as far as I'm concerned. Understood?"

"I think I'm coming down with something," said Simon.

"Your flight is in three hours."

Simon made sure to grab an expense form before skulking out of the director's office. He had already changed his Internet profiles to say he was an exhibit manager at the New York Metropolitan Museum of Art. Now when he took it down, all of his strategically chosen network would know. As Simon mourned for his résumé, he heard the clatter of several sets of footsteps down the main marble hall of the museum. Strange, since the museum wasn't open yet. Simon thought the rushing sound was coming up behind him. He whipped around just in time to see a young man with brown wavy tangles of hair running toward him with two night guards chasing behind. Simon didn't get more than a glance at the fugitive before he flew by. But he saw that the burglar was carrying a wad of crumpled pink papers. Outside, he heard cursing and the sound of a car screeching away.

Simon brushed it off and picked up his travel bag. This was an up-and-coming disaster. Simon was no fool. Everyone he'd ever met knew that he was number one in his high-school class, was chess champion of his college dorm, and had taken an online test that said he had a genius IQ. So Simon knew when someone was pulling a fast one. And he recognized that wavy brown hair. *Amateur,* thought Simon, remembering that his research assistant had been sacked for stealing office supplies. *What kind of dumb ass would come back for seconds?* Simon thought, absolutely certain that it was the research assistant who had just gotten away. Once again feeling utterly superior, Simon straightened his collar and headed to the airport.

An alleyway a few blocks down from the British Museum, full of industrial-size trash cans, was the perfect hiding place for a secret meeting. On this particular morning, seven dirty faces huddled together: seven teenage runaways, all baring that one missing tooth, the one that showed that regardless of color or height or weight, they were friends of *Peter.*

"Everybody, shut up!" shouted Tina. She was Peter's number two, assembling his LBs (for Lost Boys, but shortened for texting) wherever Peter went in the world. She was a little shorter than the rest of them, a little tougher, and always by Peter's side. She had long brown hair and tan skin, and her eyes were always half shut, as if she were appraising something or about to fall asleep. She was probably Hispanic, but nobody knew for sure. She had a dark beauty toughened by the streets. She was sexy, for sure, but not beautiful. She was just so . . . so . . .

"And if anyone else touches my can, I'll stuff your head in a toilet. Got it?"

Yeah, that was it . . .

"Peter's flying to New York in a couple of hours to start his new job. We need you guys to keep an eye out on the museum while we're gone," said Tina.

"Yeah, yeah. We know the drill," said a redheaded kid in the back. "Old Egyptian books. Got it." His name was Red. All the boys had nicknames like this so that Peter wouldn't have to bother with tedious chores like remembering their real names. *Red. Steroid. Hoodie. Newbie. Fattie. Spock.* And so on. Only Tina got to be herself, because Tina was Peter's undisputed favorite.

"What's the new gig?" asked Hoodie.

"Peter and me, we're gonna be RAs at some fancy school in New York," said Tina almost proudly.

"I heard he knicked the book from the British Museum," said Newbie.

"Nah, man, if he had the book, it'd all be over," said Spock.

"I heard he killed someone."

Tina rolled her eyes. Peter's legend just wouldn't stop growing. His fanboys knew him as a god of street kids and orphans. A phantom criminal. An underworld adventurer with a worldwide network of lost boys bent on finding one lost treasure.

"What's an RA?" asked Red from the back. "Hey, can we come?"

"Don't worry about it." Tina shrugged. As she walked away, she added, "The LBs in New York would cut y'all open and sell you for parts."

Simon sat in the airport lounge, waiting for his flight and texting his mother. He was looking down when he heard, "Anybody sitting here, pardner?"

Simon looked up to see a young man dressed like a cowboy. He had on Levi's jeans, a white shirt, and a straw hat. His eyebrows and sideburns looked too thick to be real, and they were a darker shade of brown than the hair on his head. The cowboy gave him a wink and a smile.

He had a not-too-tall, not-too-lanky body. He was a handsome boy, tan-faced, cocoa-haired, with eyes just a shade too hazel. He wasn't thin, or fat, or tall, or short. He was just an American cowboy, tightly packed and nimble, able to blend in or stand out on a whim, and completely unrecognizable as the young man who had driven Simon to his meeting that very morning.

Simon shook his head.

"Great," said the cowboy. "My name's Petey Peterschmidt. Put 'er there."

The cowboy shook Simon's hand up and down. He sat next to Simon and propped his muddy boots on the facing row of chairs. He let out a loud sigh. "Well, friend," said Petey the cowboy, slapping Simon on the back, "you headed out of town on business or pleasure?"

Simon was already uncomfortable, huddling down and putting away the message to his mom. "Business," said Simon.

"That's a shame," said Petey. "You coulda hit the town with your buddy Pete, here."

"Important business," Simon added.

"Ooh, well, don't let me stop you. You seem like one of those genius types. Am I right? Somebody payin' you the big bucks for that brain of yours?"

Simon smiled. It was nice to have his genius noticed. Maybe this cowboy wasn't as stupid as he looked. Simon didn't want to brag. "I'm a very important man, actually."

"Seems that way," said Petey.

"I'm overseeing a major Egyptian exhibit in New York."

"Like, *Egypt* Egypt? Must be at the United Nations or some such. You're like an ambassador?"

"Well, kind of. Yes, yes, I guess I am," said Simon. Simon went on telling Petey about every detail of his important exhibit, with just a few things left out or exaggerated here or there. After Simon had exhausted every subject revolving around himself, he finally turned to Petey and said, "So what do *you* do?"

"Well," said Petey, "I'm no ambassador to Middle Eastern peace-keeping, but, you know, I do well for myself." Then Petey gave a conspicuous look-see this way and that (presumably to make sure the coast was clear). He leaned in to Simon and said in a conspiratorial whisper, "The truth is, Mr. Grin, I'm in the self-help business."

"You write about how to stop being a child and get your life together?" said Simon, not stopping to ponder how the cowboy knew his name.

"Oh no, nothing like that." Petey laughed. "I help people help themselves. I give them the identity they've always wanted. Plus maybe a few added years if they're underage."

"You're saying you make fake IDs?"

"I guess so, yes. That's exactly the phrase for it. Leave it to the professor. But what I mean is age is just what you make of it, right? Look at me, for instance. Heck, most clubs *still* card me. I can't convince a daggum soul of my age. They all think I'm a teenager!"

At this, Petey put his head back and guffawed at the fluorescent ceiling lights. Simon chuckled nervously. Petey did have a baby face.

"But that's all between you and me, right, Professor?" said Petey. "I wish it was fate for me to come out a director of Egyptological studies for two major museums, but we can't all be Einstein. You know what I mean?"

An up-and-coming scholar like Simon didn't want to have anything to do with the kind of riffraff that made a living off petty fraud. But Petey was such a likable guy. And great men were always nice to the plebeians. Simon nodded and smiled. Petey slapped him on the back. "Good!" said Petey. "Now, let's get on that plane and see what kind of stewardesses they got. But first I gotta see a man about a dog, if you know what I mean."

"I don't, actually," said Simon. It stung him to admit that he didn't understand something.

"It means I gotta go to the bathroom."

"Oh, right, I should do that, too."

"Well, how about I stay here and watch your bag? You don't

wanna be putting that thing down in these airport bathrooms—get all kinds of hepatidal choleroids. I'll go after you."

"All right," said Simon. Simon headed to the men's room feeling like a smooth operator.

Sure, the cowboy was an uneducated dimwit with the slight tangy odor of a cheese wheel, but Simon had regaled him with his academic exploits, and now he was like a personal porter. Some people struck up conversations to make friends; Simon tolerated them to get something useful out of it.

The second Simon was gone, Peter grabbed the travel bag and started walking to the boarding gate. He dumped Simon's passport and boarding pass into the trash and then flashed his own papers to an attendant who looked more like a teenager than an airline employee. The attendant gave him a wink and said, "Have a good trip, Pete."

As Peter disappeared into the tunnel, he pulled out a wad of crumpled pink papers, shipping orders from the Egyptology Department dated several months ago, and examined them one more time. *New York City. The Marlowe School.* He may not have intercepted the shipment in time, but at least Simon wasn't going near Peter's prize anytime soon.

Meanwhile, back at the security gate, Simon Grin was panicking about his lost bag and trying to get on his flight regardless. He tried to explain why he didn't have a passport or a ticket or any other essential document. He called the attendant a few names and tried to run past him. But the uneducated types had a way of outrunning Simon, so he was tackled, Tased, and escorted out by security.

❖❖❖

SIMON GRIN

A HAPPY THOUGHT

Simon's Log, Stardate 3109.44

All is well in the Omega Quadrant. The triplet suns of the galaxy shine on my ship, the SS Brilliance, *with equal—no, increasing—admiration. I sense that the vast alien races in this space hub will be as much in awe of my reputation as they would of a god. I will become something of a legend in their world. After escaping the clutches of these Taser-wielding monkey-men and HALO jumping from outside the stratosphere of the planet London Prime, I will save the training facility of the famous "French Maid School," and they will see me as an avenging angel. The hottest students will beg to join my starship, but I will, of course, have to tell them that my adventures are just too dangerous for such fair maids. My weakling second-in-command, Officer Darling, will appeal as well, but my resolve will be unshaken. I'm a captain, and with that great mantle of power comes a great amount of attractiveness.*

3

THE NEVER-NEVER MAN

New York (first day of school)

Thirteen is a bad year for hair. Shiny blond curls disappear, making way for darker, coarser bundles of frizz. Cowlicks grow less and less manageable. And a whole slew of new hair-taming possibilities—not just gel and mousse, but also styling sand, highlighting pomade, and Bed Head polish—complicate a once-simple life of rinse-lather-repeat. John stood in front of his bedroom mirror in an oversize bath towel and rubbed a buttery substance with a sugary scent into his palm.

"If it's supposed to make me look dirty, then why shower, huh? Where's the logic?" he asked his reflection, wiping his greasy hands into his hair. Three chunks of it stood on end, making a crown on his head. "Yeah, oh *yeeeeeah.*" John nodded, pursing his lips the way he had seen Connor Wirth do it in his coolest moments, which were many. Connor not only had the best hair ever, but he also had enough money to cover his entire body with Bed Head twice a day. So unfair. John separated the giant crownlike middle chunk into two parts. The crown now looked like a serving fork made of hair.

John took another look at his overgreased hair and raised an eyebrow. Then he flexed his left arm. Then both arms. Nope, no change. He was still scrawny, still skin and bone. He sucked in his barely-there preteen paunch and picked at a hair on his chest. Was that there yesterday? Yep . . . still as bald as a well-oiled salamander. No problem. What he was lacking in physique he would make up for with a good dose of dirt and grime in his hair—a little more of the underground speed-metal look, and a little less of the preppy jock (which was too much work and lacking originality anyway).

Wendy walked past her younger brother's bedroom just as he was flattening a tsunami wave of hair into his signature look—slicked back and parted on the side, then tousled until it looked exactly like it had when he came out of the shower forty minutes ago, minus the hope of ever drying. She peeked in from behind the half-closed door and said, *"The Banker* again? Hurry up, kiddo. It's time for school."

"Can't rush first impressions, Sis," said John, who was still not dressed. "Especially not when it's the first day of the best year ever."

"Oh, geez," Wendy mumbled to herself as she pulled out her cell phone to text Connor. She'd need a lot of help if she was going to save John from himself. But as she was typing out her first words, Wendy stopped and clicked the phone shut. She shouldn't call or text Connor first. After all, he hadn't contacted her in two days. Maybe things would be different now that school was starting and he had all his old friends (and girlfriends?) back. Maybe their romance was just a summer thing and it would all blow over now. Would Connor want to date a teacher's daughter at school? Would he want to date just one girl?

It felt strange thinking about the possibility, because even though Wendy hated the idea of losing Connor, she wondered if she shouldn't feel more panicked at the possibility. How would other girls handle the situation? Wendy had no idea because she had no mother to ask.

Wendy and John's mother hadn't been all that great an adviser. She was too young to be a mother, too pretty, too impulsive. According to Wendy's father, she had married him when he was in the prime of his career, a dashing Egyptologist, already successful, full of adventures and stories. The perfect mix of young and old. He knew that as far as his wife was concerned, he would *never* grow old. *Never* lose his hair. *Never* grow soft in the belly and begin forgetting birthdays.

But in the real world, even adventurous men grow old, and sometimes, pretty young wives don't stop being young and pretty. Sometimes, they get bored. Sometimes, renowned Egyptologists become underpaid high-school teachers living in school-owned brownstones—happy, obscure . . . aging.

Sometimes, pining graduate students come along and sweep pretty wives away with the promise of adventures yet to come. When she left, Professor Darling had told Wendy, he felt it was entirely *his* fault. For promising too much. For being a never-never man, the way all husbands are at first.

When Wendy thought about Connor, or even boyfriends in general, she wondered if she should feel about him the way her mother felt about her father or if she should feel the way her mother felt about that grad student. Wendy imagined that Mrs. Darling's relationship with this other man was all fire and passion and illicit meetings in dark hallways. She imagined that it was thrilling, that it was the kind of thing that made you shudder in your sleep. Connor and Wendy were definitely not like that. Connor was nice to Wendy. He took her out to group events and made a point of including John in everything. Connor was definitely the "Mr. Darling" of this situation, and even though there was no magic or fire between them just yet, the comparison made Wendy want to stick with him—to show her mother that it could be done and that Mrs. Darling had been a weak and cowardly woman for leaving. That she had put her own base desires over the happiness of the entire family. Now that Wendy was sixteen, she realized that her biggest ambition in life was to become as little like her mother as possible.

Downstairs, Wendy caught her father packing and repacking his old leather briefcase, trying to fit in a stack of notes he was probably afraid would be stolen by Egyptology-enthusiast thugs while he was out of the house.

"Daddy?" she said, only to get a grunt as a response when he tried shoving his fist in after the papers. "I was gonna drop by that café after school . . . um . . . for that job I told you about?"

Professor Darling looked up with alarmed eyes. "Right," he said. "I've thought about it, and it really isn't a good time—"

"Daddy, I really could use the money. And John, too . . . I know you think all the kids at Marlowe are over-the-top extravagant, but John could use some real friends this year."

"He doesn't need the kind of friends that require cash payment," Professor Darling huffed, and looked away from his daughter. "That's not what I've taught him."

"It's not *them,*" said Wendy. "They're cool. It's all in John's head."

"OK, Wendy, let me think about it some more. But this is a very busy year for you . . . with tougher classes . . . and the exhibit."

"The exhibit?" Wendy tried not to yell, but this was exactly the kind of thing her father pulled all the time—ignore the issue and pretend you've won, until everyone forgets and you eventually do win by default. "I never said I'd do that!"

But Professor Darling was determined to plow through with his own point. "John should do it, too. I was supposed to get an assistant from the British Museum to help catalog all the items, but he was mugged by a street gang and then his flight was canceled. Or something like that. Anyway, he's not here, and I'm swamped."

"And what about my job?" said Wendy. "How am I supposed to do both things?"

Professor Darling shrugged.

"Daddy, you can't fix it so it's impossible for me to negotiate."

"Sure, I can, honey. And you'd better get used to it. Minimum-wage laborers often find negotiation impossible."

"No, they don't!" Wendy huffed, gathering her backpack. "Stop being so elitist. I hope you don't say that stuff in public."

As Wendy ran back upstairs to get John, she overheard her father mumbling, "The big difference between intellectual snobbery and elitism, my dear, is that one is *earned*—though I suppose neither is very nice."

❖❖❖

When Wendy and John had set off for Marlowe, Professor Darling finished gathering his papers and packing his briefcase. Since the day Wendy had turned thirteen, she had insisted that she be allowed to walk to school alone. *I'm old enough now,* she had argued. *I don't need to be walked to school.* Professor Darling encouraged his daughter's independent streak. He enjoyed watching her try to take care of everyone and everything herself. It made him proud. So, despite the fact that they were headed for exactly the same building, at exactly the same school, Professor Darling felt obliged to wait a full fifteen minutes before setting off. He had promised Wendy, after all, and he usually kept his promises.

"It's been more than fifteen minutes, I think," he said confidently to himself five minutes later. He strolled out the door with thoughts of the Marlowe Egyptian exhibit swimming in his head. For a long time, he had suspected the importance of these particular pieces, mostly considered minor by his colleagues. He had worked so hard, called in so many favors, to have them in his care. Now he would finally get to study them up close, use them to teach the children something new, something undiscovered. If only they would show more interest. . . . George Darling knew why Wendy wanted to do so much on her own, why she was so adamant to have her way. She was determined to never again be left behind. He could see by the way she watched him, the way she watched everyone, that she was more careful now, more guarded. He felt sad for his daughter. *I'll ask for some funding,* he decided. *A paid job for Wendy at my exhibit—where she can learn something.* He nodded, congratulating himself for the idea. He wanted to help his daughter in his own way. To make sure that she was happy. That she never had another heartbreak.

Never is a long time, he thought. But he could do it. He was the never-never man.

The front lawn of the Marlowe School was teaming with wired freshmen, sleep-deprived seniors, and sunburned teachers reminiscing about summer novels and comparing fall syllabi. John and Wendy lingered for a moment before entering the familiar crowd—even before Wendy had started at Marlowe, the two had always visited their father here on the first day of school. Now teachers said hello as they passed, and old friends waved Wendy over.

"Who's that?" Wendy said, looking across the clusters of students toward the main building of Marlowe, where a mousy brown-haired woman, probably in her thirties, was waiting, silent and motionless. She didn't look rushed or eager to speak to anyone. She just observed everyone (and no one) with her one good eye. From the distance, her left eye seemed somehow damaged. She didn't bother to swat away the moths hovering around her dark blue sweater set. Twice, she coughed into her white lace handkerchief.

"If you don't know her, she must be a new teacher," said John. "Let's go."

Wendy turned for just a second and wondered if she should greet this woman. But when she turned back, the woman was gone. Or maybe she had blended into the crowd—she was so plain, so nondescript . . . exactly the type of person that spends her life blending in, watching, never really standing out.

John seemed to forget her instantly. He began pushing his way through the crowd, and Wendy followed. They cut across the lawn and around the main building, arriving at the lacrosse field only minutes before morning practice came to an end. Wendy could see John fidgeting with a mixture of excitement and nervousness, because now Connor was approaching them with two of his teammates. John was probably trying to think of just the right thing to say. *Poor kid.*

Though, now that she considered it, *she* should probably be thinking of the right thing to say, too. She and Connor had never talked at school—not really—and somehow everything felt different here. More official. These guys didn't know her. They hadn't come to Connor's Fourth of July party or hung out with them all summer. In fact, Wendy and Connor had spent the summer in a bubble, since most of their classmates were off on summer adventures around the world. So what would Connor say now? Would he pretend it was all no big deal? That he wasn't *really* dating the teacher's kid? What would Connor's lacrosse friends think?

"Hey," she managed to mumble when Connor waved and then jogged up and slapped John on the back.

Then Connor threw a sweaty arm over Wendy's shoulder and said, "This is my girlfriend, Wendy Darling." The boys were saying hello when Connor added, "And you guys know John, right?" And then when they didn't show the appropriate level of excitement, he said a bit more loudly, "They're Darling's kids. Remember?"

Wendy looked up, amazed, because the way Connor was rambling, it was as if *he* was embarrassed that his friends didn't remember her—like he wanted her to think that he had already told all his friends about her and her whole family. He was giving his friends a look that said *Stop being jerks in front of my girlfriend.*

Wendy tried to play it cool, but she couldn't help the giant smile that was spreading across her face. *What a good guy,* she thought. And then he leaned over and gave her a hard, sweaty kiss on the lips. Wendy wanted to pull away, because to be perfectly objective, it was really gross. But that didn't matter now, because one thing was for sure: this was Wendy's one opportunity to prove that she, Wendy Darling, was the kind of girl who would pick the nice guy whether or not he met some vague standard of fiery romance or fairy-tale chemistry. She, Wendy Darling, was sensible and good. She would never be anything like Mrs. Darling. *And look at that,* she thought. *John's loving this. Wait, what's he doing?*

John was digging into his backpack and pulling out a stack of cards. *Oh, God, he didn't . . .*

"Here's my info," John said as he handed out solid black business cards to Connor's friends. "I blog sometimes . . . you know, about underground stuff I learn on the streets: picking locks, getting clean in two weeks in your room . . . stuff you need."

One of the guys rolled his eyes. Another chuckled. John looked deflated. Wendy nudged him and smiled, but he took a step away from her. Just as she was about to suggest that they leave, one of Connor's friends turned toward the dorms across the playing field and said, "What do *they* want?" From the other side of the field, four senior boys were strutting toward them with that lazy lethargic swagger that said they'd just bought another case of unpolluted urine for the monthly Marlowe dorms drug test. Wendy felt sorry for the boarding kids. They were usually some of the richest ones—their parents were willing to pay the astronomical price of housing their children at Marlowe, not to mention the guilt money that lined all their designer pockets. Still, Wendy thought it was sad that they were forced to live away from home. Most of them were international, with homes in faraway places. Just looking at them, Wendy felt a little backwater, even though she'd lived in New York all her life. All those accents and fashion trends she'd never heard of—and all of them too *street* to give a second look to the unoriginally preppy day students. Of course, every year there were a few boarders whose parents lived in New York. Those were the worst ones. Or maybe they had the worst parents. Either way, they were the truest orphans, the ones that caused the most trouble.

Now the four boarding boys, all wearing the Marlowe gray-and-navy uniform, were approaching Connor and his two teammates. They stopped a few yards away and motioned for the lacrosse boys to go over. Connor told Wendy and John to wait while he and his friends went over to the boarders. After a few minutes of talking, Connor was looking more and more pissed off. "Be right back," said Wendy, starting toward them. But of course, John followed one step behind. He was fascinated with all things Connor-related. As she approached, Wendy could hear them arguing about last week's preseason game.

"Hey," said one of the boarders, a kid whose parents were some sort of South Asian royalty, "your boy took the money, and now you're trying to punk out. Pay up, bro."

Connor's face was growing pink. "Nobody on this team would agree to fix a game. Go sell your bullshit somewhere else."

"Yeah, I get it," said the kid in the fake street accent they all cultivated. "You're sticking up for your boy. That's cool. But he *did* agree, and now he owes us."

"Relax, man," said another one of the boarders. "It wasn't like we asked him to lose. Just shave a couple of points to cover the spread."

"Same thing," said Connor, the anger rising in his voice. "He'd never do that." He glanced at his friend with his blond eyebrows in a furious tangle.

"So we're in agreement there," said the Indian boy, trying to sound suave but coming off sleazy instead. "He didn't do it. Now he has to pay for all the lost bets."

Wendy wondered why these guys cared about a few lost dollars, anyway. It was probably nothing to them. Maybe they just wanted to bring Connor down a notch. People were always trying to do that. She felt a tingle of pride at the thought. Just as she was trying to decide whether she should approach Connor or keep hanging back, she saw someone running toward them from the direction of the dorms. He was tall, his brown hair bouncing as he dashed toward them with long, easy strides. He was wearing the dorm crew shirt, a white polo with the Marlowe crest.

"What's going on here?" he asked with an air of authority that made even the lacrosse boys take notice.

"Who're you?" asked Connor.

The handsome newcomer gave a friendly grin that made Wendy smile involuntarily. He held out his hand. "I'm Peter, the new resident adviser. Everything OK here?"

"This punk won't pay up," one of the boarders, a Chinese boy with a crew cut, blurted out.

Wendy noticed that all four boys were looking eagerly at Peter. One of them had on a smirk that revealed a large gap in his teeth. *Wait,* thought Wendy, glancing at the Chinese boy. *Do they all have a missing . . . ?*

But then her attention was diverted by Peter, who spoke with the cool confidence that had belonged to the Indian boy only a second before. Not uncomfortable *adult* authority, but the kind of confidence that Connor always had—the kind that only one person in every group can display. "Pay for what?" Peter said blandly, and Wendy thought she saw him warn the Chinese boy with his eyes. "Let's go. *Now.*"

The four boarders fell in line in a way that Wendy had never seen any Marlowe kid do for an RA, or a teacher, or even the principal. From the corner of her eye, Wendy could see John staring with awe, his admiration finding a new target. *Not again,* she thought, since John's hero roster was growing longer and longer with each passing day. And now that John's plan to change his online image had totally failed with the lacrosse boys, he would be looking for a new group to admire—probably a group that didn't care as much about image, a set of friends that didn't have time for Facebook, who were more *street,* as John would put it, which was bad news because the boarding kids were big trouble.

Peter leading the way, the boys walked to the other side of the field, where a girl Wendy had never seen was waiting for them. She, too, was wearing the white crested polo shirt. Wendy was still staring with curiosity in Peter's direction when she felt Connor's arm around her shoulder. He was still sweaty, and she pulled away a little, then chastised herself for being shallow in front of the hot new

RA and forced herself closer to him. Connor didn't notice, anyway. If they were alone, Wendy would have thanked him for sticking up for John, for being so perfect in every important way. She would have done something to show that she wanted to *deserve* him. But they weren't alone, and the RA with the brown curls was turning around to take one last look at the scene, capturing the attention of everyone around him with every minuscule gesture, making Wendy notice Connor's youth and his tight grip and his sporty smell, forcing her to think of grad students and disloyalty. The RA's dark gaze caught Wendy's for just a second before she turned sharply into Connor's arm. Again, Connor didn't notice. As they walked toward the locker rooms, he rattled on about weekend plans and last week's game and entitled druggies who spew lies about his teammates.

❖❖❖

CONNOR WIRTH

A HAPPY THOUGHT

"We're late in the fourth quarter of the New York Prep State Championship here at Madison Square Garden, and these two teams are matching each other punch for punch—a slugfest between two heavyweights. Demarcus Marchand, captain point guard for Bard Academy, has almost single-handedly carried his team through the second half. But Connor Wirth, the Marlowe captain, hasn't slouched on the other side. It may be presumptuous for me to call, but I see hints of Larry Bird in that young man. From the floor, this

reporter has seen Wirth call a number of his shots, right at Marchand, and then execute. Wirth has been playing with a superstar swagger. . . .

Marlowe comes out of the time-out with the ball, down by one. A double screen, in to Wirth at the top of the key, Marchand is in his face, ten seconds left, he fakes left, goes right, Marchand stays with him but Wirth pulls back, a spin, Marchand is WAY out of place, Wirth with a turnaround jumper pulls the trigger at the buzzer . . . it's in! Marlowe wins! Marlowe wins! Marlowe wins the state championship off the last-second heroics of Connor Wirth!"

INTERLUDE

PETER

Peter woke with a start. At first he didn't recognize his dorm. He was always in strange beds, in houses that didn't belong to him. He ran his fingers through his sweat-soaked hair. *Another nightmare.* They were getting worse, more intense, and the stress was getting to him. He spotted the moth in the corner. He wished for someone, a protector, to ward off his dreams. *But what if the one standing over your bed is the one causing it all?*

More than anything, Peter still hated getting older. But a close second was the dark. The night was when Peter was most alone. No Tina, no LBs, no one but Peter himself, alone with his thoughts, his fears, his deepest regrets. All those monsters that lurked after dusk. The broken eye that was fixed on him always. Night is the time when everything can go wrong. Twelve hours, twelve chances for disaster. Night is when his oldest nemesis tried to haunt him, to hurt him, to scare him away. *All nights come to an end,* Peter assured himself.

THE FIRST LEGEND

"Sorry I'm late, class. . . . Class. Quiet down, please."

Professor Darling stumbled through the door, holding a pile of books, notes, a laptop, some rolled-up schematics, and his third cup of coffee. He unloaded the heap on his desk. Wendy and John were already nervous.

"You got lucky this time, Professor," said Marla, from the back of the class. "Two more minutes and we were going to invoke the ten-minute rule."

Professor Darling picked up some notes that had fallen to the floor.

"The ten-minute rule?" he said distractedly.

"Yeah, ten minutes and the students get to walk out," said Marla.

The professor adjusted his notebooks, pushed his glasses to the top of his nose, and snapped back to the present.

"I assure you, Marla, that the Marlowe rule book does not contain any kind of clause allowing students to walk out on their own education."

"Well," said Marla, crossing her arms, "it should."

A few students made some noncommittal sounds of agreement.

"That's a great idea, Marla," said the professor, pulling out his lesson plan. "Why don't you prepare a five-page paper on why young adults today are not given the kind of respect and freedom as those of the ancient Nile Delta? I recommend working with me at the Egyptian exhibit, where all of you can see documents from the reign of Ramses II, who was a ruler before he was a teenager."

"Are you kidding me?" said Marla, sitting up.

"Of course not," said the professor. "It's well documented. I think you'll also find some compelling research on children of peasant families, who didn't have to go to school at all. In fact, they were allowed to work in the fields as early as six years of age."

"I mean about the five-page paper," said Marla.

"Well, it'll be six pages with the bibliography, but, yes. You can present your findings to the class on Friday."

As Professor Darling was absentmindedly giving Marla an assignment, Wendy and John sank farther and farther in their seats. The others kids never really understood their dad. He was like the ultimate head-in-the-clouds, nose-in-the-books, good-intentions-but-terrible-attention-span kind of history nerd. And it wasn't exactly doing wonders for them on the social front. It was even worse for John, who was accelerated into classes with his older sister. His dad may as well have spoon-fed him his lunches in the cafeteria.

Marla rolled her eyes and shut her history book with an irritated clap. John ventured a glance her way, but she caught it and glared back. He gulped. Marla was the kind of rich kid who thought she was badass just because she dressed in black clothes and played guitar—never mind that *real* street kids couldn't afford to go Goth in cashmere.

"The items in this exhibit came from the British Museum," said Professor Darling, clapping his hands, "and they've included artifacts dating from the late Coptic period all the way back to pre-Antiquity. I'm sure you all know how exciting it is to have the pieces from the world's largest collection. I mean, we could be looking at undiscovered history here."

Here we go, thought Wendy. Every time Professor Darling used the phrase *undiscovered history,* it meant he was about to start waxing poetic about humankind, oral traditions, myths, and the stories we tell one another around the fireplace. He loved the phrase because it was full of mystery. Anything could be discovered and join historical fact. Any impossibility could become possible. "Every fiction," he'd say, "is a fact that hasn't been proven yet."

"I'll be needing as many volunteers as I can get to help catalog the pieces before the exhibit goes up."

Someone in the back said, "Oooh, where do I sign up?"

Professor Darling didn't seem to hear.

"The theme I've proposed for the show is the *Five Legends.* That sounds cool, doesn't it?"

"Super cool," said Marla, in a tone so sarcastic that even their father must have noticed.

As always, he ignored it and went on with undiminished enthusiasm. "Some of the pieces we've acquired are fascinating. For example, we have in our exhibit several canopic jars used in Egyptian funereal rites. And we have a very old copy of the *Book of Gates,* which, I should add, *could* be a set of original bound papyri dating back thousands of years." The professor's eyes sparkled and he added, "Of course, that isn't what the museum community believes, which is why they let us borrow it. . . . You know, the original *Book of Gates* is said to have magical powers."

The professor waved his fingers in the air, obviously trying to seem mysterious, or even interesting. He deflated in the silence that followed. "OK, well, no one has really suggested *magic*, but I've presented theories that mystical occurrences have surrounded this lost artifact. Personally, I believe the original book may be the key to unearthing the truth behind the five great legends . . . *myths*, as they are called by . . . most scholars. The historicity of the stories is doubted by many, but I think anything is possible."

"Five legends?" John asked.

"Yes, yes, John," said the professor hurriedly. "The five stories that are told in the *Book of Gates*. Remember, I showed you an English translation in our library at home?"

John flushed and dropped lower in his seat. Professor Darling was getting excited again, talking with his hands above his head and walking around. Wendy groaned. Her dad's fairy-tale theories about Egypt had given him a reputation as a kook. No one denied that he was preeminent in the field, but maybe he just believed more than he should have.

"Well, an English translation from our house is one thing . . ." Professor Darling stopped. As soon as the professor said the words *our house*, someone in the back snickered.

Someone whispered, "We can't all live in a free house on Marlowe's dime."

Someone else responded, "I wonder if our tuition pays for his storybooks."

Professor Darling reddened but continued, pretending not to hear. "An English copy is one thing, but the long-lost original . . . well, some people say that it can do a lot more than just *recount* the five stories. It has the power to *unlock* their mysteries to the world."

Professor Darling wiped a bead of sweat off his brow. Wendy knew that discussing his less conventional theories with a Marlowe crowd always had this effect on him. He switched to something less risky. "The five legends in the *Book of Gates* revolve around great loss. Five people—unknown to history, but tied together by a single cursed bloodline—who have suffered injustice on an eternal scale, the life of each becoming a legend in its own right."

"What do you mean, *unknown to history*?" asked a soft-voiced girl in the back, a freshman also accelerated into the class along with John. "I mean, *you* seem to know about them."

"Ahh," said Professor Darling. "We know of them through *myth*, Jenny. But these stories have not made it into conventional Egyptian history, or even mainstream mythology. They are part of a much more obscure, much more *secret*, lore. A lore that is shunned by scholars and Egyptians. A lore that would tell us that even the death god was something different from what is commonly believed."

The class was quiet for a moment. The professor went on. "As I was saying, each of the five legends tells the story of a grave injustice. In one story, the injustice may be the loss of a person's heritage. In another, maybe great love. But in all of them, there is something that caused a great bitterness to grow and fester inside—a bitterness over a life not fully lived. The ancient Egyptians used to say that this bitterness, this desire to take back what was lost, has a life of its own. It lingers in the world of the living. And so, these five characters continued to *linger.* You see, none of this would matter if the heroes of the five legends had just had a normal death and burial. But that isn't *exactly* what happened, now, is it?"

Some of the sleepy students perked up. The professor was pacing the floor with a far-gone look, lecturing wistfully, from memory. Even Marla was interested. "What did happen, then?" she whispered, an almost sadistic look in her black-lined eyes.

Professor Darling shot Marla a smile. "Well, they were mummified, of course! We all know that the Egyptians believed that mummification was the way to transmit a body into the afterlife. But we also know that it was only the pharaohs or the extremely wealthy who could afford to be mummified. These five characters were certainly not historic icons. But legend has it that they were each *somehow* mummified, which is an astonishing fluke in itself. It was the mummification that preserved the bitterness in their bones."

"So, wait a minute," said John. "You're saying that the reason *these* five made it into the legends and not anyone else was because they had something really bad happen to them and then they were mummified?"

Professor Darling nodded. "There were *three* commonalities among the five legends that made them unique. One, the grave injustices. Two, the mummification. And three, the fact that they were all in the same family—a shared bloodline. Through the workings of fate," the professor continued, "these five doomed souls were first born into the same cursed line and then were serendipitously and undeservedly mummified. It is said their lives were trapped in their bones, their souls unable to leave the mortal world. Not while the wrongs against them remained unavenged."

The professor trailed off, and the children's expectation hung in the air. The professor was staring off into nothing.

"So?" said Marla finally.

The professor blinked. "So, what?"

"So, what happened? What happened to their bodies? Did they get revenge?"

Professor Darling smiled. "Well, no one knows. Their bodies disappeared. They weren't alive, but they couldn't die. Some people say the god of death took them away, knowing what great magic was hidden in their bones. The force of injustice on such a massive scale . . . well, it can't just disappear. These five mummies are believed to possess within them a substance that treasure seekers and storytellers call bonedust. It is said that the bonedust from the five mummies, when mixed together, can give everlasting life—a real-life fountain of youth, if you will—that it can overcome death and undermine the death god's greatest power. Bonedust is her greatest enemy."

"What do you mean, *her*?" asked Wendy.

Professor Darling's eyes flashed blue-gray as he leaned on his daughter's desk. "Well, *that*, my dear, is one of the most fascinating parts of the legend. According to five legends lore, the death god is not Anubis, as is believed by historians and Egyptians. It is a *woman*." Professor Darling scurried behind his desk and grabbed a stack of notes. "You see, every legend starts and ends the same way. Each one starts by telling us what that hero's injustice was. And it ends like this. . . ." He began to read from a yellowing page:

"The bitterness of this injustice devoured his soul. And so, he died with his life trapped in his bones. The goddess of death took the mummy and the bonedust with it. She shielded it with her greatest weapons, fearing that someday death might be conquered. The Dark Lady hid the mummy in a place where no one could reach it, a legendary labyrinth of the gates. . . . And so, [our hero] was gone, but he can never fully die . . . his wasted life forever trapped as grains of immortality in his bones."

"You see?" the professor continued. "The legends say that the death god is a woman. They call her the *Dark Lady,* but I believe she appears in the fifth legend. . . ." He trailed off, then began again. "This is why most people believe the five legends are rubbish. Because everywhere you go in Egypt, you see statues of the jackal-headed Anubis. You don't see a female death god. But *we* have a statue of her in our very own exhibit. I suggest you all go and look at it."

"So is the bonedust around somewhere?" asked Jenny, the quiet-voiced ninth-grader.

"Most people would say it isn't anywhere. They're just myths, remember?"

"But according to this legend?" asked John.

"According to this, the bonedust is hidden in an unidentified labyrinth. And some say that the original *Book of Gates* is the key to unlocking it."

"Tell us one of the legends," said Marla.

Professor Darling didn't have to be asked twice. He sat on the edge of his desk, looked each rapt student in the eye, picked up a tattered spiral notebook and a smattering of crinkled notes from his desk, and began reading his own meticulous English translation of the first legend.

The First Legend

A legacy is a precious thing. If a man is robbed of his life's work, of his chance to achieve the basic immortality granted to all who work and raise children, a bitterness builds inside.

This is the story of one family with a curse on their line, a dark legacy full of the cruelest injustices. Tales of their fate have wafted through Egypt for centuries, like smoke clouds that refuse to die. They cannot die. Their stolen lives linger on, still flowing in their bones. Life has been mummified inside them, forming an ever-living bonedust—a new kind of immortality.

Their tombs are hidden, for they bear a great secret. When ground together into dust, the remaining bones of these five mummies give eternal life—a chance to escape death and defy the goddess. Natives have long told ever-fading legends about the secret of the dust. For centuries they have searched and failed, for the family name is buried, their saga hidden. Those who decipher the ancient relics and find their way through the gates meet obstacles that have killed many.

A legacy is a precious thing. So it was for the first father of this wretched family. In the time of the ancient pharaohs, when the people of Israel were slaves in the land of Egypt and little hope of freedom yet existed, Elan worked to save his family. Born in the tribe of Benjamin, Elan was proud of his heritage and of the heritage he would one day create. Every day, he toiled under the taskmaster's whip. His greatest hope was to have children and to watch them grow up free.

One day, as he hung by his waist from a rope near the top of a half-erected palace—the future home of Akhara, a high official of the pharaoh—Elan received the news that he had become a father. With difficulty he lowered himself to the ground, ready to rush to his wife's side. But the taskmaster was loitering below. Elan tried to slip away to his wife, freed from all reason by the elation in his heart. But the taskmaster was too quick. When the broad-faced guard raised his whip, Elan did the unthinkable. He reached up and grabbed the man's hand, bringing the whip down with a slight jerk.

The guard's eyes flashed.

Another guard arrived. Then another.

Within minutes, Elan was beaten and dragged to the court of Akhara. There, the high official offered him a bargain. "Build me a tomb worthy of a god, and upon your death, your family will be set free. There is only one condition: from today onward, you will have no tools and no help from your brethren."

That night, Elan held his son for the first time. He turned Akhara's bargain over in his mind.

Soon after, Elan had a daughter, and with each passing day, he threw himself more fiercely into his work. He gathered straw from the discarded piles of the other slaves, from the stables and fields. He built his own bricks, one by one. He fashioned his own rods and rope pulleys. He erected the pieces of Akhara's pyramid little by little, so the very walls were soaked with his sweat.

Through all this, the gods ignored this insignificant man.

For twenty-five years, Elan worked.

Then, one day, when his back was bent with work and his hair had become like wisps of gray cotton, he looked up and saw that he was finished. He had built a five-headed pyramid of clay and stone, with five pointed pillars protruding from the pyramid base. It was painted a golden color since he had no gold of his own, but it was a tomb without equal.

That night, Elan knocked on Akhara's door with his cane. But he was greeted with silence. He called into the house, but his aging voice did not carry far. He waited until the sun went down, leaning on his cane outside Akhara's door.

When he returned home, Elan found Akhara's answer waiting for him. Four guards were holding his wife and children at the point of their spears. Elan rushed toward them but was held back by a leering guard. There, before his eyes, they killed Elan's only son. Elan fell to his knees, the screams of his wife and daughter fading behind the thundering in his head.

Then, through the blur of tears and aging eyes, past the sandaled feet of the guards, he saw the rich robes of Akhara. "Slaves do not make bargains," said the high official. "No slave should fancy himself so strong, or he and his sons will be cut down. But you have done good work, and I am a just man. I will marry your daughter as fair compensation."

Elan and his wife were returned to a life of slavery. His daughter, Jobey, was swept away by the guards, and Elan never saw her again. She might have been his legacy, but she was stripped of his name, of his heritage, and of his God. She was not free, but a slave to a cruel husband.

For years, Elan wallowed in the fact that his life's work had been for nothing and that he would have no legacy. His children's children would be swallowed up by Egypt, their blood diluted long after he was dust. To Elan, that was the greatest injustice of all. The bitterness devoured his soul. He died with his life trapped in his bones.

But Elan's daughter did not forget her father. When he died, she asked her servants to steal his body and take it to the tomb that he had built with his own hands for the thief Akhara. There, she mummified his body, preserving his bones and all the venom they contained. The body of the old man rested in Akhara's tomb undetected until the story of Elan the builder passed to legend, and the magic that he held with him found its way to the goddess of death.

When Akhara died a few years later, his family finally discovered that the great tomb had been used. They found pieces of Elan's burial clothes and a few of his remaining belongings, but they could not find his body. Elan's daughter, too, was shocked to see that her father was gone. For desecrating Akhara's tomb before his death, Elan's daughter was put to death, and her children were given to Akhara's other wives. The women were ordered never to speak of the children's true heritage. As for Elan, the goddess of death had already taken the old man's mummy, and the first bonedust with it. She shielded it with her greatest weapons, fearing that someday death might be conquered. The Dark Lady hid the mummy in a place where no one could reach it, a legendary labyrinth of the Gates, guarded by powerful deities that no human could overcome.

And so, Elan was gone, his legacy lost. But he can never fully die. His wasted life is forever trapped as grains of immortality in his bones.

INTERLUDE

PETER

Peter sat alone on the front lawn of Marlowe watching kids in sports gear rushing this way and that, teachers heading home, and that Darling girl playing around with her boyfriend, the lacrosse player. He wondered if she'd ever had any other boyfriends, a pretty girl like that. He wondered what she really wanted—how much effort it would take him to pluck her away.

Soon it was dusk and all the kids cleared out of the school, all the sports ended, and the Darling girl went home, too. Peter sat on the lawn—even after the dark overtook the school and that fearful part of him began to shiver.

The Dark Lady was present. Peter could feel it. She had drawn him here. And now the school would begin to change. It would become like the world below, because now it was linked to that world. The fog would seep into every crevice and slowly infect Marlowe, just as it had done to every other place the book had been. The air would become harder to breathe. The walls would grow moldy and unwelcoming. Everything that was once fresh would become rancid and spoiled. Peter could see it happening now. It would start with just a feeling, and soon not a single happy thought would remain.

Across the lawn, Peter spied a matronly nurse in a blue sweater set walking toward the girls' dorm. She swept across the lawn lithely, quietly, moving the way his own nanny had all those years ago. The nanny who had first shown him the book, thinking he would just forget about it like any other child. The ageless nanny with the moth-eaten clothes who had tried to corrupt him with her stories but had created a hunger instead. The hateful nanny with the antique metal hook, a gray mist in his mind that chased him for all these years.

PETER PANIC AND THE MARLOWE LBs

"All right, everybody gather around." Peter waved a hand to the eleven boys who made up his advisee group—the kids who lived in the hall he now ruled. To these longtime residents of the boys' dormitory, the guy standing in the doorway of the RA room and signaling them to follow him inside didn't seem much older than a student. Usually, resident advisers were twenty-something burnouts desperate to sidle up close to one of Marlowe's famous professors. Once there was a girl who became an RA just so she could advise the daughter of a music mogul. Apparently, she had a demo CD. But Peter looked young, like he could be a senior at Marlowe—not an authority figure, but one of their own. They had already met the girl next to him, Tina, who had a bridge 'n' tunnel sleazy-sexy bad-grammar thing going on that made the boarding kids imagine she'd treat their parents like garbage. Basically, they fell in love with her image. No one bothered to ask why she was at the boys' dorm meeting. She was just always there. And they loved it—even though she had been the one to rip out their tooth with pliers (except for the two senior boys, Poet and Cornrow, who had been members of Peter's crew for all the years they had attended Marlowe).

"Listen up," said Peter, standing in the middle of his sparsely furnished room. The eleven boys of his hall were now packed inside. The room was old, and badly lit, with a nonworking fireplace and mismatched bricks in the walls. Apparently, Marlowe couldn't be bothered to revamp historical buildings like the dorms. In one corner, two twin beds had been pushed together to form a king, which was covered with a gray-and-navy, standard-issue Marlowe comforter. In another corner stood a desk and one chair. Peter hadn't bought a couch or a coffee table, as most RAs did. He wasn't exactly planning to throw weekly study breaks. "I know you guys are new, but you have to use your heads," he said, tapping his forehead. "You can't just go up to a bunch of players and demand money." He spoke slowly, as if they were very dumb children. "If you need to shake 'em down, you pick the weakest one. And always, *always*, leave a physical reminder—nothing huge—just a bruise, a cut. These guys aren't from the streets. No need to break bones. Oh, and do it off campus."

The boys were nodding excitedly.

"That Connor kid's a bad target," said Peter. "He's the kind that goes running to Mommy. Watch him, though. His girlfriend's a teacher's kid, right?" Peter looked thoughtful. But he didn't say any more about the Darlings or the exhibit he had chased all the way from London. Tina was now picking up his lecture where he had left off.

"And if someone doesn't pay, you call *me*, got it?" said Tina.

Once again, no one objected.

When the new RAs had first arrived and Peter had taken out the boys from his hall and introduced them to the real New York and all the destructive possibilities of being LBs, not a single one of them had hesitated. Peter was an underground god—a legend that Cornrow and Poet had spread throughout the Marlowe dorms.

"Look," Peter went on, "I'm supposed to give you an intro meeting." He looked at a stack of papers that had been mailed to him by the residential advising department of the school. He looked disgusted as he read through it. "So, let's get this over with. I'm the new RA. You got crap to deal with, help with your homework, or life advice, find it online. I don't do 'life coach,' and I don't counsel overprivileged monkeys on the existential questions of youth." The boys shuffled around, smirking and nudging one another as they drank up his every word. "In fact, don't think of me as your RA at all." Peter took a permanent marker out of his pocket. He turned and crossed out the capital *A* on his door. Next to it he wrote a lowercase *a*. One kid in the back (probably the only one who had ever heard of Ra, the sun god) snickered. "Think of me as a figure in your life that is bigger than you, harder than you, and willing to cut you to pieces. Think of me as someone you want to keep on your side."

The advisee group, the new LBs of the Marlowe School, grew quiet, none of them willing to admit how nervous this guy made them. In his haste to look cool, one of them pulled out a cigarette. Peter waited for him to light it before yanking it out of his mouth and putting it out on the kid's jacket.

Then Peter went to the mini-fridge next to his desk and pulled out five cartons of ice cream. "Now, I'm supposed to host something like five events every semester." He tossed out the half gallons to several kids. "This is your first one. An ice-cream social. Eat in your rooms." Peter walked to the door and held it open, expecting them to leave.

"Wait, that's it?" said the South Asian kid with royal parents, who was now covered in bling and holding a carton of cookies 'n' cream. "What about the . . . you know . . . the thing?" He pointed to his missing tooth. "What's the next thing?"

"We tell you when to talk about the *thing*," said Tina, playing with the pliers like she was itching to pull another tooth.

"I got business with one of your professors right now," said Peter.

"Psh," said the Chinese kid with a crew cut. "Shoulda figured you was a punk. Man, you just another old wannabe. Whatever, man . . ."

A droplet of sweat shivered down Peter's thumping temple. A twitch. He said, "Did you just call me old?" Peter snapped the pliers out of Tina's hand and walked toward the smart-mouth. The kid stepped back.

"Yo, Peter Panic, ease up, son," said one of the boys in the back.

"What?" said Peter, lifting an eyebrow, clicking the pliers like the jaws of a crocodile. "What did you just say to me?"

Even Tina seemed unnerved. She leaned toward the two veteran LBs. Cornrow, a banker's kid with baby-pink skin and blond corn-rows, was well known at Marlowe for getting away with all sorts of crap. Everyone knew that this guy never got in trouble. And anytime something went wrong, everyone knew he was behind it. The kid was like a money-dropping, school-skipping, trouble-shirking ghost. And not just because his dad had the best lawyers. The other boy, a thick-shouldered black guy with thin-rimmed glasses and an adult-size goatee, looked like he had been held back for ten years. Peter called him Poet, not just because his dad was a famous rapper but also because of his poet glasses.

"That is *not* a happy thought," Tina said, leaning over to whisper to the two.

Cornrow nodded and smiled. Tina looked on curiously as the two boys began to whisper to each other.

"What are you doing?" she asked.

"Just watch," said Poet. "One order of happy thoughts, coming up."

Cornrow and Poet each pulled out their fancy phones and started searching the Internet. Peter had the Chinese kid by the collar and was lining up the pliers to pull more teeth. The kid was wrenching his head so that Peter couldn't get a good grip.

"OK, what about this?" said Cornrow, showing Poet a story about stock prices.

Poet shook his head. "That's stupid."

Poet pulled up a video of a cat jumping out of a hedge and pouncing on a baby.

Tina laughed, but said, "Nah, he only cares about one thing."

"Got it," said Poet with a nod.

One thing they all knew about Peter was that he hated the idea of growing old. He stared at Marlowe's middle-aged teachers with revulsion, counting each line and wrinkle, assessing every sunspot, crinkling his nose at every bald spot and paunchy belly. He critiqued the signs of their surrender with nothing less than scorn—those cowardly reading glasses, that outmoded hair, the pathetic layers of amorphous cloth meant to drape and hide. Peter had a complex—a need to live forever, sort of like the ancient Egyptians who couldn't stand to let their dead decay and be lost. Peter was like them, with his never-ending quest for bonedust. He had a hunger. A mummy complex as rigid and unchanging as the ages. A rigor mortis of the spirit.

The Chinese kid squealed as Peter took hold of one of his teeth and prepared to yank.

"Here!" said Cornrow loudly. "Check this out."

"What?" Peter turned, loosening his grip on the boy.

Cornrow continued, "Some fifty-year-old lady that still gets carded at clubs. Pig placenta in the antiaging cream. Can you believe it? It has, like, a ninety-percent success rate."

"Really?" said Peter. "Huh." He turned back to the Chinese boy but seemed a little less interested in hurting him.

"Hey, Pete," said Poet. "Just got an e-mail from the school."

"So?" said Peter.

"It's about the new staff," said Poet. "There's a bit about you, man."

Poet handed Peter his iPhone. Peter dropped the Chinese kid and began reading the e-mail out loud. Suddenly a smile rose up from his lips and spread all over his face.

"Introducing three new staff members: Ms. Neve Verat, our new nurse, and two resident advisers . . . including the youngest member of our staff, the new resident adviser for the boys' dormitory . . ."

"Nice," said Peter.

"I wonder if the new nurse is hot," said one of the boys.

"Nah," said another. "She's a mouse."

Tina looked at the two veterans with obvious admiration. No, this wasn't the Cockney street gang from London, with their cheap technology and haul-ass mentality. These kids were sophisticated— rich LBs with expensive toys.

"A'ight," said Poet. "Is it cool if I bounce, Pete? I got an essay on *The Picture of Dorian Gray.* Gotta keep the numbers up, know what I mean?"

"Yeah," said Peter, his interest piqued. His eyes twinkled as if he was thinking all kinds of very happy thoughts. "Keep up the numbers . . . know what you mean," he said. Peter slapped the Chinese kid on the back; the boy rubbed his cheek and backed away as fast as he could. With a dreamy expression, Peter motioned for them all to get out of his room.

That day, Wendy was particularly aware that none of the boarding boys showed up to any classes. She still saw them hanging around the main Marlowe building and the dorms, but that was no indication of what they were up to, since they *lived* at school. Maybe they were planning a ditch day. She saw them huddling as a posse on the street corner, smoking and whispering to that new RA who had appeared randomly on the lacrosse field. *Since when do these guys hang out with an RA?*

Normally, she would ignore all this. Wendy had no interest in delving into the lives of self-absorbed, spoiled boys who thought they were above the rules. She wasn't one of the girls who followed their every action eagerly, checking each Facebook update, (which there weren't many of, anyway, since these guys liked to keep low profiles online), waiting for an iota of attention. But something about the new RA intrigued her. He was dark, moody, obviously their leader despite his lame job title, and most unnervingly, he stared blatantly at her each time they crossed paths. And not just her. He observed the *school* like a thief staking out a house—taking in everything and everyone. He was dark and peculiar, with a satisfied smile curling on his lips each time one of the other guys vied for his attention. He ran his hands through his hair and glanced at his shadow—just to make sure that every strand was still in place. He was good-looking, but standing here with his posse of rebels in private-school uniforms, he looked nothing like any of the guys she had ever known. How old was he? Wendy wondered. Sixteen? Seventeen? *Must be older to get the RA job. Probably a college student.*

When Wendy came back out after third period, Peter was standing by the girls' dorm, helping an eighth-grader figure out why her ID wasn't working on the doors. He was obviously bored with the task (though he was nice enough to the girl) and cracked some joke about teaching her to break in. Wendy walked by with her gaze on the ground. His long, thin silhouette extended out, imposing itself on the sunny sidewalk as his shadow hand smoothed his shadow hair. Somehow, every time Wendy passed by the crosswalk near the dorms, he froze, his hand in midair. She felt singled out—as if he was watching her. She liked the idea very much, but she couldn't help but notice that he had a girl, the other RA, who had been waiting for him on the far side of the lacrosse field, a girl that Wendy noticed stood very close to him when they spoke. And what did she care, anyway? She had a boyfriend who had been amazing to her.

Later that week, Wendy saw the handsome RA walk toward the dark-haired girl and whisper something in her ear. She seemed delighted, leaning forward and looking down at her feet as he murmured his instructions. Lingering only a few feet away, Wendy could see that he was reaching for the girl's hand and that the girl let him hold it—for only a second—before she threw her head back and laughed, raising her eyebrow at something he had told her. *She must be his girlfriend.* Wendy stepped closer. She couldn't help it. Something about this boy made her want to listen, despite the guilt and the shame of wanting to be closer to him. So she pretended to walk by several times, hidden by other bystanders. She heard him say something about her father's Egyptian exhibit, and she grew even more curious. Why would a guy like that, one who probably rides a motorcycle and goes to college parties and only has an RA job for the cash, care about a stupid Egyptian exhibit?

One day, as Wendy was walking down the halls with Connor's arm on her shoulder, Peter passed by with the girl, and he and Wendy exchanged a long look, a look that made him smirk and put his arm around the dark-haired RA. A look that made the angry brunette glare as though to say that she was very capable of doing Wendy bodily harm. Wendy pulled away from Connor just as she came shoulder to shoulder with Peter, but she was pretty sure neither boy noticed. Next time, she would introduce herself—just to legitimize their future interactions, because after all, why should she be avoiding a member of the Marlowe staff? She had done nothing, would do nothing, to make herself behave with so much guilt and awkwardness. And she wanted that involuntary part of her mind, the part that turned on when she was asleep or exercising or was supposed to be thinking about homework or exercising, to stop.

She didn't have to wait long for an introduction. After school, as she was leaving the building, she saw John at the center of a very amused circle of boarding boys, including Peter the RA.

"Lost Boys?" John was saying. "I can dig that name. . . . LBs . . . that's cool. How about you let me join your crew? I got mad skills."

"Our crew?" said one of the boys with a laugh.

"Yeah, crew. Like, lookin' out for the otha. Poppin' caps in the suckas. Rollin' ten deep. Havin' love for the street. Hustlin' till we're bustlin'." John made all the appropriate hand signs to illustrate his point.

"Where did you learn to talk like that?" asked a newly minted LB.

"Gaming, mostly. Everyone talks like that on Xbox LIVE. I got brothas and hos all up on the World Wide Weezy, you know?" said John.

"We don't really call girls hos anymore," said Peter.

"Why?" said John.

"Although," interjected Peter, "we should definitely start saying World Wide Weezy."

The boys had a laugh. One of them slapped John on the back, which almost knocked him down. John grew red.

"I'm just kidding," said Peter. "You can roll with us anytime you like. Might need to catch up a little, but that's cool."

Wendy instinctively reached for John and pulled him back by

his shoulder. He jerked her hand off and muttered, "Leave me alone, Wen." He was obviously insulted and humiliated by Peter's brush-off. Still, Wendy knew John wouldn't back off. She didn't like that he was beginning to idolize the boarding kids. Everyone at Marlowe knew how rough they could be. They had all the money and freedom in the world and absolutely no one to give them rules or advice. The Marlowe faculty didn't care. They received massive donations to keep these kids happy and educated—and to overlook any infraction that could be chalked up to loneliness or lack of family. Wendy felt sad for them. They were like a super-rich version of herself, because they too didn't have mothers who loved them enough to stay. They were like orphans, forced to live at school because no one else wanted them. But then again, they were the most entitled bunch of playboys she'd ever met. So her sympathy only went so far.

She wished that John could see all that: that the boarders were nothing to idolize, that they were very much like John and Wendy. But nowadays, all John cared about was looking cool enough or wealthy enough, and he brooded constantly over his failed Facebook reinvention maneuver. Well, at least she could give him *some* help, Wendy thought, making a mental note to ask Connor to invite John to work out again. It would be so much better for John to hang out with the lacrosse boys than with these criminals.

The thought of Connor made Wendy suddenly aware of Peter watching her. "I'm Wendy Darling," she said.

Peter nodded as if he already knew, and he didn't offer his name, as if he expected her to know it already. Instead he said, "Don't worry so much about your brother, Wendy. These guys are cool. We're just talking about this exhibit we want to see."

Wendy raised an eyebrow. Peter may have been cute, but this was exactly the kind of pretend-do-gooder comment that made her suspicious. She wasn't the kind of girl who let herself be manipulated. If she knew anything, it was that people always lie to get you to like them just before they do something to disappoint you. That had been Wendy's experience all her life. Might as well start off with a healthy dose of suspicion and never get caught off guard.

"Look," she said distractedly, "the exhibit isn't even open yet—" Wendy stopped herself, but it was too late. Peter was giving her a strange sideways glance.

"How'd you know we were talking about the Egyptian exhibit?"

A smile grew on Peter's lips as Wendy blanched and the boys laughed. Peter knew she had been watching him, and now she looked like some kind of stalker. Peter didn't take his eyes off Wendy.

"Well, Wendy Darling, since we're on the subject, what's up with this exhibit? Have you seen it yet?" He said the *Darling* with emphasis, as if it was a very important part of her name.

Wendy stifled a laugh, amused at the way Peter allowed himself to be so transparent in his manipulation—as if, for him alone, it wasn't such a bad thing to do.

Peter kept prodding. "Is there an old book called—?"

At the mention of the book, Wendy remembered something. She interrupted Peter—"I have to go"—and checked her watch. She had been on her way to the basement, where the exhibit's items were waiting to be dusted, cataloged, and readied for display. The job her father had finagled for her didn't pay as much as the café, but Wendy wasn't going to turn down a paying gig. And she appreciated the trouble he had gone to. Besides, for once John didn't object (since she was tucked away in a basement, away from judgmental eyes, working on a project that even John secretly geeked out over). "I'm starting a new job today. John, let's go."

"Why do *I* have to go?" John whined, and then caught himself.

"Come on, little bro." Wendy put an arm around her brother's shoulder. "You love poking around in Dad's junk. And if you keep me company, I'll share the paycheck."

As they walked away, John again shrugged off her arm and said (loud enough to ensure the LBs heard), "Only 'cause I need the dough." When they were out of earshot, John said, "That guy's kind of a punk. He talked to me like I was five or something."

"He's an RA. He's just doing his job," said Wendy.

"No way. He rolls up like he's 800 on the verbal. Look at the way he keeps looking at his shadow and fixing his hair."

"You fix your hair all the time!" said Wendy. "I don't even think hair's supposed to stand up like that." She ran her hand over his spikes.

"Whatever," said John, for once not pushing away his sister's hand.

I've met that kid somewhere before, Professor Darling mused as he watched his children through the glass of Marlowe's giant double doors. He had been observing John's conversation with the boarding boys, hoping that he would lose interest in that particular social group, when he had noticed the new RA. Now the old man stood watching Peter, wondering where on earth they could have met before.

When John and Wendy had disappeared into the back entrance that led down into the basement, George Darling decided that he would introduce himself to this new Marlowe staff member. He strolled outside and approached the pack of boys that were still hanging on to Peter's every word. As he stepped outside, he couldn't help but notice the strange gloom hanging over the school. *Strange,* he thought, since New York was usually beautiful this time of year. The last few days had been bizarre. First a moth infestation, then the strange smell that seemed to permeate half the classrooms on the first floor, and now this dark, dreary weather.

Peter stepped forward and offered his hand in that overtly deferential yet clearly superior manner that future politicians use with their elders when they are still rule-breaking, troublemaking teens. "I'm Peter," he said. "Pleasure to make your esteemed acquaintance."

Professor Darling looked hard into the boy's face. He pursed his lips, then looked away, coughing into his hand.

"Have we met?" Peter asked suddenly. He peered at Professor Darling, trying to connect him to a place or time before this trip to Marlowe. Peter looked with disgust at Darling's wrinkled face. He squinted, as if trying to take in the look of the man's face while sifting out all the irksome signs of old age. "It couldn't be. I don't know any old people."

One of the boys grinned.

Then another.

Like a stroke of lightning, the sight of their missing teeth sent shock waves through Professor Darling. He stood dumbfounded a few feet away from the group.

CORNROW

All I used to be is

Five times two

With nuthin' to do

Just a kid on the stoop

Always lovin' my troop

Always list'nin' to Snoop

LBs took mah teeth

So my nanny packed soup

But I didn't have a care

'Cuz I didn't have a coop

I was quick to the hoop

My eyes didn't droop

If my daddy was rare

At least Peter was there

Peter

The city lights were like ten thousand little lamps keeping the bedroom monsters away. A night wind swooping across the avenue
chilled the back of Peter's soaked undershirt. He had woken up in a
sweat again and needed to distract himself. Without really thinking
about it, he headed toward the Darling house. From the street corner
on the residential block, he could see Wendy's window. The light
was still on. She was reading at the window, probably something
for class. Her hair was up in a bun, with a pencil holding it up. She
had another pencil in her mouth and a mild scowl of concentration
on her face. Peter barely knew her, but just staring at her seemed to
calm him. Maybe it was that she had lost her mother, too.

Peter closed his eyes. The nightmare was still there, waiting
behind his eyelids: He is young, very young, and his mother sits at
her mirror. He holds on to her knees. She leans forward and exam-
ines her gaunt cheeks, her sunken eyes. The sickness will take her
soon. Peter stares at the sparrow on her jewelry box in order to save
himself from crying. His mother looks down and attempts a smile.

She says, "Don't worry. I will be old, very old, before I go." But only one week later, Peter is standing at a fresh grave.

Peter opened his eyes. Wendy was gone. He turned and walked back down the avenue, thinking of Wendy's disheveled hair, the freckles on the back of her neck, and repeating his mother's happy mantra that death is not for the young.

6

THE EXHIBITION

If there's one thing John understood about being *street*, it was that you give people their props when they help you out. And even though Wendy was too busy being this super-cool junior, hanging with her boyfriend and basically rubbing it all in John's face, he knew why she had taken the job at the exhibit. There was a wad of ones and fives in his pocket that said he owed her *something*. So he'd agreed to go and meet the British guy who was supposed to watch over the exhibit items. Besides, his dad had been hounding him about giving this guy a chance. Anyway, John didn't mind helping—the exhibit was pretty cool. He caught himself thinking that and shook his head sadly. If his classmates could read minds, they'd give him the gold medal for the dweeb Olympics. He wished he could be one of the LBs—just change his image completely and be a badass.

Then he remembered his misfire with the lacrosse boys and pulled out his phone to update his Facebook status:

John Darling says screw this.

John Darling doesn't give a damn.

John Darling is

John tried to imagine what the new exhibit assistant could be like. Most people who worked for John's dad were suck-ups— jumping over one another to assist the kindly professor, with his whimsical beliefs in myths and his amusing stories about dig sites. Then again, his dad could be a slave driver when it came to his work. It reminded John of Thutmose III's ironfisted rule in the Eighteenth Dynasty, culminating in his campaign against the Nubian tribes in the Upper Nile. *Oh, no.* John glanced around to make sure no one saw him thinking about the fifteenth century BC.

As he rounded a corner toward his dad's office, John saw Connor slamming shut his locker. "Hey, little buddy," said Connor, a big smile spreading across his face.

"Hey, man," said John, trying to think of something cool to say. He wished Connor hadn't called him *little buddy.*

"I was just looking for you," said Connor, hoisting his gym bag over his shoulder. "Sorry about the guys the other day. Tim's just a jerk. Anyway, my parents have a box at MSG and a bunch of us are going to watch the Knicks. Wanna come?"

"To watch the Knicks?" said John excitedly. "At Madison Square Garden?" This definitely sounded like something for *real* friends only. Connor nodded. "In your parents' box?" John knew what that meant. A private box meant *free of charge.* And that meant he wouldn't have to make up some excuse to avoid spending money he didn't have.

"Yep," said Connor, throwing an arm around John's shoulder as they walked down the hall. John pulled himself to his full height. He was still several inches shorter than Connor. "And afterward, we're all going for steaks and imported beers at a new place near there. I know a waiter, so European party rules apply. No IDs."

John was practically salivating. He'd never even tasted beer before, much less beer from Holland or wherever it was they imported it from. He fingered the small stack of bills in his pocket. Would thirty-seven dollars be enough for a steak and beer? Plus tax and tip? *Probably not*. And Connor's mom wouldn't be there to pay for the steaks. Probably, it would be one of those things where all the guys split the bill equally, so John would end up with a huge charge, even if he didn't order much. For a second, John considered asking Connor to cover him. He was only thirteen, after all, and these kids were so casual about their cash. He might even look *less* poor if he just admitted it. But that thought only lasted for an instant before John dismissed it as utterly stupid.

"Nah, man," John mumbled, hating himself for having to miss out on a private box just because of some dinner afterward. But he couldn't go to the game and then skip out on the meal. Then everyone would know. "I have things to do."

"Are you serious?" said Connor. "You don't have to worry about the guys. They'll be cool. And I already told Wendy—"

"I'm not worried about the guys," John snapped, and quickened his pace, his fist tight around the wad of useless bills. "Thanks, Connor, but I have to go."

Connor shrugged as he turned to walk away. "Suit yourself, kid."

Stupid school. John would definitely have to join the LBs. He'd have to become as street as he possibly could so he'd have something other than money to offer the crew. And it wouldn't be easy, because that stupid RA was out to make him look like a little kid—and on top of it all, the jerk was sweet-talking his sister. *Gross.* John had overheard Professor Darling talking to Wendy about Peter. "Honey," their dad had said, "I don't want you spending time with older boys. Focus on your grades." And John couldn't agree more. Peter was a poser. Why did he have to make fun of John's street talk? Couldn't he just be *cool* about it? John was just chillin' with the LBs. That's what dudes did. They chilled like villains. Which is exactly what John was doing, with some possibly new friends, and Peter had called him out in front of his new bros. But still, maybe he should give Peter a chance. It wasn't like John was in any position to be weeding out his friends' list. Last week, even the gaming geeks had told him to get lost (Sanjeev said John was a poser online), and so John's social calendar consisted of hanging with his sister and waiting for her boyfriend to ask him to tag along (and half the time he had to say no).

John wondered if his dad would get mad if he knocked out one of his teeth to match the LBs. That'd be pretty sick—like he was in the club. Then the next time someone picked on him at Marlowe, he'd be like, "Biznatch, we can take this to the street, go crew by crew, na'meen? They'll cut you, son." John felt so gangsta just for talking with the LBs that he almost popped the collar of his polo shirt.

Too bad now he had to go watch some assistant professor hit on his sister. John knew more about Egyptology than all the assistants combined. But they all tussled his hair like some puppy. John walked past the computer cluster, where his ex-friends had loaded a low-grav golden gun match with no mods—his specialty. He gritted his teeth as he approached the office.

It was brutally unfair, Wendy thought, that she—a junior who was already taking college-level classes and working on museum-quality artifacts (which her father had taught her to clean and preserve professionally), a girl who was pretty much independent and running the household—was forced to work with some pretentious British research assistant when she could very well handle the exhibit alone. Besides, she had John's help. Wasn't that enough? For a thirteen-year-old, that kid was an authority on Egypt. He had read every one of their father's books, and, frankly, if he hadn't been around, she would have categorized at least two Old Kingdom vases as Early Dynastic.

Not that John joined her in the basement *that* often. The hour after school ended was strategically crucial for social standings, and he was busy trying to fit in. After school was the time for practicing football drills, or working on debate speeches, or even getting a workout at the Marlowe gym. Wendy felt a spark of happiness when, after she had spoken to Connor, she had seen John resolutely lifting ten-pound dumbbells with the lacrosse team (twice). Something like that was worth mislabeling a few jars.

Recently, every time Wendy thought of Connor, her mind drifted in the direction of Peter. She knew that John didn't like the new RA, that he thought Peter was too cocky and was stung by the way Peter had dismissed him. Besides that, her dad had warned her to stay away from Peter. Wendy suspected that Peter was misusing his position with the boarding kids. She wouldn't be surprised if he was the one who set up the whole point-shaving scheme with the lacrosse player. And on top of it all, he was a little too interested in the Egyptian exhibit. Still, something about him intrigued her, and despite the guilt of spending so much time thinking about someone other than her boyfriend, she reminded herself that Connor hadn't been her boyfriend for that long.

"Excuse me," said a deep, hollow voice that resonated down the hall. Lost in thought, Wendy had run right into the mousy new nurse—the same woman she had seen loitering alone outside the school before.

"I'm so sorry," said Wendy with a smile. "Just thinking."

"Happy thoughts?" the woman asked in her cryptic voice, then coughed into a lace cloth. There was a dead moth on her shoulder, and she watched Wendy with those observant eyes.

Wait—Wendy stared—*her eye.* One of the nurse's deep blue eyes was broken. Suddenly feeling a wave of gloom and dread, Wendy forced another smile and rushed away, not waiting to hear nurse Neve Verat introduce herself. She searched her jacket pocket for her basement key and bounded toward her father's office to meet the new exhibit assistant—thinking how much she hated grad students, fast forgetting every detail of the nondescript nurse whose talent was to blend in so easily.

The sound of John's excited chatter reached Wendy even before she opened the door to her father's office. He was already inside, talking animatedly with a stranger Wendy assumed was Simon Grin, while their father rifled through notes on his desk.

"Hello," she said, and dropped her backpack on the ground.

Instinctively, she put an arm on John's shoulder, but he pushed it off with such force that Wendy swallowed the rest of her introduction. She looked at John, confused, but he was glaring straight ahead, almost fogging up his glasses with the heat coming from his eyes. *Right.* John's most recent hang-up was being treated like a kid. Sometimes, Wendy felt like talking with John was like walking through a minefield. She tried to be sensitive, but sometimes it felt like he just wouldn't let her off the hook.

She turned to the thirty-something man with thinning, greasy red hair, who was now showing John his state-of-the-art multi-watch.

"Slick," muttered John as he pushed buttons on the timepiece. The constant tick-tock coming from Simon's wrist was irritating, but John didn't seem to notice.

The man stared rudely at Wendy. "Who're you?" he said. The leering way he looked at her made Wendy want to turn and run out of there.

"I'm Wendy Darling," she said, already hating him. "You know . . . the name on the door?"

Professor Darling cleared his throat and said, "Wendy . . . manners."

"Are you the new assistant?" asked Wendy, putting on her most detached authoritative tone, a skill she had developed since her mother left.

The man straightened himself, but his jacket stayed wrinkled.

"I'm Simon Grin, here by request of the British Museum. I'll be supervising the exhibit."

"Um, Dad," said Wendy, turning to her father, "you said that *I* was supervising the exhibit. I thought I was getting an assistant."

Simon laughed loudly (which made the always-polite professor go red in the face) and said in an oily voice, "Sixteen-year-olds, no matter how charming"—he winked and Wendy almost gagged—"don't get PhD assistants from the world's premiere museum."

"Well, that is true," muttered the professor.

"Don't worry, Wen," said John. "Simon's cool. Not old or a kiss-ass or anything like the other poser assistants . . ."

Simon gave John a strange look. Professor Darling coughed loudly, and John said, "Sorry, man."

"What took you so long, anyway?" Wendy demanded.

"I was held up by *official* business. I won't bore your delicate ears. . . ." He obviously thought that he was being charming, but every time he looked at her, she wanted to whip out any proof of her underage status and have him arrested for being so disgusting.

"Dad said you got your bag stolen," challenged Wendy.

Simon sneered. "I was attacked by . . . a splinter cell . . . possibly made up of nativist Egyptian operatives . . . looking to steal artifacts. . . . I stayed behind to . . . gather intel." He cleared his throat.

"Wow," said Wendy. "I didn't realize assistant history professors had such action-packed lives."

"As I said, you're far too delicate a young lady for this talk, *Darling*." He looked at the professor as if he expected him to appreciate the jest, but Professor Darling didn't look amused (and Wendy had heard this joke about five hundred times already).

"*I* heard you spent two nights in the airport until they replaced your passport," said Wendy, her tone cold.

Simon ignored her.

"Well, we'd better get to work," said Wendy. "I want to clock in a few hours before dark. Daddy, can you sign my time card?"

Professor Darling nodded proudly.

She turned to Simon, deciding to ignore his protests and pretend that she was the boss. As her father always said, *Do the job you want, not the job you have.* Or, as John would put it, *Fake it till you make it.* "Follow me. The three of us are supposed to start cataloging the artifacts in the basement."

"Dr. Darling"—Simon's Brit accent seemed to intensify just then—"I suppose I'll need the keys, cataloging papers, et cetera." He held out his hand.

"Wendy already has all that," said the professor, already busying his mind with other things. He sat behind his desk and was opening research files before Simon had even withdrawn his hand.

Wendy smiled at Simon, who glared back. "Yes, well," he said, "you'll have to turn over at least the paperwork. We wouldn't want any liability issues . . . as a result of mishandling. I'm sure you understand, Wendy."

"We'll see if I can find them," said Wendy sarcastically. "Teenagers tend to be so flighty when it comes to misplacing things. Can we get to work now?" She picked up a couple of clipboards and walked toward the Marlowe basement. The whole way, John examined Simon's multi-watch, holding up Simon's limp wrist to his face. He rapid-fired questions, and Simon answered indifferently with line after line from the owner's manual. John didn't seem to notice the irritation in Simon's voice. Wendy hoped desperately that John wasn't finding a new role model in *this* guy. Those spoiled dorm felons were bad enough. Why couldn't he just hang out with Connor?

The basement was a huge open space that extended under most of Marlowe. The room was piled high with mounds of trophies, old equipment, and textbooks. The stacks were so tall that they formed a maze. One could see that the janitor had tried to create a path winding around each stack. Along the walls of the room, doors webbed out in each direction, leading to broom closets, boiler rooms, and other utility outlets. It seemed that over the summer, the basement had gone into disrepair—full of mold, dirty rags, and discarded paint buckets. Wendy was shocked to see so many colonies of moths and flies in the corners of walls, in the cracks of doors, and nesting in every nook and on every box. "Gross," she said.

John and Simon immediately headed to the pile of old computers, pulling out scrap parts. As far as computer nerdery was concerned, Simon seemed like a thirty-year-old version of John. This worried Wendy because in the few minutes that she had known him, Simon had already won the prize for the most socially stunted man-child she'd ever met.

Wendy let the boys pick through the electronic rubble and went over to the artifacts. Professor Darling had already opened the crates. Packing materials were strewn all around the pieces, like colorful paper on Christmas morning. Wendy had to admit, even though this job cut into her time with Connor and her friends (unlike the café, where they would have been able to hang out), the ancient relics filled her with excitement. She had grown up hearing the stories of Cleopatra and Hatshepsut, the most powerful women of their time.

Wendy picked up the inventory list and began organizing the

timeworn vases, placing them in groups chronologically, using her best guesses to date the items. A statue of an ibis bird was astonishingly intact. Its impossibly long thin neck had endured centuries of jostling without snapping in half. A few small statues looked like pieces of a child's game. She placed them with the other Middle Kingdom artifacts. Wendy paid close attention to the papyrus scrolls, which were delicate and discolored. One especially rare item was a book, bound in the European style but obviously containing pages made of ancient papyri. Maybe it was the copy of the *Book of Gates* that her father had mentioned. She laughed as she remembered her father's high hopes for it. Wendy had no idea what to do with it, and John was too busy shirking work to read the hieroglyphs. The book seemed ageless. There was no category for it. Brown and brittle pages showed images Wendy had seen before in her father's notebooks. She set it aside to show John when he was done goofing around.

Then Wendy came across something strange. It was a set of canopic statues, which were really jars containing a mummy's liver, lungs, stomach, and intestines. Usually, there were four jars with four different heads (man, baboon, jackal, falcon) to represent the four sons of Horus, the gatekeeper god. The idea was that the mummy would need all those organs in the afterlife, so they'd put them in the jars for safekeeping. But these jars were all carved to represent the death god, the jackal-headed Anubis. But were these really Anubis? The jars were jackal-headed, with sharp listening ears, ravenous long jowls, and piercing eyes, but their bodies . . . they seemed almost female—as if someone had tried to combine Anubis with someone, or something, else entirely.

The strange thing was that one of the statues was missing. The inventory list expressly stated that there were four alabaster statues, but all Wendy could see were three. Three jackals. She wondered if anyone had been down there. What was even more odd was that next to the three statues Wendy found an alabaster ball. It looked like one of the eyes of the jackal god. It must have dropped from the missing statue. Professor Darling would be appalled if he knew. Wendy stared at the globe, wondering what it had seen, where its body had gone. But she was overcome with an uncomfortable feeling, as though the eye was staring back at her. And the creepiest part was that the eye didn't seem vicious, the way she imagined the death god would be, but scared, as though it had seen something truly terrible.

"How's it going?"

Wendy jumped at the noise. It was John. He and Simon were holding a few scrap pieces they had found.

"Are you OK? Did we scare you?" said John.

"No," said Wendy. "You two should be helping."

"But look what we found," said John, holding up his scraps. "Simon showed me all kinds of stuff."

Simon stood to the side, taking the compliments like tributes laid at the feet of a pharaoh.

Wendy wasn't in the mood. She had been doing all the work by herself, and the afternoon was wasting away.

"You guys can start over there," she said. She reached out to hand Simon the inventory list, but Simon didn't reach out to take it.

"You two go ahead and finish up here," said Simon, changing tack from his previous attempts to get his hands on all the paperwork. "It looks like you've got it under control."

It seemed that now his game was to play boss by *not* doing work.

A flare went off behind Wendy's eyes. "What? You're supposed to help."

"I'm supposed to make sure that you children don't harm the artifacts," said Simon. "I've monitored the quality of your work, and I'm willing to let it slide."

"You weren't monitoring anything. You were playing with that pile of electronic junk and your stupid watch," said Wendy.

"*Adults* can do two things at once," said Simon. "I've been tested and can do five."

Simon turned and marched out of the basement as Wendy tried to control the anger rising up from her chest. *What a total prick!* Did he really think that kind of crap would work? She was sixteen, not twelve. And she could see right through this guy. Just another résumé-padding loser who thought that if he ordered people around with enough condescension, they'd just blindly do everything he wanted. Wendy let out a frustrated groan. She went back to the daunting task of organizing the exhibition by herself. John put down his scraps and knelt by her side. Wendy was too angry to give him any instructions at the moment. So he hovered, waiting for an opportunity to make himself useful. Wendy worked in silence. A few times, she reached for something and John jumped up to get it and hand it to her.

When she placed a limestone vase in the Thirteenth Dynasty section, John made a little coughing sound to catch her attention. Then he nodded at the Fourteenth Dynasty artifacts, and Wendy realized he was right. She placed the vase in the right pile and smiled at her little brother. John grinned. "Thanks," said Wendy.

"No problem," said John.

They were silent for a little longer, until John said, "Wendy?"

"Yeah?" said Wendy.

"You know, you probably shouldn't have insulted the multi-watch."

"Shut up, John."

As they sat cross-legged in the semidarkness, sorting statues and scrolls into piles, the thick walls of the Marlowe basement ricocheted the sound of their laughter.

PROFESSOR DARLING
A HAPPY THOUGHT

We walked through the museum gardens my colleague Russell had been cultivating for months. Pink cherry blossoms like big clouds right above us. I had my research assistant set up a picnic on the grass, and when we sat down, I think she thought that I was going to ask her right then. But I didn't. We had Brie and olives, and the whole time she kept interrupting her own sentences to look at me. She was trying to figure out when I'd ask, but I never did. I couldn't help grinning like a fool, but I talked about Russell's trees, and my newest exhibit, and how we'd tried to harmonize the museum and the grounds. And when we'd finished, she was obviously disappointed. Then I took her into the exhibit—Old Kingdom artifacts—and I prattled on about a set of combs under the glass case. In the reflection I could see that she was uninterested. I pointed out an emerald necklace. Then we passed the ring—even Cleopatra would have drooled over this one. I said, "You know what? Let's just take that one out." I opened the glass case. She was shocked. I pulled out the ring and gave it to her. She cried. She'd never seen anything like it.

THE BOOK AND THE GATES

"Can you believe we're allowed to do this?" John asked Wendy as he carefully swirled a Q-tip in one of the cracks of an old statue. He came up with a clump of grayish grime.

"You mean can I believe our nerd-core dad subjected us to a childhood of learning to restore priceless antiques at museum quality only to force us into his lame-sauce career?"

"Yes!" exclaimed John.

"Yes," mumbled Wendy.

"Did you know that the *Book of Gates* used to be called the *Book of the Netherworld*?"

"How do you know that?" said Wendy. She was dusting a papyrus scroll and sorting through a stack of placards—wishing that there was just one other person at Marlowe qualified to take this job. She glanced at a clock. *3:10 p.m.* They'd been working for only ten minutes, but it already felt like hours. Outside, she heard her friends laughing and making weekend plans. She felt a momentary hint of jealousy—that they were born into a particular family and so had license to do whatever they wanted with their free time. No need to work. No need for money. But, hey, some of them had really overbearing parents, always pushing them to get ahead. Get in to this school. Get in to that club. At least her father didn't do that. And after finally meeting Connor's mother a few days ago, she was starting to think that she was lucky not to have one around.

"It was in Dad's notes," John answered. "The gates apparently open the way to the world of the dead. That's why they're called gates, see? They lead to the *other side.*" John flicked the Q-tip aside and pulled out another.

"Creepy. Do you have the death god placard?" Wendy turned in place a few times, scanning the room for the missing placard, then got on her knees and started peeking under the display tables.

"Just make another one," said John. He was now elbow deep in a vase, cleaning out the bottom with a dry sponge. "Hey, you know what else I found in his notes? The ancient Egyptians used to divide the day into twelve hours and the night into twelve hours. So during the summer, when the night was short, the night hours were shorter. But there were *always* exactly twelve between sunset and sunrise."

"Huh," said Wendy. "You shouldn't be snooping around in Dad's notes."

"He left them out on the coffee table. What's he expect? So anyway, in the underworld, there are gates that lead to the afterlife, each with its own guardian, which, by the way, are supposed to be the worst kind of monsters. So the book is all about the journey of the dead soul through the night when he is carried to the afterlife, passing through each gate one by one. Cool, huh?"

"I thought the book was about the five legends."

"That's not *all* there is, Wen. It's a big book. Geez."

"And what're the guardians for?" Wendy asked.

"To protect the gates to the afterlife!" said John in his most irritated *this-is-obvious* voice. "Come *on,* Wen!"

Wendy laughed at John's enthusiasm—a quality he showed only to her. She wished he would be this happy, eager John more often instead of the John that came out in public. "Don't scrub that one so hard." Wendy cocked her head, and her hair tumbled past her shoulder like a strawberry-blond waterfall.

Wendy was about to return to her search for the missing placard when a strange ticking caught their attention. *Tick-tock. Tick-tock.*

"There's that cretin"—Wendy rolled her eyes—"with his lame-ass scuba watch."

"Don't be a hater," said John. "Me and Simon are bros. You're just mad because he's way smarter than you."

"Everyone keeping busy? Keeping on task?" Simon's eyes flitted this way and that as he walked down the steps to the basement. He glanced at the exhibit items and gave a cursory examination to each without bothering to properly inspect it. "Things look shipshape here," he said, pointing to John's vase. "Wendy, get busy on those placards. Chop-chop."

Wendy was about to mention, for the fourteenth time, that he wasn't doing his share of the work, but Simon had already turned to leave. He walked distractedly toward the stairs, knocking old, discarded items out of his way as he went. Just as they were going back to work, Wendy and John heard a sloshing sound followed by a frenzy of curses. Simon had stepped into the large puddle near the steps, the result of a recent leak, that both Wendy and John had known to avoid. There were electric cords all around the puddle, and Wendy had seen a spark or two flying from exposed wires touching the water. She had called the maintenance crew, but they were backed up till tomorrow.

"Careful, there," said Wendy. "You don't want to get fried."

"This place is a disgrace," said Simon bitterly. He waved a hand on his way out, like a king dismissing his subjects. "Put a towel on that," he said. "I'll be doing important research in Darling's office. Don't disturb me unless it's life or death."

"No problem, Simon!" John shouted after him.

"No problem, Simon," Wendy mimicked in a squeaky, mocking voice. "How can you kiss his butt like that?"

"If you cared at all about this stuff," he said, pointing at the artifacts, "you'd understand how important the guy is. The *British Museum* sent him to protect them." He said the words *British Museum* with extra emphasis, as though the entire question would be settled on the strength of the museum's credentials.

"John, can't you see that the guy doesn't *actually* care about this stuff? You and I know more than he does. Who cares about his title?"

John ambled back toward the vase, and Wendy began cataloging items again.

"Dad thinks he has an early version of the *Book of Gates* somewhere in here," said John.

Wendy, who was thumbing through a stack of papyri, looked up. "Oh, right," she said. "I was gonna show you the other day. There's an old book in here that I figured was the one Dad was talking about. I put it over there." She pointed to a far table where she had laid the book, but before she had put her arm down, John was across the room.

"It's probably not the original, John," she said. "Back then they used scrolls."

John picked up the book, which was hidden behind a statuette. He flipped through the pages carefully, lowering himself to a sitting position on the floor. "You don't know anything, Wen. It *was* a scroll, but a million people have been searching for it over the years. Everyone knows it was cut up into pages and made into a book to disguise it."

Wendy got up and walked toward him. She said in a teasing tone, "Riiiight . . . so, Professor, what's your expert opinion. Is that the original?"

"Well, obviously I don't know, Wen," John snapped, insulted. But they were alone now, so he didn't go into his usual brooding silent treatment. Instead, he turned the book over in his hands. "But it's definitely a copy of the *Book of Gates*. Who knows if it's the first copy or the thousandth or what . . . ?"

John spoke with confidence, and Wendy was amused by how much he knew about this subject—much more than she did.

Wendy took a seat beside her brother, and they carefully lifted each page, examining the pictures and hieroglyphs. Many of the pages were empty, and everything else was in ancient Egyptian—besides being worn-out and just barely visible.

"These must be the guardians." John pointed to a picture of a long snakelike creature and another one that seemed nothing more than a blur of ink. "And look, you can tell where each hour starts." John pointed to each of the sections as Wendy leaned over to get a better look. The book was ancient, the pages so crinkly and delicate that any sharp move would have snapped them. When John turned the pages, they crackled like dry leaves. The color had worn to a sort of pale yellow, and the edges were frayed, sometimes torn. On each page, color pictures of mummies and jackals and serpents gave hints about the contents of that hour.

"I can't believe they let us have this at Marlowe," said John with obvious awe.

Wendy chuckled. "It was a political thing." She decided to let her little brother in on what she knew. "I heard Dad on the phone. The museum director called Dad a loon in some magazine and one of Dad's big-shot fans was offended. This was payback. Besides, Dad's the only one who believes in five legends lore, so they probably think it's safer with him."

"Maybe we shouldn't be touching it," said John, his tone blasé, as if he didn't really want what he was suggesting. "Dad was really clear about how to handle the artifacts."

Wendy shrugged, also too curious to care. "We're wearing gloves."

After that, neither of them pushed the topic of setting the book aside.

"I wish I could read this," said John after another few minutes. He shut the book and opened it again, somewhere in the middle. "See these titles? They must be the names of the hours."

"How do you know?" Wendy asked.

"That's not so hard to know." John shrugged. Then he pulled out a piece of notebook paper from his pocket. "See?" He held it out to her, and she opened it. Inside were words—English letters in her father's handwriting—that read like gibberish.

"They're the Egyptian names of the hours," said John. "For some reason Dad's been pretty obsessed with them lately."

"You shouldn't have taken Dad's notes," said Wendy, looking toward the door. John shrugged again. Wendy began to read aloud from the paper, sounding out the strange words one at a time.

"*Shesat-maket-neb-s,*" she read. "That's the name of the second hour. Why don't they just call it two o'clock?"

"Shut up. You're not even pronouncing it right." John made to grab for the paper. But Wendy was too quick. She pushed him away with one hand and kept reading.

"The third hour is called *thentent-baiu*. At least that one's shorter."

"Fine," said John. "You have fun with your little list, and I'll just sit here and read the original in ancient Egyptian." He cradled the book in his lap.

"*Urt-em-sekhemu-set,*" Wendy read, enunciating the name of the fourth hour. As soon as the last syllable had left her lips, something stirred in the Marlowe basement. A tremor passed between John and Wendy and they both leaped back.

"Did you feel that?" said John.

Wendy laughed nervously. "It's a creepy old basement. It's probably just someone banging around upstairs. . . . Let's finish up, OK?"

"Yeah, one sec," said John. He was trying to read the title page, based on the very little he knew of Egyptian lettering. As he brushed the dust off the book, the corner of a page snapped off in his hand.

Wendy let out a little scream. "John, Dad will *kill* you! Do you know how much it would cost to—?"

"Stop distracting me!" John said. He tried to fit the corner back on the page. But then they noticed something changing. The ink on the page began to fade, until there was nothing there for John to decipher.

"Put it away, John." Wendy's voice trembled as she spoke. "Just put it away and let's go." But John didn't say a word. His gaze was fixed on the blank page of the book, and he motioned for her to come closer. She leaned tentatively across him, holding her breath. Words, in English letters, were appearing on the page, faint and unreadable at first and then stronger and stronger, so that they could have been printed off a modern printer.

"What . . . what's it doing? John, what's it doing?"

John's face was pale. He looked the way he used to just before he was about to throw up at someone's birthday party. Wendy thought for a second about pulling the book off his lap. "Well?" said Wendy. "Read it. What's it say?"

John pulled Wendy by her sleeve so that they could read it together.

You speak truly: this fourth hour of Egypt's night

Open the gates and enter here

Next to the final word appeared a black symbol, the Eye of Ra, which both John and Wendy recognized. They were silent for another moment. John moved to turn the page, but Wendy grabbed his hand. "I think we're supposed to open something."

John's eyes sparkled. "So you *do* realize that we're about to open the door to the freaking underworld, right?"

"OK. Don't have a nerdgasm," said Wendy, faking bravado. "It doesn't really lead to anything. It's a trick. Don't you want to know if someone's messing with Dad's exhibit?"

It took only a second for John to be convinced. "OK, fine, what do we do next?"

Wendy was silent. John looked at the book and asked again, "What next?"

"John," said Wendy, one eyebrow raised, "it's a book. It's not gonna start talking to you. Gimme that." She snatched the book from him. She read slowly, all the while chewing one nail nervously.

A barely perceptible tremor ran through Wendy's fingers. Otherwise, everything was exactly the same. They swiveled around on their haunches, clinging close to each other, wondering what horrors they had unleashed. But nothing happened. The Marlowe basement was still the Marlowe basement. The exhibit was in the same state as before. And the book sat, still and harmless, in John's lap.

Neither John nor Wendy noticed the minuscule detail, the tiny alteration that occurred in their basement hideaway almost at the same moment as the appearance of the message in the book. Silently, it waited there, during all the minutes they spent trying to figure out the next step, while they passed the book back and forth between them, and while Wendy read and reread the passage. It took Wendy several minutes to notice it, and she only did so after a second and then a third glance around the room. A barely perceptible etching of the Eye of Ra, no bigger than a quarter, appeared above the nearest door, the one leading to the janitor's broom closet. Its elegant curls shone coal-black and fierce, boring deep into the wooden door. Wendy approached, thinking at first that it was some sort of projection or hologram. She looked around for its source, but then, as she came closer, she saw that it was embedded into the door, its creases branded on and singed like scorched firewood.

As she drew closer, John got up and followed. They stood in front of the door, unable to decide, their mouths too dry to articulate all the possibilities that lay beyond the broom closet. Finally, Wendy said, "We might as well open it and see. Hold on to my hand."

John looked behind to make sure Simon wasn't there (since he wasn't about to let his sister hold his hand like a little kid).

"OK, ready," he said finally, grabbing hold of Wendy's hand and squinting his eyes into a ready-for-anything frown. Wendy pulled open the door.

"I don't get it," spat John.

Brooms. Brooms and buckets and an old toilet. That was all they saw in the tiny room. They looked at each other, puzzled. John dropped Wendy's hand and rolled his eyes. He threw his arms in the air and began pacing. "That's it? So this is what—?"

And then he was gone. Vanished in mid-sentence. One step inside the little room and John had disappeared. Wendy was about to scream, but a pang of instinct kept her silent. Without wasting another second, she took a step into the broom closet.

Wendy expected to fall a long way down some black hole and land hard. So when her feet prematurely hit an ordinary stone step, she lost her footing and stumbled right into her brother, whose mouth was hanging open. He was standing on the step above her, on a patch of stringy green lichen. The first thought that went through Wendy's mind was that they had lost their way back, that they were forever trapped here. She whipped around frantically, her heavy breaths almost too loud in the perfect silence of this place. But when she turned, there it was, the same glowing black Eye of Ra that had appeared on the door, now hanging in midair behind her, in the exact spot from which she had emerged. She took John's arm and approached the eye, inching closer until it was above her. Beyond the eye she saw stone pillars and more winding steps leading up and down all around them, but Wendy guessed that this didn't mean anything. After all, beyond that invisible curtain in the broom closet they had seen brooms and buckets. In one quick motion, she thrust her hand into the space past the eye. Her arm was gone, cut off at the exact plane that contained the charred black symbol. There was Wendy, just standing there with a bloodless stump and empty space where her arm should be. John screamed, his voice reverberating through the space behind them. Wendy pulled her arm back. "OK, at least we know how to get back."

"Look what's over here," John said, pulling Wendy away from the invisible door and toward one of the many sun-bleached staircases leading downward into a black space beneath their feet. "I might be going nuts here, but does all this look a little familiar?"

Wendy shrugged. She had never seen this place before, but she did get that strange feeling of familiarity when she looked around her. The columns had a cluttering effect—not all that different from the basement they had just left. The pillars looked strangely similar to the pillars holding up the basement staircase—though the ones here were much bigger and greater in number. They were made of mud, hardly the elegant pillars of the Marlowe School. And the steps . . . the steps were the most prominent feature here, just as they were in the Marlowe basement. Except here, they all led downward, deeper into this strange world, instead of upward into the Marlowe School.

Looking around, Wendy could see now that the space they stood in had exactly the same angles and proportions as the basement, though it was definitely bigger. And just like in the Marlowe basement, the stacks were so tall that they formed a trail, exactly like the winding path the janitor had cleared around each stack of junk.

Wendy looked up, but there was no sun in the gray expanse overhead—no sun, no stars, and no clouds, so that she couldn't tell if it was day or night here. She noticed then that the sky wasn't a sky at all, but gray rock. She felt confined, as though they were breathing borrowed air. Were they underneath Marlowe? Were they still in the basement? There was something intriguing about the labyrinth that extended out from where they stood, the way it continued on past her line of vision, toward the unknown spaces beyond this eerie clone basement. But then, it couldn't lead far. The whole place felt like a giant stone prison. *It's like the inside of a tomb,* Wendy thought.

Wendy motioned to John, and they started walking along another set of steps. They drew closer to the maze, which didn't seem at all like a part of the fake basement now. In fact, it was as if the room with the pillars and stairs was a part of *it*—a colossal snakelike labyrinth with no end. "As long as we know how to get back," said John, "it should be OK." They quickly walked past another set of steps that descended into the oblivion below. They avoided the temptation of the stairs, choosing instead to explore the columned space, with its unruly shrubs and discarded spires. It was dark, and they couldn't see the entire space the way they might be able to in the Marlowe basement. They fumbled around for another few minutes before they spotted a small circular lake in a clearing a few yards away. It started underneath a pillar and continued on into the bushy maze beyond what should have been the end of the basement. The lake was an icy blue, but sparks were flying from it. Every few seconds the water flashed and a giant flame licked the air above the lake, floating up toward a nonexistent sky, died out, and returned to the water.

Wendy drew a breath.

"What?" John asked. But Wendy couldn't explain. It seemed so crazy to tell her brother that the lake reminded her of the puddle in the basement—like a larger, darker, more foreboding version of it, this time with huge sparks instead of the tiny flashes of light from exposed electric wires. *Are we still in the basement?* Wendy wondered. *Are we underneath it? Maybe this lake is what caused the basement leak.*

But then something else caught Wendy's attention. She took a step into the maze beyond the periphery of the twin basement, John following on her heels. Wendy walked tentatively, making mental notes of exactly which turns they took. Five minutes later, when they were already past the lake, they caught sight of a far-off building. Wendy whispered to John, reciting from their father's lecture. "A tomb made of clay and stone with five pointed pillars and a pyramid base—"

"Painted a golden color since he had no gold of his own," John finished for her.

"Oh. My. God," whispered Wendy.

"We have to go there," said John. "We have to! Do you realize what we could find? That's the castle from the first legend!"

"No way. No way I'm going farther through this maze, risking getting lost just to find some old bones. Forget it. I want to go back."

Something inside Wendy was absolutely certain that she could never cross the whole maze. She turned around. The pillared space was still close behind them. Something told her that the castle in the distance was much farther away than it looked.

Frightened, they turned to go. Almost as if the labyrinth had heard them, a shadow passed over the maze. A cold breeze blew through Wendy's hair, and she stiffened, as if she had been brushed by an icy hand. The rocky sky seemed to lower and began to turn into a darker, more menacing gray. Above the tiny gold-painted castle pyramid, Wendy saw a shadow pass to and fro.

"OK, this is scary. Let's go," she said. As they made their way back through the maze (two rights, two lefts, another right), past the fiery lake, and back toward the pillared space, the shadows above them grew darker. They hurried toward the eye that signaled the invisible door. Wendy pushed John forward. "You go through first," she said. John was chewing his lips nervously. He let go of Wendy's hand and disappeared into the empty space beyond.

John stepped into the broom closet for only a second. He dove back through the gate just as suddenly and practically fell on top of Wendy. "What are you doing?" Wendy asked. "Let's get out of here!"

John's face was as white as a blank sheet of paper. He began muttering. "Simon . . . Simon's snooping around out there. He might have seen me. If he comes in here—"

"We can't stay here forever," she said, looking up at the shadows gathering up above. "How do we know when he's gone?"

John thought for a moment, and then he jumped up. "I've got it," he said. He dug deep into his pocket and took out a ballpoint pen.

"What are you doing with that?" Wendy asked. The shadows above them were becoming grayer. Wendy's legs shook as she began to smell a stench coming from over her head. Everything was getting darker now. Looking at the fire-spewing lake, just barely visible in the far corner of the space, Wendy glimpsed a solid figure, the shadow of someone wrapped in thick cloths, passing back and forth, inspecting the ground they had walked. Once in a while, the figure stopped and bent its head, as if it were a person coughing.

"You'll see," said John as he unscrewed the bottom of the pen and tossed out the ink tube and the ballpoint. He held the hollow, strawlike casing of the pen and carefully approached the invisible door. He pushed one end of the straw just inside the hidden barrier so that a tiny circle from the tube's end was inside the broom closet and most of its length was with John and Wendy, in this other world.

"Genius," said Wendy as she heard Simon's footsteps through the makeshift periscope. They stood there holding the pen tube for one or two minutes, all the while watching as the ominous figure overhead drew closer, darker. They clutched each other as they heard a dark whisper, somewhere far off. The air was cold now and more confining. Shadows were still hovering above, darkening everything.

Simon's steps grew louder. John got on one knee and held the end of the tube to his eye so that he could see Simon on the other side of the invisible barrier. Simon was going door to door through the basement, opening closets and bathrooms, peeking under tables.

"He definitely saw me for a second," said John, watching the curious way Simon searched the basement, like a mental patient trying to prove that his hallucinations were real. Then Simon came to the broom closet, whose door was already ajar. He peered inside. Through the pen tube John could see his huge face. John drew a breath.

John's pen quivered. Across the curtain separating Marlowe from the underworld maze, they were face-to-face now—Simon in one dimension, staring into a broom closet full of mops, his face only an inch or two away from John's (only an inch from stumbling into this career-making secret), and John and Wendy in another dimension, their pen-tube barely poking through the barrier, its tip lightly touching Simon's sweater. They held their breath, hoping that Simon would not lean forward, praying that he would not feel the sharp circle on his belly or see the eye above the door.

"Why doesn't he go away?" Wendy whispered.

"He's probably trying to figure out where we went," said John, putting his thumb over the end of the tube so Simon couldn't hear. "Just hush and we won't get into trouble."

"No." Wendy shook her head. "I bet he would be all over this if he knew. He's one of those weasel résumé padders who'd totally screw Dad if he could."

Wendy looked up again at the impending darkness and began grinding her teeth nervously. For a moment, she thought she might just jump back into the broom closet and take her chances with Simon. Who cares if she got into trouble or if Simon the sleaze took all the credit for a discovery that her father had been so close to making? At least she'd be alive.

Wendy turned around. The figure by the lake was no longer pacing. It stood by the water, its hooded head and female body reminding her of the statues of the death god from the exhibit. Again it seemed to cough, and the humanness of the sound was frightening. The figure was looking right at her, and even from this distance, Wendy felt the force of a deep-blue left eye that she couldn't see.

Just then, through the pen tube, they saw Simon squint suspiciously, turn, and march out of the basement. The sound of his footsteps faded away. Then, overhead, they heard a voice. A thick, raspy voice echoing through the labyrinth, whispering words in a dead tongue. John and Wendy threw themselves into the broom closet and stumbled out. They lay on the floor, panting, for only a second before they grabbed their backpacks and started running out of the basement.

They didn't make it far. Simon was waiting just above the banister, on his way back down to check on the exhibit.

"What are you two up to?" he asked, his eyes narrow slits.

"We're done for today," said Wendy. She glanced at the now-ominous puddle near the staircase. "We're leaving."

"Why are you all flushed like that?" Simon asked.

"Heavy lifting," said Wendy, still panting.

"And where were you a minute ago? I came down and you were missing."

"We took out a few bags of garbage," said Wendy, trying to sound very justified and therefore annoyed at his questions.

Simon's eyes scanned them up and down, examining closely.

His arms were folded across his chest. "I'd better not find any of the artifacts missing."

Wendy took a frustrated breath. "Why would we steal from our own dad?"

"Don't be silly," said Simon, laughing. "I wasn't suggesting *that*. . . . Besides, these things belong to the British Museum, and as the only representative of said museum, *I* am their sole guardian here."

Wendy didn't bother to refute him, to defend her own role. She was too freaked out and couldn't care less about titles right now. There was a moment's silence, then Wendy made for the door. Like a parking lot barricade, Simon's arm swung up to block the way. Suddenly, his voice sounded casual, as if he was trying to feign indifference. "Find anything cool down there?" he said. "You know, none of this stuff is that important, anyway."

He must think we're morons, thought Wendy, but she saw that John wanted to share something with Simon. He wanted to impress him. She grabbed John by his backpack and said, "We're going now."

Simon shrugged and dropped his arm.

On the walk home, when Wendy and John were alone, they started to puzzle out what had happened.

"I bet he won't tell on us," said Wendy.

"I know," said John. "He's cool. He's just protecting the stuff."

"No, John. He won't tell because he's got his own little agenda and he has no respect for Dad. Can't you see? He's too stupid to know what's *really* down there. He probably thinks we found something important and he wants credit."

"Why would he need to?" said John. "He's gonna be a famous Egyptologist. He told me so himself. He's just doing his job."

"His job is to be Dad's assistant," Wendy shot back. She shook her head and added, "Let's just focus on the more important question. What the heck just happened?"

They walked home, shivering with excitement. They talked about the door, and the book, and how they might have caused the book to react. They puzzled at the location of the door ("Why the broom closet?") and the words that had appeared in the book ("Why were they in English?"). They wondered how they had opened the gate to begin with. John had broken the corner of a page. Could that be it? He had tried to read the title page in the original Egyptian. Did any of those things bring the book to life? They even considered that scrap of paper in John's pocket, the one with the names of the hours.

Neither of them remembered the still-open door of the broom closet, or the Eye of Ra, still freshly scorched and ominous in the white-washed wood. In their rush to get away from Simon, neither of them had seen that it lingered there. As Simon slapped the light switch on his way out, he, too, missed the details. He left the exhibit, muttering about bratty kids, never noticing a silhouette, perhaps a woman, lingering in unseen corners. Why would anyone notice such an ordinary person, after all? She wasn't strange. She didn't have the animal head of Egyptian statues or the putrid breath of the underworld on her lips. She was just a person, just a shadow that had become accustomed to blending in and going unnoticed—a sick soul whose illness had gone unnoticed in the fast world of Marlowe. And so Simon, too, overlooked her. But there she was, a silhouette that looked a lot like the new school nurse, picking lint balls from her overworn blue sweater, caressing moths in her palm—such a tiny, unimportant person holding open the broom-closet door, covering the recesses of the dusty closet in black thoughts and shadow.

The Dark

Darkness isn't confined to one place. It can't be held down by brick walls, by alabaster statues, or even by flesh and bone. The dark inhabits vaster regions. It searches for purpose. Sometimes, one home is hospitable, and so the dark lingers, reinfecting the same space again and again.

In the labyrinthine corridors of the underworld, the new school nurse walked alone, as comfortable as if she were walking in any ordinary living room. She examined the marks left on her home— a fiery lake, the discarded rubble—her unchanging eye surveying the gloomy replicas of a happier place. Now she, too, could leave her mark on the world above. She coughed again and wished that the intruders would leave her alone to recover, to gain back her old strength. She wasn't used to being the one chased . . . the one on the defensive.

Below, the darkness walked, circling the water, contemplating the intruders who had entered here. Sometimes she moved upstairs and watched from among them, seemingly an ordinary person, a sick mortal body—fallible, forgettable—walking in the midst of people who thought themselves *special*.

Above, students rushed through Marlowe's halls, unaware of why the air felt heavier, why images looked murkier, and why happy thoughts were so much harder to summon.

❖❖❖

JOHN DARLING

REACHING FOR A HAPPY THOUGHT

When Sanford's dad said it was lights out, we all got our sleeping bags, and it was a little weird since Rory was there and he's younger than us by a year. But he's still bigger than me, so I said "seniority" and put my bag next to Sanford's, but Rory just pushed it over and put his down in between. I was gonna punch him on the shoulder, but he and Sanford play on the same football team, and Sanford says he hits the hardest out of everyone. It didn't matter anyway 'cause we decided to circle all the bags together and take turns telling stories with the flashlight. Everybody agreed mine was the best because I told an old Egyptian legend about real mummies. They all said Egyptology is super cool.

Everything in our first apartment was magical and had a story. It was only me and Mom and Dad (before we moved to the Marlowe house, and got rid of all the furniture, and John was born). I'd say, "Mommy, tell me about the monkey table," and she'd sigh ('cause she'd told me a hundred times). Everything was oddly shaped and multicolored and one of a kind. I thought it made us a special family. When Mom would tell me about the caribou lamp, I'd imagine them adventuring together all over Africa, finding lost cities, jumping out of boats, and kissing. I used to imagine that when Dad's work at the museum was over, the three of us would pick up where they left off. I'd put on a safari hat and Mom would get out of bed.

THE SECOND LEGEND

"And so, if you think about it, ancient Egypt isn't all that different from a modern high school, like Marlowe," said Professor Darling during his next lecture to his class.

From all the way in the back row, he could hear Marla's sarcastic commentary and the snickering kids around her. John and Wendy were running late to class again, so there was no reason to care about the other students' sarcasm . . . *nobody around to be embarrassed by their old man.* The professor sighed and continued with his analogy.

"For example, the Bedouin were nomadic, fierce warriors with honor codes that have lasted to this day. That's a lot like these *gangsta* types I see after school." He put *gangsta* in air quotes and made every effort to pronounce it the way he had heard John do. "They seem to have a code for *posers,* the uninitiated who try to infiltrate their ranks, versus the *dawgs* (more air quotes), who have been cleared to *roll* with them." By the time the professor had reached his fourth set of finger quotes, Marla's clique was already busting a gut.

The professor was encouraged. He knew that they were making fun, but they were listening for a change. And what good teacher wasn't willing to make a fool of himself if it meant making history accessible and fun?

"They would ride camels, and later Arabian horses, across the Sahara, able to strike like lightning. I guess this part doesn't have a *direct* corollary, since you kids don't ambush each other at water wells, but it could be similar to bicycle gangs."

"I pantsed some kid while he was drinking from the water fountain," said Marla.

"Or that," said Professor Darling. "But you couldn't *pants* a Bedouin, since they wear beautiful long robes."

Marla spoke up again. "So they're basically the dudes from *The Mummy Returns*?"

Professor Darling thought about it for a second. "Yes, basically. Except they don't have English accents."

The door of the classroom suddenly flew open, and Wendy and John Darling came stumbling through. "Sorry we're late," said Wendy, dashing to her seat. John wrestled with the straps of his backpack in an attempt to get settled as fast as possible. They had spent the passing period back at the exhibit, trying to figure out what they had done to make it work. But no matter how many of the previous day's tactics they repeated, the door didn't open. The charcoal-black eye was gone (which seemed strange to Wendy, since it had been etched into the wood), and the door to the broom closet was closed (something neither of them remembered doing). The professor coughed into a fist, then fiddled with his notes, then adjusted his glasses.

"All right, well, we'll discuss this later . . ." said the professor.

Marla said something under her breath.

The professor added, "In detention."

Wendy looked up from her book. "What?"

"You heard me, Wendy. You were tardy, so I'll see you in detention. You too, John."

"But we're *never* late," protested John.

"We were working on *your* exhibit," said Wendy.

"Don't worry, welfare girl," said Marla, "you can do my homework in detention. How's twenty bucks a page?" When the professor wasn't looking, Marla flicked a rolled-up twenty at the back of Wendy's head. Marla's friends laughed. Wendy whipped around. Marla whispered, "It's all right, you can pick it up. Go ahead."

"Try and shut up when you're not spoken to, Marla," said Wendy, almost shouting.

"Wendy Darling!" said the professor. The entire class swerved back toward Professor Darling. Having their complete attention was jarring to the professor. He stammered, "That's—that's enough. Where were we . . . ?"

"The syllabus says something about another of the *five legends*. Perhaps you were discussing the *Book of Gates*?" Simon had slipped into the room in the wake of the commotion. He nodded respectfully to the professor. "I imagine you were getting ready to lecture on the myths and legends surrounding nomadic groups, such as the Bedouin. It's all socioreligious hullabaloo, if you ask me."

The professor was almost relieved to see Simon. If anything, he would make sure they stayed focused on the syllabus. But Wendy and John seemed even more flustered than before.

"Quite right," said the professor. "But myths aren't necessarily untrue just because they're myths, Simon. They are just stories that our worldview hasn't made room for . . . yet."

With that, Professor Darling was back on track. When he spoke about supernatural subjects, it was hard for people to take him seriously. He seemed so much like an old dreamer caught up in his own fairy tales. But since the events of yesterday, Wendy and John would never doubt again. In fact, they were listening more intently than ever, hoping for some information about the magical things that had happened to them in the last day. Partway through the professor's speech, Wendy felt an itch in her right ear, as though she was being watched. She looked at the window just in time to see Peter grin and duck down. Wendy almost yelped, but caught herself. What was he doing here? She could see the top of his head, all covered with brown curls, as he hid behind the windowsill. She turned back to the front of the class, hoping no one would see her and look at the window. Why was Peter hiding, anyway? What did he care about this lecture? And if he cared, why not just come in? Wendy put aside these questions when the thought struck her that Peter had chosen to reveal himself only to *her*. Then she chastised herself for thinking like one of those idiot freshman girls with their constant crushes.

"We talked last time about how the legends are on the subject of great injustices. Last time, it was the character Elan, who was robbed of . . . Who can tell me what he was robbed of?"

Marla ventured a hand into the air. "His heritage?" She made sure to roll her eyes while she said it so her friends would know she wasn't actually interested.

"Not the word I'd use for the loss of one's children, but basically, yes," said the professor. "And after the crimes against him, we all remember that his daughter . . ."

Marla was more confident this time. "The daughter mummified his body."

"Exactly," said Professor Darling. "Each of the five legends features someone getting mummified in some way or another. This is very important, not only because they were given the chance to enter the afterlife like pharaohs, but also because their bones were preserved, each carrying a glimmer of lives unlived—preserving the famed 'bonedust.' "

Marla jumped in. "The five of them together make a person immortal, right?"

"None of this is historically accurate," interjected Simon.

"But you're right, Marla," said the professor. "The legends say so."

"The *myths*," repeated Simon.

"So what's the second one? What's the great injustice?" asked Marla.

"Well . . ." said Professor Darling, sitting down and letting the pause build their anticipation, "the second one is love. . . ."

The Second Legend

Love is a precious thing. If a man is robbed of his life's passion, of his chance to walk in the most excellent way of life, if his love is ripped away, a bitterness builds inside.

So goes the story of one family with a curse on their line, of Elan's dark legacy, full of the cruelest injustices. The house that cannot die. Their stolen lives linger on, still flowing in their bones. Life has been mummified inside them, forming an ever-living bonedust—a new kind of immortality.

After Elan's heritage was no more, his daughter, Jobey, lived as Akhara's unwilling wife. She bore many sons and daughters, all unaware of their Jewish blood. Akhara taught them to be cunning and cruel. They ruled over their Jewish servants, unaware that they were subjecting their own people to pain and death. They grew up in Akhara's image.

All except for Garosh, the lonely son, the last born. Too young to know his brothers and sisters, he was never subject to the torture of their wicked childhood games. And so his heart was never clouded by their meanness. As the boy grew, he fell more and more out of favor with Akhara, who had become a decrepit monster. Garosh insisted on rebuilding the slave quarters and scolded the harsher taskmasters.

One day, as Garosh glided up the Nile on his boat, he saw a vision. At first, he thought it could be a mirage. He had caught only a glimpse before the figure passed behind an outgrowth of papyrus plants. She was wearing white Bedouin robes, and she bent like the sacred ibis to wash her black hair.

Garosh leaped into the languid waters and stood in the deep. The water reached his neck. She looked on from the shore as he approached like a supplicant. When they stood in the marsh, Garosh spoke to his pleasing hallucination. She told him that her name was Kala.

Garosh rejoiced in his fate, knowing he could never again be alone. He begged Kala to give him her hand in marriage. She laughed. He pleaded. Garosh swore his love upon the names of the gods. He cried and coaxed, until finally, Kala realized the depth of his love.

The two lovers vowed their lives to each other. But his family would never accept a Bedouin maiden, and so Garosh forsook his father's boat. Together, they walked into the desert, hoping Kala could convince her father to accept Garosh as her bridegroom.

As the lovers approached Kala's home, Kala's brothers rode out to meet their sister. The Bedouin warriors saw the wealthy stranger touching her and were filled with rage. They said to one another, "Brothers, let us be rid of this foreigner, here to take our sister."

The brothers embraced Garosh as a brother, but in their hearts, they plotted evil.

The youngest warrior said, "Come, Sister, I will take you to our mother, who will prepare you for a wedding. And we will welcome your bridegroom to our tribe."

Kala bid Garosh a happy farewell. But as she rode over the horizon, the rest of the brothers took Garosh by the arm, saying, "Every Bedouin boy must pass three trials to become a warrior and worthy of marriage. To be Bedouin, you must learn to shackle our horses, to dig a well, and to raise a tent. These are the three tasks we require."

Eager to prove his worthiness, Garosh accepted the tests. The brothers took him to far reaches of the oasis and dismounted their horses. They presented Garosh with sharp iron shackles. "Tie these horses to the palm tree."

A simple test. Garosh took the shackles and began to tie each of the mighty horses. But just when he leaned on a horse to clasp the metal hooks, the brothers sent out a mighty blast from their battle horns. The startled horses galloped away, and the shackle hooked into Garosh's belly, ripping out his innermost parts. Garosh stumbled but did not fall. The brothers were startled to see him alive, his organs strewn in the desert by their horses. But his heart had remained. His love for Kala still beat in his chest.

They took the wounded man to a vast desert salt flat. "You must now dig a well," they said. They offered no tools, but Garosh did not mind. His thoughts focused only on Kala. He fell to his knees and began to dig with his hands. The salty wind cut at his face and poured into his open belly. As he scooped the sands, the salt crystals pushed into his skin, drying up his internal fluids. Soon, Garosh was nothing but bones and jerked flesh.

When Garosh climbed from the well he had dug, the wicked brothers were afraid. Garosh had become a preserved monster. His skin was leather. His hair withered in the sun. His chest was frail and thin. But the brothers could all still hear the young and happy heart of Garosh, thumping against his bare bones.

"Well done, brother," they shouted. "One very simple test remains." The evil brothers helped Garosh to a clearing where he would raise a dwelling for Kala. With his body destroyed, Garosh struggled with the parchments and stakes. He weakly pounded the corner spikes and limped under the tent to place the center beam.

This was the moment the brothers had waited for. They pounced on the drape, beating Garosh. But he did not die. He did not need his body.

They pulled up the four stakes and wrapped the tent around him. But he did not need air.

The brothers had tricked Garosh. In his eagerness to prove his worth, he had mummified himself. But the mummy did not die. The wicked brothers were astonished. Some ran away, fearing his revenge. Others listened and heard the beating of his lovelorn heart.

The mummy Garosh stumbled toward the oasis, moaning in a broken language for his beloved. As he approached, he heard the joyous music and laughter of a wedding feast. When he broke into the clearing, the music stopped. Children shrieked at the sight of the monster. There at the center sat Kala, dressed in matrimonial robes. When Kala recognized Garosh, both their hearts tore and the love that had kept the mummy alive finally gave way to despair. Kala cried out, but her brothers held her back. Garosh lurched from the clearing into the desert night.

No one knows the fate of the mummy. The Bedouin say he roams the desert still, crying for his lost love. But those who know the dark history of this ill-fated family, those who have studied it, know that this cannot be. The goddess of death took the young lover's mummy and the bonedust with it. She shielded it with her greatest weapons, fearing that someday death might be conquered. The Dark Lady hid the mummy in a place where no one could reach it, a legendary labyrinth of the gates, guarded by powerful deities that no human could overcome.

And so, Garosh was gone, his love lost. But he can never fully die. His wasted life is forever trapped as grains of immortality in his bones.

At the end of the second legend, Professor Darling took off his glasses and spoke the last lines from memory. This was a loss he knew well.

❖❖❖

Wendy glanced toward the window and caught Peter staring at her. What they shared at that moment Wendy thought she would never lose.

MARLA
A HAPPY THOUGHT

Belarus? Do you even know where Belarus is? Probably not. It's a country. My family used to own seven factories out-side Minsk. (The capital. You didn't know. Don't pretend.) Everything was so much cooler than here. My friends were twenty years old, and they drove me to all the clubs, nothing like these Disney bars in New York. My nanny was an old Russian hag who fell asleep so much I could get away with anything. I went to a lake in Turkey for three days and she didn't notice. People think everyone is poor over there, but we had anything we wanted. I drank champagne with everything.

THE SECRET OF THE BOOK

Later, John and Wendy meandered through Marlowe's empty halls at a lazy pace. No one else was here now, and the lights were turned down, so the school was washed in shadow. *So depressing,* Wendy thought. Despite the opulence—the colorful art on the walls, the state-of-the-art lockers, a discarded Hermès scarf—Marlowe was dismal at this hour. You could barely imagine that only two hours before, these halls had been teeming with uniformed, overly energetic kids crawling all over one another, jockeying to win this position, or grub that grade, or finagle this recommendation. Now the only noise came from the crinkling of candy wrappers underfoot, the clicking of Wendy's heels, and the rubbery squeak of John's shoes as he purposely slid across the linoleum to annoy her.

But then Wendy heard something else. A low moan—or no, maybe it was the wind. There it was again—now an excruciating moan, like someone sick or in a lot of pain. It was coming from somewhere upstairs. She stopped, took hold of John's arm, and pulled him back. This time, he heard it, too. It was a crackling sound louder than a breath but softer than a whisper, like the unconscious murmur of a person lost in ugly dreams.

"What was that?" said John, looking up in the direction of the sound. What could possibly be up on the top floor? Only the attic and the nurse's temporary office, which was housed up there at the insistence of the new nurse.

"Just the wind," said Wendy. They continued to walk, but then they both heard something that couldn't be mistaken for wind or pipes or the hum of a lethargic old teacher alone after hours. It was a flutter—the swift whoosh of a million tiny wings rushing away. They both froze. Wendy wanted to shout out, *Is someone there?* but then she remembered that this was what stupid people in horror movies did right before running into a dead end, or deep into a deserted forest, or up the stairs to the soundproof, windowless attic.

"Let's get out of here," said John. They began walking faster than before, not running and not daring to look back. He stopped in front of the big Marlowe double doors. There was something blocking the exit. A stick of some kind, a long, twisted wooden rod was jammed through the brass handles, holding the doors shut. "What is this?"

Wendy tried pulling on it. It was jammed.

They turned down a dark hallway and stopped, frozen by a movement in the shadows. Something unseen crept past them. It was close—close enough to make Wendy's hair flutter and leave her fingertips cold. Almost involuntarily, her head snapped toward the motion. Had someone rushed past? The hairs on her arm were standing up as if they had almost been touched. Yet when she turned, there was no one in sight.

Then Wendy noticed something strange.

"John," Wendy muttered, "was *that* there before?"

Wendy was looking at the staircase that led up to the second-floor classrooms. She had walked past this staircase a thousand times before. It was one of her favorite spots, an elegant staircase made of marble flanked by two thin white marble columns with beautiful Roman-style designs encircling them. But now one of those two columns was different. It looked much older, as if it was made of mud. In fact it looked exactly like one of the columns they had seen on their trip into the world beyond the broom closet.

Wendy approached it. As she got closer, she realized that the column wasn't entirely transformed. Patches of marble peaked out from underneath the mud. It was as if the old, ugly column was overtaking the marble one, eating it up, transforming it into something different. Inside the mud, Wendy spotted the carcass of a moth, trapped, dead, and mounted into the structure.

"Whoa," said John. "This has *got* to be a trick." All around the infected pillar, tiny vines were beginning to grow, just like the ones in the other world.

"I . . . I want to leave," said Wendy, taking John's hand. She had spotted something else. John followed Wendy's gaze toward the stairs. It was such a small detail; no one would notice it in this dark. But one of the steps, the third one from the top, was different from the rest. It was no longer made of marble but of rough stone.

Wendy and John turned back down the hall, toward the back exit. As they crept quietly along, Wendy's eyes kept darting back and forth, trying to spot the source of that feeling of almost being touched. Suddenly, in the shadowy far end of the dark hall, a hooded figure seemed to appear. Someone small, a woman or a girl, glided into their line of vision gracefully, like a witch, then just as quickly disappeared into one of the classrooms. Before the phantom was gone, Wendy thought she saw her turn, and she glimpsed a broken blue eye—like one she thought she had seen somewhere before . . . but where? Maybe on TV? Or on someone she had forgotten, someone unremarkable and small . . . someone easily forgettable in the course of her important daily routines. An eye not quite human. The sight of it made all the blood in Wendy's body go ice cold, full of jagged edges pricking from the inside. She wanted to scream, but she held back. They stumbled backward into the main corridor toward the barricaded door.

It seemed that ever since they had entered the world beyond the broom closet, everything felt so much gloomier. Even the hallway seemed gray—every object grungier, every sound more muffled. Taking a step felt like a chore, and the once pristine Marlowe School actually looked *dirty*. Above the lockers, Wendy saw gray gunk, the kind of grime that builds up in cracks, and then, mingling with the filth she saw something move . . . were those more *moths*? *Didn't they kill them all?*

As Wendy and John approached the other end of the corridor, the point where they would have to decide to take a left or a right, John heard a rustling and some muffled whispers. He was about to speak when a hand reached out and pulled Wendy into a classroom. She let go of John's hand, screamed, and began thrashing about. Whoever it was had her by the waist.

John shouted, "Wendy!" and dove after her into the classroom.

"Stop . . . making . . . all . . . that . . . noise," whispered a familiar voice. The room was dark, but after a few seconds, their eyes adjusted, and they could make out Peter and two of the boarding boys, still in their Marlowe uniforms.

"Peter!" gasped Wendy. "There's something there—some seriously messed up—I dunno, something."

Peter slapped his hand over her mouth. "Shhhh," he whispered. He quickly pulled John and Wendy inside and shut the door. They all crouched together, staring into the hall through a small window in the door frame. The only sound now was Wendy's frantic and John's asthmatic breathing.

Through the dark corridor, the hooded figure passed slowly by the window. She walked deliberately but elegantly, noiselessly, like a demon tracking, like a spirit that somehow sees all, so there is no need to crouch or hide or hold your breath. She moved so subtly, so smoothly, that they could only sense her presence though the deep ghostly gloom that hung over them when she was close. Her steps were as quiet as a snooping nanny or a mother looking for guilty secrets. For ten long seconds, they held their breath. The intruder turned toward the classroom, touched the glass of the window, her hood still obscuring her face. She brought a pale hand to her invisible mouth, as if clearing her throat or coughing. Wendy squeezed her eyes shut. John shivered. None of them knew why this figure was so scary. Even Peter seemed frightened. Then the figure was gone.

"Nice going," said Peter when the intruder was out of sight. His voice was unconcerned, almost elated. "You shouldn't go playing around with six-thousand-year-old portals to the underworld."

There was a second of silence, and then John and Wendy spoke simultaneously.

"We only went the once!" said Wendy.

"What do *you* know about it?" said John.

The boys gave a mocking laugh, revealing the matching gaps in their mouths where a tooth had been pulled. Since that day when Wendy had first seen Peter, Wendy's curiosity had led her to eavesdrop on the boarding boys—just once or twice, in the hallways, in class, outside the dorms. She had learned that this tooth was the price of becoming one of Peter's boys. Among their gang they called it the Peter tooth—top row, left canine. Peter, too, had a wry smile on his face, and he nodded to one of the boys. It was one of those lazy half nods, the kind where the head moves upward only once. She knew it infuriated John.

There was a rhythmic knock on the door. Three knocks, then two, then two more. One of the boys opened it, and Tina rushed in. She was wearing her usual RA crested polo shirt and holding the twisted stick that had been barring the door.

"How'd you—?" Wendy looked at the stick that had left welts on her hands and still refused to budge.

"Cornrow," said Peter, "go watch the halls."

"We'll text you," said one of the boys, the famous Marlowe criminal with pink skin, three blond cornrows, and an affected streetthug accent, "if we see anything else."

"Good," said Peter as the two boys left the room. "Just one more thing." He turned to Wendy and John. He pulled the teacher's rolling chair toward him, then flipped it around and plopped himself onto it. "You have to tell me where the book is."

John snorted. "No way," he muttered. "Who the hell are you to tell us what to do?"

Wendy noticed Tina creeping toward Peter, her dark eyes sparkling

with curiosity. Or maybe it wasn't curiosity. She sat on a desk immediately behind Peter and leaned over to put an arm across his shoulder, resting her head in the crook of his neck. He stroked her arm
absentmindedly and stared intently at Wendy.

"So the poor little rich kids have gotten into trouble," crooned
Tina, with a bit too much sarcasm and disgust for an RA. "What
would Mommy say?"

"For your information," Wendy hissed, "we're not rich, and we
don't have a mom."

Peter caught her glance, but Wendy looked away. She wished
she hadn't said that. But Peter was smiling sympathetically and then
he changed the subject.

"So you had some fun with the *Book of Gates*," he said. "Great.
I don't blame you. But I need that book now, if we're gonna fix
the leak."

"What leak?" said John, his eyes narrow with suspicion. "How
do you even know about this stuff?"

"The wall that separates the underworld from Marlowe," said
Peter. "When there's a leak, that means the underworld takes on
more and more qualities of the overworld, and vice versa, until you
can't tell them apart. Our friend out there . . . she's from the underworld, and I'm pretty sure you two unleashed her into the school.
You're lucky no one's dead."

Wendy drew a breath. "How . . . ?"

Tina cut her off. "You went snooping around the labyrinth,
that's how," she said. "And you left the door open."

"No." Wendy shook her head. "No, it wasn't us. I've seen that
eye somewhere before."

"What eye?" Peter sat up, his voice was suddenly harsh. "You've seen her eye before? Where? When?"

"I don't know!" said Wendy. "But I don't think it's our fault. . . . I've definitely seen it." Wendy tried to remember. She tried so hard, but a place as large and busy as Marlowe is so full of unimpressive faces.

"Well, if you didn't cause a leak," Tina snorted, "then how do you explain the *physical* changes to the building in the last two days?"

"Now *you're* an expert, too?" John said.

Peter had been rubbing Tina's arms for seventeen seconds now, not that Wendy was counting. But Peter didn't seem to care. He was mumbling something about the eye.

Then Peter abruptly looked up and said, "Your call. It's the book in exchange for getting rid of the leak. I'd say that's a fair trade, especially since you don't even have a clue about how to use it."

Tina started rubbing the tip of her nose on Peter's neck.

Wendy (who wasn't looking) shouted, a bit too loud, "No deal."

"Suit yourself," said Peter. "I'll just be on my way, then." He got up from his chair and started toward the door.

"No," said Wendy, and Peter stopped. "You get rid of the leak *and* tell us how the book works, and then you can use it . . . along with us. Otherwise, I call my dad, get you two fired, and put the book through the shredder."

"And if I say no?" said Peter. "You'll let all your friends get killed?"

"I don't have any friends," said Wendy, her tone unflinching. "I don't care what happens to the school." She felt guilty for saying that, but she had to play tough here. This was her father's exhibit, and it was her job to protect it, to protect her father's career. Not to mention the fact that she wasn't about to let Peter the RA out of her sight. And even if she didn't get involved, she was pretty sure that John would, not only to impress the LBs, but also because he was crazy about all this Egyptian stuff.

"This doesn't make sense," said John. "What does an RA want with—?"

"Fine," Peter interrupted, looking bored. He eyed Tina. "Out!" he said. Tina shot Wendy a murderous glance as she headed for the door. Wendy beamed back, relishing the idea that she was about to share a secret to which, evidently, Tina wasn't privy.

Peter dropped into one of the student chairs. His legs were too long, and he pushed the desk away from him and leaned back. "So clearly, one of you speaks ancient Egyptian."

John and Wendy exchanged glances, a dumb, confused look on both their faces.

"You have to say a word in Egyptian. The name of the hour," said Peter. He was picking the gunk out from under his dirty nails.

"Yeah, yeah," said John, pulling his father's list from his pocket and studying it. "The fourth one from the top. We said it like ten times. It only worked the once."

"Did you try any of the others?"

"All of them. So?" said John. He mouthed the names from top to bottom. He had practically memorized them.

"Aren't you two supposed to be the spawn of the genius professor?" said Peter with a wink to Wendy. John clenched his fists. Peter continued, "You have to say the name of the *current* hour of the night. So if you said the name of the fourth hour, you must have said it during the fourth hour of the night."

Wendy shook her head. "Nope," she said confidently. "It wasn't night. It was right after school."

Wendy thought she saw Peter suppress an eye roll. A sharp sting ran through Wendy's chest. He was still laying on the charm, but he looked almost annoyed. "The current hour of the night in *Egypt*. Egypt is seven hours ahead. So three o'clock would be ten o'clock at night there. The sun sets at six thirty this time of year. So ten o'clock is the fourth hour. See?"

Now John was practically salivating. "I can't *believe* I didn't figure that out!"

Wendy was chewing the polish off her pinky. Her next words were a little less confident, a little more hushed. "But we've tried all of them. We tried all of them all at once. Why didn't that work?"

Peter shrugged, sinking lower into his seat. He put his thumb under his belt. "It could be a bunch of reasons. Pronunciation. Proximity to the book. But most likely, you did it during the Egyptian daytime, which wouldn't correspond to any of the twelve night hours."

John was pacing and nodding furiously. "Right," he was mumbling. "Sunset to sunrise. Those are the only hours in the *Book of Gates*."

Wendy blushed. Shouldn't she have figured this out? "Yeah," she mumbled, "it was before school . . . mid-afternoon in Egypt."

"OK, so then what?" John said.

Peter sighed. "You say it aloud . . . and you have to be close to the book, as if you're speaking the hour *to* it."

John began biting his lower lip.

"Then"—Peter got up from his seat, walked toward the door,

and turned the knob—"you just open a door—any door that's closest to the book. You'll know it because it will be marked with the Eye of Ra. But once you've opened the door, it's an active portal until you shut it and the eye disappears."

"What if someone shuts the door while you're inside?" asked Wendy.

"You just say the name of the hour again," said Peter. "You can open a portal pretty much anywhere inside the underworld. But you have to be careful, because every location in the underworld corresponds to a place in the overworld. So if you open a portal in one place, you end up in the matching spot."

"What's the overworld?" said John.

"For the moment that would be Marlowe," said Peter. "See, the underworld melds itself to what's above, like a parasite to a host, and replicates it. It's sort of like . . . like an evil twin. Its parts match up with the school in some way. The biggest difference is that the underworld version is always bigger, much more dangerous, and a whole lot less . . . academic, let's say." He laughed at his own dumb joke.

Wendy remembered the columns forming a clutter eerily similar to the basement from which they had entered the underworld. She remembered the lake of fire that had looked so much like the puddle and the electric cord. And of course, she remembered all the things inside Marlowe that had begun to look like the underworld—the dirty, grimy hallways caked with dead moths, the stone step, the marble column turning into mud.

"We were in the basement," she whispered.

Peter nodded knowingly. "So you probably ended up in the base of the pyramid. It's attached to Marlowe right now, but the Egyptian underworld is always shaped like an upside-down pyramid."

Wendy nodded, remembering all the stairs leading downward, into the dark void below, just like the steps in the basement that led up into the school. She didn't want to think about the horrors that might lie dormant beyond the first layer of the underworld.

"The main thing to remember," said Peter, his voice a conspiratorial whisper, "is to watch for the eye over a door. You could look inside a room and everything could look completely normal, but if it has the eye over it, it's the portal. And if you leave the door open, you're just leaving the gateway open and inviting all sorts of nasty things in from the underworld. And it always starts with just a feeling. . . ." Peter looked around as if to signal what he meant—because everyone had been aware of the creepy change in atmosphere, the tainted air, in Marlowe over the last few days.

"So once we fix the leak, everything will go back to normal, right?" asked Wendy.

Peter shrugged. "Some things," he said, as if he didn't care.

"Peter," said Wendy, "when people come back to school tomorrow, they'll see the step and the column and all that . . . ?"

"You'd be surprised how little people notice," said Peter. Then he added, "Don't worry. The big things will fade away. But you can't have your happy fairy-tale school back as long as the book is hidden here. The overworld only becomes more and more tainted the longer it's attached to the underworld."

With that, Peter pulled the door open. Tina stumbled into the room, having been pressed tightly up against the closed door. She looked dissatisfied, clearly not having caught more than snippets. *How strange,* thought Wendy, *that he doesn't trust her with the secret of opening the gate. How strange that she still does what he says.*

Peter shook his head and clucked his tongue like a disapproving parent. "Hey, babe," he said to Tina, sarcasm dripping from his lips. "Can't even go a second without me?"

Tina ignored the comment and pushed past him toward Wendy. "Can we do this already? I have disturbed advisees to counsel and condoms to hand out."

"Funny." Peter turned to Wendy. "I need the book *now*. Whether *she's* been out there for days or weeks, we still need to force her through a new gate." The way Peter said *she*, with so much disdain and malice, signaled to Wendy that he had met this figure before. That he had a personal vendetta.

"OK," whispered Wendy, wondering how you force a shadow or a phantom through anything, and, more important, where she had seen that unearthly eye before.

As they crept out of the classroom, they spotted the two LBs coming back toward them. One of them shook his head as if to say he didn't see anything else.

"OK, Wendy, lead the way." Peter took Wendy's hand with such ease that for a second she didn't even realize it. But then, as his grip tightened, a warm feeling spread over her, like the first time Connor had kissed her.

Tina made a disgusted sound with her throat. She grudgingly took her place out of the spotlight while Wendy led them toward the basement. The group shuffled along quickly but noiselessly, with only the occasional whisper of "Left here" or "Round that corner" dotting the silence. Soon they passed Wendy's locker, and then half-way down the main corridor, one of the boys stopped in front of a floor-to-ceiling trophy case. "That douche still owes me for the game," he whispered.

"Stupid sport," said Cornrow, also falling behind to look at the trophies and victory photos.

From up ahead, Peter motioned for them to move, and they continued on.

This time Wendy heard Cornrow whisper, "It's that prick Connor Wirth's fault. Too worried about his shrine getting tainted with a little side bet."

Every time Wendy heard boys from her school talking, she felt ashamed to even go here. None of them really appreciated Marlowe, with all its everyday excesses: the marble trophy case, the vending machines full of organic treats, the sign forbidding handheld devices, and the distance-learning lab full of flat-screen TVs. As they were making their way down the hall, a couple of girls from Wendy's English class wandered past. They swayed along easily, carelessly, completely unaware of the chaos that was going on around them. They were in their cheerleading uniforms—stragglers who must have stayed late after practice. They glanced at the boarding boys invitingly. When they saw Wendy with Peter, they began whispering to each other. Wendy caught the words *Connor* and *holding hands with an RA*. One of them said loudly, "He's too hot for her. She must be putting out."

Wendy turned to watch the girls walk away. They took a left turn at the end of the long corridor where the hallway branched in the shape of a T. As they ambled out of sight, their chattering heads close together, oblivious to everything around them, Wendy saw a long, elegant shadow appearing over their shoulders, a few moths fluttering behind it. One of the girls shuddered. She turned around as if she felt something behind her. She ran her hands through her hair, trying to remove some invisible pest. Without noticing their own reactions, the girls quickened their steps and left through the back door.

"OK, another left here," said Wendy. She rushed into the turn and immediately stopped. Halfway down the hall was her locker again. "Wait. Something's not right."

"What's wrong?" said Peter. "You said you knew where the book—"

"No," said Wendy. "Look, we've been down this hall before."

John ran a few yards ahead and peeked down one of the hallways. "Are you sure?" he said. "There are three hallways before the basement."

"Yes," said Wendy, irritated, "and we've been down all three."

"You sure?" said John, looking around as if he was trying to remember a much longer journey. The confused look on his face gave Wendy a sinking feeling in her stomach.

Peter ran one hand through his hair. "I know what's wrong," he said. "This happened when the British Museum was the overworld." Tina and the boys were now gathered around them, waiting for Peter to explain. "We're lost," he said.

"I don't get it," said the boy with cornrows. "I've gone to this school for ten years, man. I can take you to the friggin' basement. Follow me."

He hadn't taken four steps before he stopped cold, face-to-face with the trophy case full of Connor Wirth's achievements. "What the f—?"

"Stop wasting time!" Peter snapped as he marched toward the boy and pulled him roughly by his arm. To Wendy's surprise, the LB just accepted the rough treatment. He didn't object to being man-handled by his RA. Didn't try to fight, or threaten to have his dad sue, the way most Marlowe kids would have done. Wendy wondered if he was on drugs or something, but then Peter continued, "We're lost because the hallways are turning into a maze. The underworld is a labyrinth. And now Marlowe is, too."

For a moment, they all stood there while Peter deliberated. Wendy expected him to have some grand plan for unraveling the maze that was now their school. But all Peter said was "Getting lost in the maze could get dangerous." Then he turned to Tina and added, "Tina, you go and scout out a route. The key is to find a way *downward;* doesn't matter where you find it." With that, he turned away from her, pulling Wendy along with him. He turned only once to say to Tina, "Text me when you find a way."

Tina's gaze fell, but she obeyed.

"Don't worry," said Peter to Wendy. "Tina can take care of her-self." Wendy could see Tina's chest rising up and down, heaving with a mix of hatred and disappointment. She wondered what Tina had wanted to hear. Did she want Peter to tell her to stay in a safe spot, too? Was she hurt that he was sending her to face dangers that he was shielding Wendy from? Wendy wondered why Tina would let Peter treat her like this—one of the boys one minute, his favorite girl the next. But then again, Tina had serious skills. He probably just needed her to back him up.

Just then, as she watched Tina disappear down a hallway that could lead anywhere, Wendy felt her hair flutter. She whipped around. Again, there was nothing there. She grabbed John and pulled him close to her, but John pulled away from her and went to stand by the two LBs.

"Careful, kid," said Peter. "She doesn't look like much, but she doesn't mess around."

"What do you mean *she doesn't look like much*?" John shot back. "Stop pretending you're not scared!"

"I don't get it," said Wendy. "What does she want?"

"Me," said Peter with an almost proud smile. "She wants me."

It seemed like they had walked in circles for hours when Tina finally sent a text message. In reality, it had been only twenty minutes, and Tina said that she had found it easy to get to the basement. But no matter where the rest of them went, the maze seemed to encircle them like a man-eating snake, always moving, coiling around itself so there was no escape.

Try service elevator, Tina's text said, **NW corner of Mrlo. Leads down.**

But despite the simplicity of the instructions, another fifteen minutes later the group was back in front of the trophy case. Somehow, Wendy got the feeling that the maze was targeting them. That it was adapting to them specifically, moving and changing around them so they couldn't get back to the basement—and to the book. But why had it let Tina get away?

Peter turned to the boys. "You two. Go and find the elevator . . .

and . . . we need some sort of string. Something really long."

The boys checked their pockets. Wendy, too. But John was already running down the hall.

"Where are you going?" she yelled after him.

He stopped at the end of the hall. "My fortress of solitude," he yelled back as he opened his locker, all the way down from the trophy case. When he rushed back to them, he was carrying two packets of dental floss.

"Brilliant," said Peter. "Here, take this," he said to the boys. "The maze is focused on the three of us—me, John, and Wendy—because we're the ones who have been through the door. So you have to find the way down to the basement holding one end of the string, and we'll hold the other. When you get there, text us, and we'll follow the string down."

Soon, the text came and they began gathering up the floss across the halls of Marlowe. Peter said that they had to run, because who knew how long this plan would work. They bolted down the hallways, with Peter gathering up the floss in his fist so that it would remain taut—a signal to the LBs that they were still on the other end.

Wendy was exhausted. The flight down the hallway and into the service elevator was a blur. All she could sense was the fuzzy outline of things. The outline of Peter's free hand on her back. The outline of John running ahead. The outline of two girls from English class in the adjoining wing of the school whispering frantically now that Wendy Darling was racing down the hall with the infamous rule-breaking RA. And finally, when they reached the elevator, there was the outline of Tina waiting for them. Tina, who even in all this excitement and hysteria hadn't missed the fact that Peter had protected Wendy, while he had let *her* navigate the maze alone.

When they were safely out of the elevator and standing at the top of the rickety basement steps, Peter signaled that they could relax. John was wheezing heavily as he took out his inhaler. He bent double and rested his hands on his trembling knees.

"So I still don't get it. Why was the maze zeroing in on the three of us?" Wendy asked.

The boys were waiting at the top of the basement steps, waiting for someone to unlock the door leading down, holding an empty case of floss, high-fiving each other and cheering their triumph.

"Don't flatter yourself," said Tina. She was the last to step out of the elevator.

"It only targets the ones who've been inside," said Peter. "The ones chasing bonedust."

"So you believe the mummies are real?" John panted. "The stories about the five victims of great crimes being stolen by the death god. You think bonedust might actually exist?"

"Evidently," said Peter, trying to sound bored. Then he added nonchalantly, "I would've had it a long time ago if the overworld didn't keep changing. Every time that book gets moved, I have to jump on a plane and start all over."

Wendy wondered how old this guy was. He didn't look any more than nineteen. "So you got the RA job just to be near the exhibit?" she asked. Peter just looked at his nails. He took a second to think, then said, "It's the *underworld*—not exactly a part-time gig."

"But it feels so small," Wendy muttered.

"Things aren't always laid out for you to see," said Peter. "Some things are much bigger than their visible parts."

Then Peter said something that sent chills through Wendy. "This part of Marlowe—the dark side of it—it's always been here, even if you didn't see it. It's what drew all the pieces together to begin with."

Peter didn't have to say it. Wendy already knew what the "pieces" were: the *Book of Gates;* Peter, who was forever chasing it; and the Dark Lady, who was ever conscious of the danger Peter presented. This place was predestined. There was an evil here. Maybe it would always be here—even if they closed the leak, found all the bonedust, and destroyed the book. The labyrinth might go away, but what scared Wendy was the idea that the devil that had attached itself to Marlowe was much harder to get rid of.

"Was that . . . woman with the hood . . . was that her?" Wendy asked. "The Dark Lady . . . um . . . the death goddess?"

"You saw the eye," said Peter, "the broken one. I've seen that on only one other person . . . years ago." Wendy thought he would tell her more, but he trailed off.

"OK, let's do this, then," said John. "Let's force her back in . . . or whatever."

"Guys." Peter turned to Tina and the boys. "Go back to the dorms."

"*What?*" said Tina, not bothering to hide her anger.

"Do it," he said. "This is *my* thing." This time, Tina and the boys obeyed.

Peter went to the basement door. "So the book's in here?"

Wendy hesitated. Then she nodded.

Peter's lips curled incredulously. "I can't believe you left it next to the last open door." Then he whispered something to himself and said, "Let's move. I have an idea."

TINA

A HAPPY THOUGHT

My mama used to call me Martina Fabiola

My papi used to call me his little preciosa

*My girls, Ronnie and Lia, used to call me the genius 'cause I
passed pre-algebra*

*Richard Lubenstein used to follow me around and call me
"regina di mi corazón," bad Spanish for "queen of my heart"*

Mrs. Waxman used to call me Ms. Vazquez

Poet used to call me his muse

Cornrow used to call me a dime-piece shorty

Peter used to call me his girl

10

BONEDUST

"So what's your plan?" Wendy asked Peter as she unlocked the door at the top of the basement stairs and watched him take the steps two at a time.

"Relax," said Peter. "I have it under control."

"How, exactly?" Wendy asked in her most rational tone. "Tell me."

Peter ignored her, which made John glare at him through razor-thin eyes and mumble curses. He ran down the steps after Peter, as always looking for every opportunity to hassle the arrogant RA. "I bet he doesn't actually know what he's doing," John said, as if Peter weren't right there within earshot, "but we're *still* walking down to the creepy basement, chasing after some undead thing that's trying to kill us."

"Give him a chance," whispered Wendy.

John, who was losing all patience, turned and yelled at his sister, "We're going to die, Wendy! Do you get it? Game over? Brutally shredded corpses? *Tú no more está alive-o?*"

"Look, Peter knows way more about this stuff than we do," Wendy whispered. "And he says he has it under control." John hated her mature act.

"And how, exactly?" asked John. "Is Peter one of the X-Men? Excuse me, Peter, did you by any chance train at Charles Xavier's School for Gifted Youngsters? Do you have a field degree in kicking superevil ass that we don't know about?"

"You're such a colossal dork," said Peter. "Stop freaking out like some old lady."

"Oh, I'm sorry," John shot back. "I should stop freaking out now. Because valuing your life is *so* lame. . . . Stop acting like you're not freaked out, too."

Peter didn't seem fazed by any of this. He was acting like it was all a game. John swore he was doing it just for effect—another guy trying to get next to Wendy. He wanted to whip out his phone right now and scream all his frustrations into his Facebook status update.

Peter's a poser. Tim the lacrosse player blows. Sanjeev is a tool. Everyone sucks SO MUCH! I swear I'm gonna blow past all these guys, figure out this whole Bonegate thing, and tell y'all ta suck it!

"She'll follow us when we open the gate," said Peter. "John, take this and dial 1 if anything goes wrong." Peter pulled out a sleek new cell phone. John was impressed. It was the most expensive phone on the market. *He probably stole it.*

"No way," said John, crossing his arms and staring at Peter. "I'm not your secretary."

Suddenly Wendy, who'd been looking more and more nervous as they descended the stairs, took Peter's phone, marched up to John, grabbed him by the arm (this was probably the last year she'd be stronger than him, John swore to himself almost every day), and pulled him to one corner. "John, stop this *right now*! You're acting like a brat, and we're in real danger, and if you don't get a grip, I swear I'll—"

John glanced at Peter, who was watching them with a sneer. He couldn't believe his own sister was humiliating him like this. "You'll what?" John shot back.

"Just stay here," said Wendy, tightening her grip on his arm. "Take the phone and do what you're asked, or I'll show Connor your *Battlestar Galactica* collection. I swear I will."

"Traitor," John whispered, his eyes rolling into the back of his head, his glasses fogging up, his voice full of resentment. He grabbed the phone from his sister.

Wendy and Peter rushed to find the *Book of Gates* while John fumed and killed time by fiddling with Peter's phone. At first, John cast only cursory glances at the phone and watched with fury as Wendy hurried across the basement, winding around the set pieces of the exhibit, straight to the ancient book. Peter's eyes almost welled up in excitement. When he put his hands on the book, it was with familiarity. He brushed his hands across the surface, lifted it, and bounced it on his palms a few times, as though he was weighing it. But then, just as John was about to throw a spiteful comment about the RA's creepy interest in all this, he stumbled across Peter's contacts list and his attention was diverted.

"Five twenty," said Peter, glancing at his watch. He closed his eyes and held the book up to his mouth. Wendy didn't think you had to do that for the magic to work, but it looked like he was breathing in the smell of the pages. Then Peter whispered the name of the sixth hour of night in ancient Egyptian. *Does he have all the hours memorized?* Wendy also noticed that he pronounced the word differently from the way John or her dad had on the many occasions she had heard them practice ancient Egyptian.

Peter opened his eyes and opened the book to a random page. The message began to appear just as it had done for Wendy and John. Wendy leaned over his shoulder to get a better look.

You speak truly: this sixth hour of Egypt's night

Open the gates and enter here

As she bent over Peter's shoulder, Wendy heard him whisper the words and then mumble something in a language she assumed was ancient Egyptian. It sounded like a prolonged sigh of relief or a prayer of thanks. Wendy knew she was geeking out a little, but she couldn't help finding it attractive. The way his lips spoke the words in a hushed breathy tone made her quiver. She imagined the damp contact of those lips barely brushing against her face as he whispered little temptations in her ear. Then Wendy remembered Connor and all the promises to herself, and she pushed the thoughts of Peter out of her head.

Wendy was busy admiring all of Peter's less academic qualities when suddenly he looked over and caught her staring. Wendy flushed and looked up at him. Peter just smirked. "Well," he said, "do you see the door?"

"Oh," said Wendy, her tone a little squeaky, her hand instinctively fixing her hair. She glanced around, hoping to spot it first. But a moment later, Peter pointed to a door nearby.

Wendy turned to see the Eye of Ra slowly appearing over the door frame.

"Now we wait for her to come," said Peter.

John had only managed to get through the *D*s in Peter's contacts list when they finished opening the gate. Apparently, this Peter guy was the most connected jerk on the face of the planet. He had contacts all over: a guy named Agro in the Canary Islands, someone named Behamut Iron-Arm, who lived in Bhutan, the Kingdom of the Dragon. There were almost a hundred contacts in Cairo.

In the time it took for Wendy and Peter to open the gate, Peter's phone had gotten thirty-five texts and seven calls that left voice mail. After a while, someone answered a group text. The response was signed *LB53*. John figured out that it stood for Lost Boy 53. Apparently, Peter was even lamer at remembering names in cyberspace, where there were no physical clues to provide easy nicknames. Soon, more texts started getting responses.

It was like they were some kind of underground organization. The questions would be in one language, and the response would be in another. Sometimes the subjects would be small-time, like "How do I get the change out of a soda machine?" And other times it'd be big enough to make John squirm: "Posting the blueprints to the prime minister's HQ on secure FTP, encryption codes to follow . . ."

And it was always signed with *LB* and a number. All the texts went through Peter's phone. *Geez*, thought John, *he's not an RA. He's the boss of an international syndicate.* The central hub. The center of the Lost Boys' universe—not just at Marlowe; apparently, there were LBs all over New York, London, Tokyo, and a dozen other places. Knowing this made John feel a moment of admiration for Peter . . . but only a moment.

John scanned the contacts list again, then started reading more messages. Close to twenty more texts had shot back and forth. He took a few steps away from Peter and Wendy, who were now engrossed in a conversation about what to do with the open gate. Shrinking into a corner with the phone, John was tempted to text back, to write something to the LBs and be a part of it all—oh, and to screw Peter by infiltrating his network. But trying to enter the conversation was like trying to jump into those rivers at the water park that are always changing, always rushing ahead. He quickly typed out a message: **LBs in Marlowe. Damage under control. The Johnny.**

That was a pretty badass message. John was starting to get into this. He grinned as text after text started pouring in from all over: **The Johnny? Who is this? How did you hack the secure line? Has Magnus Unus been compromised?**

"Magnus Unus?" said John. Do they *really* refer to Peter as the "Great One"? As John ate up the sudden infamy, he failed to notice the slow changes, the tiny shifts in atmosphere that were taking hold all around. He didn't notice the lights dimming, didn't bother to look down long enough to see the patches of stone taking over the floor, didn't breathe in the rot all around, or see the moths, like curious minions, appearing in hidden corners. He was too busy imagining his name flying all over the servers, like Morpheus or aXXo. And as the room grew darker and darker, he had the light of the phone to read by.

He looked up just as his sister's trembling voice traveled across to him in the now pitch-black basement. "Wh . . . where's John?"

John held up the phone, trying to use it as a flashlight. He felt his way across the basement. "Wendy?" he whispered, forgetting his anger and trying to find his way to her. He could hear Wendy and Peter breathing, calling him to come to them. Or was that them? He couldn't tell. He felt like he was in a stone prison, just like inside the labyrinth. Suddenly, everything felt scary and urgent. He couldn't seem to swallow the pooling spit in his mouth. He just stared as an elegant shadow closed in on him.

In those brief moments, he thought perhaps he should run. But he didn't have long enough to process the idea. Instead, random facts began to flutter through his mind, like the fact that the shadow looked like a woman, or the fact that it really *was* zeroing in on the three of them. The three who had been inside.

And then, in the dark basement, as the Dark Lady drew closer, John thought he saw a familiar face under the layers of coarse fabric. He squinted to try to get a better look, but something shiny caught his eye instead. She was holding something in her right hand.

By the time John snapped out of it, it was too late. His survival instinct kicked in and he whipped around to run up the stairs, but the figure was too close. She seemed to be whispering, and each time he turned to look, he saw that her steps were slow and almost painful. John thought he heard her cough, and he peered into her hood one more time. Her face was completely obscured by a cloud of moths. He whimpered and tried to run again, but as he did, his hand brushed the fabric of her sleeve and he felt her cold flesh . . . and something else . . . something hard and metallic. It was some kind of hook.

A second later, John let out a horrible shriek.

For a few agonizing seconds, John leaned forward, halfway up the staircase, his body slumping over the banister, his arm caught between here and another place, an agonizing place made of pain and fire and torture. He saw blood spilling from the part of his arm that was still connected to the sharp hook, and now it was pumping in spurts from his veins, to the beat of his quivering heart. The pain was hot and cold, white and black, mute and shrill, all at the same time. John felt his body going into shock. His knees were giving out. He was losing too much blood.

Self-preservation was the only instinct left. Before he passed out, John made one last effort. He yanked. With everything he had left, he yanked his arm free of the hook's grip. The meat on his arm was stripped like a kebab and he fell forward. And John's limp form went tumbling down the stairs.

As the figure approached them, Wendy stood crying, with her hand on her mouth. She wanted to run and help John, but Peter was holding her back.

"Come on, now," said Peter. "We both know you're looking for me."

"What are you doing?" Wendy asked.

"I have to go in," said Peter. He looked ashen, like a kid about to get his punishment.

"*What?*" Wendy panted, looking up at the moths that were now circling them overhead.

"She wants *me*. She'll follow me, I promise. It's the only way." He looked up at the moths as if he expected them to be watching, and then, in an instant, he was gone. He just stepped through the door with the eye and vanished.

The lights flickered once. There was a brief pause, and the room was bright again. The smell was gone; the patches of stony floor disappeared as if it had been a mirage. Even the moths in the corners had gone. The figure hobbled into the gate behind Peter.

Wendy wondered if she should shut it. *Yes,* she thought, remembering what Peter had said. *He can just get back to the overworld by saying the name of the hour.* Peter had every name and secret and story in the book memorized. Though she hated closing the gate behind him, Wendy ran over and slammed the door shut, watching the eye disappear over the threshold. Then she rushed to John. She was overcome by guilt. How could she have been so cruel to him? And now he was lying here, his arm torn to shreds—the same arm she had so violently squeezed just a few minutes before.

Wendy felt her brother's cheek, tried to take his pulse. She would have thought he was dead if not for the barely perceptible movement in his chest. His arm was almost completely stripped. It was bone with a few threads of white pulp. Wendy winced. It reminded her of a twig after it's been used to roast a marshmallow. And it was her fault.

Wendy sat there next to John, waiting, trying to figure out what to do. She considered going upstairs to find a teacher or the school nurse. Instead, she found a cloth in the exhibit cleaning supplies and wrapped it tightly around his arm. Five minutes passed and Wendy began to panic. She was about to leave the basement when suddenly Peter came bounding down the staircase, shouting triumphantly as if he'd just won a tennis match.

"Where were you?" Wendy shouted.

Peter was taken aback, as if he expected her to rejoice with him. "You shut the gate, remember? Good job, by the way. But I had to get away through the labyrinth. I opened a gate at the first possible chance and ended up in the art studio upstairs."

Wendy had stopped listening halfway through the explanation. She began to shake John. "Wake up. Please, John, wake up. I'm so sorry." Then she looked at Peter. "Peter, we have to get him to a hospital."

But Peter didn't seem to grasp the urgency of the situation. He walked over to the *Book of Gates* and closed it gently. He set it on its stand before wandering over to John's body.

"Come on, *hurry*," urged Wendy.

"Don't worry so much," said Peter.

"He might die," said Wendy. She noticed she was trembling when Peter put his hand on her shoulder to steady her. She looked up at him. *Why is he so calm? Doesn't he care?*

Peter knelt down beside John. Wendy tried to regulate her breathing. But instead of tending to John, Peter reached down and grabbed his phone from the floor next to John. He was checking his messages.

"What are you *doing*?" said Wendy.

"Shh, shh, this one's important." Peter quickly texted something, oblivious to Wendy's panic. "The prime minister. That's good."

Peter looked up from his phone. Wendy was dumbfounded by his callousness. "Oh, right," said Peter, turning his attention to John. He dug into his pocket and brought out an item wrapped in gauze. From the other pocket, he pulled out a multi-tool. Wendy watched with curiosity as Peter slowly unwrapped the gauze around the item to reveal a stubby rock, or maybe a dried mushroom. Wendy leaned in. "It's a bone," said Peter, "from a toe."

He pulled out a nail file from the multi-tool. Carefully, very carefully, Peter started to grate the bone over John's thrashed arm. A fine dust began to snow, and Wendy gasped, finally realizing what she was witnessing.

At first, nothing happened. But soon, as the dust settled and soaked in, John's wound began to heal. A ripped strand of muscle began to grow like a cartoon vine, wrapping itself back around the bone. John let out a weary groan as he gained consciousness. Wendy gaped as she watched veins and tendons growing in John's arm. And just as the final layer of skin wrapped itself tightly, a rush of blood coursed through the tissue, swelling it up like a sponge.

And then it was back to normal. Peter immediately stopped grating. He didn't waste a single speck. He wrapped the remainder of the petrified toe and put it back in his pocket. They'd have to clean the bloody mess, but John was perfectly fine. They'd also need to get rid of his blood-soaked clothes. But for now, Wendy was overjoyed. She helped John sit up. And while John got his bearings, she threw her arms around Peter.

"*Thank you,* Peter," said Wendy. Her face was buried in his shoulder, and she felt him tap her absentmindedly on the back, the way he had done to Tina. She lifted her head slightly to look at him, hoping that his mind wasn't with myths or bonedust or some other faraway distraction. For the first time, that feeling of mistrust that Wendy had toward anyone who showed interest vanished. She didn't think about being left behind or betrayed. She didn't think about Connor or how this moment with Peter would stack up in her life's quest not to be like her mother. She watched Peter's smirk, a self-satisfied, happy grin—maybe he was happy *for her*. Wendy didn't move. She just waited, her face inches from Peter's.

After a slight pause, the smirk left Peter's face, and she thought she felt him inching forward, his hand creeping toward her neck, so that she could feel the first tickle of warm breath—when John moaned, "Gross."

Wendy jumped back, only now realizing what strange timing this was for Peter to try to kiss her. She didn't care. She didn't even allow the niggling thought that Peter might be the type of guy who got kissed whenever and wherever the idea struck him.

"I'm so sorry, John," she whispered, falling on her brother and hugging him.

John pushed her off and shrugged the way he always did when he wanted to say it's OK.

"*The Johnny* speaks," said Peter, looking at his phone. The idea of a kiss seemed to have flown out of his mind just as suddenly as it had flown in.

John sat up and examined his arm, then his bloody clothes with increasing alarm. "H-how—?" he asked, gawking at his tattered shirt with awe.

Wendy eyed Peter. "Someone neglected to mention he has bonedust."

Peter put his hand through his hair. "You put it together, did you?"

"How else could you heal a wound like that?"

"Maybe I'm Superman."

"Superman can't regenerate carbon-based tissue," said John in a still-groggy voice.

"Wow," said Peter. "He's even dweeby in his sleep."

Wendy changed the subject. "So Daddy wasn't just *right* about the legends and the five mummies; he was close to finding where they were! He's the one who said that the book holds the key to the mysteries of bonedust. And he commissioned these artifacts from the British museum. Do you think he knew about the labyrinth, or do you think he expected to find a treasure map or something? Like, a more . . . um . . . earthly one . . ."

"Your pops isn't as crazy as everyone thinks," said Peter.

"We saw one of them," said John, perking up. "The pyramid with five pillars, that must have been—"

"The temple Elan built," said Peter. "That's where I got the first bonedust. The toe was all that was left of him." He tapped his pocket. Then he turned to Wendy, a look of hungry curiosity on his face. "So at Marlowe, the Elan temple is at the base? You said you went only to the *base*."

Wendy shrugged.

Peter began mumbling to himself. "It can't be," he said. "How close did you get?"

"It looked about that big." Wendy made a fist.

"Hah!" Peter laughed, almost triumphantly. "You weren't even close. Distances in the underworld are bigger than they look. You'd have had to go in using a completely different part of the overworld. There's no way she'd put one of the five mummies near the base. No way." He shook his head vehemently. "In the last overworld, Elan's temple was halfway in the middle of the pyramid. I had to go in through a construction site. Get it? Because Elan was a builder. . . . It always corresponds like that to the overworld. The pyramid is like a leech. It gets its energy from the world above it. It can't survive without a host, so the two worlds share lots of features. It's a good thing, 'cause I can use clues from the five stories to find my way— like a construction site for Elan the builder."

A leech. Wendy thought about the eerie feeling she had lately, even before today's events, every time she walked through the halls of her school. She thought about all the creepy similarities she had already seen between the two worlds.

"So the gates . . ." John started, his voice a bit weak.

"As far as I know, there are five major gates," said Peter, "each with a guardian and one of my mummies. The rest of the labyrinth is just designed to keep intruders confused."

The way he said *my mummies* felt uncomfortable to Wendy.

"Do you have more?" she asked. "If you have all five, you'll be immortal. Is *that* true?"

"It's all true, Wendy," said Peter.

"Do you have any of the others?" asked John.

"Just the second one . . . sort of," said Peter.

"I figure it should be in a desert. That's where Garosh went to die, or not die," said John.

"Yeah, I know. I *had* it."

"What happened?" asked Wendy. "Did you make it past the gatekeeper?"

"Oh, yeah." Peter smiled. "That wasn't a problem. But then—"

"The death god," whispered John.

"Death *goddess*," said Peter. "If we're gonna get technical."

So that part was true, too—the Anubis legend that all the scholars studied was wrong, and the obscure five myths lore about the Dark Lady was real. They had just seen her. John had even touched her.

"Anyway, I had to hide the second batch of bonedust inside the labyrinth," said Peter.

"You hid an entire mummy?" John asked. "Must be one heck of a hiding spot."

"Uh . . . yep," said Peter proudly. "No one's ever gotten closer than I have. Why do you think she's after me?" Wendy saw a serious look, a hatred, overtake Peter's features. This was obviously an intensely personal grudge, and one that Wendy could understand. Peter didn't just want the bones. He wanted revenge—to defy her, the way a child wants to defy a selfish mother. "I hid it in the best possible spot. . . ."

"How about a hint?" said John, his tone not all that hopeful.

Peter laughed. "I'll just tell you, kid. It was in the mouth of a giant sphinx."

"So that's why you want to go back," said Wendy.

"Wanna come?" said Peter, grabbing her hand. "It's the biggest adventure in the world."

Wendy blushed. "We should clean up the blood. Someone must have heard the noise." They stood up, taking one last look at the door that had served as the gate. On the other side was just another utility closet.

"We were almost killed," Wendy mused as they prepared to leave.

"Nah," said Peter, relishing his success as if it were something much bigger, a victory over all forces of evil, a blow to every power-mad teacher and abandoning mother and wicked, black-hearted nanny. "That was Peter *one*, Dark Lady *zero*."

"How about a half point for nearly ripping my arm off?" said John, rubbing where his gaping wound used to be.

"No," said Peter. "One–zero, me."

A turning knob, a clicking lock, and the echo of a door slowly creaking open—a door without the Eye of Ra to mark it.

When the children had cleaned up the mess and left the basement, Nurse Neve crept out of the basement broom closet, wiped her pale, squinty face with her handkerchief, and walked back into the school.

THE DARK

In the halls of Marlowe's underworld, the dark nurse moved in secret. In the school corridors, too, she walked unseen, the way all aging, plain-faced women without public accolades go unseen. She was hindered by the frailties of this most ordinary of human bodies, but she could see that Peter had found his way back. And he had brought others, intruders looking for fame, fortune, long life. With her broken eye, the darkness watched them, assessed them. Now there were two who had used the bonedust to heal themselves, and she could afford no time for rest. Until the boy had all five mummies, death would not be conquered, and so the Dark Lady held the most powerful bonedust close. She might be weak, but she had once used this very body to accomplish epic things. She didn't need to be a stunning governess to conquer worlds, because Neferat was so much older, more experienced. She could do it all again now. She sat in her attic office, the one she had requested from the school, and coughed blood into her napkin.

The moths, these tiny messengers, circled around frantically, looking for approval from their mistress, sharing in the stench of her gloom. She was beginning to like this humbler form—it was a subtle disease infecting the school, a forgettable nurse in moth-eaten blue, seemingly harmless but in truth the crucial lulling ingredient in a dark trinity. In the meantime, let the children play in the underworld maze. Let Peter play his games just as he had done when he was a child, a wayward, unrepentant child who rejected her plans for his own. Let them all come a little closer. Each time they opened a gate was a brand-new opportunity to infect the world with malice, hatred, and sorrow. Every time someone new entered, another soul could be corrupted forever.

SIMON/PETER

It wasn't that John was invisible in the halls of Marlowe; that would have been too easy. And he wasn't exactly an object of scorn; that would have been too maudlin. No, after his attempt at reinventing himself, Marlowe had prepared the perfect torture for little John Darling, who couldn't help how smart he was (well, maybe he could stop darting his hand up every time the teacher asked a question). And he couldn't help that his dad was a brilliant and respected, and only slightly kooky, professor at the school (well, maybe he could stop reminding everyone all the time). And especially, John couldn't help the fact that everybody knew he had his pick of top colleges even though he was only thirteen and college was five years away (well, three years for him, actually, and before the aborted Facebook makeover, he kinda blogged about it).

It must have really ticked off all the upperclassmen angling for leadership positions and teacher recommendations that this thirteen-year-old freshman (accelerated into high school, naturally) had already aced the SATs. Not just aced them; he really beat the living crap out of that Scantron. John was the king of computations, the sultan of smarts. He was a badass of books. No matter how much he fought it, he was a big . . . fat . . . nerd.

OK, he was a big fat nerd. Whatever. He couldn't help it. This sucked. Maybe he could help it. He shouldn't be so arrogant about his brains. But then, if he wasn't, it felt like he didn't have *anything* to bank on. He wasn't ripped like Connor. And it wasn't like he had a phone full of contacts calling him the "Great One" all the time. He wasn't six feet tall like Peter, with chicks licking his neck and a crew of boarding students helping him live a real-life Egyptian fantasy. He didn't have that smirk. Geez, John really hated that smirk.

So basically, John was doomed to be invisible to everybody, until he decided to make his talents known (which just happened to be unbridled genius), and *then* he was the object of scorn. And if he tried to be someone else, more scorn. *Sweet.*

Just three more years and I'll be someplace where prodigies get the girls, thought John as he skulked down the hall through passing period. Hundreds of classmates were gabbing, grabbing books from lockers, laughing, playing jokes, and doing ninety-nine other things that didn't involve John. Some guy bumped John's arm as he chased his friend, sending a tingling feeling all the way up to John's shoulder. John couldn't tell if he'd been hit in the funny bone or if this was some aftereffect on the arm that had been mangled yesterday. John rubbed his forearm. It was fine. In fact, it was better than fine. It was a weird thing to say, but it felt new. Even the burn mark he'd gotten from a Bunsen burner last year seemed to be faded and gone.

The bell sounded for next period, and everyone had a buddy to walk with. John still hadn't made it to his locker. It was so freaking difficult just to navigate between all the stupid cliques standing in the middle of the halls, getting in the way. John had to zigzag the whole time. As the space cleared, John heard a few girls in an animated discussion.

"Ommagod. He was *soooo* hot; he should be in a musical!"

"I know, right? He's so college."

"Tell us, Wendy, are you dating? What about Connor?"

"And isn't dating RAs against the rules?"

John realized that the three girls with their backs to him were facing his sister. They were three of the richest witches at Marlowe. All they ever cared about was shopping on Daddy's plastic. To them, cachet was cash. The only sin was not to be *in*. They'd all had work done. They all thought the Darlings were peasants. And John hated them completely. But Wendy had been hanging around them a lot more since dating Connor. Even though she had heard them call her Trendy Wendy as a joke, she still tolerated them. She played like she didn't care, but John thought that Wendy had been really lonely since their mom left.

John perked his ears. "No, we're just friends," said Wendy, "We met outside school."

"Outside school?" said one of the girls. "Like, was he cleaning up?"

"RAs don't clean, stupid," said another one.

Wendy interrupted. "He was just hanging with his advisees."

The girls were still confused. "I don't get it. Boarders hanging with staff? Why?"

"He's pretty hooked up," said Wendy. "And it's not like they have parents around."

"They have bodyguards."

"Nope," said Wendy. "Not allowed in the dorms."

"Wow, it's like olden times."

"He almost kissed me," said Wendy, for a moment forgetting caution. It was almost as if she *wanted* them to tell Connor.

"He *did not!*"

Their voices were full of glee, and suddenly Wendy looked nervous. "Not really," she backtracked "Well, almost, but I didn't let him. I'm with Connor."

They didn't pay attention to the recant. "I bet he has a tongue ring."

"It'd be so romantic if he got fired because of some illicit affair."

Wendy shook her head vehemently. "No! Do *not* say anything. If he gets fired, he won't have a job or money . . . and there's nothing going on, OK? I lied."

"Figures," huffed one of the girls.

"I've seen him hanging around that Hispanic chick."

"She's not his girlfriend," said Wendy. "I don't think he's into labels."

"What does *that* mean?"

"What does he write on his profiles? *Single? Seeking?* What?"

"I don't know," said Wendy. "I don't spend that much time checking online profiles."

The girls were boggled. One of them pulled out her handheld device to make sure she still had hers and they hadn't teleported to the Land of Lame.

"Okaaaay," said one of the girls. "Well, you've got to dish the rest on this Peter sometime."

"Yeah, OK," said Wendy.

"Come on, girls, let's go somewhere . . . else."

The girls walked away. Obviously they were finished with Wendy and weren't inviting her to join them. As they left, John could hear them whispering about Peter, about how insane it was that he'd *almost* gone for Trendy Wendy when he could have had one or all three of them. That would have been way more *college* of him.

John hurried around a corner before Wendy could notice that he'd witnessed the scene. The halls were empty now. John would be late to class. He heard Wendy's slow steps on the marble tiles. He leaned on the wall, waiting for the sound to recede. The mud column and the stone step were gone now. Marlowe looked pretty much normal. But that strange feeling, the weird smell, and even a few moths were still hanging around, reminding them that Marlowe was still attached to the underworld. No one noticed, of course. Once or twice, a janitor was called to find the source of the smell, or more fumigators were hired, but that's it. John didn't want to go to class. He didn't hesitate very long. He knew what he wanted to do instead. Cutting class was new to him. But dreaming about being the kind of guy who cuts class, well, that was a rerun.

He was still daydreaming when he crashed into Connor Wirth, right by Connor's locker. He dropped his gaze and tried to think of something cool to say. Ten seconds passed. *Too late.* John waved weakly and kept walking.

"Hey . . . John." Connor's thick voice called him back.

John turned. "Huh?" John was trying to play it cool, hoping desperately that Connor wouldn't offer him another Wendy-inspired charity outing he couldn't afford. Connor had an amused look on his face.

"Dropped something." Connor held up a shiny piece of metal. It was John's Swatch. It had a broken clasp that he hadn't bothered to fix, so it kept falling off his wrist at inopportune moments.

John shuffled over to Connor and took the watch, doing his best to avoid eye contact. *This sucks*, thought John. *Now he'll think I didn't get the watch fixed because we're poor, which we totally are not. These people need to get some perspective.*

"You should get that fixed," Connor said as he handed the watch to John. John glanced at Connor's six-thousand-dollar timepiece and sighed.

"Oh . . . yeah . . . well, no point," John muttered. "I have three other ones at home . . . way better ones . . . back at my house . . . well, not *my* house. My dad's. Actually, not his either because he sort of works for . . ." John trailed off. He was doing himself no favors.

"Cool," said Connor. "Listen, man, I'm gonna head to class. But good luck with that." Connor smiled and walked away.

John skulked off in the opposite direction, now completely determined to skip class.

John snuck through the hallways of Marlowe. The only noises were the muted sounds of teachers trying to speak above their class. It didn't take him long to reach the door to the basement. Here, he paused. It was on those stairs yesterday that he had been attacked. John instinctively looked over his shoulder, down the long hall, to make sure no one was there. Then he descended the stairwell.

The basement was no longer the mad mess it had been just a

few weeks ago. Thanks to him and Wendy, most of the crates had been broken down and recycled. The exhibition pieces had been cataloged and were sitting in organized rows.

John walked straight to the book. He didn't waste time marveling at it. He didn't sniff it or treat it like a delicate pastry. He was a lone wolf. He was Indiana Jones, exploring the hidden dangers of the labyrinth alone. No man could ever keep up with him. No woman could ever understand him. He tucked the book under his arm and ran out of the basement. He wasn't sure where he would go, but he wanted to see something new. He wanted to explore an uncharted part of the underworld. He paced in the empty halls, hoping that the answer would come to him. When he was outside Barrie Auditorium, the future home of the Egyptian exhibit and the book, he got an idea. *I'll know what piece of the underworld matches with Barrie before anyone else. If they want to go, I'll have to be the guide. If some unsuspecting kid opens the gate accidentally, they'll call the Johnny to save the day.* It didn't cross his mind that the Egyptian names of the hours weren't exactly the slang-of-the-moment at Marlowe.

Inside the auditorium, John wasted no time looking around. He was just relieved that it was, once again, deserted. No one ever went into the auditorium unless there was a required event going on. It was the most deserted place in Marlowe—plus it was always stifling hot, since the air-conditioning was always off in the cavernous room to keep costs down. He had no desire to linger. He said the words, and he watched the message appear. It wasn't anything to dwell on. When he saw the Eye of Ra appearing above a door leading offstage, John's confidence waned for an instant. Then he remembered that smirk. The smirk that Peter had had when he looked danger in the face. The smirk he'd had when he'd come and saved John's life. *Geez*, thought John, *did he have to save my life?* It was so humiliating.

John didn't want to think about it. He closed his eyes and rushed through the door. He knew he had passed through to the underworld when a hot wind met him like a punch. Sand scraped at his face. John opened his eyes. It might have been the first time he was grateful he wore glasses that looked like lab goggles. In front of him spread a desert so vast that it looked like an ocean. The dunes were undulating in the wind like golden waves. Gone was the pillared clutter of the ruins. Gone were the green hedges twisting and turning away from the fire pond. The sunless sky poured some kind of burning light, like a lamp; the sands shone back in an eerie way that left John feeling cold. John stood and wondered. Then he laughed to himself, thinking of the giant sandbags attached to the pulleys backstage. The auditorium was the only place in Marlowe with sand.

This was exactly what he wanted. He wanted to be a hero, traveling by foot through a barren desert. The cinematography would be stunning. His grizzled face would be so renegade. This beat advanced biology class by about a googolplex.

John tried to step into his new role, but his feet wouldn't move. He looked down. The sands had shifted around him. He had sunk in to around his knees. John panicked.

"Help! Help!" he yelled. The sound died in the lifeless plain. John tried to lift his feet out, but each time he lifted one, he had to shift his weight to the other, causing it to sink deeper. He grabbed one leg and tried to yank. No use. He was breathing heavily. Maybe it was an asthma attack. This sucked. He was going to die during advanced biology class. How could someone who had read so many comic books, played so many desert levels, surfed so many websites on survival scenarios, be *this* terrible at the actual experience?

But wait, that was it! John remembered reading an Adventurators comic where the Dust Devil ambushed the hero, Brody Dudecool, in an abandoned putt-putt course. The villain used the powers he'd gotten from a magic ant farm to flood the golf course with sap sand. For a while Brody tried to use his hyper-strength to get out of the quicksand, but it didn't work because his muscle mass was too hyper-dense. Then he tried to use the windmill in the golf course to create a makeshift hovercraft, but the Dust Devil jammed up the engine with a sand missile. Just when it looked like the end for Brody Dudecool, the hero came through with the right idea. Though it went against all his awesomely valiant instincts, Brody Dudecool gave up. He went limp and lay face-first in the sand. The Dust Devil thought he had won. Soon the world would be his. But to his surprise, Brody Dudecool hadn't actually given up. No, he had let his body go limp so that he could slowly raise his legs out of the sand without putting pressure on any one part of his body. It was über-brilliant. His punch to the Dust Devil's face sent a tornado to the moon. Binky Lacelass was saved from the hydraulic jaws of the putt-putt clown.

As he performed the dead man's float from his waist up, slowly leveling out his legs, John was dreaming about a kiss like the one Brody got. He didn't know how long it took to free himself. All he knew was that he'd have to find a way to explain the crimson sunburn blistering the back of his neck as he was finally able to escape the sand. As he struggled to stand, making sure to keep his feet moving, John realized that he was dizzy with dehydration. All he wanted now was to get back to Marlowe, find a water fountain, and stumble to biology class.

John surveyed the scene. It was desert unending. If he squinted, he thought maybe he could make out an oasis in the distance. Tiny palm trees and the slightest hint of blue water waved in the distance, probably a mirage. His adventurous spirit wasn't in the mood anymore. The strange, closed-off feeling that was ever present in the labyrinth was starting to affect him. It was as though this underworld had a way of physically sucking out a person's enthusiasm. He felt gloomy and hopeless. John looked in every direction for the Eye of Ra, hanging in the air where the portal would be, but he couldn't find it.

The sudden fear struck him that maybe a janitor had shut the door in the basement, sealing him in this desert until he could remember the name of the hour—or until the Dark Lady found him. John whipped around, splashing sand, frantic, when he caught sight of the eye. It was directly above him, about ten feet up.

Oh no, thought John. The sands must have shifted while he was freeing himself. The eye was ten feet up, so the bottom of the door must have been just barely above his head. But it didn't matter. There was no way he could jump to catch the ledge in the soft sand.

OK, think, think. What would a boy genius do? John took a look around to find something, anything, that he could use. Still nothing but sand. John was afraid to shift around too much, but when he moved his foot over a little, he thought he felt something solid. John precariously bent over and dug near his foot. His hand touched something. It felt like a baseball bat. He pulled it out, slowly, so as little sand would shift as possible.

As soon as the item came into view, John recoiled and dropped it. It was a piece of a skeleton. A human arm. It was shattered at both ends, but he knew it was a forearm. (He *was* the best student in advanced biology.) The desert sand had grated any shredded flesh from it, bleaching it a whitish gray. Some tattered wrapping flapped around it in the wind. *Must be some poor jerk who tried to navigate the desert without Adventurator training.*

Well, don't look a gift bone in the mouth, I guess, thought John. He picked up the bone again. It would make a decent grappling hook. He took off his hoodie and tied one sleeve to the bone. While he did this, he estimated that he lost about three more inches of height from the sand. He had to work quickly. Squinting to make out the charcoal eye above him, he swung the bone through the lowest point of the door, which he could just barely reach with his fingers. It slid uninterrupted and disappeared through the bottom of the door. But just as quickly it came back down to him. He needed the bone to catch onto something on the other side.

This wasn't good. He tried again, this time holding it farther up the sleeve to give a large swing. Just as he let the bone fly, he lunged as high as he dared on the shifting sands. The bone flew upward and went sailing through the middle part of the door. At the height of its arc, it disappeared and kept its momentum. "Yes!" shouted John when he felt the bone catch. Now to reel it in. Slowly, John began pulling his hoodie back, hoping it would stay connected to whatever was holding it. "Come on, come on," he muttered. To his disappointment, the hoodie kept coming, appearing out of the space in the air, until he could see the edge of the bone. John grunted and pulled the bone back, letting it fall to the sand.

He couldn't let disappointment get to him. He knew that the longer he waited, the more his probability of success plummeted. John coiled the hoodie again and gave a few small swings. Then, with his best lunge, he launched the bone. It flew farther and disappeared much farther up the sleeve. Almost immediately, John could feel that it had hooked onto something big. He gave it a tug. It was solid. He put half of his weight on it. It held.

John looked in the distance at the oasis one last time. He saw a dust devil coming toward him, swirling sand like a miniature tornado. *Not this time, foul villain.* John grabbed as high as he could on the hoodie and began to climb. Coach K would have been dumbfounded to see Little Darling climbing a rope. It helped that it was a life-and-death scenario, without the girls watching.

John struggled up to the invisible door frame, using the floor as leverage as soon as he could reach it with his forearms. He grabbed the ledge and pulled himself up. When his head broke the plane, he saw the bone jammed among a pile of props behind the stage. His arms were throbbing. He couldn't breathe. Sand was glued all over his sweaty body. But finally, he managed to pull himself out. With the last of his strength, he reached up and shut the door. A few seconds later, he rolled over to make sure that the eye had disappeared.

John lay in the heat of the auditorium, panting, relishing the idea of water. He began to laugh, which turned into a cough. He'd almost died a horrible death. How awesome was that? No one could take that away from him now. He had been to the underworld and survived. Now when he walked through the halls, invisible, or felt the scorn of some remedial like Marla, he could always remember the badassery it took to survive the labyrinth. At the thought, John began to shake uncontrollably. Maybe it was fear, or the aftershock of all that adrenaline, but John was pretty sure his sweat was drying and he was getting the chills—even in the heat.

He got to his feet, a little wobbly, and unhooked the forearm bone from the junk all around. It was a pretty awesome souvenir. He turned it over in his hands—the bone had been strong enough to hold his weight. *Must be pretty new, then. Probably the last hero who tried to get out of the underworld.* He imagined a babe like Binkie Lacelass on his arm, exploring his Batcave, asking, "What's that?" And he'd say, "That? That's just a little something I took from a god." And she'd swoon and say, "Oh, Johnny." And it'd fade to black, 'cause Adventurators don't kiss and tell.

John was smirking as he walked down the hall, still a little disoriented and woozy, the book hidden in his backpack, the bone flung over his back the way James Bond flings a tuxedo jacket over his. As he strolled the marble halls, John saw Connor Wirth passing by, flanked by a group of jocks. He walked up to Connor and tapped him on the shoulder with the bone. "Hey, Con-man," he said. "Wuzzup, bro?"

The guys burst into laughter, slapping Connor's arm for a reaction. But Connor smiled indulgently at his girlfriend's quirky brother. "Don't be late for class, kid," he said, tapping his watch in a way that told John that he was making the watch thing their own inside joke. John tucked the bone into his backpack and zipped it tight.

"No worries," he said, slurring his words just a little. "I have the hours memorized." He knew Connor didn't get it. But John didn't care. He was his own adoring audience. An audience that now, as the heatstroke hit him, was getting more and more audible inside his head. John had taken two more steps when he collapsed in the hall.

He woke up twenty minutes later in the tiny, stuffy nurse's office on the highest floor of Marlowe. Connor, who must have delivered him here, had already left for class.

"How's that arm?" said the new nurse. Her voice had a creepy reverberation to it.

"That what?" said John. He looked at his newly healed arm, still tingly from the bonedust, and wondered if there was some sign of the injury still left.

"You landed on your arm," said the new nurse as she picked up a clipboard and swatted a fly away from her face. "When you fell. . . . Just want to make sure everything's OK."

"Oh . . . what happened to your eye?" John said as the nurse turned toward him, giving him a full view of her face. She was wearing a black patch on her left eye, like a pirate.

"Infected," said the nurse. "But let's focus on you, dear. How are you feeling?"

"Great," said John, remembering his exploits. He made an instinctive grab for his backpack and breathed out when he found that everything was still there. The nurse was looking at him inquisitively, as if she was trying to read his mind. Something about her made John feel nervous . . . fidgety. "Um . . . thanks, ma'am, but I have to run."

"Call me Nurse Neve," she said. "What were you doing before you blacked out?"

"Having the world's awesomest adventure," said John proudly.

Then he added, "Um . . . I was just hanging in the auditorium. It's hot in there."

"Why would a cool kid like you be *hanging* in the auditorium by himself?" said the nurse. She looked at him with her one good eye, almost lovingly, almost knowingly, though there was something off about her. John thought he knew what it was. She was so ordinary-looking, so plain. She had probably spent her whole life being overlooked, just like John. She probably used to be a little too smart in high school, too. John shrugged. "I know your father is a teacher here," said the nurse. "It must be hard to make friends."

"I don't have a hard time," said John defensively. Who was she to lump him in the same category as all the losers in the world? She was probably just projecting her own issues.

The nurse continued as if she hadn't heard. "I'm just saying, you shouldn't hide out alone in auditoriums. It seems to me like the answer to your problem is right in front of you."

"What are you talking about?" said John, getting up to leave. "Look, I've got to go. And I don't have any problems."

"Suit yourself," she said, brushing off another bug that was buzzing around her eye patch. She coughed a few times, demurely, probably because of all the dust. "I've seen you trying to make friends with that new RA. Peter, is it? Anyway, people like that will never be your friends, John. And why would you want them to be?" Then she leaned over and whispered in his ear, "*Real* winners don't need validation from people like that. They don't need to tag along. They just do what they want."

Now John was listening. He had never heard an adult talk this way before.

There was a minute of silence when the mousy nurse went back to arranging her instruments. Needles and stethoscopes, and . . . was that *a hook*? John thought he must be crazy, because ever since his attack, everything looked like a hook.

Finally, she spoke again. "I recently met Simon Grin . . . your father's new assistant." She turned away again, and John realized that each time she did that, he forgot the details of her face. She must have had the most forgettable face on the planet.

"So?" John said.

"Nothing," said the nurse. "He said you were the smartest kid he's ever met."

"He did?" John asked, trying not to seem too excited.

"Yes, but . . ." She trailed off for a moment and then said in a soft, almost worried voice, "I just hope you don't screw it up for yourself . . . waste time that could be spent with a real mentor by chasing more lonely auditorium *adventures*."

John began chewing his nails. Worry lines began to form around his eyes as he got up. "Thanks for the checkup," he said before bounding out of her dusty office.

As he headed back down the hallway, John thought about what the nurse had said. Why should he follow Peter around? Why should he follow anyone around? This realization felt so new, so exciting, because now that he thought about it, John realized that he didn't need anyone at all. He had friends. He had a friend in Simon, and in the Egyptian exhibit, and in his books and computer. *Everyone else can shove it.* This felt good—as if a lifelong desperation had suddenly come to an end. . . . But he'd have to be careful not to screw it up. What if he already had? He turned left, realizing that he needed to freshen up and shake the sand out of his underpants. John swaggered into the boys' room, unafraid of a swirly.

As John was washing his face at the sink, he heard a flush and Simon came out of one of the stalls. "What're you doing here?" demanded Simon.

"Nothing," said John—the paranoia of having picked the wrong idol already taking over.

"Where's your hall pass?" Simon asked.

"How do you like the exhibit so far?" said John, hoping Simon wouldn't bust him.

The subject of himself immediately distracted Simon. "What? It's amateur. The only good thing about it is that it's short."

John couldn't help but wonder about the exhibits Simon oversaw at the British Museum. They must have been pretty amazing.

Simon walked over and began washing his hands, making sure to stick his watch conspicuously under the water. *"It's waterproof up to 300 feet below sea level."* He looked over and noticed the deposit of wet sand in John's sink, the miniature dune at his feet. He shook his head knowingly.

"The track-and-field kids buried you in the long-jump pit?"

"Uh, yeah," said John, "something like that."

"You should get some baby powder. Helps with the chafing," said Simon.

John gave a knowing half smile that only a couple of dorks like he and Simon could understand. Simon may not be stacked like Connor, or slick like Peter, but he really *was* a lot like John. He was smart, and sad, and bitter . . . and that was only because he'd probably spent his entire childhood, like John, being misunderstood by the bigger, dumber, less-visionary plebeians of the world. A guy like Peter could never understand the two of them, and John wished that Wendy would just *get it* and stop her obsession with the new RA. And even though John liked Connor and the LBs, they could never get it either. It was like the nurse had said: *Real winners don't need validation from people like that.*

When John unzipped his backpack to look for his eyedrops, Simon noticed the bone inside. "What is that?" he asked.

John sucked in his breath. "That? Uhh, that's—"

"Is it from the exhibit?"

"Uh, yeah, *yeah,*" said John. "It wasn't cataloged."

"And you were going to use it to bludgeon the track kids," added Simon.

"I thought about it," said John. They both laughed at the shared fantasy.

Simon patted John on the back approvingly. John couldn't help but admire Simon. He remembered what the nurse had said and realized how badly he wanted to be liked by Simon. "You can have it," John blurted out.

Simon paused, then said, "If it's not in the catalog, it's not on any of the books."

John thought he understood Simon's meaning. One of them could keep it. It would make quite a paperweight for the up-and-coming preeminent scholar in the field. John could see that Simon wanted it.

"Go ahead and take it," said John. He knew that only a guy like Simon could really appreciate the artifact anyway. Why should it rot away in an exhibit for the rich Marlowe kids who had no clue?

And this way, he wouldn't lose Simon's respect, as the nurse had implied. Why burn bridges?

"You sure?" asked Simon.

"Yeah," said John, feeling generous.

"We won't say anything to your father," said Simon absentmindedly.

"Uh . . . yeah."

"Well, thank you," said Simon with a nod. He snatched the bone.

A small pause, and John said, "I should get ready for class."

Thinking back on his adventure as he walked back into the halls of Marlowe during the next passing period, John felt invincible. He'd skipped advanced biology, as if it wasn't even a big deal or anything. He'd snuck into a lost magic kingdom of a god, where all the myths were real. He'd survived being stranded in the desert. And now he'd impressed Simon—who was ten times better than Peter—with a gift. For a second, he wondered if it was OK, if he shouldn't have shown the bone to Wendy first. Did this count as one of those brother-sister obligations that Wendy was always going on about? But then he remembered what the nurse had said about tagging along with his big sister, and how cool Simon had been in the bathroom. He would never tell on him for taking an artifact. And he had no way of knowing where it came from.

John swiveled around the cliques, oblivious to all the other kids. He'd have to go back to the basement before his next class and replace the book so no one would know. He puffed out his chest and took the steps two by two, replaying his adventure over and over in his head. This exhibit was the best thing that ever happened to him.

❖❖❖

JOHN DARLING

The next morning, I woke up and it was still dark and I couldn't breathe 'cause there was all this stuff on top of me. I realized I was buried under all the sleeping bags, and the other kids were jumping on them. I started screaming 'cause I was gonna suffocate, and it was really scary for a second. I was kicking so hard that I didn't notice when they stopped and everything was quiet. I got out from the sleeping bags, and they were snickering. I was all red. Rory said, "Hey, John, we were playing King of the Hill. Guess you lost."

PETER

Peter dreamed of himself . . . without the bonedust, with his patchy white hair and sagging arms, with his papery skin and bushy eyebrows. He saw himself as he could be, as he *would* be, if he were to fail. And then, he saw *them*—the guardians. He touched the scars from the two he had faced. During the day, these scars were his trophies. But at night, they frightened him. How could he overcome three more?

Peter breathed hard. He tried to steady himself. *Something's gone wrong.* It was a strange feeling, like a twin might have when the other dies. Had the bonedust fallen into other hands? *Give up,* the dark seemed to say, *give up and avoid tumbling into eternal night.*

THE THIRD LEGEND

"Shhh, Peter, someone will see us here," said Wendy, brushing Peter's hand away from her cheek and looking around to make sure none of Connor's friends was nearby. *What am I doing?* she thought. Over the past few days, she just couldn't think about Connor anymore. Everything had changed for Wendy since Peter saved John's life. And this morning, during her free hour, something compelled her to go up to the attic, to stop outside the closed door of the nurse's office, to linger for just a moment . . . long enough to hear voices—staff members gossiping about a scandal. It took only a few seconds of listening before she realized they were talking about her own parents.

"It's right that she left," she heard a familiar voice, a deep reverberating voice, say to her nursing office colleague. "Because it's only human instinct to chase after personal happiness. Deep passion is more important than commitment . . . less dull."

"Yes," said a second voice, "but leaving your family like that . . . it has consequences."

"Maybe," said the first, familiar voice, "but ripples are what make life interesting."

And so, for a moment, Wendy had felt validated. Maybe this voice was right, and her mother (as much of an abandoning wench as she was) had chased the right instinct. In that instant, standing behind a closed door, Wendy thought she was close to fulfilling her own greatest longing. Maybe Peter was it for her. She wasn't sure. . . . Lately, she just felt confused every time she set foot into the school.

"What's the matter? Scared of being seen with me?" Peter was wearing that all-knowing smirk again. Having been banished from Wendy's face, his hand made a subtle turn around her neck and traveled toward her ponytail. He curled the strawberry-blond coil around his index finger and leaned a little closer. Wendy shivered and looked away.

She remembered the last thing she'd heard outside the nurse's office, before she walked away. "Have you seen the new RAs?" said the nurse. "What a cute couple." She had been thinking about that last comment all day . . . obsessing over it . . . becoming increasingly paranoid, so that she cared about nothing other than finding out if it was true.

Now Wendy and Peter stood alone on the Marlowe grounds, right outside Professor Darling's empty classroom. In a few minutes, the class would fill with students (including Wendy and John) who had been waiting for days to hear the eccentric professor tell the third legend. Wendy forced herself to focus on the present.

"You can hear everything if you stand out here," she told Peter. "I'll make sure the window's open. But don't you know the legends already?"

"Maybe I do," said Peter, brushing the end of Wendy's ponytail against her neck. He tilted his head with interest, as if the rising hairs at the nape of Wendy's neck were a very interesting phenomenon. "Maybe I just like stories."

"So why not go in?" said Wendy. "You work here."

Peter leaned in closer. "Nah," he said, "not sure your dad would like me crashing."

"Something's going on with John," said Wendy, desperate to say something, anything, to prove that she could talk casually. "He's been acting weird."

"He's not stupid enough to try to go in the labyrinth alone, is he?" Peter asked.

"No," Wendy mumbled. Then she looked around and switched to a whisper. "When are we going back to find the second mummy for the bonedust? The one you stashed . . ."

"As soon as you find a desert wasteland in this country club you call a school, let me know," said Peter bitterly. He pulled his hand from her hair. The grin left his face.

Wendy cringed. She wished she could just learn to shut up, like the older girls who seemed to know exactly what to say, and not to say, to make scenes like this last long past the tardy bell. She searched for another subject. Actually, the question she *really* wanted to ask Peter didn't have anything to do with deserts or bonedust. She wanted to know what was going on with *them*. Was he ever going to ask her out? Or try to kiss her again? Or get rid of Tina? Were he and Tina really a couple, like the nurse said? None of this was clear. Peter spent just as much time pressed up against walls with Tina as ever. And with Tina, he didn't play these cutesy ponytail games. Then again, it wasn't against Marlowe rules for him to be dating Tina. When Peter started mindlessly playing with the button on Wendy's jacket collar, her every instinct screamed for clarification. But she knew enough about boys not to bring it up. Besides, wasn't this newfound sense of expectation and excitement a good thing? When Connor played with her hair or touched her hand, she felt almost nothing. So she turned back to the problem of bone-dust. "OK," she breathed out. "So let's try something. How about the recycling room? That's a *waste*land, technically."

"You can't be that half-assed about it, Wendy," said Peter in an exacerbated tone. Wendy winced again, but he didn't notice. "You can't just go in a bunch of places and hope for the best. Every time you go in there, you could die. When you're in, she knows. She may not attack, but she's watching. Every time you open a gate, you give her another chance to pour more evil into the overworld. That's the only reason she doesn't kill you the second you're inside. Who knows? She could be waiting till I've reached the last of the bonedust to strike me dead. It's been pretty good for her so far; I've opened the door for her to kill plenty of . . ." Peter trailed off. Wendy felt flushed with a mix of exhilaration and fear. She stepped away from him. Peter changed tack. "And don't even think about searching from the inside. The maze is ridiculously elaborate."

"So we figure it out," offered Wendy tentatively.

"Right," said Peter, stabbing Wendy with his impatient tone. "It's just that easy deciphering an evil maze. There are so many places you could wander into, so many dangers, that chances are if you try to cross it from the inside, you'll get so lost that you'll never see one spot twice." He dropped his head, and Wendy could see the dark curls looping on the top of his head. She wanted to touch them, but then he looked up again. "I didn't want to leave it," he said, his eyes filling with regret. "I knew how hard it would be to find it again. But I had no choice."

"How'd you carry around a whole mummy, anyway?" asked Wendy.

"Well," said Peter as he played with the crest on his RA shirt, "it wasn't exactly a whole mummy. The kid was so excited, I may have embellished a little."

Wendy laughed. "How much was left?"

"A forearm," said Peter, tapping a spot between his wrist and elbow.

Peter leaned back against the brick exterior of Marlowe and sighed. "We just have to figure out the right spots in the overworld. We have to use clues from the legends to figure out what sort of place each bone could be and then find the right place in Marlowe—sort of like matching pictures with negatives. That way, we spend as little time in the underworld as possible." His voice sounded once again determined, but he glanced at Wendy with weary eyes. "Oh yeah, and after going through all that, we get the pleasure of dealing with the guardians. . . ."

"OK, shut up now," said Simon, waving the tips of his fingers toward the classroom as if he were shooing them away. When the pre-class chatter didn't stop at his first bidding, he shouted, "I said: Shut up!"

The class went silent. Simon dismissively flipped through Professor

Darling's lesson plan notebook. "All right, you little criminals, what's on the agenda for today?"

"You're supposed to tell us the third legend," Marla said from the back of the room. A sleepy boy sitting to her right, a dark-haired, sloe-eyed European with a half-tucked-in shirt and long wisps of dramatically straight hair cutting across his face snickered and tapped the guy in front. Marla blanched. "Whatever," she said, leaning back in her chair.

Simon brought his hands to his temple in an exaggerated move to show his irritation. "I did *not* spend six full months at Oxford to teach little kids bedtime stories."

"Simon," said Wendy, eyeing the lower left corner of the open window, where she knew Peter was hiding, "either tell the story you're supposed to tell or let us out early. We're not sticking around to do busywork just because you're a crap sub."

"First of all," said Simon, "when we're in class, it's Mr. Grin. Second of all, I didn't get my master's degree to sub your little remedial story time."

"And yet, here we are," said Wendy under her breath.

"Second of all," said Simon, "the only reason I'm here is because Darling is moving the exhibit today, and I'm not the sort for manual labor."

Simon looked at Wendy sidelong. Then he glanced at John, who was sitting in the front row, staring admiringly at him. He gave John an indulgent smile, a long, lipless smile like that of a crocodile. "Before we begin, some plaudits are in order. Now that our dear old Professor Darling is moving the exhibit to Barrie Auditorium for all to see, we should give a big round of thanks to those responsible for putting it together."

John sat up in his seat, though Wendy was, as always, suspicious.

"John Darling," said Simon, extending his hand benevolently toward John, "under my supervision, of course, was instrumental in restoring the artifacts to an exhibition-worthy state. Good job, John. Keep up the hard work."

John nodded happily. He caught Wendy's disapproving glare and his face went sour.

Simon turned his sneering gaze back to Wendy. He watched her, as if daring her to read his thoughts. Was he gloating over his petty little revenge? He looked downright gleeful, as if he had caught her elbow deep in the biggest canopic cookie jar in ancient Egypt. Did he suspect something? There was no way of knowing, because by now Wendy was convinced that whatever he found on her, Simon would never tell her dad. He had his own little agenda. He wanted to know what they were up to—what juicy, career-boosting secrets they had discovered. At least he was too much of a witless peon to ever figure out about the book. She looked away, toward the window where Peter was hiding. Simon followed her gaze, refusing to let her escape his silent challenge. "There are a lot of *very* interesting pieces in that exhibit. Don't you think, Wendy?"

Wendy crossed her arms across her chest. OK, maybe he wasn't completely brainless. "I wouldn't know," she said, "since apparently I didn't work on it."

"Not very hard, anyway." Simon turned a few more pages in

Professor Darling's notebook. He pulled out a stack of notebook paper, stapled together and crinkled with use. Simon shrugged. He sat back in his seat and held the paper in front of him. "I guess if Darling's busy setting up *my* exhibit, I *could* humor him and read his little story."

"What's the big injustice in this one?" said Marla, trying to act cool. "What's the thing the guy loses?"

Simon sighed loudly. *"This* story is about a *girl,"* he said, locking eyes with Wendy, "and about knowing your place." He reached into his pocket and took out a long, gray, dusty thing. An ancient piece of bone shattered at both ends. He scratched his head with it and gave John another conspiratorial smile. None of the other kids paid any attention. It was just an old stick to them. But Wendy felt sick to her stomach. She could practically feel Peter's rage as he crouched outside. "A girl should know her place," said Simon. "Because if she doesn't, someone she trusts might just betray her."

THE THIRD LEGEND

An identity is a precious thing. If a person is robbed of her place in this world, of her one chance to shape the world in her own unique way, if her fingerprints are obliterated as though she never touched the earth, a bitterness builds inside.

So goes the story of one family with a curse on its line, of Elan's dark legacy, full of the cruelest injustices. The house that cannot die. Their stolen lives linger on, still flowing in their bones. Life has been mummified inside them, forming an ever-living bonedust—a new kind of immortality.

Harere was born two hundred years after Garosh. Descended from another of Jobey's sons, she was raised the beloved daughter of an Egyptian merchant. Throughout her village, Harere was known for being the most gentle, the most faithful, and during her youth she had many offers of marriage. Her father turned down each suitor, none of whom was worthy of his younger daughter. But Harere had a lover named Seth.

Harere's older sister, Nailah, on the other hand, was given to her first suitor, a brutal rival merchant whose only thoughts were of swelling his coffers and fathering many sons.

Soon, the family became aware that Nailah was barren. Many months passed without a pregnancy, and she was universally considered a failure in the village community. After that, Nailah's nights grew dark and she was often seen at the family table with her face completely covered, the blue skin around her eyes the only sign of her husband's cruel hand. Harere, who had a good and noble heart, suffered along with her sister. She went to her late one night when Nailah's husband was away, and she offered to help, whatever the cost to herself.

The sisters concocted a plan. Harere would take Nailah's place for two years, time enough to bear two healthy children. The two women were similar in size and shape. They had the same dark hair, the same sun-browned skin. Harere would cover her face at first, claiming modesty. Nailah's husband would never notice.

The sisters put this plan into motion immediately, giving Harere only enough time to say farewell to her lover. One winter morning, draped in her sister's rich clothes, she kissed Seth good-bye and promised to return and to marry him after two years, if he would only wait. She did not tell him of her secret errand but bade him to trust her and be patient.

Nailah's husband never questioned Harere's identity, and she became pregnant right away. The family celebrated Nailah's good fortune and was none the wiser, since both sisters covered their faces in public.

Halfway through Harere's first pregnancy, their father grew suspicious of Nailah in her role as Harere. She was much less patient, her manner much more reserved, than the Harere he knew. Nailah grew alarmed as her father began to suspect her identity. So, as a precaution, the two sisters decided that the false Harere should run away. She should hide in the next village until the two years were over and the sisters could switch back to their rightful places. Then Harere, who would surely be presumed dead, could marry her lover, Seth. Nailah would return to her own house and raise Harere's children as her own.

And so Nailah packed her bags and set off in the night, taking Harere's precious identity with her. For the remainder of the two years, she lived alone and free, working as a midwife, a nurse, even a cook, in the houses of the neighboring villagers. Now independent, she was happy for the first time since her marriage. Back in the merchant's house, Harere waited. She bore a son and soon became pregnant again.

While Harere, bloated and pining, sat counting the days until the end of her torment, her lover, Seth, grew anxious. He began to loiter around her father's house, listening, trying to find out where Harere had gone. All he found out was that she had run away.

One day, as he was asking about Harere in the market, a woman overheard him. "I know someone named Harere," she said. "She's a midwife in the next village."

When he arrived in the next village, Seth found a veiled Nailah in

Harere's clothing. Thinking he had found his love, he begged her to end her self-imposed exile.

From behind her veil, Nailah watched her sister's lover beg at her feet. She was torn by jealousy, and then by hope, and then by desperate desire. And so Nailah let him believe that she was Harere. She promised to love him if he would only understand that she wished to remain veiled for a time, to mourn her separation from her family. Seth agreed.

In the same way that Harere had convinced the merchant that she was her older sister, Nailah convinced Seth that she was Harere. Seth believed that he had found Harere, and, being lonely and eager for marriage, he gave himself to Nailah, heart and soul. They were married publicly in the village square.

When the two years were over and Nailah did not come back, Harere began to worry. Had something happened to her sister? Nailah, too, now blissfully joined with Seth, began to fret. She wanted children. She was still unable to have her own. But weren't the children in the merchant's house rightly hers? Was she not the mistress of that house and therefore the children's rightful mother? She knew that Harere had two sons. She longed to have them for herself.

For three years, Nailah brooded.

For three years, Harere waited, dejected and alone, except for her sons, whom she loved.

One night, unable to wait any longer, Nailah crept back into her home village. She stole into her sister's house under cover of night and took the children from their beds. She told Seth that she had come upon the children abandoned by the roadside.

In the morning, when Harere discovered her loss, she fell to the floor in fits of tears. Unable to account for the loss of the children, she became raving mad. Soon, everyone in the village believed that she had murdered her own children. The villagers drove her away, all the way to the edge of the Nile. There, while they stood watching, their accusing eyes pushing her forward, Harere decided that she had no reason to live. Her children were gone. Her identity was lost under the mask of Nailah. She threw herself in the Nile and drowned with a bitter heart.

Harere's body floated down the Nile to the next village, where it attracted crowds of spectators. Seth, too, came to see. He hovered above her, a vague tingle of recognition stirring inside. He reached down and took off the cloth that covered the girl's face. In an instant, he recognized her. Harere. The real Harere.

He swept her up in his arms and took her away, deep into the desert, where his own humble tomb was kept. He sought to pay homage to his lost love. He looked for a way to honor her, to atone for his betrayal and negligence.

There he gave her the burial rites of a queen. He mummified Harere's body, leaving it wrapped but without a sarcophagus in his own small tomb. There she lay, without peace, without rest, until her body was stolen by the Dark Lady.

Seth, brokenhearted, quietly left the village, choosing not to betray Nailah's secret, for the sake of the two motherless sons in her care. Though she begged, he refused to stay. "I have married the worst kind of creature," he said. "Worse than a snake whose bite is unconcealed, you are a worm that slithers underfoot, whose presence in the body goes undetected until all damage is done."

Years later, Nailah died an old woman, bearing her sister's name, mother to her sister's sons.

The bitterness of this injustice devoured Harere's soul. And so, she *died with her life trapped in her bones. The goddess of death took the young mother's mummy and the bonedust with it. She shielded it with her greatest weapons, fearing that someday death might be conquered. The Dark Lady hid the mummy in a place where no one could reach it, a legendary labyrinth of the gates, guarded by powerful deities that no human could overcome.*

And so, Harere was gone, her identity lost. But she can never fully die. Her wasted life is forever trapped as grains of immortality in her bones.

WENDY DARLING
A RECURRING THOUGHT

The first time Connor took me on a real date, I think he was trying to impress me, so he came in his family's limo. We were just going to the movies, but he'd decided to take me to his mom's favorite pastry shop in Westchester. John got to the door first and interrogated him, which, when I think about it, was kind of sweet. Much better than Dad inviting him in and treating him like the board of trustees or something. Dad even pulled out a chair for him. Connor was so nervous, he said, "You have a lovely house, Professor," and John said, "It's not ours" (I don't know why, 'cause he's always hiding it, but I think to show that he was cool with it). Connor made the mistake of trying to cover for him by saying, "I know," politely, but then John pushed, saying,

"How?" I've never seen Connor so tense. He stammered, "Oh, it's nothing. My family's foundation kind of, um, oversees, um, part of the Marlowe endowment . . ." And John blabbers, "Oh, so you own it." The room froze. Dad was maroon. He said, "It was nice meeting you, Connor. You two have a great night." We spent the whole night not holding hands and not kissing and not anything, really. Things like that don't happen with Peter, because Peter and I connect somehow, and he doesn't have parents.

The Mystery of Harere

"Explain!" Wendy and Peter shouted at once as they marched from both ends of the hall toward John, who was trying very hard not to cower as they approached. John had run out of class the second Simon had stopped reading the third legend, and Wendy had followed him out. Peter was approaching from the opposite direction so that John had nowhere to escape. John decided to go with a two-part approach: passive-aggressive freeze-out combined with oblivious bystander.

"Ease up. I got class," he said, shoving past Peter and swaggering in the other direction. His shoulder hit Peter hard, sending a satisfied chill through John.

Peter grabbed John's arm, the newly healed one, and squeezed hard. John tried to pull away, but Peter's grip was too firm, as if to suggest that the arm belonged to him. John hated being reminded. He tried to pull away, but it was useless. Peter was barely making an effort, that annoying smirk creasing his lips with every ineffective tug from John.

"What do you want?" asked John, turning toward them.

"Where did Simon get the bone?" Wendy asked.

John shrugged. "How should I know?" *Oh, no.* Did this count as one of those sibling betrayals? Should he have asked Wendy first? *No way! Who was she to order everyone around, anyway? Real winners do their own thing. They don't need validation.*

"OK, kid. I don't have *any* patience for this." Peter took out his handheld and started texting furiously. Before he was finished typing, two LBs appeared at the end of the corridor, carelessly strutting through the hall toward them, uniforms crumpled as always, ignoring the lovesick girls who had been chasing them all semester. They were both tall. One had olive skin, long, black hair, and a backward cap. Under his Marlowe jacket he wore a T-shirt with a picture of Crazy Horse on it. His companion was the boy they had seen the other day, the banker's son who always got away with things at Marlowe, the country-club thug with blond cornrows.

"What's up, chief?" said Crazy Horse, slapping Peter's hand in greeting.

Peter nodded toward John.

Crazy Horse stepped closer. He hovered over John. The more John squirmed, the more he towered. "Are you gonna talk, or do we need to adjourn to an empty classroom?" he said, his thick voice a bit more official-sounding than John had expected.

John crossed his arms tighter.

Crazy Horse picked him up by the collar.

"Hey, let him go!" said Wendy.

"Relax," Peter whispered. Then he shook his head, as if to say nothing's *really* going to happen.

John tried to keep a cool look on his face (not easy from three feet off the ground). "It was just a souvenir," he said. "I found it in some desert and I gave it to Simon to shut him up. And it worked. See? He hasn't hassled us all day."

The LB dropped John to the ground. Rather than rushing to his side, Wendy called him out.

"You gave Simon the second batch of bonedust," she said through gritted teeth.

"What are you talking about?" said John. "Peter stashed that. This was just a stupid piece of junk I found in the sand. Besides, it was a *new* bone . . . not even dust yet."

"It was Garosh's forearm, smarto," said Peter. "I stashed it in the sand two hundred paces from the tomb where I found it. The bones don't crumble. They're *alive*."

"N-no," John stammered. "You have it all wrong. It was *in* the sand. I didn't take if off a mummy. There was no shroud. No shrine. No marker. No hiding spot."

"I don't *need* a marker," said Peter. "And that bone was all that's left of him."

John went silent. Then his face grew red. "*You* said it was in the mouth of a sphinx!"

"I lied," said Peter. "Can't you tell playful banter when you hear it?"

"Well, then it's your fault, isn't it?" said John. "You didn't trust us with the truth, and see what happened?"

"I don't know what you were expecting, little man," said Peter, barely hiding the annoyance in his voice. "This isn't some video game. You saw the Elan toe. We're looking for little tiny nothings in a big giant mother of a haystack."

"Why did you have to give it to *Simon*?" Wendy wailed. "*Simon, of all people.*" She repeated the name as if doing so would make it all untrue.

John was seething. Peter's video game remark stung.

After a minute of squirming under the glare of everyone's scrutiny, John relaxed and told them the whole story. Peter turned to Wendy and said, "What's the likelihood this jerk's figured out what he has?"

Wendy shrugged. "If he knew, he'd have stolen the book by now. He thinks the legends are just stories. Besides, he's not that smart."

"That's what *you* say," said John.

Peter was typing on his handheld again. Without looking up, he said to the boy with blond cornrows, "Draw up a plan to get it back. A level three at least. We'll need two guys or more, plus Tina. A whole lot of supplies. Possibly some rappelling and/or pyrotechnics. Can you figure something out in an hour?"

Cornrow was about to nod when Peter said, "Good. Get on it, then." He started walking away, with Wendy right behind, and John ambling reluctantly a few steps back. "For now, let's focus on the other three, before Simon figures out what's up."

"OK," Wendy said, and turned to John, who was brooding over how he was a lone wolf and how much he didn't need anyone in the world. "We need your help. Please come?"

John shrugged and tried to suppress a smile. "Only 'cause the labyrinth's awesome," he said. "Not because I'm helping *him.*"

"There's just one problem," said Wendy. Peter just glared. He clearly wasn't used to being bothered with every single minuscule issue. "We have to get past my dad."

Professor Darling had been supervising the exhibit move from the basement to the auditorium all day. Even now, as the trio approached the auditorium, they could hear his thick cello voice telling the workmen how to handle each item ("Oh, no, no. Not there . . . That's precious, you know. . . . Be careful with the neck; it's extremely fragile!"). Wendy motioned for Peter to hide within earshot while she and John searched for the book.

Barrie Auditorium was a huge, two-hundred-seat domed space usually reserved for matriculation ceremonies, lectures by foreign dignitaries and minor celebrities, and maybe one play a year (if the writer managed to finagle a *New York Times* mention or donated obscene amounts of cash). The seats were a deep cherry, each with its own writing surface. They shone red in the sunlight streaming from the top of the dome and contrasted with the mahogany paneling to create an old-world academic effect, though, even here, the workers and the professor seemed to fidget, as if they knew something was wrong with the atmosphere. Something foreign was affecting this space, too. For the next few weeks, the stage area had been reserved for Professor Darling's exhibit items.

When he saw his children, the elderly professor straightened up and waved proudly. "Come in, come in," he said. "Look what your hard work has accomplished." John and Wendy climbed the wooden steps to the stage. Professor Darling checked his watch. "How was class? Did Simon do OK?" He seemed worried.

John nodded, still eager to defend Simon. After all, how could he have known what the bone was? It wasn't *his* fault John had made a mistake. He wasn't *trying* to steal the bonedust—not that he would give it up now, whether he knew what it was or not. "He told us the Harere story. It was pretty good."

"Ahh, Harere," said Professor Darling, turning the name over in his mouth. "In many ways the most fascinating of the five. Perhaps the most difficult to *truly* grasp."

"What's not to grasp?" said Wendy brightly. "She loses her identity to her bitchy sister."

"Wendy!" Professor Darling reprimanded.

"Sorry," said Wendy.

Professor Darling was humming something to himself. "Yes," he mumbled as he turned back toward the artifacts. "Identity is a complex thing."

"Daddy, so . . . um . . . where's the book?" asked Wendy as she scanned the tables and the stage floor for the *Book of Gates*.

"My office," said the professor, already distracted. "I wanted to examine it a bit further before I put it on display. Don't worry. It'll be out here for all your friends to see."

Wendy and John made a series of quick and barely convincing excuses that would never have worked had their father not been preoccupied, then hurried toward the spot in the back of the auditorium where Peter was hiding. He was already gone. They ran down the hall and he was there, briskly marching toward their father's office. When they reached the door, he was already prying the lock open with a jet-black AmEx Centurion card.

The book was lying on Professor Darling's desk, in plain view. Peter grabbed it without a word. He checked his watch. It was afternoon, so the Egyptian night had already begun. As he approached the office door, Peter hesitated. He had a look on his face as if he was about to confess something. "I haven't really given Harere a decent search," he said. "I spent so much time chasing my lost Garosh bone, I've been neglecting the others."

John snorted.

Peter ignored him, but he switched back to his usual confident tone. "I think she would be in the Nile. That's where she died."

"Isn't that a little obvious?" asked John, arms tightly crossed over his chest.

"I already tried the desert where the story says Seth had his tomb," said Peter. "It's final. We're going after the Nile."

"That's an easy one," said Wendy, trying to speak over her brother's sarcastic murmurs. "The Nile has to be the hallways. Think about it . . . the Nile connected everything in Egypt and everyone gathered around it, right? Exactly like the halls at Marlowe."

John was already shaking his head, even before she had finished her sentence. "No way, Wen. You have to think simpler than that." He puffed out his chest, knowing that here was his opportunity to talk about his solo trek into the underworld. "Garosh's desert was the auditorium because that's where we have sand. Peter said that Elan's castle was attached to a construction site just because that's where *building* happens. So wouldn't it make sense that the Nile would be someplace with water?"

Peter nodded thoughtfully. "Plus the halls match up to the maze itself. If we went in through a hallway, we'd probably end up lost in the twists and turns of it."

Wendy's face melted into a smile. John was beginning to feel better, too, more useful. Maybe this was his second chance for a big adventure.

"I say we try the pool," said Peter, in a voice that suggested that he'd come up with the idea all by himself. He ran out of the office with John and Wendy following behind, Wendy eager to keep up, John trying not to burn up from hatred for Peter the Poser.

Standing beside the empty swimming pool, Peter whipped out the book and began reciting the name of the hour, just as fluently and elegantly as he had done last time (Wendy could see John seething with jealousy). Peter scanned every door from the locker rooms to the buoy closets. The eye wasn't above any of these. Then Wendy saw it.

"Ah, geez!" she said, shaking her head disbelievingly.

John and Peter followed her gaze to the bottom of the pool. The black Eye of Ra, blurry and muddled under seven feet of chlorine water, was slowly appearing in the upper right-hand corner of a drainage hole at the bottom of the pool, a slot about the size of a clothes dryer with a sliding grate-like door that allowed the water to pass through. The eye was etched in the metal part of the door the same way it had been in the door of the basement broom closet. It was charred, burned black, as if on wood.

"I say we stand close to *that* door and try again," said Wendy, pointing to a locker room.

"Too late," said Peter. "If we want the eye to appear somewhere else, we would still have to open and close that grate. We made the mistake; now we have to get wet."

With that, he dove in, fully clothed, and within seconds was pulling at the metal bars.

Peter stayed underwater for a full two minutes before coming back up for air. Without a word, he pulled himself out, ran into a nearby cleaning closet, and took out a broomstick. He dove back in the water, dragging the broom behind him. He jammed the long broom handle into the bars. From where they stood, Wendy and John could see him throwing his weight into the broom, trying to make the door budge. Finally, a muffled gurgle escaped from the pool, and the door slid back far enough to let Peter through. On hearing the screeching metal, John and Wendy waited for Peter to resurface and tell them it was OK to go in. When it became obvious that he wouldn't, they jumped in simultaneously, Wendy stopping just long enough to pull off her new faux-leather shoes.

Peter didn't look back to see if the Darlings were following. He simply slid inside the hole, his body as graceful in the water as an eel. He didn't seem to mind the size of the door, which scraped across his body and snagged his clothes as he pulled through. He simply thrust himself in, headfirst, and disappeared down the hatch, past the piles of pool gunk into the oblivion beyond.

They stood, lost and confused, in the middle of an endless maze. Wendy tried not to look up at the stone sky. Being in the labyrinth made her chest constrict. It made her panic and despair at the same time.

After plunging into the pool, about an hour before, they had appeared in a river full of sludge and black muck. It was a winding, snakelike river with dark, bottomless water and a menacing feeling that reminded Wendy of the stories she'd read about the River Styx. Strangely enough, the river also reminded her of Marlowe.

When they climbed out, Wendy could see a reddish plank exactly where the red kickboard had rested in the second lane of the pool. Blue sludge grew in straight lines, dividing the river the same way the bouncing rope of blue buoys divided the pool. Equidistant between each stony horizon, a tree, ash-white and leafless, stood in place of the white lifeguard chair. Wendy almost expected to see an evil version of Connor swimming laps, which he did every morning before school.

They had walked around the river for an hour, and all they had accomplished was to get hopelessly lost. Meanwhile, Peter had told them about the guardians and what they should expect. "The first two mummies had guardians from their stories," he said. "Creatures that used to be people—all tied to the mummies somehow. I had to fight a Bedouin monster for Garosh."

"My guess is that it'll be a snake," said John. "I remember something in the story about Nailah being called a snake."

But the river had led them nowhere, and after an hour of walking around, losing the water entirely, and ending up inside the maze, Peter had decided that this was not it. There was no shrine, no sign of a guardian. There was something about the story that they had missed. There was some clue that they'd overlooked. They would have to go back and start again.

How did they lose the river? Wendy wondered. It was so long and winding. Sure it was so dark and gray that it was almost a part of the deathly miasma that made up the air they breathed and the fog that touched their face, but its stench would surely keep them close to it. But no. It was as if they had sleepwalked away.

Peter shook his head. "See? This is what this labyrinth does. It's the worst kind of maze—the kind you don't even see coming. By the time you realize it's not a straight line, you're already lost."

Wendy glanced around at the empty landscape. Suddenly she noticed the menacing stone walls of the pyramid bearing down on them, moving closer and closer until she could barely breathe. "Anyone else feel that?"

The walls continued to approach, and Wendy could feel a rough rock jutting into her back. "Peter, just say the name of the hour," said Wendy, breathing loudly. She tried to swallow some air, but there was very little of it. The space around them was shrinking.

"We could appear anywhere in Marlowe," said Peter.

"Well, we can't stay *here!*" shrieked Wendy.

Peter checked his watch. He grabbed both of their hands and shouted the name of the third hour into the tiny space around him.

None of them saw the eye appear over their heads. The second it appeared, they were on the other side, jammed in a dark space so small that Wendy again found it impossible to breathe. It was like being in a coffin, but at least that dreadful, ominous feeling of the underworld was gone (almost). The three of them were pressed up against one another in the pitch black. Wendy could feel a number of hard objects poking her in the back. She could smell brand-new books, erasers, and Magic Markers. She reached for a doorknob and threw the door open.

The three of them fell on top of one another, right in the middle of AP calculus.

Mrs. Flanagan, the calculus teacher, jumped back.

A roomful of students stared.

John's jacket was still dripping black goo.

Wendy rubbed her eyes.

Then the room erupted in laughter. Wendy heard one of the cheerleaders snicker and say to her friend, "You'd think someone would have told her that you're not supposed to invite your little brother into the closet with you."

Wendy, John, and Peter were standing in the hallway, long after everyone had cleared out. John, visibly exhausted, was sitting cross-legged on the floor. Wendy was leaning against a locker. Peter was pacing. Wendy and John had both been dragged into the office and written up for hiding in the closet and skipping class. Professor Darling would hear about this for sure. Peter had been reprimanded severely, received a pay cut, and only avoided being fired by explaining that he was there first, looking for supplies, and that the Darling kids had just shown up, presumably wanting to avoid class and listen to music instead. What could he say? He didn't want to antagonize their father. For the past forty-five minutes, the three of them had been sitting in the hallway, ignoring the eerie, unclean feeling that told them that Marlowe was still contaminated, trying to figure out why the river wasn't the right spot. Wendy suggested that maybe they had the wrong river. But there were no other options besides the pool. John had suggested that maybe they had missed it, but Peter said that the mummies were always in a shrine. It would be hard to miss if they had the right spot.

Finally, just as Peter was returning from a detour to the pool to retrieve the *Book of Gates*, Wendy had a thought. *"Identity is a complex thing,"* she said.

"Huh?" said John.

"I can't believe it!" said Wendy, her eyes lighting up. "I can't believe we missed such an obvious clue."

"What are you talking about, Wen?" John got up off the floor. Peter had stopped pacing.

"We heard the story, but none of us really understood the nature of the injustice." Wendy was breathing hard, rushing through her words, her excitement pouring out all at once like a burst water balloon. "Daddy said this story was the hardest to grasp. To *truly* grasp. But I think I have it."

Peter looked at her sidelong, as if, after all this brainstorming, he didn't want her to have it. Wendy got the feeling that Peter still didn't trust her—that he didn't trust anyone except himself. Maybe he didn't even care what she thought she knew. Then, reluctantly, Peter pulled a rolled-up stack of notebook paper from his back pocket. It was crinkled from multiple readings. He handed it to Wendy. "I thought I'd find something in your dad's margin notes. Something we'd missed," he said. "But no luck."

Wendy recognized the pages. They were her father's third lecture, written out for Simon and read to the class earlier today. She flipped through the pages. How did Peter get his hands on Simon's notes? "Did you steal these?" she asked, and he shrugged. He must have gotten them as everyone was leaving class, or maybe when they were in the auditorium talking to Professor Darling. It seemed that Peter, with his black Centurion card and his army of street-savvy, designer-clad boarding brats, was a world-class thief.

Wendy skimmed the pages, eager to tell Peter what she thought she knew. The pages captured her attention. Even a cursory glance through them revealed that Simon had rushed through the lecture; he had skipped details, rolled his eyes over the parts he considered overly sentimental. He even crossed out a line here and there and added notes. *Not likely. . . . Internally inconsistent. . . . Would never occur in ancient Egypt. . . . Anachronistic. . . .* And so forth. Wendy's eyes fell on a segment about Nailah and Harere's childhood. She read it fast and skipped ahead to the part about the merchant husband. The full extent of his evil hadn't been mentioned in lecture. Simon had marked it *Implausible.* Then Wendy's eyes fell on a line near the end, words in italics, underlined twice by her father. She recognized the shaky double lines he always used under the sign-off on his birthday cards.

Nailah of the Nile.

A few lines later, Wendy spotted another line marked by her father's unmistakable double lines.

Nailah the elder. She was condemned in all their hearts to die a watery death.

Wendy reread that line, her heart pounding. Her theory had been right. Now she had proof. *Nailah of the Nile. Nailah of the watery death.* She started bouncing up and down with the paper in her hand.

"Peter!" Wendy shrieked. "I knew it. This is why we couldn't find Harere."

"Why?" Peter asked, trying to hide his excitement.

"It's because we didn't really understand the nature of the injustice," said Wendy. "The tragedy here is that Harere's identity was gone. Gone *forever*—even in the afterlife. She's the one that died in the Nile, but everyone thought that was *Nailah*! We should look in the place that *Nailah* died, because everybody thought *she* was Harere."

Peter considered that for a moment. "I don't know, Wendy." Then after some thinking, he conceded. "But I guess it *does* make a good hiding place for the real bones. . . . No one would look for the boring other girl who lived a normal life."

Wendy spotted another line in the lecture notes that Simon had neglected to read. He had marked this one *Logical fallacy.* "Listen to this," she said, her voice shaking with excitement as she read out loud. "*And the other, an heiress to a stolen life. Wiling away her ill-gotten days. Wilting in a merchant village. Harere, the old crone in the marketplace.*"

"Total injustice," said John. "She can't even get her identity back in the afterlife."

"It makes sense," said Peter. He was staring at Wendy with obvious admiration, as though she were an equal. Even Tina, his right hand, had never deserved *that.*

"So we're looking for a village," said John.

"A marketplace," corrected Peter.

"A 'marketplace' could mean lots of things," said John as they made their way through the halls. "Maybe it means stock market. There's a Bloomberg machine in the econ lab on the second floor."

Peter raised an eyebrow. "You guys have an econ *lab?*" He shook his head thoughtfully. "Food," he said, after a moment's pause. "Merchants usually sold food."

"Yeah," said John. "The other connections were that simple. Sand for the desert. Water for the Nile. Food for the market."

Wendy checked her watch. It was night in Egypt, happy hour in

New York, which for teachers at Marlowe meant another drawn-out faculty meeting. Professor Darling wouldn't be back for an hour. The trio slipped unnoticed down the hallway and, without another word, headed straight for the dining hall, trying to ignore the moths and the unexplainable nimbus of rot overhead.

Once inside the underworld pyramid, Peter immediately ducked behind a fruit stand. Wendy and John stood on a step inside the invisible doorway and gaped at the site. It wasn't some august land-scape or a terrifying sea. It wasn't a goblin market or a skeleton bazaar or a market for shrunken heads and dusty old bones. It was just an ordinary food market, which—even though they were look-ing for exactly this—was really scary when they stopped to think about it, or if you stopped to look at the way every row of stalls exactly matched the rows of Marlowe's dining tables. Or the way the soothing cream walls of the dining hall translated to a sickly hue between gray and bone, and the sweet smells of muffins and coffee had become rank, putrid, and thick with death.

Row after row of covered stands gridded the space in front of them. Each stand was heavily laden with pomegranates, clemen-tines, dates, and a hundred other fruits they'd never seen. Burlap sacks leaned on one another, filled with sunflower seeds, sesame, and chickpeas. On the ground, lining the front of each stand, stood wooden barrels with pickled vegetables bobbing in brine.

Nailah's market should have been teeming with bodies and noise, peddlers and customers, bargaining for the right price. But this deserted market felt unnatural and eerie, as if something had run the people off.

"Get down!" hissed Peter. John and Wendy squatted behind the stand.

"Hey," said John, "did you guys notice this?"

John had a habit of asking vague questions so people would have to admit not knowing.

Wendy breathed out and said, "No, we didn't. What is it you noticed, John?"

"Just that every stall is the same."

"They're *stalls*, John," said Wendy. "What do you want?"

"But look," said John through gritted teeth. "Every stall is the same. It's really hard to tell, unless you step back a little. The whole market is a grid, and each stall is so cluttered with bags, and barrels, and stuff that it's easy to look at all the variety in each one. But if you look from one stall to the next, they're carbon copies." John tapped his foot impatiently.

Peter and Wendy got up from their cover to take in the view. "It's obvious once you see it," he said. "Like, look at the stall keeper."

At the right of the stall nearest to them, Wendy and Peter saw a figure, hunched, barely distinguishable from a burlap mound. It looked like an old crone, like a gypsy fortune-teller, a beggar woman of the East Indies, or a Salem witch. The only part of her body exposed under the draped cloth was her nose, hooking out from under the shadow of her hood. Maybe she was the proprietor of the stall. Except, of course, she was dead, or a mannequin. She didn't move or breathe.

"Once you see her, you see them all," said John.

Wendy and Peter realized it at the same time. At the right of *every* stall huddled the same dead stall keeper, with her burlap covering, her hooked nose.

"It's like someone cut and pasted the same little food stand over and over again," said Wendy, scanning her eyes over the identical burlap sacks, the jars of pickled vegetables stacked in exactly the same numbers, with exactly the same vegetables. Where two pomegranate seeds had fallen to the floor of the first stall, two pomegranate seeds had fallen to the floor of *every* stall.

"And arranged them in a grid," mused Peter.

Wendy glanced at one of the stall keepers. "Looks a little like Tina," she joked.

Peter raised an eyebrow, as if he was trying to decide what to make of the comment. "If this really *is* Harere's tomb," he said, "then Harere's mummy is somewhere in this grid."

"And it's protected by this puzzle, where you can't figure out which stall is the right one!" John interrupted Peter's speech to show he'd figured it out, too.

"Well, that and some kind of guardian," added Peter. John thought he was just adding it to get the last word.

"Whatever," said John. He started to walk down a row of stands, fingering the dried fruit carelessly. "It's probably one of these old lady statues. Let's just find the old bag that looks the most like Nailah, or Harere . . . or whichever. Ancient puzzles are so level one."

"Thanks, Indiana," said Wendy. "We don't know what they looked like. We need a clue."

"And we need to keep an eye out for the guardian," said Peter.

John turned and walked backward. "What're you, scared?"

John was sneering at Peter, daring him to come along. But Peter only shook his head and smirked. *Stupid smirk,* thought John. *"What?"* said John.

"Nothing," said Peter. "You're just so obvious."

"You mean, you're scared," John shot back.

"No," said Peter, "I mean, you're being that kid in the movie."

"The one who isn't scared," said John, trying to get under Peter's skin.

"The one who's making a fool of himself," said Peter. "You're walking through this market like it's that rich-kid nursery you call a high school. You've already gotten shredded for trying to act cool, but you still think you're invincible because you get too much 'positive reinforcement' from all the adults in your life who're all too afraid to tell you that you're acting like a spoiled idiot, just in case you try to shoot up the school."

John was taken aback. He stammered, "Well, well, you're nothing but a-a—"

"Shut up," interrupted Peter. "Don't say anything. Just come back, before you hurt yourself or get us killed."

Wendy didn't say anything to defend him, and John thought he saw Peter's hand brush hers. He glared at his sister and mumbled, "You're totally doggin' Connor."

Wendy blanched and Peter said, "Scratch that. I'm gonna hurt you myself."

Just as John was about to respond, a tremor shook the dirt beneath their feet. A distant rumbling began to increase, as if something was coming toward them from behind the spot where John stood frozen. Peter and Wendy looked wide-eyed at John, who was shaking visibly, and at the ground rising up beneath him.

Over John's shoulder, a mound of earth barreled toward them down the aisle between the food stands. It moved like a shark in the water, tilting the stands on either side with the wake it left behind. "John," Wendy shouted, "run!"

John didn't dare to look, but Wendy's voice got him moving. He ran to one side, hoping the mound would follow the course it was already on. Peter and Wendy ran parallel to John, two stalls down. John wasn't very fast, but it didn't matter. Just as the mound was about to overtake him, it veered and circled around in another direction, tearing up the dirt and sending it high into the air. As it moved away, the sand near its front end broke, and John saw a slippery brown head break through, for just an instant, before it retreated back into the ground. It had no eyes, just a big, round opening where its face should be, jam-packed with a circular set of gigantic teeth. The rest of its body was just a long tube, covered with moist brown rings marking each segment.

The trio sprinted for another few blocks of the marketplace before stopping to catch their breath, an effort made far more difficult by the gelatinous, unhealthy air of the underworld. Every breath was like sucking pudding through a straw.

"Now *that*," said Peter, "is a proper guardian."

"You didn't say it'd be a giant sandworm," said John between breaths.

"You didn't ask," said Peter. "Also, I didn't know."

"Well, what do we do now?" asked Wendy. "We need Harere's bones, and the thing doesn't seem to care that it's wrecking stalls. How do we know it hasn't already destroyed the right one?"

"Because this is the tomb. And that thing is Nailah, Harere's sister. She's been turned into the guardian," said Peter.

John suddenly remembered. In the story, Nailah had been called a *worm*, not a snake, as he had thought. "Gross," he muttered.

"No matter what she looks like," said Peter, "her whole purpose is to protect Harere's bones. It's her punishment, just like the Bedouin I fought to get Garosh."

"Hey, wait a minute," said John. "I think I got it . . ."

"What?" Wendy said impatiently. "Will you please be specific?"

"All right. I'm just catching my breath. Geez," said John. He took a big breath and began: "We know the worm isn't following the grid, since it went under a few of the stalls and uprooted them, right? And we know it's protecting Harere's bones."

They nodded.

"I figure, it's going in a circle *around* Harere." John pointed to the horizon, where the worm was taking another turn and uprooting a patch of earth parallel to them. For lack of a proper sky, the rising sand made the entire scene look like one giant dirt wall. It was grim—dirt below, dirt above, and over their heads, the gray stone ceiling of the pyramid. But it *did* look like a circle. "So, basically, all we have to do is look at the area the worm is circling, and we can assume that if we calculate the center of that circle, we'll more or less have the location of Harere's stall. We could use the standard geometric equations for the derivation of the center, but I would enter a few variables to account for the elliptical nature of the perimeter, caused by the worm's inertia, which will narrow the results slightly but, I think, significantly."

Both Peter and Wendy blinked a few times.

"Wow," conceded Wendy. "That was really specific."

"Sweet, let's do it," said Peter.

"You're welcome," muttered John.

Peter and Wendy had to do some reconnaissance, running around the perimeter of the market and counting the number of stalls on each side. Though the market looked and felt stifling, running around it showed that it wasn't much longer than the dining hall, which was, incidentally, as massive and grandiose as any dining hall in New York. John made the calculations using a stick to draw in the dirt. After some time, he got up and patted the dirt from his knees. He drew an X on a rudimentary map he'd sketched in the dirt and said, "It's somewhere around there."

"That's the best we can do?" said Peter.

"We could wander aimlessly till the sandworm eats us," retorted John.

"Let's just go," said Wendy, surveying the long run toward the middle.

The three of them paused, made sure that their shoelaces were tight, gave one another a last look, and started running toward the center of the invisible circle the worm was protecting. The mounds of loose dirt the worm had made when it chased them had already receded back into flat earth. They threaded in between the stalls, zigzagging the grid in as straight a line as they could. When they crossed what John had assumed was the perimeter, they picked up the pace.

"That way!" John shouted, squinting to see the trajectory of the worm.

It wasn't long before a chunk of earth shot up behind Wendy and gave chase. Wendy screamed and sprinted. The mound wormed along, just under the surface of the earth, crashing through the stalls and making them explode with clusters of dried fruit and clouds of spice. Wendy bought some time by making a quick right. The worm was too big to make quick turns.

"It should be somewhere around here," yelled John. "Hurry!"

Peter took hold of one of the old crones by the hood of her burlap robe. He yanked back. The figure crumbled. Decayed old bones . . . either that or this thing was carved out of rotting clay. "They're all the same," said Peter, grunting in frustration. He was growing visibly angry. He went from stall to stall, pulling the old crones down from their perches. Wendy couldn't tell if it was adrenaline from running from the worm or if he was becoming furious for not finding the bones he so desperately wanted.

Just then, John yelled, "Wait!"

Peter stopped in the middle of ripping down another body.

"Look at that one," said John, pointing to one of the figures now lying on the ground. Instead of the withered old clay, it seemed to be carved out of smooth pine. It was hunched over in the same position, but the face was young.

"That has to be it," said Wendy. "Harere died *young*."

All three of them jumped onto the stall, digging into the sacks of figs, pistachios, and dried thyme. "It has to be here," said John.

As they rummaged through the piles of goods, they heard the rumbling of the sandworm coming closer. It would reach them soon, and then—

They didn't know *what* would happen when the worm reached them. Wendy thought of those enormous teeth, all packed together in that disgusting circular mouth. A wild-eyed Peter upturned entire barrels at a time. John kept looking over his shoulder, trying to locate the rumbling. Then Wendy cried out. John and Peter and saw her pulling a skeletal hand from under a pile of rice. In an instant, Wendy was mesmerized. It was withered, its long, thin fingers shriveled to nothing. But it wasn't ugly. Its fingers were curled delicately toward the center, the thumb and middle finger reaching for each other in an elegant pose. Wendy imagined what this gray, ashen hand must have looked like eons ago. Long fingers under soft, creamy skin. Short, glossy fingernails much like her own.

Peter jumped over a few barrels to where Wendy stood. Together, they began digging the entire skeleton out of its rice grave, working outward from the hand, up toward the wrist, and then revealing an entire arm. The rumble was deafening as they uncovered the skull and the neck. But as they continued, the rumbling came to a sudden stop. Silence. A whirring of wind. A flapping of tent coverings.

"What's happening?" whispered Wendy.

Peter shrugged.

Behind them, a young voice was whispering. They turned, all three at once. But the only thing there was the discarded figure of the stall keeper. She was sitting at her perch, hunched over, hood over her face.

"Wait," said Wendy. "Wasn't she lying on the floor a minute ago?"

Wendy brushed the rice off her hands and stepped closer. In the still silence, the figure moved. There was another whisper. The young stall keeper was calling to something.

Slowly, it lifted its head. Its hood fell back and Wendy saw the beautiful face of Harere, no longer carved in wood, but in the flesh, reeling with anger over the desecration of her mortal body. Her almond-shaped Egyptian eyes were narrowed with rage. Her red lips barely moving as she continued the chant summoning her monstrous sister. She bored into Wendy with her eyes. She grew louder, speaking words that sounded like ancient Egyptian. Wendy looked back at the mummy. Peter was still digging. The stall keeper grew so loud that her voice echoed in their ears and shook the ground at their feet.

"Look," said John. Fear struck the three of them as they saw a fence of jagged teeth rising out of the sand, encircling their entire stand. At the outer edge of the stall, sand was beginning to pour into a growing chasm. The worm's mouth surrounded them. The stall keeper sat silently once more.

"It's below us," said Peter. "It's going to eat the whole stand to protect the mummy."

John scrambled to his feet and jumped beyond the worm's mouth. "Come on!" he shouted to Wendy.

Wendy looked at John, outside the worm's mouth, then at Peter, who refused to stop digging. She implored him to come with her.

"Go," said Peter. "I'll be right there."

Wendy hesitated, then turned and ran. When she reached the wall of teeth, it had already risen to her waist. She climbed and almost cut her hand on the tip of a tooth. Then, with John's help, she fell to the other side.

Peter frantically dug through the rice, pulling every few seconds to loosen the mummy. The worm continued to swallow the sand. An inner row of teeth started to chew, while the outer row of teeth pulsed to help shake and direct everything downward. The outer-lying barrels dipped and then fell into the abyss of the worm's belly.

"Leave it, Peter!" screamed Wendy.

But Peter didn't seem to care. He would get eaten before he left the bonedust. Finally, the mummy came loose from the rice. Peter didn't stop to celebrate. He lifted the skeleton and ran to the edge of the worm's mouth. The teeth were too high, even for Peter to jump. He tried, but failed, cutting his hand open on the edge.

"Get a barrel to stand on," said John, looking on from the other side.

"No, it's too late," said Wendy. "Stand on the mummy."

Peter looked almost angry at that suggestion. Then he rethought the idea. Quickly, as the last of the stand began to waver and plunge, Peter situated the mummy into a sitting position. While holding on to one of its hands, Peter placed a foot on the mummy's shoulder and scrambled up and over the worm's teeth. As soon as he landed on the other side, Peter turned and began pulling the mummy over by the hand. Just as it seemed that Peter would be able to pull the skeleton over, the worm chomped its jaw.

"Nooo!" shouted Peter. He wrenched the hand of the skeleton, but the worm had bitten down on all the rest of the mummy. The mummy shattered at the wrist bone, leaving a severed hand in Peter's grip.

They didn't have much time. The worm's mouth closed and just as suddenly burrowed back under the earth. The three of them dashed deep into the marketplace as fast as they could. The sand in the air scraped at their lungs. The worm chased after them. It knew that a piece of the mummy had been stolen. It would eat all three of them to retrieve it.

The mound gained on them with every step they took. Wendy closed her eyes and sprinted, tears squeezing out of her ducts. The mound was about to overtake them. Teeth punctured the earth's surface to claw at their heels. John was calculating out loud, trying to figure out the location of the still-open gate. He yelled, "Jump!"

All three leaped blindly across some unseen barrier that only John's calculations could have guessed. John prayed that he hadn't made a mistake—that they were in fact jumping through the portal. They fell to the ground and rolled, waiting for the painful crunch of the monstrous teeth. But none came. Wendy opened her eyes. The mound was gone. They were lying on the cold floor of the dining hall, right next to the lunch line. Thankfully there were no students around. The book was lying next to John, and the kitchen door behind them was wide open. Without getting up, Wendy reached over and slammed it shut. Slowly, the Eye of Ra disappeared from the doorpost. Peter was looking at her, smiling wide. He had the bones in his hand.

John opened his eyes, too, and let out a relieved hoot. "We made it," he said.

"We made it," echoed Wendy, focusing only on Peter now that they were safe. Watching him lying there, clutching his prize with everything he had, Wendy was sure that she was falling for him, a lot worse than she had ever fallen for Connor. And judging from the way he looked at her just then, she was starting to believe that maybe he had fallen for her, too. But then Peter turned back toward Harere's hand and his attention was gone. He looked at it with all the affection of a lost love.

In the quiet of the dining hall, once they had caught their breath, all three of them noticed that Peter's handheld was beeping in twos and threes. He ignored it at first, too absorbed with the hand of Harere. Wendy nudged him, and finally Peter picked it up. He flicked through the messages with his thumb, then said, "The LBs are a go. We're gonna get the second batch of bonedust back from Simon."

"I'm getting out of here," said John. He and Wendy got up and dusted themselves off. But, for the four and a half minutes it took to properly wrap and stow the hand, Peter sat still.

The Dark

The nurse with the limp hair and dull eyes stormed through the ruined market in a rage. The underworld thundered and cracked under the weight of her fury. Billowing plumes of smoke suffocated the maze, filling up the labyrinth and seeping into the Marlowe school. After all these years, the third batch of bonedust had been lost.

Again, death had been robbed. The ageless demon was desperate to be rid of Peter—a boy who vowed revenge against the one who had raised him. In the daily hours she spent up above, she sat in her forgettable nurse's body and watched the unhappy children that ran unguided in the halls of the school. She squirmed in her weak form, unable to see or hear more than ordinary human eyes or ears can. She hated covering her shattered eye, the one true part of herself . . . but not the *only* true part, because this pathetic form, this mousy wreck of a girl, was her original body. Not the beautiful governess Vileroy. Not the goddess of death. No, this brown-haired girl with dull eyes and thin lips was older than them all.

Up above, the Marlowe school was shut down for the afternoon in order to investigate strange fumes, air out the tufts of unexplained smoke, and find a solution to the rising humidity. Teachers and students walked around in a fog of gloom, wondering whom to call for an entire school afflicted with depression and paranoia.

OPERATION *LBs R Go!*

Peter looked at the text message on his phone. The LBs were ready. The Garosh bone had been in the overworld ever since John used the priceless relic as a grappling hook. Now it was in the hands of an ambitious twit, who so far hadn't figured out that it was more valuable than everything in the British Museum put together.

During his lecture, he'd used it as a pointer, a pretend drumstick, and a back scratcher. If he did manage to figure out the secret (for instance, if the bonedust miraculously healed him from his idiocy), then he'd never let it see the light of day again. Of course, he'd take it on *60 Minutes* and pretend he'd found it after years of research and digging in the Sahara. Or before that happened, the Dark Lady would ruthlessly kill him and take back the bone, which would guarantee that no one would ever see it again.

The next day, John, Peter, and Wendy hurried to the rendezvous point, a smoothie bar a few blocks away from Marlowe. When they arrived, Wendy spotted two of the boarding boys and Tina leaning on the fresh-fruit counter. The twenty-something worker was trying to pick up Tina, who, even in her advising uniform, looked good enough for clubbing. No guy at Marlowe—LBs included—was stupid enough to try to hit on her.

Tina glided over and wrapped her arms around Peter's neck while Wendy glared.

The two LBs stepped away from the smoothie counter. One of them was the blond with cornrows, who had obviously risen to the top of the ranks. As far as guts and connections were concerned, this kid had it all. He was probably using his dad's company to get funds to Peter by now. He was lanky; every time John saw him, the LB reminded him of the ghost twins from *The Matrix Reloaded*. "Everything's in place," he said to Peter.

The other LB was the rapper's broad-shouldered son with thick-framed poet glasses. He spoke with a calm confidence. "We're at launch sequence, T minus whatever."

"Good," said Peter, nodding like a unit commander. "Any variables?"

"None that we've reconned from the op site," said Cornrow.

"Our point is a perimeter guard, code name: Poopinski," said the buff Poet.

"The guard's name is Poopinski?" asked Peter.

"It's Roy Boykins, but we liked Poopinski," said Poet.

"Hmm," said Peter, weighing the comment, "I would have gone with RoyBoy."

"We can switch to RoyBoy," said Poet immediately. He put his hand up to his earphone and spoke, "LB29 to world, make Poopinski RoyBoy. Repeat. Poopinski is RoyBoy."

"Never mind," said Peter. "Don't even worry about it."

Poet broke off his transmission.

"Cancel that, world. RoyBoy is no go. Repeat, ixnay Oyray Oybay."

"Why do you guys talk like that?" asked Wendy.

The two LBs and Peter turned from their strategizing. Wendy was looking at them as though they were little kids playing with LEGOs.

"What do you mean? It's pig Latin," said Peter.

"No, like *that*. Like soldiers in action movies."

Peter's eyes widened. Cornrow's hand slowly came up to his ear. He whispered something into his iPhone.

"They *are* soldiers," said Peter, still staring at Wendy.

"They're boarding boys," said Wendy.

"Oh, no, she didn't," said Tina under her breath. For the first time, Wendy saw a hostile look in Peter's gaze.

Now Poet forgot about his earpiece and brought his phone to his ear. She heard him whisper, "Transmit happy thoughts, stat! For the love of humanity, launch the happy thoughts now, now, now."

Peter's phone was suddenly alive with buzzes and beeps. He broke off his stare, the hypertense moment between him and Wendy, to check it. Wendy spied text after text streaming into his phone from all over. One said: **The Highlander series just came out on DVD.** Another said: **Hollywood Rumor: Ra's al Ghul is next Batman villain.** A text came in about Dracula, and another about Mrs. Whatsit, the immortal character from *A Wrinkle in Time*.

Peter's scowl slowly turned into a wistful smile. By the time he had scrolled through every text, he seemed to have forgotten any angry feelings he may have had. When he looked up from his phone, he seemed almost surprised to see everyone. "Where were we?" he said.

Wendy wondered how often the boarding boys had to manage Peter's moods.

Meanwhile, John shifted closer to Tina. He turned to her and said, "So, maybe you and me should find some time later."

Tina looked down at him and chuckled. "Gimme a wildberry, large," she said to the vendor, and walked away.

Simon sat at the teacher's desk in history class, grading inarticulate, illiterate backwash that somehow passed for essays these days. His red pen slashed at the papers like the samurai that he was. He had three katanas and a kodachi blade in his apartment in London, which he'd gotten in a seedy Chinatown mall. They were sharp enough to slice through any intruders—not to mention the shuriken he had under his pillow. Now he was performing a ritualistic slaughter of every three-page response paper in the stack in front of him.

"Stupid."

"Inane."

"Asinine," he said to no one in particular, as he scrutinized each assignment.

"Garbage."

"Archeologically inaccurate."

"Grade-school material."

"Wrong font."

"One-inch margins? Right."

Simon took immense pleasure in imagining their smiley young faces dropping as they saw their grades tomorrow. Somehow, the professor had managed to slough off the work of grading these essays onto Simon, just because they were response papers to *his* lecture. It was ludicrous and beneath him, but of course, he couldn't say no. The old man had connections far above Simon.

As Simon wrote a particularly cutting remark on the cover page of Marla's paper *(Try to think on a higher level—at least where the rest of the class is),* he heard a creak. Simon jerked his head upward. He didn't see anyone. It could have been the pipes. Or it could have been spies sent from the Egyptology department of Duke University trying to plagiarize his work. Simon pretended to go back to the papers. Then, nonchalantly, as though he didn't suspect anything, he pretended to yawn. The dramatic arc of his neck allowed him to look into the vent shaft above his head. There was no one in there.

But he couldn't be too careful with his work. Simon decided to do something else, something that he could do while laying a trap for any archeology spies from Duke. He picked up his new trinket, the arm bone he'd gotten from John, from atop an old, dusty book with a broken spine and wrinkled pages, *The Undiscovered Histories,* by Professor George Darling. Simon didn't have much respect for it. It was written before carbon-14 dating, and it may as well have been a work of fiction. But Simon thought he should scan it a little, if only for amusement. He flipped to a random page.

And so it's important to remember—no, it is absolutely criti-cal to understand that everything you have ever heard or believed, everything in the great story of the world, has been passed to you by someone else. Even in the sciences, it is a rare individual who has gone back to the beginning of his knowledge and conducted experiments to lay down the very foundations of his own thoughts.

Peter used the crowbar to pull apart the grate. He let it fall to the ground. There was no one but him in the back of the building where the air vent led outside. The LBs were distracting Boykins now— that was phase one of the plan. Phase one: Distract Boykins so Peter can climb in. Phase two: Make a big noise to draw Simon out. The key was for Peter not to be on record going into the school. He couldn't use his RA badge or be caught on security cameras, because if anything went wrong, Peter couldn't be implicated. Right now, Tina was using Peter's ID to open the front door of the boys' dorm, all the way across campus. She would do this once every ten minutes for half an hour to establish his alibi. He couldn't lose his job at Marlowe. Not while the book was here. If anything happened, the LBs would have to take the fall. He stretched a little and swung his arms like a swimmer about to take a dive. Then he bent over and crawled in.

It was Isaac Newton who said he stood on the shoulders of giants. All those with knowledge stand on such shoulders.

But all I present in this book is that perhaps our giants are dwarfs. Perhaps as we gaze at what we once thought were the farthest horizons of truth, we're standing at the cliff side, its peak far above us.

Down the hall, Officer Boykins was reading the *Post,* trying to figure out why in the world people were famous for doing nothing but shaking what their mama gave them on a tabletop in fancy clubs. As Boykins was unscrewing the top of his thermos, he saw a figure walk in that he couldn't quite make out.

"ID," he said to the figure.

"ID?" mimicked the boy. "I left my ID in my locker. I have a . . . um . . . a game of, um, polo to attend to, participate in, and likewise."

It was the rich kid with crazy hair that was always causing trouble around Marlowe.

Boykins wasn't sure if he was being played or if this hooligan was acting a whole lot stupider than usual. "You're not going anywhere with that gasoline, son."

"What gasoline?" the boy mumbled, blatantly hiding a sloshing drum behind his back. Then he reached into his pocket and a whole bottle of pills (a club drug called *W*) spilled out. This was definitely out of Boykins's jurisdiction. He picked up the phone.

"Administrators' office," said the gruff voice on the other end of the line. Boykins backed away from the receiver and looked at it. Was it broken? Because that was definitely not Sally, the assistant. Must be a temp.

Boykins hesitated. "Can you come down here? We have a situation."

"What's the situation?" asked the temp with a grunt. "'Cause I'm supposed to wait here for the polo players to check in."

The smile on Boykins faded. "Did you say polo?"

"Yeah. Gotta stay here and make sure they've all got their . . . um . . . cornrows."

"What in heavens are you blathering on about?" said Boykins. "What's cornrows got to do with polo?"

"Tons," said the temp. "Cuts down on wind resistance. And it's better to bleach it, makes the hair weigh less."

"Are you serious?" said Boykins. Somebody was playing him for sure. He was starting to think this was some kind of hidden-camera TV show. "Look, buddy, maybe you should come down here."

Simon could hear people talking in the halls. He tried not to pay attention to anything that had to do with children. He flipped to the middle of the book. He was scoffing before he even finished one paragraph. How did this gullible old man climb so far in the field?

> *Once we establish that the claims of the* Book of Gates *are true, then the testimony of the legends is consistent. Each of the five figures undergoes tremendous punishment (figurative and literal), enough to create an extraordinary amount of emotional energy. In the instance of Garosh, it is quite easy to assume that some massive amount of stress-induced*

toxins could contaminate his very bones. Of course, this is all conjecture.

"You got that right," said Simon, trying to ignore the noises from the hall, which sounded more and more like an argument. This book was pure science fiction. The old man didn't present a shred of evidence.

The evidence of this claim would come from direct examination of Garosh's bones (had we access to them). Since the mythic figure is said to have walked the desert for years in the undead state, it stands to reason that his bones would present highly abnormal osteographic patterns. The vertical pressure on the decaying bones, as the mummy staggered in the desert, would create vertical striations, unlike any we have seen in the past.

"Hmm," said Simon, glancing at the bone sitting on his desk. It also had vertical striations. Proof that Professor Darling didn't even know basic science. If this bone had those striations, too, then how could they be proof of the mythic bone with all its special *bonedust.* Whoo. Magic beans, all of it.

Outside in the hall, Officer Boykins was trying to pacify the punk kid, who was irate at not being allowed into his own school.

"This is outrageous," said the boy. "I mean, seriously, man, me and my can of fuel have a polo game to get to. Now. Do you want me to call my father?"

Boykins kept thinking that this was all wrong. "You're in serious trouble, son. I suggest you surrender the gas and the pills right now."

"Bite me," said the kid. And then it got even worse.

"What's the matter, Roy?" came the temp's rough voice as he strolled down the hall. It was that rapper's giant son, who had been going to this school since who knows when.

Just last week Boykins had busted this one for smuggling drinks onto campus.

"*You're* the temp?" Boykins asked. "But you're—"

But before he could finish, the so-called temp jumped in with serious anger in his voice.

"What? What am I? I'm *black*? Is that what you meant to say? Is this a racial thing?"

"Whoa, whoa, whoa, now wait a minute," said Officer Boykins. "I was gonna say—"

"*You* called *me* in the office," said the temp, "because you can't do your job, and then you start getting racial? And what are you doing with my boy over there? What do you need? Fingerprints? Would you like to Tase him a few times to see if he screams like a real Marlowe student?"

Officer Boykins began to cower and worry about his job. And Poet was just warming up.

In addition, of the five mummies (and, in fact, of all mummies and human bones to date), only Garosh's bones would

exhibit the odd trait that the ends, where the joints meet,
would have crumbled away in a circular pattern after years
of grating against each other postmortem.

Simon still wasn't impressed. His new paperweight had its ends crumbled away as well. *And look at that—the markings are circular. . . .* The noise in the hall was impossible to ignore at this point. Simon would have to go tell the children to shut up.

And last, the most convincing piece of evidence would come
from the bones themselves. The dust from the decayed bones
would have some sort of regenerative effect on carbon-based
material. For instance, the legends claim that when treated
with bonedust, all decay on human flesh (scar tissue, for
instance) would be reversed.

Simon was disgusted. He slapped the book shut, pushed away from the desk, got up, and walked to the door, taking the book with him. He opened the door and stuck his head out to yell. To his surprise, two boarding boys were standing over a terrified Officer Boykins, screaming something about a color-blind world where people are judged by their abilities in polo, as opposed to the color of their cornrows. It looked like the big one was about to beat up the officer. Simon would have to intervene somehow.

"Hey," he shouted. "Hey, you!" he said again, using the book as a pointer.

Suddenly, Simon saw something. The three people in the hall had turned. The boy with cornrows said, "What do you want?"

But Simon wasn't paying attention anymore. All he could do was stare at the book. The wrinkled, old brown-stained book with a broken spine, which had rested under his new paperweight, looked brand-new. The spine was perfectly whole; the pages were as white as the day they came from the printer. Simon couldn't bring himself to believe it. He heard a noise and turned back into the classroom. There was that new RA he'd seen hanging around with the Darling brats. He had jumped down from the air vent. He had Simon's precious bone in his hands.

"No, it's mine!" shouted Simon. It was all he could get out.

The punk smirked at him and said, "Not anymore." Then he ran and jumped out the window.

I knew it! thought Simon. *I knew it was true!*

PETER

It *was* true. Peter had known for ages. Now he sat alone in his dorm room, away from Tina or the LBs. The Garosh bone—the second batch of bonedust—rested in his lap, and he examined it inch by inch. Ever since he'd arrived here, Peter's anxieties had multiplied. He didn't have much time. Every time he had found the book, he had been discovered, or else the book had been moved again, before he could make multiple trips.

He remembered now that it was the Darlings who had helped him get this far. *Three bones down.* That Wendy, she was good to have around. She was inspiring, beautiful, innocent. He liked that about her—her innocence. He could tell each time he touched her face that Wendy felt guilty about her boyfriend. She was the loyal type. Maybe he would ask her to visit him sometime, when there weren't so many people around. Maybe he would ask her what she dreamed about at night. Did she ever wish she could live forever?

As for Peter, he had had another nightmare last night. He had seen the broken blue eye again. And this time, it wasn't his decrepit, hunchbacked old nanny, with her quiet steps and her moth-ridden clothes. It wasn't the woman who had shown him the book and then yanked it away. The nanny who had lived forever and always hungered for more children to corrupt, the one who beat him with her antique hook, the ageless governess against whom only one child, Peter, had ever plotted payback. No, this was a far more beautiful woman, with blond hair and a black overcoat, an exciting woman like all the ones that he let into his life every day. He wondered if he should trust them so easily. He wondered if he should trust Wendy.

THE CON-MAN

For a few days after getting the second batch of bonedust back from
Simon, Peter disappeared, taking all three bones with him. John and
Wendy didn't have any idea where he was or what he was doing,
just that he wanted to be left alone. John had a fit. ("He just *took* the
bones? We could've *died*. Worse, we could've gotten *expelled!*") Wendy
didn't mind, though. She was beginning to trust Peter. She knew
that he was obsessed with bonedust, that the quest consumed him,
and that he had been chasing it for a long time. If she had to guess,
she would say that bonedust days were extremely rare, and that he
had been walking around with Elan's toe in his pocket for a while.
So maybe he deserved some time with it. She knew he wouldn't steal
the bonedust or jeopardize her father's work—unlike Simon. She
wondered if she should break up with Connor. Even though she had
agonized over whether leaving one guy for another was despicable,
she was beginning to think that maybe things weren't so black and
white. Wasn't dating Connor just to help John make friends equally
dishonest? For some reason, the conversation she had overheard

through the closed door of the nurse's office kept coming back to her, reminding her to chase her own happiness.

As for Simon, ever since Peter had stolen that bone, it had been all-out war. Now Simon knew that the legends were true—or at least true enough to make him rich and famous. Did he believe that bone-dust could give eternal life? Maybe. Maybe not. But one thing was for sure: he knew there were five mummies out there that had been unaccounted for in all of history. He knew they were the five mummies from the legends, with verifiable backstories and an identifiable time period. The possibility of magic powers was a bonus. Finding the mummies would be enough to make his career. Finding a gate into a hidden treasure trove would make him a legend. Simon didn't care about ever-living dust the way Peter did. He wasn't desperate to live forever—except in history books. His name was the entirety of him. *Rich and famous, acclaimed and renowned, the untouchable Professor Grin.*

Meanwhile, Wendy and John were grounded indefinitely. Professor Darling was livid about the AP calculus closet incident. He ranted and ground his teeth over the fact that this irresponsible RA had not been fired. Apparently, Peter had done nothing expressly wrong . . . and he was part of a union. So Professor Darling took his anger out on his children. Had he not warned them that this Peter character wasn't their sort? Had he not expressly forbade them to fraternize with him? Was any of this unclear? Wendy and John didn't protest too much (even Wendy, who was way too old to be grounded). Any new provocation, even the smallest detail they might accidentally reveal, and they would have to spill everything to their dad. And for now, they had Simon to deal with.

"Thank God he's too selfish to ever say anything to Daddy," Wendy had remarked.

John hadn't responded. Because, to be perfectly fair, Simon hadn't done anything John wouldn't do—if necessary.

A few days later, Peter returned. John demanded to see the bone-dust. "What have you done with it? It belongs to all of us!"

Peter just stared at him with an amused look. Then he straightened up, looked John square in the face, and said, in the most serious tone they had ever heard him use, "Let's get one thing straight, little man. The dust belongs to *me*. All five of them belong to *me*. If you're not cool with that, I don't need your help."

When John didn't respond, Peter flashed a bright, toothy grin and put an arm around both of their shoulders, taking them into his confidence the way a bird takes its chicks into its nest. Even though he didn't like Peter, John accepted the gesture, telling himself that it was some kind of acquiescence. Besides, he liked feeling included, like one of the LBs. LB77NY. That would be his handle. He would change all his online accounts later tonight. For the past few weeks, John had looked on every website and in every chat room for LBs. He had found a few. None of them talked to him. It seemed that to be an LB, there was no getting around Peter. So, as much as John disliked the cocky RA, he would accept this gesture. Maybe now

Peter would tell the LBs they had to talk to him. And maybe later, Peter would be gone and he and Simon could be head of the LBs.

Tina sat on the bed in her RA dorm room, trying not to slap the poor, rich white girl that had been yammering on about her stupid problems for the past half hour (what kind of loon names their daughter Yale, anyway?). *Oh, my thighs are fat, my face is too square, there's a lump in my breast, my boyfriend is not really my boyfriend, Chelsea bought the exact same skirt as me. Can you feel this lump?*

Tina pretended to listen as she stared out of her window and watched the perfectly trimmed front lawn of Marlowe, with its resident squirrels that looked just a little plumper than the squirrels in Central Park, its trees that looked a little more lush, its Gothic buildings trimmed with spires and gargoyles and family crests carved into brick. Even after the underworld infestation had turned the school into a pit of despair, it still looked nicer than any place Tina had ever lived. *Please, please, someone show me the rule that says you can't stab your advisees. 'Cause I don't think it's actually written anywhere. Right? Right?*

Tina had never seen such needy teenagers in her whole life— and she had lived among *real* orphans, *real* runaways, kids with *actual* problems. The girls in her hall were at her door every chance they got, with every made-up reason and crazy need imaginable, and Tina was starting to suspect that they just wanted attention. *What kind of wack-jobs do they have for parents?* Tina wondered, putting out another plate of boxed donuts. Apparently, the superrich haven't heard of Entenmann's, and, what do you know, they can pack it away just like everyone else.

"OK, *chica*." Tina took a deep breath. "I got about thirty seconds of patience, so I'll make it fast. You don't have breast cancer, you're dangerously underweight, and all the purging is making your breath stink. If you wanna be loved, stop talking and get a dog." Yale started to whimper. *Oh, geez.* "Kidding, kidding!" Tina patted Yale on the head like a puppy. She hoped the girl didn't expect a hug. "Stop crying."

"I can't"—sniff—"because I have"—sniff, sniff—"a boyfriend . . . but"—sniff—"he's not . . . really my boyfriend."

Tina sighed. "You know what, Yale? I get it."

Yale stopped crying.

"Yeah, I get it," said Tina. "I have a guy just like that."

"*You?*" Yale said, because not even Tina could deny Tina's hotness.

"Yeah, girl," said Tina. "It happens. I've been with this guy— let's call him Mr. Dirtbag . . . for years. *Years.* And now he's running around, feeling up this new chick every chance he gets, making lame excuses, and I'm still sitting here, waiting for him to gimme the time of day. How's that for fair?"

Yale sniffed and took another donut. "You mean Peter?"

"No, I do *not* mean Peter," Tina snapped. She started roughly pulling a loose thread off her Marlowe bedspread.

"'Cause he's kind of cute," said Yale. She started digging for her diet pills in her Lady Dior handbag.

"All right . . . time for you to go," said Tina. She wondered why she wasted her time with Peter. Why she did everything he asked. Why she stood by and watched him slowly seduce that private school brat away from her boyfriend. And Wendy . . . she was worse than Peter. Just another rich girl who can never be satisfied. Tina had seen how close Peter and Wendy had become in the past few days, and especially since getting that third bone. She hated Wendy for being the one to help him find it—for replacing Tina as Peter's useful right hand. Tina had seen Peter and Wendy together in the halls, in empty classrooms, when they thought no one was looking. . . . Wasn't one guy enough for her? Didn't she know how hard it is out there just to get one man who'll stick around, one decent guy who'll take care of you? This Connor character wasn't as bad as the other boys around here. Tina saw how he befriended Wendy's nerdy brother and how he stood up to the LBs for their game-fixing scam. Couldn't Wendy be happy with one good, honest man in her life? *Why does she have to come after mine?*

Ever since the last time Peter, Wendy, and John had gone into the labyrinth, the changes to Marlowe had become impossible to ignore. Strangely enough, the students and faculty managed to do just that. Sure, there were cleanup crews dispatched, air purifiers installed, plumbing inspected, pest control called, and hallways fumigated. But in the end, no one acknowledged that this was all *one* thing—a single thread of changes that were very much related to one another. No one thought that the sadness they felt when they entered the grounds—now just a little grayer, drearier—had anything to do with the school itself.

This morning, Wendy had walked in on four faculty members marveling at a classroom that was filled—*filled*—with moths and flies. They were everywhere, inhabiting every nook, covering every surface, leaving no air for breathing and no ground for walking. No teacher could explain it. They all just stood back and watched. The assistant principal shook her head and said, "It's an old, historic school. There are quirks with ancient buildings like this. Comes with the territory." And weirder still, the new school nurse stepped right into the middle of it, as if she didn't mind, and let the moths cover her for a second before stepping back and agreeing with the assistant principal. And so they had left it, the entire buzzing, fluttering mess. Wendy stayed a bit longer to watch, because this was not the kind of insect swarm you see every day. Peter had said that the moths were spies. . . . The darkness from below was watching them.

Peter and Wendy walked through the halls, trying to figure out what to do about Simon, while John followed behind with one of the LBs, a geeky-looking one that was probably the Marlowe-branch webmaster, trying to convince the guy to add him to the text-message group list, and occasionally chiming in on Peter and Wendy's conversation.

"We're so close," said Peter. "If we just figure out the last two, then who cares about getting in trouble or losing my job?"

"Uh," said John, "you might not care, but we still have a couple of more years here."

"Simon won't tell," said Wendy. "He'll work his butt off to get the other bonedust first, but he won't tell. If Dad finds out about any of this, Simon'll lose all leverage."

Peter was lost in thought. He didn't seem to be listening, which made Wendy mad and anxious. She wasn't used to these erratic feelings. She was usually very levelheaded. She wished things with Peter could be clearer and that she wouldn't have to keep going back and forth between elation and rage.

"Enough of this crap," Peter finally said. "Time to go after the Nubian."

John perked up. "What Nubian?" he asked excitedly.

"The fourth legend," said Peter.

"I say it's a desert," said the LB, never taking his eyes off his phone.

John's eyes were shining, and his mind was already working full time. "Nubian, huh?" he said, though neither he nor Wendy knew the fourth legend. "Then I bet it's someplace with horses. Nubians were known for horse skills. . . ."

"Nah," the LB said. "What about a battlefield? They were warriors."

John jumped in, clearly feeling competitive with this fellow nerd who had the privilege of being an LB, while he was still a nobody. "An army barracks!" John countered.

"I've tried all those," said Peter. "Hey, you," he said to the LB, not bothering even with a nickname. "Get me a smoothie."

The boy rushed off to the dining hall. "How did *he* get to be an LB?" John asked.

"He's on my hall," said Peter with a laugh. "Plus, he can hack into anything. I don't know how I ever lived without one of *him* . . . oh, and he does whatever I say." Peter handed John a five and said, "Forgot to ask for a bag of chips."

Wendy could see John seething and considering at the same

time. Poor kid. He really wanted to be an LB, but he obviously hated doing anything for Peter. He finally settled on taking the money and showing his contempt by huffing and stomping after the webmaster to the dining hall.

When Peter reached for Wendy's hand, she felt her stomach tighten. She knew Peter was a good person, but sometimes his selfishness made her worry. She remembered when they were outside the school before Simon's lecture on Harere, when Peter had almost admitted to letting someone die. She shook the thought from her head. For the first time ever, walking through her own school frightened her. Every two minutes, she felt chills, as if someone was running cold fingers up and down her back. More than anything, she sensed a lingering evil here.

"Don't be scared," Peter said when Wendy shuddered.

"I'm not," said Wendy a little too quickly.

A tiny smile curled Peter's lips, and he interlaced his fingers with hers. Out of nowhere he said, "Wendy, what if there were enough for two?"

"Huh?" she said, and then wished she had said something more graceful.

He leaned close to her and whispered, as if he thought someone else were listening, "If there were enough for two, I'd share it with you. I'd let you have half the bonedust, and then neither one of us would ever grow old."

Wendy's heart started to beat faster. What he was inviting her to do was huge. It wasn't just a gift, a little present you give to any random girl. He was offering her an eternity. He might go away, run to the far reaches of the world, meet a hundred different girls, live a dozen different lives, but in seventy or eighty years, *she*'d be his oldest friend. She stopped walking. Despite the thumping of her heart, she wasn't sure what she would do if given this chance. Living forever wasn't necessarily a blessing to Wendy. She looked forward to growing up, even to growing old.

Suddenly Connor appeared at the other end of the corridor. Wendy was so taken off guard that she didn't realize she was still holding Peter's hand. But Peter didn't let go.

"I can't believe you," Connor said, his voice more high-pitched than usual, his eyes darting. "What's *this*?"

Wendy was dumbstruck. She couldn't tell if Connor's anger was genuine or caused by the school. He stared at Peter, his eyes angry and sad. "Aren't you the RA?"

"No, Connor . . ." Wendy began.

"No, what?" he said. "No, you're *not* one half of a statutory?"

Wendy wasn't sure who moved first, but in the next second, three things happened almost at once: Peter dropped Wendy's hand. Connor lunged toward Peter and shoved him against a locker. John reappeared with the webmaster and, seeing Peter in the middle of a beat-down, made his own contribution by drinking Peter's smoothie.

Wendy tried to pull Connor off, but she just got shoved out of the way. Peter didn't need help anyway. He kneed Connor in the stomach, then pulled back and punched him in the jaw, just as Professor Darling and two other teachers came running down the hall in time to witness the massive violation of the resident adviser code.

Peter was fired on the spot.

Wendy was dumped faster than she could say "Nothing happened." Connor just said, "We're through," and walked away.

Professor Darling glared at his children, shooting them looks that said *Did I not tell you he was trouble?*

John just stood there, sipping a smoothie, watching Connor walk off as if nothing had happened, probably wondering if he was still invited to lift weights tomorrow after school.

Simon sat at his desk and, for the hundredth time since losing the Garosh bone, thought about how he could get the book away from the Darling kids without giving away what he knew. He could not let that kook Darling get credit for such a discovery (which Simon had known *all along* to be real). "I am going to win the freakin' Nobel Prize. Forget it, they're going to rename it and give Mr. Nobel the Grin Prize."

Once he had discovered that the legends were real, Simon had gone on a research rampage. He had perused all of Darling's published works and even thumbed through several of Darling's source materials—works that until now Simon had dismissed as garbage. He had camped out at the Egyptology Library with a sleeping bag and a thermos of coffee, bribing the guard not to kick him out at closing time. He read and reread all the seminal works on the *Book of Gates,* and even some of the obsolete ones, until finally he had found something. It was no more than a footnote in a dusty old volume from a hundred years ago. A book that had been tucked away in the last row of the back shelf, unread for decades. The footnote alluded to an old story about a portal and referred the reader to yet another volume, which Simon had to crawl through the cobwebbed stacks to find. But finally, he had it. He translated it and committed it to memory. The words were vague, but enough.

The next day, he was back at the library, rereading all the obscure books he could find. He now understood the connection between the guardians and the five mummies of Elan's cursed line. He quickly linked the earthworm to Nailah, never admitting to himself that he had been wrong when he scribbled insults all over Professor Darling's notes. For days, Simon researched. He read about Garosh and the Bedouins, Elan and his quest, and all the details surrounding their lineage. He tracked the generations using obscure genealogical records, filling in the holes from Elan to Garosh to Harere and beyond. He even made rough blueprints of the school, attempting to tie every little nook to its twisted underworld twin. Soon, he thought, he would figure out how to cross the barrier between the overworld and the underworld. And then those stupid kids could do nothing to stop the up-and-coming scholar from getting his due.

CONNOR WIRTH

A RECURRING THOUGHT

"After leading his basketball team to a state champion-ship, setting national records at three different golf courses, and anchoring the 4 x 200 m butterfly relay earlier today, Connor Wirth has got to be the favorite for this race, even

considering the other two excellent swimmers on his team.
Connor scoops some of the water over his arms to warm up
his muscles, gets a pat on the back from his teammate, and
climbs onto his starting block. The gun sounds and they're
off. Teammate Christian Faust gets a HUGE dive off the
block. Wirth seems to stumble. His kick seems off, a cramp
maybe? I think . . . I think Wirth is suffering some kind of
injury. His rhythm is completely off. He seems to be flailing.
Faust is on pace to shatter the school record, held by none
other than the struggling Wirth. Something must be wrong.
Wirth has put up his arm for assistance. He can't even tread
water. He's sinking. I've never seen anything like it. The best
swimmer in the state is drowning."

The Dark

In the innermost depths of her chamber, the Dark Lady fumed. Her home had been breeched, and now the boy had three of the five immortal bones. It would no longer be so easy to kill him. Now he had the power to heal, the power to fortify his mortal body. He must be captured. He must be stopped. *He is nearly there. . . .*

She stood in the lowest part of the underworld, the very tip of the pyramid, the deepest part of the abyss. She was covered by a cloud of her companions, her minions, her eyes. They whizzed around her as in a mist, making her seem like a giantess made of black billowing specks. And this is what she was. This was her natural state. She was their mistress. Lord of all flies, mother of all the creeping, buzzing things of the world. She lifted her shoulders, and the insects gave her strength. When she bent her weary body to cough, they propped her up and soothed her throat.

As for the meddlesome children above, the darkness would draw them in. She had been a nanny, after all, before she was ever a nurse. She would distract them with their own petty problems—

infatuation and obsession and the longing for validation. She loved these weaknesses most of all, and she would use them to turn the children's focus from the quest. If that failed, she would fool them with tricks of the eye. Then, if they persisted, she would guide them through the murky depths, to the place where she lived alone—all the way to the heart of the underworld maze. It would not be enough to kill them then. If they persisted in disturbing her slumber, she would bring them deep into the underworld and take back the bones that had been lost. And so the dark nurse schemed. . . .

16

THE FOURTH LEGEND

Wendy stood breathless in front of the boys' dorm building. *Am I hallucinating?* She had come to visit Peter as he packed his dorm room to leave Marlowe for good. After the incident with Connor, Wendy had spent hours obsessing about their relationship. Now that she was officially single, she analyzed everything Peter had said. She thought about Tina, who had known Peter for so much longer. She just *had* to know where things stood with Peter.

But now, as she stood in front of the boys' dorm, she was sure the paranoia was getting to her, because there wasn't just one but *two* black Eyes of Ra singed into the door frames leading into Peter's hallway. "Is there an open gate here?" she muttered aloud. Should she avoid going in? But she wanted to see Peter. And besides, why would there be an open portal here, in Peter's (soon to be ex-) hall?

"What gate?" said someone from behind her.

Wendy jumped a foot and screamed at the unexpected voice over her shoulder.

"Sorry." Wendy turned and saw that she had startled the school nurse, whose hand was hovering just over her chest. "I'm jumpy today."

The nurse was wearing an eye patch. "Are you OK?" Wendy asked.

"Yes." The nurse smiled and touched the patch. "Just an infection. Were you talking to yourself, dear?"

Wendy laughed nervously. The way the nurse said *dear* was nice, like a mother or a confidante. "No . . . I mean, yes . . . I'm here to see my boyfriend."

"You mean Connor?"

Wendy was surprised that the nurse knew about her love life. She scrunched her brow, and the nurse smiled and said, "You hear things around here." Then she looked away and took out her handkerchief and wiped her forehead. She coughed once while averting her eye and then looked at Wendy again, waiting.

"Right," said Wendy. "I'm here to see Peter."

"Peter?" The nurse raised an eyebrow. "Ooooh . . . I heard about what happened, dear." Then she leaned in like a practiced gossip and said, "I suppose he won't be moving far."

"What do you mean?" Wendy asked.

The nurse shrugged. "He can just bunk with his Spanish friend, like he always does."

Professor Darling kept pushing his glasses farther and farther up the bridge of his nose. Wendy knew the students were waiting anxiously, hoping that he wouldn't call them out on the fact that none of them had gone to see the Egyptian exhibit. She was livid and full of unanswered questions. What did the nurse mean when she said Peter could bunk with Tina? Peter was supposed to be *hers* . . . or so she thought. She could barely focus her attention on the class or on her father or on the worrisome fact that Simon had been eerily quiet about the Garosh bone incident, which meant that he was up to something.

Wendy was desperate to talk to Peter alone, but Peter, now fired, was reduced to lurking in the background and getting his information through Tina and the Lost Boys. Wendy's eyes darted from where Peter was hiding, on the other side of a windowsill, to the classroom door. Every passing custodian made her jump at the thought that a faculty member could storm in any minute now, followed by police looking for Peter (and Wendy, too, since she had helped him sneak back onto campus). Wendy glanced at her brother. John had been awfully quiet since the breakup with Connor. He was obviously taking it hard—not that he ever thought Connor was his best friend or anything. But even the occasional charity invitation was better than total friendlessness. Wendy pressed her fingers to her temple. She didn't think she could handle all this at once.

Simon sat nervously in the corner, but he was *always* nervous, along with nosy, narcissistic, and nettlesome. Since losing his precious artifact, he had been humiliated and had promised himself that he would unlock the labyrinth no matter what. He had drawn up a plan. In fact, he had drawn out maps and charts and all kinds of schematics during his off-hours. On the margins of his plan, there were doodles of a stick figure version of himself dancing on a pile of money. And in a few other doodles, his head was poking out of a poorly drawn biplane as he shot down the Red Baron with photon torpedoes. The plan itself was nothing more than a diary of how he had John wrapped around his little finger, and that he could use this "mole" to extract further information about the book. What more did he need? The schematics were mostly of the huge house/arcade he was going to build after he became the richest Egyptologist ever.

When the bell rang and it was time to start class, Professor Darling walked to his podium. He was still staring off into a distance as he flipped to the right page in his workbook. Wendy knew that whatever was occupying his mind, it wasn't as simple as the success of the exhibit. To the outside world, the exhibit was going great. The governor's office had even asked the professor to attend a gala, where they would present him with some kind of award. Whatever was bothering her dad, thought Wendy, it had to be big. Not many things could turn the jolly professor to such brooding behavior.

"Hey, Professor," said Marla from the back of the class. The professor was flipping the pages while staring out the window with a far-gone look on his face. "What's the story?"

"The story?" echoed the professor.

"Why's he so out of it?" Wendy asked John. He didn't respond. He probably thought it was Wendy's fault—that their dad was worrying about her relationship with Peter.

"Yeah," said Marla, ignoring the snickering. "The fourth legend of the *Book of Gates*."

"Ah," said the professor, "Marcus Praxis, the Nubian god-warrior."

Marla sat up in her seat, intrigued. Something told Wendy that these legends were going to make their way into the lyrics of Marla's psychedelic goth rock band soon. Well, at least she wasn't making fun of their Marlowe-owned house or flipping twenties at her head anymore. "What did Praxis lose?" asked Marla.

"Everything," said the professor.

"But all of them lost everything," said Marla. "That's the point."

"Yes," said the professor, "but they didn't *have* everything. Praxis alone collected a fortune, found requited love, and conquered the world."

"Cool," said Marla.

"Praxis would have been as famous as Alexander the Great."

"So he really lost his fame," said Marla.

"His place in history," amended the professor. "His figurative immortality."

Wendy glanced again at the windowsill, where moments before she had helped Peter hide to hear clues from Darling's fourth lecture through the open window. She knew Peter was smirking at that last comment.

Professor Darling sighed as he glanced at his notes. "I do encourage you all to visit the book in our exhibit and see the sketches that go with each of these stories. Take advantage of these last hours of its stay at Marlowe."

"*What?*" said Wendy, a bit too loudly. She could almost hear Peter panicking outside.

"What do you mean, *last hours?*" said John, also alarmed.

"Well," said the professor distractedly, "I'm taking it to the gala. I'm presenting the governor with a token from the exhibit. It's customary."

"But you can't!" said Wendy. Her father flushed at her volume, and a few kids looked up from their doodling. "I mean . . . it belongs to the British Museum, right?"

"Yes," said Professor Darling. "I have the proper permissions, of course. It's on loan to the governor's offices only for a short time."

"The governor's *offices?*" said John. "You mean in *Albany?*"

Professor Darling chuckled. "Yes, that *is* still where they keep the capitol."

"But I thought . . ." Wendy searched for the right words. "I thought you said this book was the original gate book . . ."

"*Book of Gates.* No, I've long abandoned that notion. Sometimes, Wendy, the smallest, most inconsequential items are the most important. I'm focusing my research now on the figurine and the small jars. Don't worry—the book will be in good hands. Simon's mentioned something about applying for some sort of curator job in Albany, correct?"

The professor looked at Simon, who nodded solemnly. Wendy wondered if John understood that Simon had engineered this loss, that he was isolating the book for himself. Probably not. He probably thought Simon was protecting a valuable artifact for posterity. Still, it was obvious that John did see one thing: opening the gates without the book—or getting their hands on it once it was sent to the capitol—would be impossible.

"Now," said Professor Darling, "back to Marcus Praxis and his great loss."

Wendy knew that Peter was fuming on the other side of the windowsill. She could practically hear it as her dad began the fourth legend.

The Fourth Legend

A just reward is a precious thing. If a person is robbed of the rightful credit for his deeds, of the right to be praised or punished according to his own humanity, then he is nothing. If his place in history is obliterated as though he never touched the earth, a bitterness builds inside.

So goes the story of one family with a curse on its line, of Elan's dark legacy, full of the cruelest injustices. The house that cannot die. Their stolen lives linger on, still flowing in their bones. Life has been mummified inside them, forming an ever-living bonedust—a new kind of immortality.

Hundreds of years after the betrayal of Harere by her sister, Nailah, the House of Elan languished in desolation. With each passing generation, the family became more and more entrenched in a legacy of regret. Soon, they were nothing but bandits, floating up and down the fertile Nile, ambushing caravans led to water, and hijacking merchants.

The Children of Elan were the most feared gang in all of Cairo, roving the City of the Dead, desecrating family tombs for precious objects. Ambitious officials often hired them to assassinate rivals. If they paid extra, a lot extra Hurkhan the legend, leader of the infamous gang, would personally attend to the matter.

It was said, only in the quietest corners of the city, that Hurkhan had a taste for killing. He was an abomination to Elan's bloodline, to Egypt, and to humanity. He had used the blacksmith's sharpening wheel to grind his own teeth into a jagged bracket of razors. His smile was grotesque. No one would speak of Hurkhan and prayed that he would not speak of them. But this legend is not of Hurkhan the bloodthirsty. It was someone else who bore the weight of Elan's heritage. . . .

Hurkhan had spent much time sharpening his skills with the Nubian tribes, using his fearsome reputation and grotesque acts of violence to frighten the elders into allowing him to stay among them when he needed to hide. There, he had fathered a son with one of the Nubian princesses. When Hurkhan's son was born, no one could deny that he was beautiful. Somehow, by the gods, he had taken the best of his parents' odd coupling. He was strong, shrewd, and courageous, like his father. He was also kind, just, and generous, like his mother. His skin was a dark bronze.

When the boy came of age, Hurkhan returned to the village to claim his son. In the alleys of the City of the Dead, the underground began to whisper. The Children of Elan had arisen with a new son. But no one had seen this new street prince. No one had seen him because Hurkhan had other plans.

Lately, Hurkhan had been uninformed of the goings-on within Cairo and the pharaoh's palace. He needed a new spy in the royal house. As it happened, his son was the same age as the new pharoah, Amun-Ra, who was a petty and jealous young man.

No one would suspect that the Nubian boy was the rumored son of Hurkhan. But his tribal name was not suitable for the sly affairs of courtesans. Hurkhan gave him the name Marcus Praxis, knowing the young pharaoh's fascination with the Roman clans.

Marcus Praxis did not know he was a spy. He only went to the court of Amun-Ra to find a friend. Hurkhan lived, as always, in the shadows, watching the two boys grow as close as two brothers, waiting for his chance to use Marcus for his purposes.

Amun was not nimble, like Marcus. Nonetheless, all the courtiers let the frail pharaoh win at games. He could not win chariot races, as Marcus did, but the courtiers pulled back their horses to let him pass. Marcus was the only one who would soundly defeat Amun at every game they played.

Amun-Ra grew envious, and even though Marcus Praxis was his best friend, somewhere, deep down, the pharaoh hated him—especially in the presence of Layla, the daughter of a minister. To young Amun-Ra and Marcus Praxis, Layla was the ocean. Her splendor outshone Alexandria's lighthouse. She was famous for her fiery nature. People called her fierce, an unstoppable force: a windstorm.

Over the years, Marcus became a great soldier, courageous in battle, and the commander of the most elite warriors. When it seemed as if the wars would tear all of Egypt apart, his spear shone and struck fear and regret in his enemies. He was given credit for saving the empire from ruin, and he rode into the city to a hero's welcome.

"Amun-Ra is pharaoh. Marcus Praxis is pharaoh builder!"

"Amun-Ra is god. Marcus Praxis is god maker!"

What Marcus Praxis had achieved was monumental. Poets wrote songs in his honor. Craftsmen built him statues. Artists painted his image throughout the kingdom. And most important, Layla chose him as her companion. Word spread that he would become the greatest name among all the peoples of the East. Amun-Ra burned with hatred.

But soon, Hurkhan showed his wicked face to Marcus once again.

In the palace garden, one dusky evening, Hurkhan approached his son, the commander of all Egypt's armies, with a scheme. He had amassed a horde of barbarian warriors, mercenaries, and thieves, in the desert just outside Giza. Marcus Praxis could purposely lose this battle, letting Hurkhan's criminal army overrun Cairo. Hurkhan would ascend the throne. But so would Marcus Praxis, after his father's eventual death. It was a devious plan.

Marcus could not deny that Amun-Ra was a terrible ruler. His taxes starved the people. His law had become overly severe. But Marcus Praxis would not betray his people to Hurkhan's army. His father snapped his teeth in frustration, for Marcus was too strong to kill there in the garden. Hurkhan retreated into the shade, and back to his army.

Marcus returned to his loving wife and their children. It was not long before the Egyptian army heard of Hurkhan's men. The people of Cairo squirmed under the threat of more war. They called for Marcus Praxis to bring peace once again. Marcus Praxis kissed the beautiful Layla's tears and promised to return. Then Marcus rode to Giza.

Deep in the desert, the two armies faced each other. At the head of Egypt's army stood Marcus Praxis, the legend of the day, his soldiers shouting in perfect unison. Among the roguish horde stood Hurkhan, the myth of the night, his men cackling and cracking their teeth. All the empire stood between them. From the palace balcony, Amun-Ra and the court waited for sounds of battle. Layla would not listen. Amun-Ra grinned, for he knew there was nothing to listen to. . . .

Marcus Praxis lowered his sword, the signal for his soldiers to attack. He sprinted ahead of them, unafraid of leading the charge. But when the great general reached the middle of the battlefield, he knew that his army had not followed. Hurkhan's men had also stayed in place. Marcus knew he had been betrayed. His spurned father smiled like a crocodile as he watched his son standing lonely between two armies.

At the command of Hurkhan, both armies raised their bows, and together they wiped the memory of the great general Marcus Praxis from the earth. Far away at the palace, as the court awaited the sound of war, Amun-Ra returned to his chamber, but not before ordering Layla to be his wife. Hurkhan's army was allowed to ransack all of Cairo, but would stop short of the palace. For days the city burned. The bandit army took all that they pleased. They had only one command. All statues of Marcus Praxis were to be shattered, all murals scratched out of the stone. His name would be erased from the histories of great men. Marcus Praxis would be no more, and the great achievements of Amun-Ra's kingdom would be credited to the pharaoh alone. Amun-Ra the brave. Amun-Ra, great warrior. Amun-Ra, savior of his people.

Before the carnage was done, Hurkhan claimed the body of his son. In a ritual of debasement and desecration, the monster removed his son's organs and preserved the hollow body as a trophy, a relic of war that he hid in the winding alleys of the City of the Dead. He used sawdust to stuff it and linens to wrap it. And so, in creating his grotesque monument to himself, Hurkhan mummified his son's remains, trapping in his bones so much more than he knew. It is said, only in the quietest corners of the city, that beautiful Layla, who died soon after her marriage to Amun-Ra, wanders the dead city to this day, searching the intricate maze, looking for a token of her beloved.

The bitterness of this injustice devoured Marcus's soul. And so, he died with his life trapped in his bones. The goddess of death took the general's mummy and the bonedust with it. She shielded it with her greatest weapons, fearing that someday death might be conquered. The Dark

Lady hid the mummy in a place where no one could reach it, a legendary labyrinth of the gates, guarded by powerful deities that no human could overcome.

And so, Marcus Praxis was gone, his rightful place in history lost. But he can never fully die. His wasted life is forever trapped as grains of immortality in his bones.

MARLA

A RECURRING THOUGHT

Of course, my father becomes a diplomat. If you are rich and you want to keep your money out of the hands of all the corrupt officials, you have to become one of them. So we move. Overnight. No bars. No cars. No hot Russian boys. No champagne. Just Marlowe and a bunch of boring rich kids who only care about getting into good colleges. Who are these losers? They hear that my father is a diplomat from Belarus and are impressed that he can park anywhere he likes. Then they ask, "Where's Belarus?"

INTERLUDE

PETER

Peter tossed and turned, twisting his blanket around himself, sweating through his pillow all the way to the scratchy feathers inside. He was in a barely furnished room, in a strange house that the LBs had found for him—someone's attic outside Manhattan. The nightmares were unbearable now. His demons would not leave him alone. The night would never end. He had barely slept in days. Still, the desperation for bonedust drove him onward.

He thrashed in his bed and kicked away his blanket. The book would soon slip away from him. It would be moved to Albany, and he would have to start all over again. It was already so much harder getting close to the exhibit since his firing from Marlowe. Now he would have to move fast. "Don't worry—I always think of something," he had said to Wendy only hours ago, when they met in secret. But now that he was alone, he wasn't so sure his plan would work. Time was running out. And yet the night . . . it was unending.

Peter buried his face in his scratchy pillow and turned his thoughts to Wendy. He smirked at the thought of Connor trying to beat him up over her, the memory of Tina fuming with jealousy when she saw them together. He liked being with Wendy, especially now that her father had expressly forbidden it. Then he remembered how Wendy had hesitated, how she had shown no trace of happiness, when he had offered her the world. . . .

17

PROFESSOR DARLING'S GALA

Professor Darling had researched the *Book of Gates* and its surrounding mythology for years. He had read books, written books, given speeches, and been laughed out of half the lecture halls in Europe and the U.S. for trying to further his theories on the veracity of "the five myths." The fact that this formerly legendary, now defunct professor had gotten his hands on such an important collection of ancient artifacts did not escape the attention of the academic world. Yes, Darling was still perusing the items for clues about five absurd myths. Yes, his motives were still frivolous and questionable. But no one could deny that his exhibit was an achievement for the community. So, of course, they wanted to recognize him for his efforts— even if only to give the governor a photo op.

Shortly after the unveiling of the exhibit, Professor Darling had received phone calls from Egyptologists all over New York. One of them had come to see the exhibit for himself. Others had simply sent their regards and moved on. A small news piece had been written about the exhibit, followed by another about Darling's career.

When the article had reached the hands of the alumni association at Darling's alma mater and was published in the alumni magazine, it gained a much more privileged readership, including New York's governor, who had attended the college some years after Professor Darling and whose current education-focused campaign was sorely in need of a media boost. Professor Darling was informed that he would be given a gubernatorial prize at a special gala in honor of his contributions to the education of New York's youth.

Professor Darling hated to say good-bye to the *Book of Gates*. But the old man knew when it was time to let go. And by now, he was convinced that it was no more than a copy. Since the exhibit had come to Marlowe, Professor Darling had gone to work trying to figure out which item could possibly unlock the mysteries of the legends. Could it be the almost female death god statue—so life-like, so intrinsically tied to the underworld narrative? Could it be one of the several canopic jars—built to hold human remains and therefore the natural vessels for the mythic remains of the cursed family? Or, he had often asked himself, could it be the *Book of Gates* itself? Professor Darling, though he was a seasoned scholar, had lost the vigor and patience of the youthful researcher. He didn't read every footnote. He didn't follow every lead. He didn't dig in the back rows of the obscurest libraries or bother with the giant creaking wheel that moves the stacks back and forth to reveal the most rarely touched volumes. So, by the time Peter and the kids had found three of the bones, Professor Darling was still grappling with the question of what *form* this unlocking of secrets would take. Was the underworld a metaphor for a place on earth? Were the mummies in another country? Would the key to finding them be a map of some kind? Early on, he focused his research on the statue labeled *Neferat*—the strange female figure that could be the death goddess from the legends—deciding after many perusals that there was nothing to be found in the book, which was, at best, an ancient copy of the legendary original.

In this mistaken notion, Simon played no small part. He subtly encouraged all of Professor Darling's false assumptions.

"Yeah, that book came to us at the British Museum a couple of years ago. I think from Rome," he said one day, keeping a very casual tone as he flipped through the pages, his heart pounding with greed. "Or was it a Spanish copy? Yes, it was the Prado in Madrid."

Then, on another occasion he remarked, as he placed a small cracked bowl behind a placard, "The book was marked for permanent storage a few months ago. It was spared because the papyrus is in pretty good condition."

"Oh, is that old thing still here?" he said one afternoon as they were wrapping up for the day. "I read a paper in the Cairo Museum archives about the original being tracked to somewhere outside Alexandria."

Each time Simon made one of these comments, Darling would sigh and resign himself to the fact that his mission was proving to be a failure.

And yet Professor Darling's mind was troubled by more than just a failed theory. He had noticed a strange aura all around Marlowe. A weird presence seemed to inhabit the school, lingering just around his exhibit—possibly even making people sick. Maybe it was asbestos or dust or lead, but the new nurse was practically tubercular. She should really quit. And yesterday, as he was packing up for the day, he thought he heard a raspy groan, a muffled murmur, coming from one of the locked classrooms. . . .

Despite Wendy's nine hours a day spent in the pristine classrooms of Marlowe, despite a lifetime of mandatory birthday parties at the lush homes of her Upper East Side classmates, and despite all the years of tiptoeing around a borrowed house far above her family's means, the lobby of the Four Seasons made her stop and stare. Though the room was bustling, the sound of Wendy's shoes echoed through the vast space as her soles tapped a nervous rhythm across the chocolate-and-cream marble floor. Wendy ran her fingers along one of the massive ivory-colored columns, then followed John and her father inside, where a sign directed them to the reception. Wendy could see that her father was nervous. He almost bumped into a table holding a vase so huge that it towered above them, bursting with hundreds of blossoms in burnt shades.

The entire restaurant had been converted for the event. The dining tables, covered with silk and decorated with lily centerpieces, held place cards with the names of prominent Marlowe patrons and campaign donors. In the front of the room, a sculpture the shape of a large coral looked out onto the diners. Below the sculpture, a long table was set up with places for Professor Darling, his children, Simon, the governor, and three of her reelection campaign staff.

"Well, helllooooo, Professor Daaaarling!" cooed a slim, designer-clad woman of about fifty whom Wendy immediately recognized as the governor. She said the professor's name as if it were her pet name for him. Professor, *darling*. And Wendy, *darling*. And John, *darling*. And their *darling* assistant, Simon.

Professor Darling coughed into his hand and nodded politely to the governor. "Pleasure to be here." He made to sit down at his assigned seat.

"Oh, no, no," said the governor, taking his arm. "It's only the cocktail hour. Let's go and mingle. Show off your vast knowledge of . . . um . . . Egyptian art."

"Artifacts."

"Of course," said the governor as she pulled the professor away from the head table. "Let's walk."

Wendy could tell her father was embarrassed. No one else was seated yet. All the other guests seemed perfectly comfortable, busily mingling in small groups around the room, drinking champagne and observing one another. *He's all wrong for this,* Wendy thought, feeling a pang for her father every time he made a clumsy comment or stared timidly into his glass.

A waiter whizzed by them with a tray of drinks.

"Let me guess," said the governor as she coyly tucked a strand of hair behind her ear. "You don't do this too often." She flashed a smile and a sizable sapphire ring on her right hand. Famously single, the governor had devoted her life to politics, but, as Wendy knew, single women of fifty don't do well with the all-American family-values demographic. The governor eyed the professor's rented tuxedo, patted his arm, and began to make introductions.

Half an hour later, the professor, moderately relaxed after his third drink, was fending off strings of admiring politicos, most of whom couldn't name a single Egyptologist other than George Darling and Indiana Jones.

A waiter strutted past, brushing Wendy's hair from behind. "Salmon tart?" Wendy waved him away.

Professor Darling had started to regale the governor's friends with the story of Elan the builder when Simon interrupted with a phlegmy clearing of the throat.

"Madam Governor," he said, "it is *such* an honor that you've decided to give *us* this prestigious award. We are so very happy to be here."

"I'm sorry . . ." began the governor. "But you are?"

"Simon Grin. We met before," he said. "Curator. Director, actually. From the British Museum." When the governor didn't respond, he added, "I'm the one who brought the exhibit here."

Professor Darling coughed into his hand.

Wendy nudged John in the ribs.

The governor went back to schmoozing donors. She turned to a plump man with pasty skin and beady eyes and said, "James, I hear the merger was—"

"Actually," Simon interrupted, planting himself between Wendy and the governor, "I understand you might be needing your own curator soon, at the capitol." He winked. The governor smiled the way you would smile at someone else's child who's made a mess on your floor. Professor Darling mumbled something about not having given the governor the gift just yet.

"This is insane," Wendy whispered to John. "We can't let that book go to the capitol."

"I know," said John. "I don't want that either."

"Is that because you care about Peter's quest or because you don't want Simon to go to Albany?" Wendy asked. "Or do you finally believe me about Simon?"

John shrugged. "I just want to go back in the maze. See more stuff. Hang with Tina and the guys . . ."

"What are we gonna do?" Wendy wondered out loud. "We're gonna lose the book, and we have no way to contact Peter. And I saw something really weird outside the dorms."

"Stuffed mushroom?" Wendy heard the waiter call over her shoulder.

She shook her head and kept watching Simon. She sighed and despondently tapped her cheek with her index finger.

"Whipped duck . . . mousse . . . thing?" the waiter pressed.

"Huh?" Wendy turned and gasped.

There he was. Peter was standing in front of her in a tuxedo, a white cloth over his arm, holding a tray of appetizers. He gave a childlike grin and said, "I told you I always think of something."

Wendy finally took a moment to look around—to *really* look around. She laughed inside, thinking of all the things that people miss—things that go on all around, all the time, and escape everyone's attention, though they make all the difference. She had spent the last hour admiring the table settings, marveling at the coral sculpture, gazing with awe at the crystal chandelier that cascaded toward them like an upside-down fountain, but she hadn't seen the most obvious thing: LBs in tuxedos. They were everywhere. A flawless waitstaff, impeccable in its professionalism, each with big indulgent service-industry smiles . . . Every one of them missing that same tooth: top row, left canine.

A tall Indian boy with a feathered haircut was serving champagne to one of the investors.

A short one with red hair, freckles, and a large headset was explaining the lack of suitable vegetarian options to a woman with tight lips and an upturned nose. He nodded, turned, and called into his headset, "Valet LB12, I need Mrs. Spencer's car pulled up now."

The Marlowe principal was tossing his umbrella to a coat checker with cornrows.

Tina was behind the bar in a tiny black cocktail dress, sidling up to a famous banker as she capped a cocktail shaker and explained coyly how you make a *really* dirty martini.

"How'd you pull this off?" Wendy asked. "I mean, forget the fact that getting those spoiled boarders to *work* is by itself a miracle, but you were fired and kicked out!"

"Mad skills, that's how," said Peter. "I've had this gig lined up for weeks. Besides, Marlowe isn't running this show."

"They are so freakin' *awesome*," said John, spotting a stocky boy with a German scowl (and platinum hair to match) taking coats and unburdening a few wallets. John shook his head. "That's it, I'm joining up."

"LBs are loyal to *me*," said Peter, hardening his eyes and glaring at John. "Not to weaselly assistants who try to steal my stuff."

John ignored that.

Wendy grabbed Peter's arm and whispered, "Where have you been? You won't believe what I saw outside the dorms! I think it might be a clue about the next loc—"

"Not here," Peter warned. "We'll talk about it later."

Wendy glanced at Tina. Ever since the conversation with the nurse about Peter and Tina, she felt more confused than ever. "Where are you staying?" she demanded.

"With friends." Peter flashed a charming grin. "Off campus."

Wendy breathed out. "I don't get it," she said, happy to change the subject away from Peter's sleeping arrangements. "So none of the faculty members or parents care that you're here?" She noticed Tina looking back at her, glowering. Tina accidentally spilled half a cosmopolitan on her hand. When Peter leaned in to whisper in Wendy's ear, Tina dusted the rim of the governor's drink with salt instead of sugar.

"I'm union," Peter whispered, his lips so close that his breath made Wendy's hair flutter against her cheek. "Now, you better take a salmon tart or I'll get fired from this gig, too."

She took a tart.

"We had these jobs before your dad decided to give the book away. My guys knew the second the event was planned. And I always work the Egypt-related stuff—museum openings, book readings, fund-raisers. Have been for ages . . . I told the guys in my hall they had to learn to serve drinks or they're out. The rest of them aren't Marlowe kids. Just regular New York LBs without trust funds."

"Why didn't you tell me?" Wendy asked, feeling a pang that Tina knew.

"It didn't come up. Besides, I leave the paying gigs to the guys to handle. They run it through the network and just let me know where to be." He opened his jacket and flashed his phone. "They know what I want done . . . where I need to be."

Wendy imagined all the places Peter had been, all the cities where he had his gangs of boys, just waiting for him to show up. And in each city, it would be the same. Peter would have access to every important event; he would have his ears propped against every door, ready to hear the secrets and happenings of each major metropolis. Not because he was some big shot with money but because he knew how to become invisible, because he was the one who controlled the people you don't see: the bellboys, the valets, the waiters, and the gas pumpers. The window washers, the delivery guys, and the errand boys—the unseen eyes and ears of the world.

"Simon's been trying to weasel a job with the book," said Wendy. She wondered what Peter had planned for getting the book back. Was he just going to steal it?

"Yeah, I saw," said Peter. "Let him do it. Lucky for you, the book isn't going anywhere."

"Lucky for *us?*" asked John. "See, Wen? He doesn't appreciate anything. Besides, how do you know it's not going anywhere?"

"Because I know," said Peter, irritated. "I won't let it. And it's lucky for *you*, because I don't need to get the book back. *I* can follow that book anywhere. Let him schmooze all he wants. There isn't a job in this world I couldn't beat that moron out of."

"What about Egyptology assistant?" said John with a smirk.

Peter shrugged. "I have forty different résumés. A dozen or so degrees. Do you think anyone ever checks on that crap? People don't need verification once they love you. They'd rather just believe." Wendy bristled at that remark. It sounded like something her mother would say. Peter didn't notice. His eyes lit up as he poured John more iced tea.

Still, Wendy could tell that Peter was worried. She could tell by the way his brown eyes darted between Simon and the governor. The way he was shuffling, itching to get closer to the action but not able to for fear of being conspicuous. It was clear that Peter didn't want the book to go to Albany. And that he knew he needed their help. Wendy wished he'd just admit that, tell her that he needed her around. Instead, he texted one of his boys.

Magnus Unus: **20 on Crocodile Smile?**

LB28: **I got a 20. Head table, next to gov.**

Magnus Unus: **I know, numb nuts. Tell me what he *says*.**

Simon was finally getting somewhere with the governor. She had stopped eyeing him as though he were crazy and was laughing at one of his jokes. "Well, dear, I never *did* think of it like that." Wendy hung back, chewing her nails, spying on Simon's conversation.

John watched, fascinated, as the boys circled the room, listening and serving cheese balls.

Even after they were seated and dinner was served, Simon wouldn't shut up. He was leaning over the governor's food and whispering things in her ear, and she was lapping it up as he shamelessly complimented her on everything from her gaudy brooch to her purplish hair. Meanwhile, the amiable professor seemed oblivious to Simon's scheming. The weasel was obviously trying to step over him to get credit for the exhibit, and now he was also asking for the governor's personal recommendation for a chairmanship at the Met. Most important of all, he was asking her permission to "study" the *Book of Gates*.

Wendy eyed the book, which was on display in front of the podium. She wanted so badly to be the one to get it for Peter. But she'd never be able to get to it without everyone at the party seeing.

Simon was still going on about his credentials when Professor Darling got up and approached the governor. He whispered something to her and nodded toward the book. Wendy watched as she got up, stroked the cover of the book, and nodded several times, smiling indulgently at the professor. They were probably agreeing when in the program he would present her with the gift. She heard the governor say, "Yes . . . Grin told me of its historic importance . . . yes, thank you very much . . . on loan, of course . . ."

When her father sat down again, Wendy spied Simon lean over and say, "Madam Governor, I really think your offices could use a monthly exhibit. Reports show that incorporating art into the work environment boosts employee productivity by thirty percent. Of course, as I have been saying, you'd need a curator. We could call the position 'official curator laureate to the state of New York'. . . ."

"Nice," said John, looking over at Simon. "See, Wen? At least Simon's proactive. Instead of trying to steal the thing, he's creating his own opportunities. See?" John had one eyebrow raised as if he thought he was teaching her a really big life lesson. She was getting sick of how much John had picked up from Simon, especially in the self-important-tone category. Lately, everything was all about résumés and credentials and important titles. John had never cared about those things before. In fact, the old John would have thought those things were for posers.

Meanwhile, the governor was blabbering on, giving in to Simon's oily charms. "Oh, why, thank you, Mr. Grin, I've always been proud of my cheekbones. Ha-ha-ha. Blah-blah, ramble, yadda yadda, whatever."

Wendy couldn't even bother to register the litter coming out of the governor's mouth. But then something actually caught her attention: "Curator laureate does sound like a good idea. I'll speak to my chief of staff about it. It could help with my future campaigns. *From the Art House to the White House*. How does that sound?"

"Deliciously ambitious," chirped Simon.

Spew, thought Wendy. Then the alarming part . . .

"I'll start with a *Book of Gates* exhibit," said Simon.

"Sure, sure, whatever you like."

As the governor went back to schmoozing her donors, Simon looked back across the table at Professor Darling. He caught Wendy's gaze and smiled. He had made his move, and now Wendy could swear he mouthed "Checkmate" to her.

As Wendy mouthed back, "Loser," her dad looked up from his speech cards. Wendy buttoned it before he could catch the exchange. She tried to focus on her coq au vin.

"How are you enjoying yourself, Wendy?"

"Umm, great, Dad," said Wendy. "Good chicken."

"The situation is under control," said John from her other side.

"What?" said the professor.

"Nothing," said Wendy. "John's quoting a, um, website."

"Yeah," said John. "Adventurators dot com backslash divert your attention dot net."

Wendy turned and burned a hole into John's face with her glare. The professor went back to his note cards. "You kids and your Internets," he said.

But Wendy knew that her dad was getting sabotaged at his own gala. She had to do something. John wasn't much help. Peter was still serving drinks. Every one of the LBs (including Tina) was eyeing the book while passing canapés. Yet not a single opportunity to snatch it presented itself. So it was up to Wendy. As she watched Simon worm his way further and further into the governor's graces, she knew it had to be drastic.

If the MC got up to the podium and introduced her dad for his speech, it would be next to impossible to make a grab for the book or to figure out some way to ruin Simon with the governor. Her dad would ramble for forty-five minutes, then the night would be over. Some attendant for the governor's office would take the *Book of Gates*, Simon wouldn't let it out of his sight, and they could kiss the rest of the legendary mummies good-bye. No, she had to make her move now.

"Can I refresh your drink, miss?" Wendy snapped out of her fearful musing to see a familiar hand pouring champagne into her glass. Peter. She was about to tell him about her plan to get the book when her dad looked up from his cards and spotted Peter.

"What's this?" he said. "I thought I asked you two to stay away from him."

It bothered Wendy that her dad wouldn't even address Peter directly. Was Peter beneath him? But in true Peter fashion, he took it in stride. He patted Wendy on the shoulder and said, "Just refreshing the lady's drink," and walked away.

"I don't know what that miscreant is doing here," said the professor, "but we'll speak about this later." Wendy was boiling with anger. She wanted to scream that that *miscreant* was her friend, but she knew he wouldn't understand.

"I didn't invite him," said John.

Wendy whipped around. "Whose side are you on?" She got up from her seat, picked up her glass, and started walking toward the governor.

Wendy strolled across the podium, doing her best to put on a perfect Marlowe-girl fake smile. "Madam Governor," she squeaked, "would you sign my program?" She placed her champagne on the podium and bounced toward Simon, leaning across his body so he'd be cut off from the conversation. "Ommagosh, you are *such* a role model for our debate club. We all think the way you handled that labor union strike was totally fierce."

The governor was charmed, of course, and a bit perplexed to have such a bubbly admirer. She took out a pen and replied with some bland pleasantries.

Simon tried to horn in on the conversation, leaning awkwardly to poke his head around her. "Wendy, dear—"

"Wendy *Darling*," interrupted Wendy, keeping up her kiss-kiss tone. "My dad's the one you work for, remember?"

Her hands were shaking. She glanced at the tables of guests eating and chatting. No one was paying any attention to the young lady getting an autograph. She caught Peter's eye in the crowd. She nodded to him. He wasn't the only one with mad skills.

As the governor handed back the program, Wendy gushed, "Thanks a billion. I can't wait to show this off!" She stepped back, taking care to bump into the podium as she walked. She knocked over her glass of champagne, right on the *Book of Gates*.

A synchronous gasp from Simon, Professor Darling, and Peter brought the hubbub to a halt. Every guest, waiter, and coat checker stared as champagne soaked the ancient artifact. Professor Darling was the first to act, scooping up the book and dabbing it with his napkin. Simon wedged himself into the fray, not really being helpful.

The governor stepped to the podium and addressed the crowd. "No need to be alarmed. That was just a small gift from Marlowe, which will be presented at another time. After our Professor Darling has had a chance to take the artifact back for cleaning. No need to worry yourselves. It's just a little moisture at the edges."

"So sorry," said Wendy, secretly cheering.

"I'll give the speech, and then we'll need to take the book back home, where I can clean it," said Professor Darling.

"Maybe you kids should wait outside," said Simon, glaring at Wendy. He couldn't hide the fury in his voice.

Wendy glared back. She said, "Yeah, come on, John."

While John was off trying to find Tina, Wendy leaned on the car, staring up at the New York high-rises shining in the night.

"Nice job," said a voice a little too close.

Wendy jumped. Peter was standing right beside her.

"How do you do that all the time?" she asked.

"Skills, remember?"

"Right . . . that," she said. Even when they weren't saying anything, she felt like she was in the middle of a conversation. "Well, the book's not going to Albany," she said proudly. She was still exhilarated from what she'd done. "What now?"

"Don't worry," he said. He didn't thank her. He just leaned beside her on the car, as if he had known all along that things would work out. "You worry too much."

When he didn't say anything else, Wendy felt a pang. Connor would have thanked her. She wished Peter would just do something to make her stop doubting all she'd given up for him. "I don't worry as much as you think," she said coldly, knowing that they were no longer talking about the book. "In fact, I don't care at all."

"Don't say that," whispered Peter, feigning hurt.

Then, right there in front of the banquet hall, and all the people on the street, Peter reached out and pulled her close. He kissed her full on the mouth—no more cutesy games. His lips were warm in the chilly air. Wendy's head began swimming. Her heart started to race even faster, but she didn't care. Her mind emptied of all the worries of the past few days. She forgot about Peter's strange behavior, about Tina, about the labyrinth and Simon and her dad. She didn't wonder how many girls this strange boy had kissed or whether he would leave, the way her mother had. And best of all, she didn't second-guess giving up Connor. It was perfect until . . .

"Wendy Darling!"

Wendy's eyes flew open. Peter took a step back. Her dad was standing right there, looking irate. Wendy stumbled to explain, but Peter spoke first.

"Well, anyway, thanks. I'll see you later." He began to walk off as if this was just an ordinary greeting, a chance meeting of two old friends. He nodded to the professor.

Wendy was about to say something, explain that it wasn't Peter's fault, that she had been panicked and he had just been trying to reassure her. But right in that moment, she looked up and saw Tina, her hair a mess from the night's activities, watching from a dark alley nearby. Suddenly, all the latent worries rose to the surface again. Why had Peter stepped away from her so casually? What was Tina doing there? Had she been there this entire time? Wendy had imagined herself being kissed by Peter in front of Tina many times before. But in her dreams, it had always been a victorious moment, one of those magical movie scenes when the heroine is chosen and the vixen is cast aside. But looking at Tina's face, Wendy didn't feel like a winner. She felt like the worst kind of girl, selfish and uncaring. Maybe she had inherited this trait from her mother. Tina slinked back into the alley, the expression on her face unchanging as she disappeared.

"No, you won't," said Professor Darling. "Stay away from her, Peter!"

Wendy bit her lip. This was the first time her father had called Peter by name. Peter turned, cocked his head, and said, "Huh," as if trying to remember something. He looked Wendy up and down, then fixed his gaze on her father.

"Why should I?" he chanced, recognition flooding his brown eyes. "George . . . is it?"

Wendy gasped. Peter had *not* just called her father by his first name. Didn't he realize how much trouble she was already in? Now John, too, had joined the audience.

Professor Darling laughed and shook his head. He rubbed his hands over his balding head and said, "Because I'm asking you, Peter."

"You still have that gap in your teeth, George?" Peter said, now smiling, his arms crossed. "Of course not. Now you got a case of *old*."

John's jaw dropped.

Wendy said, "I don't get it."

Professor Darling tapped his tooth. The canine, upper left. It had always been a little bit whiter than his other teeth. "I had it fixed with my very first paycheck. Now, for old times' sake, I'm asking you to stay away from my daughter."

"I don't take orders from my boys," said Peter as he turned and started down the nearby alley, as though he knew Tina would be waiting there. "Even if they are grown and washed-up."

There was nothing Professor Darling could do. After all, Peter had done nothing wrong.

Wendy had never seen her father so angry, not even when their mom had left. And she'd never seen him so confused, so nervous. It was obvious now that her father, and Peter, and the exhibit hadn't just come together by accident or luck. And it was obvious that her father's interest in the *Book of Gates* wasn't all that he'd let on, either. Why hadn't either of them told her? She didn't say anything. John, at least, was smart enough not to make any quips. Her dad said, "Get in." She got in the car. As they drove away, Wendy wondered if Peter had kissed her only to get back at her father, whom he obviously knew from another life. Was he only using her to get back inside the labyrinth? No, thought Wendy, Peter had chosen her over Tina. He had said so himself. She thought about Peter, keeping that withered Elan toe in his pocket for such a long time. Had it been there for decades? Had it been there so long that it had kept him locked in his teenage years through generations of LBs, including her father? She tried to imagine Peter searching through the labyrinth, finding the Elan toe (and maybe much more of Elan than she knew, used up over the years) not with the help of wireless handhelds and dreadlocked LBs but with bell-bottoms and ancient walkie-talkies. And her father, her own father, might have been there. Had he been inside the labyrinth? Maybe that's why he became an Egyptologist. Maybe that's why he didn't want them involved in all this—not because Peter was trouble but because Peter was his old friend.

❖❖❖

TINA

A RECURRING THOUGHT

My mama calls me useless 'cause I won't watch her sister's
    kids
My papi *calls me from his new family's house sometimes*
My girls, Ronnie and Lia, call me the puta *'cause Lia used to*
    crush on Richard Lubenstein
Richard calls me a tease 'cause I wear what I want (for me,
    not for his stupid pizza face)
Mrs. Waxman calls me a failure of the system
Poet calls me a typical oversexed Latina
Cornrow calls me used goods (when he thinks I can't hear)
Peter calls me Tina

PROFESSOR DARLING

A RECURRING THOUGHT

I never assumed I'd have to lie and say I'm a widower to avoid the awkward conversation. I never thought I would have to raise Wendy and John by myself. I never knew you didn't have to iron jeans. I never laugh so hard as when John does his Jeopardy! *routine. I'll never know how Wendy ever came from her mother and me. I never forgot the smell of her hand cream. I suppose I'm still the never-never man.*

PETER

Peter crouched outside Wendy's window, listening, waiting for the family to come home. It was night, but Peter didn't feel anxious. He didn't feel any doubts or regrets or other night creatures creeping back into his soul. He felt happy, exhilarated, powerful. For the moment, the night didn't seem so endless. It seemed exciting, because in those last few minutes with Wendy, he had had more happy thoughts than in all the previous decades.

An Extra Shadow

Wendy fell into her bed, exhausted. Her father had just left her room after an hour of nonstop yelling. He had paced back and forth across her pink fuzzy rug, red-faced, sweating, pointing his index finger in Wendy's and John's faces. She hadn't seen him so physically wrecked since that time he'd gotten food poisoning during a dig in Egypt. He looked even worse now. His gray hair was ruffled—sad, thinning chunks poked out in every direction, woefully inadequate for the task of covering his scalp.

Through their father's entire rant, John sat quietly at Wendy's desk with his hands in his lap, picking at a torn nail and glancing at Wendy once in a while. He was trying to figure it all out in his head, to convince himself that it wasn't true—that his own dad hadn't been an errand boy for the arrogant prick. But however you looked at them, the pieces fell into place the same way. John tried to work out the math. If his dad, who was fifty-eight years old, had been a stooge for Peter when he was, say, fifteen, then that would mean that for at least forty-three years, Peter had stayed the same age. And that's the minimum, because who knows if John's dad had been in the first batch or the twentieth batch of LBs? John thought about all the old men living all over the world who had worked for Peter—all the geezers who were written off as insane or senile for telling nutty adventure stories to their grandkids. All the wrinkled old ladies who had been the sultry Tinas of Peter's past.

"Gross," said John out loud, thinking of his sister kissing someone that old. No one heard. Professor Darling was in the middle of a particularly effusive part of his speech. In the back of their car, on the way home, Wendy had nudged John and passed him a note scribbled on a gum wrapper with lipstick. *Elan. Just toe?* She had written. She didn't have to say any more. Peter had found Elan at least forty-three years ago. He must have found a whole lot more of him than that. He must have used the mummy all this time to stay young until he could find all five parts of the immortal bonedust. He must have waited for decades for the book to fall into obscurity and go somewhere unguarded, somewhere easier than the British Museum. *What a loser,* thought John, *searching for one stupid thing for all that time.*

During Professor Darling's very loud, very dramatic monologue, Wendy had interrupted to ask if their father had been with Peter when he had found the first bone. She hinted at it without giving away too much, because after all, Professor Darling had no idea that the gates of the underworld were now attached to the underside of Marlowe. He had no idea that the *Book of Gates* was the key to it all.

He just knew that the legends were real and that Peter was living proof. Of course, he couldn't tell anyone that. So he had worked and researched, trying to pinpoint the one artifact that opened the door, and talked and talked till he was old and dry and branded a kook.

"Were you there," Wendy asked carefully, "when Peter found . . . you know?"

"Wendy Darling," he shouted. "Do not interrupt me."

That was all he said.

Then, after he had gone through the full roster of their crimes (damaging a priceless artifact, embarrassing him in front of his colleagues, burdening him with extra work, and most likely catching a lip fungus) and doled out their punishment (grounded indefinitely, no television, no phones), he dropped his tired head and started to leave. But before he left, he turned to Wendy and said, "That boy is dangerous. But if you do know something . . . about what he's found . . . I would hope that you would tell me."

After a moment, Professor Darling gave a resigned nod and turned toward the door.

Before leaving, he paused momentarily, his hand on the doorknob, a look of nostalgia on his face. Slowly, a small smile crept onto his lips. "No, Wendy," he said. "I wasn't there when he found the first mummy. He had already had it for twenty years."

Wendy shot John a look, and they both sat up. Their father continued.

"But I *was* there to witness another event. Do you want to know something about your friend Peter? He is the most single-minded creature I've ever met, Wendy. He doesn't love you. He never will."

Wendy blanched. Her father had never been so cynical. Even

after her mother left, her father had assured her that Mrs. Darling still loved her children. Wendy didn't want to hear this. She didn't want to know about another person who didn't love her. Her father didn't notice the look on her face, and so he went on with his story.

"On my last day as Peter's friend—we were living in London then—Peter came to our hideout near Leicester Square, and he was raving. He turned over all the card tables. He threw things around. He basically destroyed the place. He punched my best friend in the face so hard that his nose gushed with blood. And then he turned on me. I stood up to him, of course. I asked him why he was behaving like a loony. He had just come back from the British Museum. He was very vague about what he had done. He never told us anything back then. Back then, he didn't trust any of us with the details of his mission. All he said was that he had found something he had wanted for years and that he'd lost it again. He said he'd been poking around the museum, that he had it in his hand, and that some *guard* had found him too soon. He said he dropped it and ran out and that he'd never be able to find it now. After that, I left Peter's gang. He was too dangerous, and life with him was pointless. I went back home to my parents. I wanted to do something with my life, so I went to college, and I studied Egyptology—Peter's favorite subject. Only then did I understand what Peter was doing, what his life's goal was all about. Only then did I realize that, on my last day, Peter had lost another mummy."

So now her father had left the room, and Wendy was lying on her bed in her nightgown, torn between the people she cared about most, and as emotionally spent as a sixteen-year-old can be. On the one hand, she was still riding the high of that long-awaited kiss. On the other hand, her father had been the only person she had ever really trusted. How could she lie to him now? She kept thinking about the Peter her father had described. Sure, he sounded terrible, but he had a right to be mad, after all he'd been through. Besides, after dumping Connor and hurting Tina and doing so many underhanded things that made Wendy hate herself, Wendy was not ready to believe that it had all been for the sake of a person who didn't love her—who didn't care about anyone but himself. She wasn't ready to admit that she had deluded herself about Peter. John was sitting at Wendy's computer in his pajamas, surfing the Web. "I can't *believe* it," he kept saying, over and over. Wendy closed her eyes and replayed the scene outside the Four Seasons over again in her head. She decided that, for the moment, she would just be happy. She lay back and tried to think happier, more relaxing thoughts. . . .

That lasted for exactly two minutes and fifty-nine seconds, because three minutes later, the window blew open and Peter popped his head in, looking unruffled and relaxed, as always. He straightened his hair and gave them his classic upturned nod, as though climbing to the second story of a house in New York City was as easy as walking in through the front door. Wendy jumped out of bed, and John spun the computer chair around to face Peter. They were both stunned speechless.

Peter swung his long legs over the windowsill and hopped inside, not bothering with greetings or explanations.

"All right, where is it, then?" he said.

"Are you insane?" asked John. "If our dad sees you, he'll have you arrested."

"Don't worry," he said, "because *we* are not going to get caught."

"We?" said Wendy, flush with excitement.

"As in, the three of us," said Peter. "When we steal that book and go after the fourth mummy. Come on, now—Marcus Praxis awaits!"

"We can't steal the book now!" said John in a shrill voice. "It's in my dad's room. And besides, do you know how much trouble we're in already? We're grounded till we're a hundred, and some of us don't have bonedust to make the time worthless."

"Time's not worthless to me," said Peter quietly. "I don't have all five yet."

"It looks to me like one's enough," said John. "It kept you the same for sixty years."

"I haven't stayed the same." Peter laughed. "I was thirteen when I found Elan. Now I look, what, eighteen? Without all five, growing up doesn't come to a full stop. Elan just slowed it down for me." He looked at John's face, still hard and unsure. Then he added, "Come on, man, I need your help. I can't do it without *the Johnny.*" He took out his handheld and shook it in front of John like an invitation.

For once, John didn't make a smart-mouthed comment. He looked around for a while, searching for an answer, and then said, "Fine."

A few hours later, long after Professor Darling had fallen asleep, Peter convinced Wendy and John to climb out the window in their pajamas (much less suspicious in case Professor Darling woke up) and sneak into their father's room from the window ledge. Outside, the sky was clear, and Wendy could see a few scattered stars. She could see all the way down the street, where people were darting in and out of houses, attending dinner parties, going to the movies, or just returning home from work. As the trio stepped over the windowsill onto the thin ledge outside their house, Wendy glanced inside at her unmade bed, the comfortable yellow light of her bedroom. What was she doing climbing out the window with Peter? Boyfriends weren't supposed to lure you into a life of crime. Connor had never gotten her into trouble once. In fact, she was pretty sure her grades had gone up during the time she was with him (lots of study time during games). Those thoughts made her want to go back and put an end to this craziness. But then she thought about how much they had accomplished together. She thought about how without her Peter wouldn't have found the second bone, or the third, and about how quickly her confusion had left her when Peter had kissed her right in front of everyone. And she thought about Simon, how he was probably scheming to get the book right now, so he could build a glorious career. He might break into their house tonight or steal the book tomorrow. Or he might be waiting for them at Marlowe, knowing that they would go looking for the fourth item. She thought again about how Peter had kissed her, and how he would kiss her again. And knowing all that, how could she possibly say no?

That night, as George Darling fell asleep, he thought he saw his children playing outside, like they used to do when they were little. He saw their shadows running after each other under the yellow glow of streetlights. They had grown up so fast. Soon they would be running away for good. He dreamed that they were in his room, rifling through his drawers like they used to do, when they thought he was hiding candy from their health-conscious mother. *No,* he thought, *those days are over. They can never come back. I can never stop them from growing up.* He felt useless, helpless, powerless—a never-never man down to his aging, porous bones. Under the drunken haze of deep sleep, Professor Darling thought he saw the children take something. *Ah, they've found my candy stash, then. No harm in a little treat every now and then,* he thought, turning groggily in his bed. But then, his eyes heavy with sleep, he imagined that he saw a third figure, an extra silhouette . . . And then, the shadows of three fugitives escaping into the night.

At night, Marlowe was dark and looming, like an ancient fairy castle full of secrets and ghosts that are afraid of the sun. But none of them noticed the chill in the air, the flicker of lamps on the lawn, or the pitch-black hallways. They had the book. They were running away, in their pajamas, having just committed grand theft from the British Museum, the Marlowe School, and the state of New York. And those were just the institutions. What about the donors? The board members? The shareholders? Trying to name all the powerful people they had just robbed would take all night.

Wendy felt a rush as she clutched the *Book of Gates.* Simon could be anywhere. Had he followed them? There were faint lights coming from some of the classrooms.

On the way to Marlowe, the three of them had frantically tried to figure out where the fourth bonedust would be.

"Peter, I have to tell you what I saw," said Wendy. "There were two Eyes of Ra outside the boys' dorm."

"Can't be," said Peter distractedly.

"Why not?" said Wendy, hurt that he was dismissing her information so quickly.

"You must have imagined it, Wendy," said Peter, "because the eye appears only where there's a gate. It's not a clue."

"Can't we at least consider it?" Wendy demanded, suddenly not caring about the quest, only wanting Peter to listen to her. But Peter just ignored her and went on with his questions. Marcus Praxis was a Nubian warrior. . . . Where did that lead? John suggested something related to the military, or to horses. But Peter rejected both.

"I tried those things when the underworld was attached to the British Museum. I got to a battlefield through an exhibit on the history of warfare and to a Nubian camp through a display about horses, but it wasn't in either of those places."

"This is the part I don't get," said John. "Marlowe doesn't have stuff like that. How does the labyrinth match up crazy stuff like that with the school?"

"It just does," said Peter. "It always finds a way."

Their collective nervousness was feeding on itself, and every two seconds one of them snapped at the others. All three of them were growing more and more rushed and agitated. They knew that with every passing second they came closer to getting caught.

Wendy suggested they look for clues relating to Hurkhan.

"What about something to do with fathers?" she said.

"Where would *that* lead us?" snapped Peter.

"I don't know," said Wendy angrily. "But the story was mostly about Marcus Praxis and his dad. So why not start somewhere like that?"

Peter shook his head. They arrived in the main hallway and sat down next to a row of lockers. Peter rested his head in his hand, and John was changing position every five minutes—that is, when he wasn't pacing. Wendy just brooded.

"Can you stop that?" Wendy snapped when John began mumbling to himself while zigzagging the width of the hallway. "You're driving me crazy."

"I can't help it," said John.

"Simon's coming, you know," said Peter, his voice showing a hint of tension. "That nerdling is gonna come marching in here any second, and we've got no clue where to go."

John didn't say anything.

Wendy couldn't hold back her frustration any longer. "If you're not going to listen to me, then I don't care about this stupid quest anymore. I want to go home."

"*What?*" Peter said.

"You heard me," said Wendy.

"Yeah," said John.

"I can't believe what I'm hearing," said Peter, his voice strained. "Can't you guys see that this is just because of *her*? She's poisoning your mind so you'll quit the search. Wendy." He went up to her and tried to hold her in his arms. "Hey, now. What's the matter?" His voice was calm now, and he kissed her cheek. "You're not gonna abandon me now? I mean, now that I'm fired, we can be official. You know . . . you can be my girlfriend."

John snorted and mumbled something.

Wendy smiled and let Peter hold her. "OK," she said, feeling a rush of certainty—that wonderful feeling that comes with knowing for sure. Peter was right. They weren't at their best now. She knew that under this kind of pressure, with this kind of rush, they were bound to make mistakes. And she really did want to help him.

"I've got it!" said John suddenly.

"No, you don't," Peter mumbled into Wendy's hair.

"Yeah, I do," John insisted. "We're supposed to focus on what the person lost, right? Harere's hiding place was tied to her lost identity. So I think we need to focus on what Praxis lost. What did the people call Praxis when he was at the height of his glory?"

Wendy looked up. "I have my notes from the legend in my locker. I'll just go and see—"

But Peter didn't need Wendy's notes. *"Pharaoh builder,"* he said. *"God maker."*

"That's right," said John. "Now, imagine if the world was all about a person's accomplishments, like it should be. Imagine if people were judged by what they did, not by their family or their looks or whatever. Then what would his rightful place be?"

"As the pharaoh," whispered Peter, his eyes wide with satisfaction.

They sat quietly by the lockers, thinking about the story. Marcus Praxis had lost more than even *he* had known. He should have reached heights that he probably could never fathom, given his upbringing. They tried to think of places in Marlowe where a man who should have been pharaoh might live.

"Principal's office," said Wendy.

"Worth a try," said Peter. "He's the guy that runs this place."

So they ran to the headmaster's office. Peter picked the lock but didn't open the door—not until after the book had been opened, the name of the hour had been said, and the Eye of Ra appeared on the threshold. Then he looked at John and Wendy and nodded. All three stepped into the abyss just beyond the cookie-cutter image of the headmaster's room, with its mahogany desk and leather chair.

An hour later, they were back in the hallway, disappointed and even more pressed for time. Each time any of them heard the slightest movement, the rustling of a discarded piece of paper or a gust of wind, they jumped, thinking it was Simon—or worse.

"You know what?" said Wendy, pacing. "I think we got the leader thing all wrong. I mean, at Marlowe the headmaster isn't really the leader, is he? He barely has any power, and nobody respects him. Praxis wasn't powerful because he had a job title. He was just this awesome warrior."

Just then, John got up from the floor and ran a few feet down the hall, yelling over his shoulder as he went. "You're totally right, Wen. We need to find the biggest stud in Marlowe—the person everyone worships."

"Where are you going?" asked Wendy.

John stopped in front of the trophy case. Dozens of golden trophies, tributes to Marlowe's athletic prowess, sparkled behind the glass. Each morning, the trophy case was polished. Each week, visitors and potential donors were brought to marvel at it. Every day, students passed it and were reminded of Marlowe's talents and achievements.

Well, not so much Marlowe's talents and achievements as *Connor Wirth's*.

Almost every trophy had his name on it. Every few inches,

photos of him accepting awards were tucked beside gold medals.

"Connor Wirth is Marlowe's Marcus Parxis," said John. "He's the real leader—the pharaoh without a title."

For a brief second, Wendy was overcome with pride. But then she remembered that she had no reason to be. She had given up Connor. "So you think we should go through the trophy case?" said Wendy, dreading the idea of breaking that massive lock.

"No way," said Peter as he jogged toward John. "We're looking for Praxis's house or his tomb or something. We need a space that *belongs* to Connor. Which one is his locker?"

The trio rushed to Connor's locker, forgetting to look around for prying eyes or to speak in hushed voices. Peter yelled out the name of the hour before he had even reached the metal door, breaking the flimsy lock with a hard kick as soon as he saw the eye.

Tick-tock. Simon stood in a narrow hallway around the corner from Connor's locker. He waited and tapped his foot, checking his multiwatch every two minutes. By now, Simon had read all the literature in that forgotten shelf of the Egyptology Library. He hadn't been rushed or scared of getting caught. All night, he had been brainstorming and puzzling out clues, with his mind as sharp and clear as the day he took his college entrance exams. It had taken him very little time to figure out that Marcus Praxis would have a Marlowe counterpart. In fact, he had had that part down way before the gala. After all, every place has someone that's revered above all others. It did take Simon days to figure out who that was, though. His attempts at information gathering led nowhere, particularly because his preferred approach was to yell across the crowded hall, "Hey, you, pea brain. Who's the coolest kid at school?" In the end, he had to pay two hundred bucks to a group of cheerleaders for a copy of their *Hot or Not* poll (he forced himself not to comment on their biased data and their infantile calculations).

Now Simon was waiting in the corridor, holding a wooden box, waiting for the Darlings and Peter to arrive with the book. When they opened the locker, he would wait until they disappeared and then follow them. The fourth mummy was here—beyond that bikini-clad bimbo taped to the metal door. Simon was sure of it. He could almost feel it.

He closed his eyes and tried to imagine what it would be like to be famous. He would be on TV, of course—that was a given. He'd need a bigger apartment, and a fancy office. Simon's daydream about the honorary diplomas he would receive from all the colleges that had rejected him was interrupted when he heard Peter kick off the lock. He clutched his box and followed. A moment later, he was standing on a sand dune, with more dunes all around him and pyramids dotting the horizon. As always, the air was stifling, as if all this openness was happening somewhere underground. He turned around to see three figures running away from him into the distance, toward the largest pyramid.

"Stupid kids!" he said, and began chasing them, his box clutched to his chest. He ran through the sand as quickly as his new sneakers would allow, but still the box weighed him down. He was sweating profusely, cursing and spitting as he heaved his feet out of the sand with each labored step. The whole place was dark and musty. It smelled like old gym socks, making it even more unbearable down here. He passed many tombs, pyramids of all sizes collected under the umbrella of the giant pyramid. Simon knew what this was. He had already studied it, read every word of the fourth legend in three different languages, hunting for clues about the guardian. He knew who it was. He knew what form it would take. He knew how to beat it. He tilted his head and let out a bemused sigh, slightly curious how the children would fare under the shadow of the ghost. Finally, he arrived at the biggest pyramid, the one at the center, where Peter and the Darling children were surely in for a surprise. He took two steps forward, unafraid, grasping on to the box with all his strength.

Then, before he had taken a third step, he saw her.

Peter, Wendy, and John stood clutching one another's arms, staring, mesmerized, into the guardian's massive gray eyes. She was as tall as the pyramid, white-faced, with a robe of all white and a five-pointed star on her head. She hovered in front of the pyramid, partly solid, partly carried by the wind. A strong smell hovered around her. It was the smell of death and loss and ancient bones.

Then, in a second, she was gone, replaced by gust after gust of wind. A massive sandstorm smashed into them, driving them to their knees. Every inch of exposed skin felt grated and raw. They had to cover their faces and lie flat on the sand, hoping that the storm would subside before they were buried alive.

Then Simon arrived. The noise was deafening, but he didn't seem bothered by any of it. In fact, he made a point of stepping over the three kids as he approached the ghost-guardian. When he stepped forward, she turned her attention from the children and wrapped her body around Simon, whipping around him and creating a wind tunnel, as though she were made of dust particles. As the three watched, Simon walked directly into the center of the storm.

"Simon!" John shouted. The sound was almost lost in the storm. It didn't matter, anyway. None of them could move, or even stand.

"I hate that guy!" growled Peter.

Simon cleared his throat loudly and shouted into the sandstorm.

"I have a gift!" he screamed.

The wind stopped.

The ghost of the white woman disappeared. And then she appeared again, a regular-size person, not transparent but corporeal and wearing a sandy tunic that looked dirty and timeworn. Her face was no longer terrible, but striking—ominous in the most ravishing way. Her skin was porcelain-white, her hair jet-black, her eyes a deep, piercing gray.

"*What* is that idiot doing?" Peter asked no one in particular. They were still pinned to the ground. The sandstorm had quieted a little, but they knew it would pick up again if they stood up or moved forward.

The woman nodded to Simon, and he placed the wooden box at her feet. A heavy wind continued to twist around her body.

"Why is he talking to it?" John wondered aloud. "Hey, who in the story do you think—?"

"Praxis's wife," whispered Wendy, remembering what Layla had been called in the story: *an unstoppable force: a windstorm.* "Who else would be here? This is his house now."

With his eyes dejectedly on Simon, Peter began mumbling a part of the legend, which, like most of the stories in the *Book of Gates*, he had committed to memory. *"It is said, only in the quietest corners of the city, that beautiful Layla, who died soon after her marriage to Amun-Ra, wanders the dead city to this day, searching the intricate maze . . ."* He sounded positively mournful. Wendy wondered if this was partly the effect of the labyrinth—the way it crept into your soul and sucked the joy out of you.

"We should have looked at the passage more carefully," said Peter, "like we did with Harere. It says, she wanders the *maze*. I just assumed . . . I mean, in the story it sounds like she's wandering around the city after her husband's death. But the city isn't a maze. The underworld is. There was nothing about her ghost. . . ."

"I didn't even notice that word when I heard the story," John admitted.

"I can't believe I let this happen," said Peter, his voice shaking and angry.

"We were rushed," said Wendy. She touched his arm and smiled weakly. "We were in a huge rush this time around. There wasn't any time to read it carefully like with Harere."

"I've read that story a hundred times," whispered Peter.

"Whatever," said Wendy. "Maybe Simon figured out who she is, but that doesn't mean he'll get past her. She's a *guardian*, plus she's Amun-Ra's angry wife. She's not going to just hand over the bones. . . ."

Simon was bowing low before Layla now. "Will you accept my gift?"

Layla nodded again, and he opened the box.

Inside were four beautifully carved wooden jars: a baboon, a man, a falcon, and a jackal.

"What's he doing with canopic jars?" said John.

The other two watched silently as the woman ran her finger down each of the jars. As she picked up each one, Simon presented the gift with flourish and fanfare.

"The human, representing the South, to contain the liver. The baboon, representing the North, to contain the lungs. The falcon, representing the West, to contain the intestines. And finally, the jackal, representing the East, to contain the stomach."

"To store whose stomach?" asked Wendy.

"Marcus Praxis's?" John guessed.

"Can't be," said Peter. "His organs were removed by Hurkhan, remember? Then he made the mummy as a trophy."

Layla took the four jars in her arms and cradled them like babies. She brought them to her face and touched them gently, as if they really did contain her husband's remains. She bent over them, mesmerized. Then she began shedding tears into the jars.

"I thought I could just fight them all off." Peter shook his head angrily. "I never thought about . . ." He trailed off, then sighed loudly and rubbed his face with both palms. "The story says that Layla roams the maze, *looking for a token of her beloved.*"

"How the heck did he decipher that?" shouted Wendy. "How did he know what token she was looking for?"

"It's another injustice we missed," said John, impressed. "He was mummified, so his organs *should* have been preserved in the jars. The empty jars mean something to her!"

As Layla dropped to her knees and began losing herself in

the inspection of the jars, Simon slipped into the pyramid.

"No way," said Peter. He got up to run after him. John and Wendy followed. But before they could cross the threshold of the pyramid, the wind kicked up again and they heard a scream pierce the air. Layla had risen up, still holding the jars, and was taking back her ghostly form—a shadow on the pyramid's side. She turned to face them, stabbing them with her terrible gaze. Then she stirred the sand around them, keeping them back, while Simon was left free to search the pyramid.

For what seemed like twenty or thirty minutes they struggled. They tried to crawl on their bellies to go past her, to run into the wind with all their strength. None of it worked. They struggled until they were exhausted and parched and coughing out sand.

"Can you pull away?" Peter shouted at the others. It was almost impossible to hear one another over the wind and Layla's mournful cries.

Wendy stepped back, and to her surprise, she easily broke free from Layla's grasp. "Hey, yeah," she said. "Just step backward."

But no matter how much they pulled, John and Peter couldn't break free.

They were still battling Layla when Simon emerged from the tomb, a bandaged leg strapped to his backpack.

"No!" Peter called as he attempted to run after Simon. But the wind had formed a funnel around him and John, and Simon was long gone before they were finally able to break free.

PETER

Peter stalked the halls of Marlowe in the dead of night. He didn't seem bothered by the cameras. As he strolled, he took a path that eluded the gaze of every single one.

Last night, he had barely made it out of the labyrinth. If Wendy hadn't broken free from the ghost Layla, run back through the gate, and brought a canopic jar from the exhibit to throw into the wind, he and John could never have gotten away. Once again, she had saved him. But what did it matter? Simon had the fourth bone.

Wendy had replaced the *Book of Gates* in Darling's bedroom late last night, after their trip into the labyrinth. By the morning, the book was in a dehydrator in Professor Darling's office, and the old man was none the wiser.

Peter stopped at the door to Professor Darling's office. He slipped in the key and opened it without a problem. During the governor's gala, the valet had made copies of every key in the professor's key chain. Peter strolled into the room. The orange light of the dehydrator caught his attention immediately. He didn't turn on the lights but walked straight to the device. The book sat under the lamp, slowly drying.

He gazed at the book wistfully. Until now, no one in the history of the world had come as far as Peter had. But now Simon had the fourth bone and was probably gunning for the fifth. Peter would have to go in again. He had already promised John and Wendy that they would wait until the book was returned to the exhibit. Then they would go back for one final journey into the labyrinth— together. They would find the fifth mummy and get the fourth batch of bonedust back from Simon. Wendy was eager to help him; Peter knew that. And she had already been so useful. He liked Wendy. She brought him good luck and happy thoughts. But Peter didn't really want her there for the fifth mummy. He didn't want her to see what he was willing to do to get the fourth bonedust back from Simon. Besides, what is a promise when a whole life's work is at stake?

Peter would have to find the location in Marlowe that coincided with the fifth and final gate. All these years, and there were still parts of the labyrinth that he had never seen. But he couldn't start now. He had to wait for the Egyptian night to begin. Tomorrow, Peter thought, he'd have to make the best use of the time he had. He'd have to be quick and do most of his work while the Marlowe kids (John and Wendy included) were in class. Everything would be so much easier that way.

The only noise was the low hum of the dehydrator and Peter's cavalier humming. He gathered up the book, carefully laid the copy he had stolen from the New York Public Library in its place, and walked out.

INTERLUDE

THE DARK

Let him come, whispered the Dark Lady, her branded eye flashing in rage. *Let him come and take it from me.*

The diminutive nurse stood in front of the pyramid. She would have looked harmless if the ghost of Layla wasn't on her knees before her, pleading for her to return the canopic jar.

The fourth bonedust had been lost, but not to the boy; to the foolish fortune hunter, the one the darkness had overlooked. With her nurse's eye, she had assessed Simon Grin as nothing more than a nuisance. A pawn to manipulate John away from Peter. A distraction and an obstacle for the children. The Dark Lady hated to be wrong. She despised the frailties of humanity. It was like being blind and deaf and dumb; being ordinary was the worst of all curses. But soon Peter would have to return for the fifth and final bone. Soon he would have to descend to the farthest depths of the pyramid, to death's own chamber.

The branded eye flashed again. The nurse coughed. The ghost of Layla howled with pain. The desert wind stole the breath from her mouth.

PETER

Peter screamed and sat bolt upright. After pacing Marlowe all night, waiting for the Egyptian night to begin, he had dozed off in a small room somewhere on the first floor. He couldn't help it; he had been so tired these past few days. He opened the door of the room a crack and peered outside. The school was so different now, since the exhibit had been here. It seemed so much older, dirtier, more oppressive to the senses. Everything seemed to move in a slow, eerie way. And yet nobody seemed to notice. The change had been so gradual.

He wiped his brow. He couldn't stop panting. It didn't feel like a dream this time. It felt like something was calling to him, inviting him to come closer.

Come and take it from me, the voice told Peter.

He could feel her breath on his face. He could feel her claws around his throat. He felt her cold fingers grabbing his chin the way she used to do when she lived in his parents' house and governed his every move. When she would punish his bad behavior by threatening him with the hook. Those noiseless steps. That hunched back. Those moth-eaten clothes. Each time he heard the voice, he felt a pain in his chest, as if his body was desperate to be away from her and yet was begging him not to go.

But he was so close now. And unless he finished this, he would never sleep soundly again. Unless he went back into the labyrinth, the night would never end.

19

THE FIFTH LEGEND

Professor Darling called a specialist to inspect the exhibit items for damage. Perhaps it was excess moisture. Perhaps it was the recent atmospheric problems at Marlowe, all the leaks and infestations. It seemed that overnight a statue labeled *Neferat* had become eroded beyond recognition. And the nurse's office, too, had been blanketed in a mysterious layer of mold in just one night.

Professor Darling didn't hear the sixth-period bell ring. It was late afternoon, and he looked haggard with worry. He was pacing behind his desk, flipping through papers, once in a while stopping to scratch his chin or adjust his tie. He wasn't sure what was wrong. Nothing had actually gone wrong since the governor's gala two days before. The *Book of Gates* was drying in the dehydrator. The children had been remarkably well behaved and had even stayed away from Peter. And best of all, neither of them had pushed him to dredge up painful old memories from his LB days. They had left a sensitive situation alone, exactly as they had done when their mother left.

Despite all this, Professor Darling paced in front of his classroom, trying to figure out what this nagging feeling at the pit of his stomach could be. Simon was nowhere to be found, but that could be expected. It had been quite obvious that Simon was trying to win a spot as the governor's personal curator. When the book was finally sent to Albany, Simon would probably go, too, chasing better opportunities with more important people.

"Professor Darling," said Marla, now sitting in the front seat.

"Yes," said the professor absentmindedly.

"Are you gonna start class or what?"

"Ah, yes, of course. Thank you, Marla." He rifled through his notes and papers, scattering them across his desk until he came across the item he was looking for—his favorite English translation of the *Book of Gates*. It was his personal copy, printed about fifty years ago and bought secondhand when he was still a university student. It was full of his notes from over the years. He began to leaf through it, reading his musings on the mysteries of the fifth legend.

When Professor Darling didn't begin the lecture right away, Wendy sat up, threw a worried glance at John, and asked tentatively, "Are you OK, Dad?" Her voice was overly concerned, a trait she had developed toward her father when her mother left.

Wendy tried to find Peter's shadow, some sign of him listening at the window, but he wasn't there. Even though he was usually out of sight, huddled under the window frame so that they never really saw him, Wendy was sure that he wasn't there this time. She hadn't been able to find him since they had lost the fourth bone to Simon.

"Hmm . . . yes," mumbled the professor, pulling himself together. "I was just thinking about the fifth legend. It's very different from the others, in my opinion." He held up his book, with its yellowed pages and scratched leather cover. "It's so vague. There's so much that's hidden from us. Of course, all of them were passed down by word of mouth, but this one . . . this legend is the one that was thought to carry the biggest curse, and so people rarely repeated it. Most of it has been lost, and it's the one most shrouded in mystery . . . the one with the highest stakes."

"So who was the mummy?" asked Marla. "What was it that he lost?"

"Everything," said the professor as he cracked open the book. "An entire kingdom."

"Isn't that what Marcus Praxis lost?" asked John.

"In a way . . ." said the professor, turning the tissue-thin pages. "In fact, you could say that what Praxis lost was more important. Being erased from history is a loss far more profound than power or riches." He stopped and looked into the mesmerized faces of his students. Their newfound enthusiasm always brought a smile to the professor's lips. He lowered his voice dramatically, "Still, the fifth legend trumps them all. Because in this case, the injustice carried ripples."

"What does *that* mean?" asked Marla.

"In this final legend, we are introduced to a fascinating new character—a woman, unique because of her position as a mere servant. It is *very* unusual for a servant to be named and described to such an extent in a legend dating back thousands of years, especially one that is already so vague. This woman, this *nursemaid,* has fascinated scholars for years."

The students were sitting up now. Handhelds were put away. Portable games retreated into pockets.

"The nursemaid, a peasant woman called Neferat, is important to our story because she is said to have been one of the earliest political manipulators in history. Before Svengali, before Rasputin, Wolsey, or Lady Marlborough, she saw power in the hands of those she served, and she grabbed it for herself. Still, she escaped notice until later, when people began to whisper about something they had heard. Words said casually that, years later, seemed very sinister indeed." Professor Darling stopped to read the words from his notes. He licked his lips and read slowly. "*'Ripples,'* she said. *That is what I like. That is what I look for.'*" He looked up again and continued with a grin, knowing what he would say next would capture their attention. "So the legend was passed along, spreading the idea that the nurse was otherworldly—a servant of the underworld."

Wendy considered the name Neferat. It sounded familiar. And all this stuff about ripples . . . had she heard it somewhere before? Lately, a lot of details seemed to escape her memory.

Then her father added, "We have a statue of the girl Neferat . . . it is very eroded, but . . . some people think she carried the soul of the Dark Lady from the stories." Wendy remembered seeing the statue. It was the one with the missing alabaster eye.

"I don't get it," said Marla. "What are these ripples that make it such a big deal?"

"Ahh," said the professor. "I was just getting to that. You see, it wasn't just one person who was wronged in this final story. It was the entire kingdom. According to oldest lore, the king who lost his throne would have been great. But the one who overthrew him was the worst kind of evil. And so, as is always the case with despots, there was bloodshed. There was injustice enough that the whole of Egypt festered with it—and it was all carried in the bones of this one wronged king whose soul suffered for all the torment caused by his own youthful foolishness. . . . How's that for a satisfying capstone?"

The Fifth Legend

There is so much that is precious between a king and his kingdom. If a country is deprived of a good and just ruler, if a cursed family is robbed of its one shot at redemption and true greatness, if a rightful monarch is overthrown and replaced by one much less deserving, changing the course of history forever, then a bitterness builds inside many hearts and across many lives.

So ends the story of one family with a curse on its line, of Elan's dark legacy, full of the cruelest injustices. The house that cannot die will come to its mortal end. This is the story of the last member of the cursed family—a family whose children no longer walk among the living yet continue to clench life from among the dead. Their stolen lives linger on, still flowing in their bones. Life has been mummified inside them, forming an ever-living bonedust—a new kind of immortality.

Layla and Marcus Praxis left behind a daughter, a girl who was talented as well as beautiful and who lived in the house of the pharaohs. Growing up in splendor, she learned the ways of a noble life, passing on her skills and beauty to her own daughter and to her granddaughter after that. For seven generations, Layla's female descendants grew more talented, more accomplished, and even more breathtaking. Soon, in the streets of Egypt, the family name began to take on a new meaning. Hurkhan's tribe of beasts gave way to Layla's line of beauties, each of whom displayed a grace and charm unmatched in her generation.

Each of the women thrived in her own unique way, impressing court and country with new talents, and each made making a more advantageous marriage than her mother. If one girl married an army general, her daughter would better her by marrying a member of the high council. And so it was until one day, seven generations later, one of Layla and Marcus Praxis's descendents married a pharaoh.

In the meantime, another branch of the cursed family lingered beneath the surface of public life, unseen, unheard. Brooding. For while Marcus Praxis's line bore good and beautiful children, Hurkhan's other descendents were deprived of accomplishments, accolades, and attention— a deficit that, though it cannot create evil, can certainly bring to the surface any evil that is already within.

In this branch of Hurkhan's line lived a girl called Neferat.

She was of a middling stature, with forgettable looks and a feeble frame. Her face was too pale. Her hair too dull. And she had a strange defect in her left eye, a pupil broken like old papyrus. The eye was blue like the Nile. Despite this lack of beauty, Neferat was confident, walking proudly as though she had chosen her every flaw. She ignored the cruel rants and petty taunts, the other women who called her a witch and a conjurer.

She did not join in her family's jealous rants when the pharaoh chose her beautiful cousin as his queen.

Instead, Neferat became a servant in that woman's household.

This story begins deep in the chambers of the pharaoh's women, where Neferat went to claim her destiny, and where the seeds of hate sprouted and choked the house of the god-king, changing Egypt's history forever.

"'This story begins deep in the chambers of the pharoah's women,'" Peter recited from memory. After stealing the book, he had spent the night lurking around Marlowe, counting down the hours until the Egyptian sunset, when the gates would be open once again. Now that everyone was tucked away in sixth period, he'd have plenty of time to explore. "Chambers of the women . . ." he said again, a sly grin on his lips. He looked this way and that, made sure no one was following, before slipping into the girls' bathroom in the main corridor of Marlowe, the *Book of Gates* tucked under his arm.

Neferat proved herself a capable nursemaid for the many children of the pharaoh's court. She rose in ranks among the servants until she was the chief nurse, the one most trusted by the pharaoh. She watched the children closely, taking note of their flaws and talents. Soon, she chose a favorite, the young daughter of a minor noble and his foreign wife, a girl who had lived in the palace since birth. The girl wasn't beautiful or

charming, but she was clever, and even at the girl's young age, Neferat could see her ambition and cunning.

Within a few years, the pharaoh's wife became pregnant. She gave birth to a long-awaited son and heir, the one who would become pharaoh and ruler to all his brethren. The older children of the court burned with jealousy.

Neferat looked at the boy, now one of her own charges, and saw at once his enduring goodness and potential. She had heard the stories about her cursed family. She knew that a great pharaoh from Elan's line could redeem them all, wash away all the injustice and allow her ancestors to rest in peace. She realized that she did not wish for redemption to come through him, if at all. He won't be clever enough to rule, *she thought.* Goodness isn't enough to merit the throne of Egypt. *Then she thought of the so-called curse on her four ancestors and thought,* How dare anyone say that we need redemption. *These thoughts ran through Neferat's wicked mind when the pharaoh's son was brought to her, the most skilled of the nursemaids, to raise and nurture.*

"Ex-CUSE me? But this is the girls' room?" said a squeaky-voiced girl with big eyes and a blond bob. She was only applying lipstick, but apparently this was a sacred ritual.

"Relax," said Peter. "I won't tell anyone your lips aren't naturally fire-engine red."

"Get out!" the girl shouted, hands on hips, right above her low-riding uniform skirt.

Peter laughed to himself, then pushed open one of the stalls and said, "No, but really, you should leave. This could get messy."

❖❖❖

It was during this time in her life that Neferat's ill will and ruthless intentions filled up her body and spilled out into the world. As the pharaoh's son, Seti, grew older, his nursemaid writhed with fury over the splendor bestowed upon him—and the growing innocence and sweetness with which the boy responded. She watched the nobles of the land shower him with gifts and praise. She observed as fortune-tellers and soothsayers predicted that he would bring great prosperity to their land—and warned that a great shadow hung over his head. All the while, she groomed her own favorite, whispering ideas in her ear, planting thoughts of treachery in her mind, raising her to believe that she, an ambitious commoner, could be a god-queen, ruling over all of Egypt.

She built into the girl's heart a sense of entitlement and greed. Those who knew her said that Neferat was evil, bewitched by bad spirits, greedy and malicious—that she was possessed by a spirit much older than her body, coming after the cursed family once more. They said that she taught the girl her wicked ways and that she used her devil eye to bore deep into her soul and corrupt her to the core.

This is the story of Seti, the true pharaoh, who might have brought the cursed family such greatness that its effect would have been felt across even the previous generations. It would be triumph and justice enough to redeem all their bitterness—a reawakening of crushed souls. What would have come of having a great and benevolent pharaoh rise up from the cursed family? Would Elan the builder have let his bitterness go if he had fathered a line of kings? Would Garosh the monster have forgotten his lost love? Would Harere have stopped mourning? Would Praxis's soul have moved on? Perhaps . . . but none of them ever had a chance, for

Seti, the hope of all Egypt, was cut down and replaced by a most powerful queen.

Peter stood outside two palaces at the very center of the labyrinth. He chose the smaller of the two: the one belonging to the wife of the pharaoh and her children. *A person who'd had his kingdom stolen away wouldn't belong in the big one,* he thought. *He'd belong in the home of his childhood . . . the women's chambers, where the story begins.*

Later in Seti's life, when his father, the pharaoh, died and he took the throne, the people remembered the prophecies and expected great things. But Seti, acting as a playboy king, unconcerned with anything beyond his own amusement, disappointed them all. He was not wise enough or cunning enough to stand up to his advisers. He was distracted, not as clever as a god-king should be. Besides all that, he rarely said more than a few words. He spent his days in amusement, forgetting his position and responsibilities. He was weak and malleable, and soon he became nothing more than a vessel for his advisers.

The treasury was plundered by the pharaoh's greedy ministers, each of whom guided the pharaoh's hand as he approved their many requests. Seti himself did nothing but feast, laugh, and play, shirking his responsibilities to the people.

His seal was placed on a great many decrees in which he had no part.

He passed a great many laws of which he had no knowledge.

Soon, Seti's mother discovered the abuses and excessive privileges of her son's so-called helpers. She tried to step in and rule the nation in his place, claiming that since she was a member of the royal family, she could wield the pharaoh's seal on his behalf. Seti openly agreed to this plan, for he loved his mother and took her counsel above any other. He was happy to be free from the responsibilities of government.

Only a day later, Seti's mother was murdered in the night. Seti, too simple to suspect his own ministers or nursemaid, mourned for many days. That is when Neferat placed her favorite in the sight of the pharaoh. Having been his nursemaid since his birth, Neferat was loved and trusted by Seti. He did not question Neferat's motives when she told him to allow the girl to take his mother's place in his heart.

When Neferat engineered a union, the ministers did nothing to keep her favorite from becoming queen. Egypt was shocked by the strange marriage. People talked of Neferat's influence over the couple. Soon, rumors of the supernatural began to surround the new queen. Neferat had taught her special ways—of thinking, of behaving, and of keeping her people loyal. The queen did not shy away from Neferat's experiments in the mystical world.

One night, the queen was spotted in a private moment by her personal guards, who whispered rumors to their own families. When the queen's servants and handmaids left her chambers, satisfied that she had retired for the day, she made her way to her hidden pyramid, a secret hiding place that her mother had built. Here, she knelt like a common pauper and dug her hidden treasures out of the ground, dozens of vials of colorful liquid. Here, in this dark, damp pyramid, in a hole dug in the dirt, she mixed together a bubbling, writhing bath the color of blood. She lowered herself into this pit without ceremony, forgetting that she was royalty, that she was wallowing in dirt and excrement like a street urchin. This dark world required no fanfare. And so she closed her eyes, determined to bear the pain of the bath, a solution whose cleansing sting she craved daily now. A potion that blinded and mesmerized her people, bound them to her like opium, and made them forget their most fervent objections.

At the same time, Neferat walked the streets of Egypt, whispering in every ear, stirring up restlessness among the masses. She instilled in the people a hatred for Seti and hopes of a new kingdom. And so, before long, Neferat had an army of supporters. We know not their reasons for hating Seti. Perhaps they disagreed with his policies. Perhaps he had grown too arrogant. Or, most likely, they thought him stupid and ineffective. But soon, their love of Seti's new wife grew in proportion to their hatred for Seti. They imagined themselves prospering under her rule.

A great battle was waged, a battle unrecorded in the history of men, for in this battle, women's tricks played no small part. Some say it was a long and bloody battle between the armies of the pharaoh and the new queen, a takeover that should have made the history books. Others say it was quiet and that Seti was cut down with little fanfare, because he was sickly, nearly mute, and lacking wisdom.

For reasons lost in the fog of time, Seti's dethroning was not hard-won. The king himself put up little fight, dying quickly at the hands of his ruthless new wife. With Neferat's help and the support of the people, the new queen brought Seti down forever, naming herself pharaoh. History never recorded the coup, for the queen ruled under the king's name. Except the queen was not the equal of the king. She did not have his potential for greatness. She did not have Seti's good heart.

"Why isn't it here?" Peter spat. He had ransacked the women's living quarters, going through each of the ragged rooms one by one, tearing apart the ancient curtains and the porous, tattered wall tapestries. He had found mummies in each one, and yet none of them was Seti. He had desecrated half a dozen kings in half an hour, pulling apart sarcophagi twice as big as himself. Once, he had been so sure he had found it that he'd let out an involuntary cheer. It was a mummy propped up on a makeshift throne. Next to it reclined the bust of a nameless queen with a bitter expression. The golden face on the mummy's sarcophagus was hulking and imposing like a king. This had to be the one: Seti next to a bust of the traitorous queen who had stolen his throne. But in the end, Peter had been wrong. There was no magic in those withered bones.

"Where are you hiding?" he said as he ran down another set of crumbling steps. He was distracted but he remained agile. Anyone else would have fallen into the enormous cavern that had grown beneath his feet, extending down from the ground floor into the unknown below. To Peter, it was like an invitation. A challenge from his nemesis. The Dark Lady herself was calling for Peter to come, to take a step into the abyss, and to dare claim the final prize.

❖❖❖

On the day of Seti's fall, the young pharaoh surveyed her kingdom—its fertile soil, its mountains of riches, the endless Nile. She was only a girl, yet she had managed to become a god-queen, feared and loved at the same time. She had supreme power, complete control. Yet barely a day passed when someone, some traitorous soul, wasn't put to death for questioning her reign.

The despot queen ruled for many decades. She was a famous pharaoh, known by Seti's name, her path to power opened for her through Neferat's trickery. She was cruel and menacing, ruling Egypt with a fiery rage that swallowed up the nation and made them a fearful people. Her first act as queen was to kill all the king's ministers. She spent money zealously and brought the kingdom to the edge of financial ruin and war. By the end of her reign, the Nile was red with the blood of her victims.

She was a pharaoh that never should have been, an injustice, though unknown, that burned in the hearts of all of Egypt.

In the dark, hidden places of the cities, a rumor began to form . . . that the true king, the one that should have been, would have been good and kind. Fortune-tellers and sorcerers of the age said that they read it in the very air, in the sand, and in the sky. They claimed that if events had unfolded the way they should have, Egypt's fortunes would be very different. They recounted tales of Neferat, words she had spoken that seemed so innocent at the time. Ripples, she had said. That is what I like. That is what I look for. Had she known all along the evil that lay dormant in her protégée's soul? Stories of sorcery and witchcraft resurfaced, and soon people knew where to place the blame. It was the nursemaid, they whispered. She carried the dark spirit of the god of death. But by then, Neferat was long gone. With the taste of power on her lips, she was off to conquer other kings, to manipulate other great leaders with her bewitching devil eye.

And so, Egypt nursed a bitterness in its heart.

As for this legendary line, they came to the very brink of greatness, a greatness that would have freed them all. Yet, instead of having Seti's redeeming goodness, their line ended without fanfare, their stories falling into legend. Seti died childless. Neferat, the last descendant of Hurkhan, disappeared, leaving no children behind.

Though his rule hardly ever materialized, Seti's body was mummi-fied and entombed in the Valley of the Kings, as is customary for pha-raohs. He received no ceremony, no riches to take to the afterlife, and few knew of the manner or precise day of his death.

Peter climbed down into the abyss. He could feel the presence around him. He knew how close he was to having everything he'd ever wanted. He smelled the air. She was definitely close—he knew his old nanny's smell. The space around him was growing narrower, and Peter knew that it was leading him to the tip of the upside-down pyramid, the very lowest point in the underworld. That would be where he would face his nemesis.

He took a moment to think about that prospect. Facing her. For all Peter's bragging, he had never actually seen her—not since the days of his own Nanny Neferat. Since then, he had seen shadows and heard whispers. He had felt dread the likes of which he might never experience again. But he had never *seen* the Dark Lady inside the labyrinth. Did she really have the jackal head that Egyptians attributed to the death god? Not likely. Egyptian mythology was full of animal-headed things. Maybe it was just symbolism.

Peter had long ago considered that perhaps the foe he would

meet in the end would not be a seven-foot-tall jackal monster from conventional Egypt books. The other four mummies had all been protected by people from their own stories. As Peter climbed deeper and deeper into the putrid hole, his mind couldn't let go of the idea that maybe he was on his way not to the death god's lair but to Neferat's sinister playhouse.

The bitterness of so many wrongs—injustices to himself, his family, and his country—devoured Seti's soul. And so he died with his life trapped in his bones. The goddess of death took the mummy of the true king and with it the most powerful bonedust of all—the one that would complete the others, opening the way to immortality. She shielded it with her greatest weapons, fearing that someday death might be conquered. The Dark Lady hid the mummy in a place where no one could reach it, a legendary labyrinth of the gates, guarded by powerful deities that no human could overcome.

And so Seti was gone, his kingdom lost, taking with it Egypt's chance at a good and just king. So many lives that might have been happy. So many needless deaths. A family that might have been redeemed. He can never fully die. His wasted life is forever trapped as grains of immortality in his bones.

Simon popped his head into Darling's office. "Anyone in here?" he said casually. When no one answered, he darted toward the dehydrator to check on the book, thinking that the sooner it was dry, the sooner he could take it to Albany, where no annoying children would get in his way. He brought his face close to the surface of the dehydrator and peered through. *Wait a minute,* he thought, noting the slightly darker cover, the thickness of the pages, the smudge in the right corner that hadn't been there before. . . .

The Hook and the Crook

Wendy glanced at the clock. Class was almost over, and Simon still hadn't made an appearance. She tapped her feet under her desk, trying to keep calm.

"There you have it, class," said the professor. "The bones of the fifth mummy are special because they carry in them the collective power of multitudes of bitter souls. What happened to Seti had a ripple effect, so that this is the story of the injustice of the entire family and also all of Egypt, who lost out on a good pharaoh and got an evil one in return. Next time, we'll talk more about bonedust and the various failed expeditions to find it." Wendy could see that he was trying not to look his children in the eye, probably because all three of them were thinking of Peter, their father's childhood friend—now fired and lurking somewhere inside Marlowe—and of that toe he had carried in his pocket for all these decades.

As soon as Professor Darling dismissed the class, Wendy got up and ran to the door, slamming into it as she sprinted out into the hall. John wasn't far behind. The rest of the class was still packing up binders and chatting about the weekend. The jarring sound of Wendy's exit made everyone look up. "Whoa, there, little Darlin's," shouted Marla after them. Everyone sneered at the joke, since that was the only reaction that seemed available.

As students from every classroom began pouring into the hall, Wendy and John ran full speed, dodging left and right, barely missing a kid carrying a geography project, as they headed toward their father's office. A teacher shouted, "No running!" but the two were turning into another hall before she even finished saying so.

With Peter and Simon both missing, the search for bonedust had suddenly turned into a race. A race to get to the *Book of Gates* as fast a possible, a race to find Peter, and a race to jump into the labyrinth and find the fifth mummy before Simon, who never did show up to Professor Darling's class. Maybe he'd already made it inside, Wendy thought. Maybe they could get the fourth bone back.

They pushed past the door and ran into the darkened office. As they marched toward the dehydrator, Wendy said, "Did you text Peter?"

"Yeah," said John, panting, "with a top-priority code attached, and our twenty."

"Does he know where we are?"

"That's what *our twenty* means," said John.

"And that's what you sent him?" said Wendy, pacing around the room as though her mind refused to let her body rest.

"I just said that," said John. "With a priority signal. Will you just relax?"

Wendy kept rambling. "We should decide where to take the book, so we save some time when he gets here."

"OK, let's decide," said John. There was no use trying to slow her down.

"What do we know so far?" said Wendy.

"Well, there's this magic labyrinth underneath our school. . . ."

"Shut up," said Wendy, still pacing. "The legend was about a king. Where would a king fit in with Marlowe? Maybe it's a rank thing. What are we the best at? Volleyball? Did we win that last year? How did our Latin team do at state? Good? Probably not."

"You realize you're talking to yourself, right?" said John.

"Yeah, I realize that," said Wendy. "Where is he? He's usually everywhere. Ugh. Where would the prom king hang out? Or, wait, what about the teachers' lounge? It has to—"

Suddenly, Wendy's out-of-control talking came to an abrupt stop. She was frozen in place, staring at the dehydrator.

"What is it?" said John.

"It's . . . it's gone," said Wendy.

The book was right there, in the dehydrator. But then Wendy reached in and yanked the book out of the machine.

"What are you doing?" said John.

"It's fake, John. It's fake. The book's a fake."

John grabbed the book. She was right. This was just a dummy. Someone had stolen the real one and replaced it with this cheap replica from the library.

"It had to be recently," said John. "Dad couldn't have seen this. He'd never fall for it."

Wendy could only whisper, "Peter . . ."

What have you done? thought Wendy. Wendy staggered toward her father's desk and dropped the fake book. After everything she had done, how hard it had been for her breaking all the rules and lying to her own dad . . . After giving up Connor, who had been so good to her . . . Peter had to have known that it had been a nightmare juggling everything. *"How could he be so . . . ?"* she said. She had never trusted anyone since her mother left. She had closed herself off—to the point that everyone thought she was this cold, indifferent teacher's kid. She didn't have a best friend. Even Connor didn't really know Wendy all that well. Sure, she had dated him because she liked him, but deep down she knew that most of the happiness she got from the relationship was because of John. All that had changed when Peter arrived. The day Peter showed up, she felt like she had discovered someone she could actually understand, someone who had shown up just in time. Peter's desperation to beat the underworld, to throw off the heavy residue of a bad parent and defy his age, those were things that Wendy could relate to better than anyone. With Peter, she thought she had something long-lasting. But now he'd stolen the book and run off. Wendy felt hot tears forming in her eyes, and a hand on her shoulder.

"He didn't run out on us," said John. "I mean . . . he did, but it's not personal."

"How do you know?" said Wendy. Then she added, "Why would you care? You're the one who thought he was a dirtbag from the beginning."

"Yeah, but not the kind of dirtbag that tries to screw people just because. He's after bonedust. Are you really surprised that he got a head start? It's not about us."

"Maybe not," said Wendy, wanting to believe John but unable to shake the feeling of betrayal. They had so little time to spare, and for now, Wendy thought, she had the opportunity to believe in Peter. Maybe this is what relationships were all about, giving someone the benefit of the doubt. There was a lot of doubt, but Wendy would choose to trust Peter . . . for now.

"Besides," said John, "who'd want to leave you without saying good-bye?"

Wendy couldn't help but smile at John's clumsy attempt to make her feel better. John had been a colossal pain in the past, but when it came down to it, he was one of only two people in the whole world who was always there.

"Come on," she said. "We should go find it."

John clapped his hands. "All right, I bet he took the book to hide it from—"

"Simon?" came a voice from behind the half-closed door.

Both Wendy and John whipped around. Simon was standing in the doorway, his arms hidden behind his back.

"You've been very busy, haven't you?" said Simon. "Running around in dangerous places, doing dangerous things. And no one even asked for my help."

"What are you doing here, Simon?" Wendy snapped. Simon was holding the real *Book of Gates.*

"Come on, Simon, be cool," said John. "The book's under our dad's watch."

"What are you *doing*, John?" Simon switched to a sympathetic tone, like a wise older brother throwing an intervention for his screwup sibling. "You're a smart kid. You have so much potential. Why are you getting mixed up with that uneducated, bird-brained thug? You should have told me when all this started."

John shrugged. He reminded Wendy of a puppy who couldn't choose between two owners.

"Look, Simon," Wendy jumped in, hoping John would grow a backbone sometime before his teenage years were over. "It's our dad's exhibit, and our dad's years of research, and our dad's discovery. . . . You're gonna have to return that bone, too."

Simon chuckled. "Why don't we leave that to the British Museum to decide, huh, babe?"

"Where is it, anyway?" Wendy searched Simon with her eyes.

Simon just shook his head. "It's safely put away."

Neither Wendy nor Simon noticed the smile on John's lips. The LB smile. The Adventurator smile. The furtive look of the rogue operator hatching a plan of his own. Sure, he had trusted Simon before—after the visit to the nurse's office, he had been sure that Simon was his true friend. But there was something else he was even more sure of: real winners work alone.

"I'm going to need both of your help," said Simon. Wendy gave a loud and almost involuntary *Hah!* Simon turned to John. He put a hand on his shoulder and said, "John, you and I are buddies, right? All those hours of gaming has to mean something. And I know for a fact that you are a by-the-book kind of guy. You want those relics to be handled professionally and the credit to go to the right people."

"Like, you?" snapped Wendy. "John, he's just a title-grubbing, résumé-padding—"

Simon cut her off. "If you help, John, I promise to bring your dad in on this, and we'll start a proper, well-funded excavation. Your dad can even lead it."

That was when Wendy made a move for the door. Simon grabbed her by the arm, which sent an uncomfortable shiver all the way down her spine. "Wait one second," he said. "Wendy, if you don't help me, you'll never see your new boyfriend again."

Wendy was taken aback. Did Simon have Peter tied up some-where? "What are you talking about?"

Simon held up the book. "I hate to do this," he said. "But I've got that criminal trapped in here. He's looking for the last mummy, and he'll never get back if I destroy the book."

"You wouldn't," said John, disappointment coloring his face.

"He would," said Wendy. "If he knew he couldn't have it him-self, he'd rather destroy it."

John just stared at Simon, waiting for him to say what he wanted.

"You two seem to have a knack for finding the bones," Simon finally said. "So now you've got a choice. Either you go inside the labyrinth and help Peter find the fifth mummy, or I destroy the book and kill him inside."

"How do you know that would kill him?" asked Wendy.

"I don't. Wanna try it?"

"Peter will never give you the bones," said John.

"I'll be waiting outside, making sure the door doesn't close. That way, you'll have to come out the same way you went in. I know no one will try consuming the bonedust, because I have the fourth one. Once you find the last bone, you throw all of them out. Then I'll let the three of you out. If you try to jump out without sending me the bones, I'll burn the book. Who knows, maybe the *underworld* will catch fire then, and we'll all have a nice little metaphor to ponder while you die."

"You'd go to prison," said Wendy.

"Oh, yeah? On what charge, first-degree burning a book? Is there some kind of fairy-tale court I don't know about?"

"I thought you said you wanted to do this properly," said Wendy.

"I do," said Simon. "But I don't trust you and I don't trust that Peter. Now, let's go."

"I want to stop by my locker," said John as they followed Simon through the hallways. Now that another gate had been opened and Peter was inside, the changes they had noticed before were starting to take over Marlowe again. The floors were looking older. Walls seemed to be made of different materials. There were twists and turns where there hadn't been any before. Insects lurked in cracks and openings.

"No time for lockers," said Simon.

"Hey," said John, "if we're gonna be forced into the underworld, you think you could cut me some slack and let me bring some basic provisions?"

"Fine," said Simon.

They stopped by John's locker, where he picked up his gym bag. When Wendy asked what was inside, John just answered, "Adventurator survival kit."

Wendy tried to think of a way out of this. *Peter will have a plan,* she thought, hoping they could find him quickly. As they walked to the girls' bathroom, where Simon said he had found the book, Simon and Wendy puzzled over why Peter had chosen that location.

"Is he trying to throw Simon off?" John asked.

"No," said Wendy. "He's really after it. By why not the teachers' lounge, or the principal's office, or something like that?"

John shrugged. "Peter knows the legends better than we do."

Since it was class time, the bathroom was empty except for two freshmen smoking through the open window. "Out," said Simon as he plopped the *Book of Gates* on the sink. The girls crushed their cigarettes on the windowsill and ran out.

"Well, get going," said Simon.

Wendy and John took a deep breath. Wherever they ended up, they would have to make the best of it, because they wouldn't be able to jump back out. Not without Peter. Wendy hoped Peter had survived till now. As for the fifth mummy, they had already figured that it would be the hardest to take. But now, with Simon mixed up in all this, the search might just have become impossible.

SIMON GRIN

A RECURRING THOUGHT

Simon's Log, Stardate 3109.45

It seems the Omega Quadrant was actually one half of a twin-dimensional region full of annoyance and embarrassment. The tiny, insignificant wimp, Peter-tron, has become a thorn in my side. He even seems to be aligning himself with two of my crew, Ensigns John and Wendy, to attempt a mutiny of some kind. Of course, Officer Darling is blind to it all (Note to self: Fire Darling as soon as you are able). My inevitable rise to the head of Star Command has been delayed—for now—mostly as a result of rare oversights on my part and an incredible, almost supernatural, luck on the part of Peter-tron and his weenie crew of children.

The Dark Spirit of Marlowe

Wendy and John appeared in a dark place, facing two huge palaces, one slightly smaller than the other. The air around them was thick, and it seemed to push down on them from all directions as they walked slowly toward the palaces. John adjusted his gym bag over his shoulder. Neither one of them spoke. Neither one pointed out the discomfort all around them, or that awful feeling of not being alone no matter where you went in the labyrinth. They focused instead on trying to puzzle together the hazy, jumbled pieces of the last legend.

They were stumbling around in the dark, keeping the castles in their sight, when a reverberating echo caused them to pull back.

"What was that?" Wendy whispered.

And then they both saw it. The smaller of the two palaces seemed to be trembling, sinking just a few inches lower into the ground.

"That has to be it," said John as the palace gave another low groan and sank a bit farther. "That's where Peter is."

"How do you know?" said Wendy, hoping for any reason not to go into the sinking building. "Maybe it's that other one. . . ."

"Just come on!" John said as he pulled her by the arm.

Inside, they found themselves at the edge of the giant hole, spiraling down into blackness. Just as another bout of shaking rattled the ancient furniture and sent them both to their bellies at the edge of the cavern, John spotted a shadow flitting away down into the deep recesses of the earth below.

"Did you see that?" he asked Wendy. She shook her head. "Someone's climbing down into that thing."

"I didn't see anything," said Wendy. "Let's look around upstairs."

"No way," said John. "That was Peter, for sure. Besides, Wen, this is the *last* mummy. Do you think it's just gonna be lying around a bedroom upstairs?"

He was already lowering his body into the hole, using his feet to feel around for flat patches of solid ground. "It's not that bad," he said, already a few feet in. "It's like a cone! We can climb all the way down if we just crawl around the sides, like a marble in one of those science funnels."

"That's comforting," said Wendy, thinking of how the marble always came bouncing to the bottom. She took a careful step into the hole, lowering her body while holding on to the edge with both hands. John was right: it wasn't that steep, and the lower they climbed, the narrower the hole became. Still, the hole was as big as a house, and crawling around it was exhausting work. They crawled on their hands and knees along trenches that had been dug into the sides, swirling in smaller and smaller circles into the dark hollow places underfoot.

As they climbed, Wendy thought about Peter. Why had he left them like that, without a word of explanation? Why had he taken the book and started the last search on his own? Didn't he want to share this with her? Didn't he *just* say that she was his girlfriend? Wasn't he the one who once had asked her if she would share the bonedust with him, if she would go along with his big adventure and be his oldest friend in fifty or a hundred years? Wendy hadn't known how to answer then. But since then, things had changed. Her relationship with Connor was over. She and Peter were together. And lately, she found herself thinking about his offer more and more, until he was the only thing that occupied her mind. And when was the last time she had let something like *that* happen?

As they climbed, John whispered all his theories to Wendy. The way he rambled on, totally engrossed with the possibilities, reminded her of their dad. Wendy continued to climb down, trying hard to see John in the dark, when she heard the sound of crumbling rock. John's feet caught a softer, steeper section of the wall and he gasped, then he yelled out as he lost his footing and fell immediately out of sight.

"Oh, my God!" Wendy screamed into the void. "John!" She tried to lie flat on her stomach, but there was barely enough space. She clung tighter with her arms and legs as she tried to look down.

After some grunting and shuffling, John's voice shouted back, "It's not that far, Sis. Just jump."

Wendy breathed out, then positioned herself so that her feet pointed downward and she was facing the rocky wall, clutching at it with both hands. She closed her eyes, let go of the rung of earth in her hands, and dropped into the bottom of the gulf, the part where the funnel came to an end. The air felt like it was pushing down on her head with the force of all the soil that had once filled this hole. She felt sick with dread.

It was pitch dark, and Wendy could hardly see her own hand. "Hey, Wendy," said a voice to her right, and Wendy whipped around, because the voice was not John's.

"Peter," she said. "What are you doing? Why'd you run off like that?"

"Because," said Peter, his voice warm and unconcerned, "I didn't want you to hurt yourself trying to help me. I wanted to get it over with."

Wendy didn't want to ask anything more, because this was exactly the answer she had hoped for. Of all the dozens of reasons she had created in her mind, this was the only one that even came close to being acceptable. Sure, it had its weak spots, but Wendy had decided already that if Peter gave this answer, she wouldn't dig any deeper. Peter reached for Wendy's arms and pulled her closer. But John made a gagging sound and Peter let go.

The words began to flood out of her, and she told Peter all about what Simon had done, as if Peter could save them all—if only he knew. "Simon forced us in here," she said. "He's going to burn the book if we don't give him all the bonedust."

Peter didn't look concerned. "Let's get past this first. We can deal with Simon later. I need to get the fourth one from him, anyway." He reached into his pocket and took out a lighter. "I think we've found our friend Seti."

He flicked the lighter, and suddenly the circular space around them was awash in yellow light. It didn't take much to illuminate the bottom of the cone. The empty space around them was the size of a small room or a large closet, so they could easily walk around and explore. Looking up, John saw how huge the mouth of the hole had been and secretly congratulated himself for making it all the way down. Then he looked down and noticed something else in the room . . . the thing that had rested in this cavern for all eternity.

By the glow of Peter's lighter, they could see that this was no ordinary room, but a tomb, a resting place not for one person but for hundreds. All around them, sarcophagi were arranged neatly in circular rows. They were stacked behind one another, so that the trio stood at the very center. It was obvious now that the room wasn't the size of a closet at all. It was much bigger. In fact, if the rows of sarcophagi were removed, the space might be as big as the Darlings' living room.

Wendy and John glanced around at the coffins. Some of them were adorned with hieroglyphs, others with jewels and gold, and some were simple and timeworn.

"Seti is here," said Peter. "I can feel it. It's one of these." He patted the satchel at his side, obviously itching to add this ingredient to his immortal cocktail.

"So we just go through them?" said John. "How're we going to get through so many before the guardian or the death god gets here?"

"Can't," said Peter matter-of-factly. "And my lighter's running out."

The lighter flickered and went out. Peter struck it again and a fainter light appeared. If they took too long, they wouldn't just be clueless about which sarcophagus to pick; they'd be clueless and covered in darkness.

Suddenly, they heard a noise. Peter turned quickly, taking the light with him. It went out, and a cold chill ran through the tomb. Wendy thought she heard a sigh, then a deep sickly groan, something almost painful. But then the light came back on, and Peter told them what he had already figured out.

"See these hieroglyphs?" he said, running his fingers across the pictures on one of the coffins resting against the wall. "They're clearly from the wrong century. All the ones on this wall are from the same period, so we can forget about these."

Then he moved across the room to another section. "These over here are just decoys," he said. "They're not even Egyptian. There are inscriptions here, but you can see certain letters that don't appear in Egyptian script. My guess is that they were written to fool the really stupid bonedust hunters—the ones in a hurry, with nothing but a rudimentary knowledge of modern Arabic and too little research."

Wendy was impressed. As Peter ran across the room dismissing half the sarcophagi, spewing facts about ancient Egyptian burial rites and death rituals, she thought about how much work he had put into this. And now that it was time to make the final discovery, it was natural that he would trust himself with the task. He had only tried to keep her from harm. She believed that with her whole heart.

"So that still leaves us with . . . a lot," said Peter, waving an arm across the thick space around them. Wendy and John, too, began running their hands along the inscriptions on the coffins, trying to figure out which could be the right one.

"Is there any kind of clue in the legend about what the mummy might look like?" Wendy asked. "The others all had clues."

"This last one is really vague," said Peter. "They were all passed down through word of mouth, and this one didn't get told much, since people thought it was cursed. But my guess is it has something to do with Neferat, the nursemaid." His eyes searched her face for signs of understanding. "Do you remember her?" Wendy nodded. "She's the key to all this. . . . Besides that, the big difference in this legend is that it's more than one person's injustice." He rubbed his hands together and added with a smirk, "Should make for some real good bonedust."

Peter went back to examining the contents of this mass tomb. Wendy walked past the many coffins lining the walls of the cave. Some of them were bright and shiny, glinting beautifully by the glow of Peter's lighter. Others were covered with dirt and scratchings. John was doing the same thing, scanning the sarcophagi for any sign or clue. Wendy eyed the fading flame from Peter's lighter. She stood motionless under what felt like hundreds of pounds of heavy air, trying to figure out where to start, trying to read the pictures on the sarcophagi, and thinking about how the ancient stories depicted here would help find the last bonedust. She couldn't help but think that it didn't matter anyway, though. As soon as they were outside, Simon would take it all away from them.

"Help me move these, Wendy," shouted Peter. "We don't have much time."

"How are we supposed to move giant coffins?" Wendy asked.

Peter scanned the room, whipping this way and that, holding his lighter up against each coffin and down to the floor. "There," he said, pointing to a slab of rock beneath their feet.

Wendy noticed that most of the floor was a circular grid of carved stones covered in a thick layer of dust. Peter began wiping away the dirt with his hands to reveal the hieroglyphics etched into each one. Each cartouche tile was the shape of dog tags and roughly the size of a loaf of bread. "See this?" Peter said. "It's an exact map of this room. Every cartouche corresponds to one of these coffins. Count if you want."

John started to count, but it took Wendy only a moment to realize that Peter was right. Peter put his palm against one of the tiles and began to move it. The coffins (and the matching tiles) weren't tightly packed, so there was a foot or two of empty space between every coffin and each of its neighbors. As Peter moved each tile, the matching coffin moved, too, so that they might be able to rearrange them and create a path to the wall. It was almost like an ancient Egyptian version of John's 14-15 puzzles from when he was a kid— those rickety wooden squares with sixteen spaces and fifteen tiles that you move around until the numbers are aligned or the image unwarped. John pulled out a piece of paper from his gym bag and started to scribble strategies. The goal was to allow Peter to get a good look at each sarcophagus, deciphering the markings to find the right one, while making their way toward the wall of the cave.

They maneuvered one layer of coffins after another, moving them this way and that, up, down, and back again, burrowing deeper and deeper into the recesses created by their work. The coffins scraped across the floor, crunching and creaking like stubborn geriatrics determined not to move. Peter worked faster than all of them, working the tiles until the groaning sound returned, accompanied by the strong stench of rotting flesh. Wendy shivered, thinking that this must be the worst part of the labyrinth, this stinking place in the deepest part of the pyramid below Marlowe—it felt like the tip of the upside-down pyramid, a point far below the earth. If there were any place for the Dark Lady to live, this would be it, this shadowy place full of death, this place that felt like being buried alive. She thought about the goddess, how the Egyptian legends showed death as a jackal-headed man but the five legends called it the Dark Lady. She thought of the hooded figure that had shredded John's arm with her hook, and she wondered what would greet them once they reached the fifth mummy.

"Keep going!" Peter said as they zigzagged through the boxes, peering closely at each one and slowly approaching the wall of the cave.

Wendy was trembling, but she kept at it—until finally, something caught her eye.

"What's this?" she said, motioning the others to join her.

She had just wedged herself between the last two rows and was pushing against a dusty coffin that stood in the last row, hoping to uncover the wall. But where she should have found the earthen side of the cave, she found a hard wooden surface. She knocked on it. It was hollow. When she ran her hand across it, she noticed that there was a hole, big enough to fit her hand, like a primitive doorknob. "I think it's a door," said Wendy.

"Look there," said Peter. Above the door was a large inscription, like a sign. Peter translated. *"Throne Room."*

"That must be it," said John. "The pharaoh must be in the throne room!"

Peter put his hand in the opening and started to pull. Wendy and John waited. But then, before he had a chance to pull on the knob, Peter's face went white and he let out a gasp.

He was pulling now, but not on the door. From where Wendy stood, holding the fading lighter, it looked like Peter was trying to free his hand.

"What's happening?" Wendy said in a frightened whisper.

Peter continued to pull, his breath growing quicker and louder. "Something's . . . got my hand . . ." he croaked.

John and Wendy rushed toward him and started to pull him back. Something on the other side jerked, and the door flew open, freeing Peter in the process. Immediately, the door flew shut again. But it was too late. All three of them had seen it.

It was a shadow, female-shaped and hooded, just like the one that had hurt John. Two lines of blood snaked Peter's hand, like rivers on a map. Fueled by waves of rushing adrenaline, Peter lunged at one of the floor tiles, moving a sarcophagus to block the door.

"I knew it," he said, turning in a circle to look all around the circular cave wall. "It's a puzzle. If we pick the wrong door, we could be killed."

"What do the others say?" Wendy asked, pointing to three other inscriptions like the first one. They were spaced evenly around the cave, each perched above a door hidden by stacks of coffins.

"That one says *Battlefield,*" said Peter, rubbing his hand. "And those two are *Inner Chamber* and *Nursery.*"

"It has to be the inner chamber," said John. "That's where a king does most of his work, right? We must be in the antechamber now."

"You sure about that, little guy?" said Peter. "The kingdom was stolen on a *battlefield*."

Wendy didn't say anything. She looked over the coffins at the walls of the cave a few feet away and saw for the first time that there were dusty etchings all around them, not just on the coffins but on the cave itself. She examined them closely. There were kings, men, armies, battles. One of the pictures caught her eye: a nursemaid with a vicious face, surrounded by little children and babies. Something about the nursemaid's hungry face seemed familiar to Wendy—but then again, faces in old sketches all looked alike.

"You know what's weird?" said John as he began to map out the fewest steps to the inner chamber door. "This whole injustice depends on the pharaoh being inherently good, right? But what kind of a good pharaoh is so selfish that he lets his whole country go to hell while he parties? I mean, I've met a lot of partiers at Marlowe, and none of those guys would *ever* make a good president. Look at the boarding students—sure, they're cool, but you wouldn't want them thinking up fiscal policy."

Peter laughed at John's nerdiness. Then he turned thoughtful and said, "It's fun to be young. You can't blame the guy for having a good time. Besides, legends are full of holes and exaggerations."

"*I'm* young and I wouldn't let anyone screw *me* like that," said John.

Peter chuckled. "If we get out of here alive, maybe I'll take you out for some real fun, and you can see how easy it can be to forget everything else."

It must have been something in John's comment. Maybe she had already started to put the pieces together, or maybe it was the fact that John brought up that point right as she was looking at another picture of the nursemaid, this time with her hand extended over a crib, her back bent in a sinister bow, and her broken left eye glinting despite the centuries of dust, but suddenly Wendy had an idea. She darted to the coffins blocking the nursery and began wedging herself through the layers, pushing herself into the crevices with renewed vigor, mumbling excitedly as she crept toward the door. She didn't even bother with a cartouche this time. She just squeezed her skinny frame in.

"What are you doing?" asked John.

"Look at the walls," said Wendy. "The story is written there."

"How about you just explain?" said John, looking up from his notes about tile positions.

"The epic battle between Seti and his queen was a total sham!" said Wendy. "Just look!"

John walked toward the etchings in the cave walls. There it was, the whole story. The nursemaid with her roomful of children, the new king crowned, the epic battle.

"Hey," said John, surveying the battle scene, "are these girls? And what are they holding there? It's not swords."

No, it didn't look like swords at all. In fact, it looked as though the entire army consisted of women, fighting an epic battle with nothing in their hands except masks pinned to the ends of long, pointy sticks. From afar, it might look like warriors with spears, but up close, that wasn't the picture at all.

John remembered the battle scene from the story.

Later in Seti's life . . . a great battle was waged, a battle unrecorded in the history of men, for in this battle, women's tricks played no small part. Some say it was a long and bloody battle between the armies of the pharaoh and the new queen, a takeover that should have made the history books. Others say it was quiet and that Seti was cut down with little fanfare, because he was sickly, nearly mute, and lacking true wisdom. . . .

Suddenly, all the pieces fell into place. "No way!" shouted John. "Seti was replaced as a baby! The story never says how many years passed until Seti was crowned and his throne was stolen from him. I bet there wasn't a battle at all. He was crowned as a baby, and then the wife killed him and ruled in his name."

"Sickly, nearly mute, and lacking true wisdom," said Peter, shaking his head and looking around at the now obvious sketches on the wall, "just like a baby."

"It's funny," said Wendy, "because if you read that story thinking you're reading about a teenager, your mind automatically fills the blanks with partying and corruption and stuff, but you could just as easily read it about a two-year-old, and everything would still make sense." She tried to remember Seti from the story. She had only just come from class, and it was easy to recall.

. . . a playboy king, unconcerned with anything beyond his own amusement, disappointed them all. He was not wise enough or cunning enough to stand up to his advisers. He was distracted, not as clever as a god-king should be. Besides all that, he rarely said more than a few words. He

spent his days in amusement, forgetting his position and responsibilities.
He was weak and malleable, and soon he became nothing more than
a vessel for his advisers . . . Seti himself did nothing but feast, laugh,
and play.

She laughed at how her own mind had tricked her. "You know what?" said Wendy, looking at the scene in which Neferat presides over the marriage of her favorite pupil to Seti, who, like all children in Egyptian carvings, is depicted as a tiny adult, about half the height of his wife, but with the expression and posture of a king. "That's why the story says that the wife took the place of Seti's mother in his heart. And that's why Egypt was shocked at the marriage. I'll bet she was already a teenager."

"Nice work," said Peter. He and John began moving away the coffins in front of the nursery, using their feet to move tiles, and creating more room for Wendy. Peter tried to hide his amazement, but Wendy saw the look on his face.

When they had uncovered the nursery door, Peter didn't waste a moment grabbing for the knob hole. He wasn't scared of what might be behind the door. In fact, he seemed as confident as ever. He put his hand into the hole and pulled. The door didn't budge. He reached in farther for a tighter grip and pulled again. The door remained shut.

Without a word, Peter marched toward an old, decrepit coffin, pulled a plank right out of the side, and rammed it into the nursery door. He didn't even bother warning them to move, and John had to drop to the ground to avoid the oncoming blow.

The door burst open easily, but as soon as it did, an angry scream filled the cave.

Peter pushed the door wider and ran inside.

The nursery was as stifling as a sauna and lined with even more sarcophagi. It was smaller than the antechamber, but not as cramped, since the coffins in this room were far fewer in number.

Now that they knew to look for a small coffin, it seemed that finding Seti's mummy would be easier. But it soon became clear that the choices had narrowed too much. Everywhere they looked, the sarcophagi were big, adult-size, and adorned with likenesses of the people inside.

Wendy noticed that all around the hiding place, the rock walls were covered with sketches of the same person, over and over again. It was Neferat in many forms. First she was short, a young girl with her parents. Then she was a nursemaid surrounded by many sons. Then she was watching over many children, an evil look on her face, just like the etching in the outer room of the cave. But then, in the latter pictures she saw that Neferat's face grew longer. Her features hardened. Her image changed into someone, or something, unrecognizable. As Wendy scanned the drawings, she realized the answer to the final mystery. Why was Neferat such a big part of the story? The sketches showed her changing so gradually; it was like she was a spirit, sliding easily from one body to the next. In fact, she was drawn like a spirit, vague and incomplete at times, never standing on the same plane as the figures around her.

"Hurry, Peter," said Wendy. "I can hear someone coming."

The darkness was moving closer.

The air grew more and more crushing.

Outside the wall, a shadow was filling the cave with its deathly fumes.

Peter grabbed the plank and began working on a coffin at random. He was losing his cool—that eternal confidence slipping away momentarily—and for that instant, he could do nothing more than dig haphazardly. Peter's makeshift crowbar sank into the side of a gold-encrusted sarcophagus and cracked just as the dark figure poured into the nursery beside them.

"Peter," whispered the voice. It was gravelly and muted, harsh and soft, all at the same time. It sent a shiver through their bodies and made Wendy and John freeze in place.

Wendy tried not to scream.

Peter didn't answer. His hand twitched as he reached for his satchel.

The figure was walking toward them now, a dark, hunched form, shrouded in tattered cloths and completely encircled by some sort of insects.

Wendy thought she heard the icy voice speak again.

John gulped and squeaked something about getting out of there.

Wendy looked at the Dark Lady's strange face, then at the drawings on the wall, especially the latter ones when Neferat had begun to change, to transform into something else, something monstrous. The figure approaching them now was so much like the latter pictures of Neferat, which also depicted her covered with insects, a queen with a twisted face ruling over moths and flies. The latter sketches showed her with the pursed lips of a governess, the hunched back of a cripple, the wicked expression and careful steps of a thief. This figure now standing before them had the same look of malice and ill will all over her face. And she had something else in common with the pictures of Neferat. Despite her fear, Wendy squinted to see the face emerging from under the moth-eaten hood. Something strange caught her attention—a flash of its deep blue left eye, broken into four pieces.

"That's not the same . . ." Wendy began, and trailed off, remembering the lithe, diminutive, and almost elegant hooded figure that had attacked John. That figure, too, had the broken eye, but wasn't nearly as decrepit as this hunchbacked old woman.

"It's her, though," said Peter, staring an old nemesis, his own surrogate mother, in the face. "This is the way she *really* looks. I'd know her anywhere."

Standing here before the death god, Wendy could feel the connection between this ancient woman, Neferat, and the Dark Lady, who was said to be the immortal goddess of death—the goddess who had appeared even in the first legend, hundreds or thousands of years before Neferat, the nursemaid. Because, after all, wasn't Neferat just a body and the Dark Lady just a spirit? In her father's books, Wendy had come across this word before—*Neferat:* hatred. She now knew why the walls of this inner sanctum, the home of the most powerful bonedust, the tip of the pyramid, should be filled with pictures of this woman. Wendy knew that Neferat wasn't simply a woman who had lived thousands of years before. She was much more than that. She had something inside her that was different from all the rest. *Neferat. Hate.* That is one of many names for the darkness in the world. Beelzebub, Legion, and the god of death. Whatever form it takes, whatever cultural icon it inhabits—a horned man, a beautiful woman, a jackal-headed god—it is all the same. The same evil. The same age-old darkness by many names. And here they were, having just opened the door to its home. The sinister spirit that had a grip on Marlowe and refused to let go. The Dark Lady. She wasn't just one person, but a dark trinity that included so many forms. Young and beautiful, old and ugly, plain and sickly.

Neferat, the girl at the end of a cursed line in whom the spirit lived and worked its evil. Neferat, the beautiful governess Vileroy— and Peter's much uglier nanny . . . the wicked, hunchbacked, moth-covered nanny, the ancient child thief, the liar.

Neferat, the dark spirit that had inhabited Marlowe for so long and kept a watch over them all with her broken demon eye.

Still, Wendy thought as she glanced at the sketches of Neferat as a younger woman, *I swear I've seen that face before.*

NEFERAT

A HAPPY THOUGHT

It is 1926. I stand outside Peter's bedroom. He's asked for a story, and his father thinks the new nanny could tell it best. He's hired for his son the most beautiful governess he's ever seen, a vision of his lost wife—tall and blond. Poor, poor Peter. No mother to tell him stories. A father busy with the responsibilities of adulthood. Even his withered grandfather has nothing to say to him—the old sailor has no interest in children. Peter lives in fear of his grandfather's wrinkles, his aching rheumatism, his severed hand—replaced with a hook. They are all reminders that Peter, too, will decay. Age will wrinkle and mar him.

I think I have just the perfect story for little Peter. But first, I hunch my body and grow scars. I age my form by a hundred years . . . show him what I really look like beneath the false beauty. My silk gown becomes a black robe, and I can see that he is frightened. My fingers feel arthritic and knobby. Only my eye remains the same . . . I can never change that. I am an old, hideous crone. Peter is shaking because he knows that this will be the nanny that will put him to sleep, every night, from now on.

"Come, and I'll read to you from my favorite book," I say.

"No," he yells, and inches away. "What's wrong with your back? And you smell funny."

"Peter, you have a choice," I say. "Either you listen to my story or I'll have to show you my hook. You don't want that, do you? It's the book or the hook. Your choice."

"What's that on your jacket?" he says. "Is that a bug?"

"This is just a little friend. She'll watch you even when I'm asleep. So you see, Peter? There's no getting away."

From under my robe I pull out an antique hook just like his grandfather's. This will be the beginning of Peter's immortal fears, a mummy complex, a freezing of his soul. This will be a story about addictions and anchors and things as unstoppable as growing up.

THE DEAD ENDING

The nursery was hot, and Wendy could feel the piles of rubble over their heads. Peter was focused on only one thing: the fact that this was the very room where the bones of the baby king were surely waiting, holding the dust that could reverse time itself. Looking upward from the sketches of Neferat, Wendy could see that the room was square but that the walls seemed to slope inward as they came down—so she was certain now that this nursery was the last room before the tip of the upside-down pyramid.

With the entrance of the hunched figure, it became even darker, more menacing and strange. It was a prison for the soul, as deep and black as a void. *This must be her sanctuary*, thought John, the place death lays down her head, the place where she battles the very idea of eternal life. Inside the tip of the pyramid must have been a galaxy of souls, the kingdom of death. The Dark Lady would never keep all five mummies here together, so temptingly close to one another. And so she hid them in rooms surrounding it, to keep her wicked eye on them. All this time, thought John, terrified, although it looked liked they had crossed gardens and deserts and rivers, they had only been sneaking around the goddess's backyard.

In her hand, the nursemaid Neferat held a weapon that looked like an old, timeworn hook, like an antique from long ago. John's arm hurt at the sight of it, and he knew it was the same one he had encountered before. Its handle was shaped like an ankh, the Egyptian symbol of life. Its end was curved and sharp, like a sickle, the symbol of death.

For a moment, everyone stood still. And then, seemingly all at once, they noticed it. In the corner of the room, hidden among several golden sarcophagi, stood a waist-high pillar holding a sarcophagus about as big as a bassinet. Neferat stood motionless. Her chest didn't rise and fall, as though she didn't breathe. Wendy and John were petrified by her presence and looked at the sarcophagus instead. Peter, however, was staring straight into the nursemaid's eyes. For that instant, they were facing off, waiting for the other to make the first move. Peter's fingers twitched. He had waited decades for this showdown—this chance to pay her back for her years of cruelty. He smirked in the face of death. And maybe it was John's imagination, but death seemed to be smirking back.

In that second of rigid stillness, as they confronted the governess of the underworld, a hundred thoughts flashed through their minds.

Please, Peter, don't do something crazy, thought Wendy.

If we live to tell him, Dad is going to flip, thought John.

It's mine, thought Peter. *It's finally all mine.*

Then, at the same time, Peter and the Dark Lady leaped at the pillar in the corner. . . .

It had been more than an hour since the kids had entered the labyrinth, and Simon was starting to smell a double cross. He paced in front of the stall door in the girls' bathroom, the portal, and counted the minutes. Was there a back door out of the labyrinth?

The door of the girl's bathroom slammed open. It was that Hispanic RA and two boarding boys—the two worst ones. The girl walked right to the portal with her obviously stolen spear and said to the guy with poet glasses, "Teach him to swim, 22."

The cornrowed blond followed the girl through the portal as the broad-shouldered poet smiled a gap-toothed smile and walked toward a shrinking Simon.

Peter snatched the sarcophagus off the pillar a half a second before the nanny's hook cut through the air where the coffin had been. Peter dove to the side as another slash of the razor-sharp hook whistled through the air toward him. He rolled across the stone floor, holding the sarcophagus to his chest. The figure pounced toward him, raising the hook high in the air and bringing it down just as Peter rolled up to a kneeling position and brought the sarcophagus above his head as a shield.

To Wendy, it looked like this withered shell of a woman, almost frail-looking in her tattered robes, tried to stop the swing of her antique hook when she saw the sarcophagus of the fifth mummy in the way. But Peter had been too quick in that last second, and the hook stabbed into the front of the sarcophagus. They both pulled, there was a splintering crack, and the sarcophagus ripped open.

The mummified bones of the fifth legendary mummy flew end over end in the air. "No!" screamed Peter as he fell back.

John scrambled into the action, running under the mummy and catching it in his gym bag. He zipped up the bag and tucked it under his arm. Suddenly, the room grew darker. The figure seemed to disappear and then appear again. There was a flicker, like a bulb burning out, and Peter rushed to John.

In the next instant, they were washed in darkness. And then the very air they were breathing seemed to change. No longer the hot earthen smell of underground, the air around them suddenly felt cool, almost fresh. The light returned, and Wendy gasped at what surrounded them.

Now they weren't standing in the sarcophagus room at the tip of the upside-down pyramid—they were standing in the Marlowe nurse's office, with its sickbed and bottles of medicine and closetlike feeling. The walls were covered with sleeping moths from floor to ceiling, so that Wendy couldn't tell what color the room was painted.

"What's going on?" John whispered.

When Wendy turned to look at the ancient hunchbacked woman, she was gone. All that remained was a few of the moths that had encircled her a moment ago. The gravelly voice filled the space around them again. It was calling Peter.

John and Peter moved to Wendy as she turned toward the door, but it was shut. They were trapped inside the insect-infested nurse's office. In a corner, a few of them began to flutter and come to life. A deadly calm fell over the room, and as the moths woke, the small space of the nurse's office filled up with fluttering insects, thousands and thousands of them. Then Wendy noticed another change. "Something's wrong." She could barely breathe. It was as if the insects were sucking out all the oxygen, as if the room was not built to support so many living creatures all at once.

John whimpered. Wendy's throat went dry as she tried to breathe.

There was a rustling outside the door of the office. Wendy was sure the dark figure would come rushing into the room and finish them all off, but why were they *here*? On the other side of the door, she heard a soft echo: "Peter, Peter." It didn't sound like the gravelly voice that had called him before. And then Tina came bursting into the room, holding some kind of spear from the exhibit. Wendy had never been so happy to have her barging in. One of the LBs—the blond banker's kid, who was probably running the entire Marlowe branch of Peter's organization—came running behind Tina, and Wendy gulped the oxygen that wafted in after them.

"How—?" Wendy choked on the words.

"We were right behind you when the underworld disappeared," said Tina. "Ended up just outside this door." She looked past Wendy and John. "Peter!" she screamed, and ran to his side. He seemed to be having some sort of episode. He was writhing on the ground, his hands around his neck . . . except his hands weren't actually touching his neck. It was as if there was another set of hands, invisible fingers, wrapped around his throat, and Peter was desperately trying to pull them off. Hearing his name seemed to revive Peter for a second, and in a last, desperate attempt at survival, he took his thumb and thrust it into the air, at a point just above his own head—a point where a cluster of moths coalesced.

Suddenly she was there. The nanny Neferat appeared, complete with her flock of moths whipping around her shoulders . . . but wait . . . *was* that the death goddess?

"What the—?" said John as he and Wendy saw her at once. Not the ancient nanny but the new school nurse, complete with her blue sweater. She was coughing into a bloody napkin as she struggled against Peter, whose finger was piercing her in the one blue and branded eye.

She shrieked in pain and flung Peter at the wall, crushing a colony of moths in the process. Peter crumpled to the ground, gasping for air.

The look on the school nurse's face was pure malice. She may have been sick, but she had the desperation of a cornered animal— so much more dangerous than calculation or hate—capable of doing anything to survive.

Wendy remembered now where she had seen that strange eye before, the day she ran into the nurse in the hall. The thought that the Dark Lady had been among them all along, posing as a nurse, manipulating everything . . . Wendy felt nauseous. The nurse had been the one who made her doubt Peter, poisoning her mind with ideas about him and Tina. She was probably the one who put the Egyptian eyes above his hallway door. She was just trying to distract them away from the underworld. Though Wendy had so easily forgotten the nurse's face after every encounter, she could see now that it was very much like the sketches of a younger Neferat on the walls of the cave, before she became the hunched, crippled old nanny in the later pictures—the one that Peter knew so well. Long before she became the goddess of death depicted in the last sketch in the cave wall, she was this homely girl, not old, not young, just a face come to life from Professor Darling's stories. So plain. No wonder she was so jealous, so eager to leave her mark on the world.

"Do you have it?" Tina whispered. She didn't seem to care about the identity of the Dark Lady. Had she even ever met her, or the homely new nurse?

"Yeah, right here," said John, holding up the gym bag.

"So we outrun her," said Tina.

"How?" said John with disbelief. "She won't let us out with the mummy." They all glanced at the broken door, which was now being quickly sealed shut by the nurse's millions of tiny minions.

"She might not let us out at all," said Cornrow.

"All right, think," said Wendy. "There has to be something we know about her." Wendy frantically snapped her fingers, trying to remember all at once everything her father had ever taught her about Egyptology. She tried to muster a few seconds of calm, just long enough to gather her thoughts and figure a way out of this.

In the meantime, Tina rushed over to Peter. Wendy wanted to be the one to run to him, but she knew she wouldn't be of use there. And even though she and Tina had their petty competition, they had to put it aside for now.

The nurse was making her way toward Peter again. She seemed to have one singular purpose. "Hey," shouted Tina, rushing away from Peter and pushing the sickbed between him and the nurse.

"Hey!" Tina repeated as she drove the table into the nurse's torso, but the nurse's attention wasn't diverted. She just crept past the bed and toward Peter. "Look at me!" shouted Tina.

"Don't bother, Tina. You've never used the bonedust," said Peter as he inched away. "Besides, she's always had it in for me . . . I can't believe I didn't realize the nurse . . ."

"You didn't really look." Nurse Neve spoke for the first time, her voice strained. "You never look hard enough. You're lazy, Peter."

Peter scoffed.

"Or maybe it's not you," said Nurse Neve. "No one looks at the plain ones."

Wendy gripped John's gym bag, frantic for an idea. "Come on, come on," she pushed herself. *What'll distract her?*

"What about the mummy?" John whispered to Wendy.

"The bones," muttered Wendy. "OK, so what about the bones? They're filled with life. She hates that, because she's the god of death—wait, that's it! The bones! She hid them because she's afraid of them!" Just as Wendy made her breakthrough, the nurse suddenly stopped. Slowly, she turned toward Wendy, John, and Cornrow. Her branded eye glinted. Something had finally caught her attention away from Peter.

"Run, Wendy!" shouted Peter, pointing at the wall of flies and moths that were blocking the door, as if he wanted her to take her chances trying to break through. But Wendy was too busy struggling with the zipper of the gym bag.

"No," said Wendy, "it's the bones. She'll be weak to the bones." In the pressure of the moment, Wendy couldn't open the bag. The sickly nurse, the plain-faced ageless woman, came nearer and nearer, coughing as she struggled forward. Wendy closed her eyes and winced, but the strike she expected never came. The goddess of death passed her by, and suddenly, Wendy knew—

"John!" she screamed. She knew that the Dark Lady had only one purpose: death. And those who cheated her by using the bonedust were all she cared to reckon with. She knew why Layla's windstorm—back when Simon had stolen the fourth mummy—had held back only John and Peter but didn't bother her or Simon. John had been the only other person to use the bonedust, to repair his arm, maybe even to escape death, and now *that* death was coming for him.

"John! Run!" screamed Wendy. But John was staring into the bewitching eye, mesmerized. He never saw the shimmer of the hook, hidden beneath a blue cardigan, slicing through the air. He realized what was happening too late, when death's cold stride had brought her across the room and gouged her hook into John's stomach. Silence. The nurse's branded eye twinkled with the light of John's life. With an detached shrug, the old demon governess let the boy's body slide off her hook, her gruesome medical instrument, and onto the floor of the office, on a discarded pile of gauze.

John looked up, blinking at his sister, then Peter and Tina. A dry heave seized in his throat. As he hung on death's edge, he said, "Front pocket . . . my bag . . ."

Wendy was struck mute. She could only stare at the horrifying sight and wish that it weren't true. Shell-shocked, she stood quivering. She would rather have had any thought shouting in her mind. Absolutely anything. Any thought would have been happy compared to this one. Her brother, John, was dead.

A WAKE

In the moments directly after John died, Peter and Tina were—maybe for the first time ever—unable to come up with something to do. For Tina, it was the reality of all that blood pooling under John and the regret that she had been so mean to the little nerd.

For Peter, it might have been the unexciting manner in which the school nurse walked up and put the hook into the kid's gut. There was no sense of climactic flare. No real nod to heroic convention. It was so utilitarian, so unfun. Frankly, it was a really boring way to play a swordfight, and he resented letting such a mousy-looking wench have it. But he knew better than to say any of this in front of Wendy. *Poor girl,* he thought. She really was the best one of all the girls he had known.

But Wendy, who was most ravaged by the sight, who was most wracked with tears, who was the only older sister John ever had and the only one who could have protected him—Wendy never stopped trying.

As soon as Nurse Neve walked past her toward John, Wendy had struggled with the gym bag's zipper. As the hook had punched the hole in John's belly, Wendy had yanked at the bag's seams and stuck her nails into it with grief. And as the feeble-looking nurse stood above the body and placed her black loafers on either side of a heap of soaked gauze, content to have avenged herself on a user of the bonedust, Wendy finally ripped open the bag and grabbed the mummy of the baby king.

Wendy threw herself toward the nurse, with an agility that could only be attributed to her rage. She held the skeleton above her shoulder, like a cannonball. Peter realized her plan and screamed, "NO!" He scrambled to intercept her, but he was a few steps behind. It took a split second for Wendy to bound toward the deathly nurse, for the nurse to see her and turn, and for Wendy to smash the mummy into her face.

The bones of the mummy immediately burst into a fine dust, a shimmering cloud enveloping the lady and all her many insects. There was a shriek. The branded eye shot out a light. Her hands tore at the flesh of her own face.

"No," said Peter, rushing up to Wendy. "NO!"

But it was too late for Peter to save the dust, and it was too late for the goddess of death to escape it. The life trapped in the bones of the fifth mummy had infected her. She stumbled to the floor, like a feeble old woman looking for her cane. She crouched in a corner, twitching, her every movement confirming the fact that death cannot die. That she was only temporarily down.

Wendy wasted no time rushing to John's body. She knelt down in the blood to check for a heartbeat. But that was futile, and even she knew it. Peter, too, was hysterical, looking for remnants of the dust.

"I can't believe this," he said, almost screaming at Wendy, who was shocked at this new treatment. "You destroyed the bonedust. That was the *whole* point!"

Peter roared with frustration. He put his ear to the ground, looking for any dust particles that might have settled. When he saw the gym bag lying on the floor, he seized it.

Tina walked over to Wendy, knelt down, and put her arms around her. Cornrow cautiously swatted his way through the now disbanding wall of moths blocking the door.

"We have to hurry," he said. "We probably only have a few minutes."

"Ah!" said Peter, with relief. "Look at this." Wendy and Tina looked up to see Peter fishing out a small piece of bone from the bottom of the gym bag. "It's just enough," said Peter. "One helping of eternal youth, as soon as I get my hands on that Simon."

Wendy barely heard Peter. She looked at John's helpless form and tried to make sense of the last words he had spoken. *The front pocket.*

Peter examined the tiny piece of the fifth mummy. He dropped the gym bag, and Wendy rushed for it, suddenly realizing what John had meant. She unzipped the front pocket and stuck her hand inside, desperately feeling around for an answer.

Then her hand found something hard, like a baseball bat. Except it wasn't a bat. Wendy looked inside. "Oh, my God," she whispered.

It was the bandaged leg of Marcus Praxis. The fourth bonedust.

John must have taken it from Simon during one of the afternoons they spent together playing video games or sorting through the exhibit. All that time when Simon thought John was his stooge, his follower, his worshipful disciple. Simon must have left the bone somewhere John could easily have access to it. "Genius." Wendy marveled at her little brother.

Wendy felt a breath over her shoulder. She clutched the leg to her chest and turned to find Tina hovering over her. "What do we have here?" Tina said. Wendy was too overwhelmed to speak. "You know," whispered Tina, "the bonedust can bring your brother back." Tina nodded in the direction of Peter, who was wrapping the other four bones together.

Wendy took the leg out of the gym bag so that it was in plain sight. It took Peter only about three seconds to see it and come barreling toward them. "Is *that* what I think it is?" He grabbed the leg, and without another word, Peter pulled out all the other bonedust. It seemed he didn't want to wait another second to mix his immortal cocktail.

"John," whispered Wendy. She allowed new hope to spring in her heart, and new gratitude, for all that Peter had done. For the way he always seemed to save the day, like John's favorite heroes. He had saved John's life once before, and he seemed to always be there for her. Even at a time so crazy and desperate as this.

Wendy stayed with John's body, holding his head in her lap, while Peter pulled out the four other bones and began grinding them and mixing them in a glass vial. She watched Peter's face, furrowed with concentration, as he hovered over his instruments. His sweat had stuck a few curls to his forehead. His jaw was adamant. But even so, he still had that boyish smirk.

Finally, Peter sat up and said, "Done." He held up the vial, shaking it a little for show. Inside, it looked like diamond powder. Wendy was almost shaking with joy with the idea that she would have her brother back, that he would be healed right here in this nurse's office, and that they would grow up together, that she wouldn't have to go back to her dad and tell him the unbearable news.

Then Peter stood up, wiped his knees, and said, "All right, let's get out of here."

Wendy was confused. She sat there gaping at Peter, who was obliviously putting what remained of the mummies back in his satchel. The toe he had used for decades was finished, as was the tiny morsel of the fifth bonedust, so only three members of the House of Elan remained. Wendy was still baffled.

Peter looked from Tina to Wendy and said in a cheerful tone, "Well? Everybody ready?"

Tina was the first to speak. She took an unsure step toward Peter and said, "Uh, Peter, what about the vial?"

Then Wendy added, "Are we going to take him to a safe place first?"

It was Peter's turn to be confused. "Who?"

"John," said Wendy.

"I don't know," said Peter in a reflective tone. He sat beside Wendy and put an arm around her. "How do you want to tell your dad?"

Peter looked back and forth from Wendy to Tina, trying to gauge whether this was the right answer. But watching him flounder like that, completely unaware of what they expected, was enough to break Wendy's heart. This whole time she had cradled John, expecting Peter to come to the rescue. The whole time they had known each other, she had become more and more infatuated, letting him further and further in. She knew she had trusted him more than anyone.

And now Peter had shown himself to be untrustworthy. To Wendy, that was a horrible feeling to have again. That feeling that she was worthless. That feeling that she was so common, so stupid, that no one felt any reason to love her. That feeling that she wasn't really needed by anyone and that she had left the one guy who cared about her for something entirely physical. Wendy felt her cheeks flush, her eyes bubble with hot tears.

"Peter," said Tina, "wouldn't the vial bring John back to life?"

"Well, yeah," said Peter, "but there's only one."

"So?" said Tina, trying to emphasize with her tone the gravity of the situation.

"So?" repeated Peter. "It's mine. It wouldn't be fair." Peter was gnashing his teeth. He turned to Wendy. "I'm sorry. You know how I feel about you. You know I would have shared it. I even offered once, remember? But there's only enough for one person, and *I'm* the one who's been searching for it all these years. I'm sorry, Wendy." He tried to hold her against him, but a guttural sob escaped her lips and she pushed him away.

Peter looked like a little boy, hurt at her rejection and determined to have his way all at the same time. It seemed that he had no idea how big a consequence this was. He looked as though he thought himself innocent, as if he believed that he had acted fairly and that it was *he* who was being hurt by Wendy's cruelty.

Tina tried to intercede. "Peter, he's—"

But Peter interrupted her, his voice much harsher than it had been with Wendy. "No. It wouldn't be fair. We're leaving." He took a few steps away from them.

As Wendy watched the exchange, she felt the betrayal and sadness turn to fury. He actually wanted to leave John dead on the ground. He actually thought it would be the right thing to do. Wendy rose to her feet and walked to Peter with tears still pouring from her eyes. When she reached him, her shoulders were still heaving. Then, in a low rumble, she said, "I trusted you." Without any fanfare, she slapped Peter across the face.

Peter, just stood there, shocked.

"But you're just a childish, selfish son of a—" She slapped him again, then again. It was the only sound in the awkward silence of the room.

Wendy yanked the vial from Peter's hand and walked back to John, holding her thumb tightly to seal the top. Peter leaped toward Wendy and grabbed her by the legs so that she fell forward and hit her arm hard against the sickbed. All the sweet charm of the previous weeks suddenly vanished. When she was on the ground, Peter grabbed Wendy's arm and swung her around, so she was facing up, then pinned her down with both his legs. She winced in pain, then pulled away, kicking hard at his legs while holding tight to the vial. She hoisted herself up on her elbows and spat in Peter's face.

For an instant, Peter was stunned.

Wendy broke free from under Peter and crawled the few feet toward her brother, reaching out the arm holding the vial.

Peter tried to grab the vial away from her. But it was too late.

Her hand trembled only once before she hoisted herself up and poured the dust over John's mouth. She watched, expecting him to revive in seconds. But even though the dust hung in the air, then was absorbed quickly into John's face, nothing more happened. John still lay unconscious on the floor. Wendy waited and waited for what seemed like ages. She shook him gently. But he didn't move.

Peter was still on the floor, panting like an angry beast. He slapped the ground with unveiled ferocity. Then he got up and began to pace the small room, like a lost child without a plan.

The group must have sat in silence for five minutes or so. No one thought to just leave. They were mesmerized by what Peter would do next.

Finally, Peter gathered himself together and looked toward John and at Wendy's expectant face as she sat with her brother. Tina and Cornrow eyed him cautiously.

Peter turned to Wendy. "It'll take a little while. Let's go." He pointed to Cornrow. "Carry the kid." Cornrow touched Wendy on the shoulder to get her to notice him and let him take John's body.

As Tina helped Wendy to her feet, a low groan made them all freeze. The Dark Lady was twitching more violently now. Suddenly, Tina dropped Wendy's arm and ran to Peter, pulling him away from the death god. Wendy wanted to laugh at the absurdity of it. Even after all this, Tina wanted to help him above all others. She was still willing to put herself in danger for *his* sake. Wendy thought about the way she had looked down on Tina's love for Peter, thinking that her own was of such better quality. But Peter hadn't felt much for either of them, and in the end, it was Tina who loved him unconditionally, even after he had shown himself to be so impossibly selfish.

The exhausted group silently walked out of the office and into the larger Marlowe attic space. Wendy stayed close to Cornrow, looking for any signs of life in John.

Whatever this all had been, this supernatural stuff with a book and a labyrinth and mummies and gods, Wendy knew it was finally over. All the stress of being the only ones to know about it, the fear of Simon stealing it all, the terror of darkness enveloping the real world, all of it poured out of Wendy along with her heartbroken tears for Peter.

And now all she wanted was for John to wake up. And by the time they found a safe spot in the attic to hide from any adults, he did. At first he groaned, then, with a gasp for air, he woke. Cornrow put him down. His feet were unsteady and his shirt was sopping blood, but his stomach was perfectly healed. Wendy laughed at the sight of John rubbing his belly. He nodded to Tina, winked, and said, "How do you like me now?"

Even Tina had to smile. John would be just fine.

Peter sent Cornrow to check on the nurse's office. He came back to the hiding place and said there was no sign of her anywhere.

"There wouldn't be," said Peter. "She's done. No one can ever use the bonedust to live forever, so she doesn't have to stick around."

Then they all went back to the office to clean up the evidence they'd left there. As they wiped up the blood and swept up the dead moths, John puzzled over every detail of the underworld secrets they'd just uncovered. Why did the underworld disappear? Where did the nurse go? Would she come back? Would Peter recognize her next time?

"Figures her hideout is up here, though," said John. "We should have known it was her. Not just the eye and the name, but *look* at this place. It's the opposite of the lowest point in the pyramid." The nurse's office in the attic was the highest point in Marlowe, just as Neferat's dark cave was situated at the tip of the upside-down pyramid. And just like that abysmal hole in the ground, the attic surrounding the office was filled with clutter, with boxes and old furniture where sarcophagi had been. Just like all the other places in Marlowe that corresponded to the underworld, this similarity unnerved Wendy—the way the underworld had molded itself to them, the way it had formed a negative Marlowe, a new hellish Marlowe, dark and backward, like an image imprinted on film.

"The girls' bathroom is just below the attic," added John. "I think there are pipes that lead right up from the bathroom to the attic, just like the way the women's castle was right above the cave, so it led down to Neferat's lair. See?"

"Would've been easier just to go directly through the nurse's office," said Wendy.

"If we'd known the dowdy nurse was *her*, I'm sure we would have," shot Tina.

As Tina looked around for a mop, Poet charged into the nurse's office dragging a sloppy wet Simon behind him. When he saw Peter, Poet stood at attention. He held Simon up by the collar and said, "Yo, Pete, check it out." He clearly wanted his RA to see his handiwork, but Peter didn't even acknowledge it. He just stomped out of the attic, slapping away Tina's arm as she reached out to console him. On his way out, he dropped a pile of bones he had collected in Neferat's cave—a toe, a forearm, a hand—bones from various mummies that he was planning to use to trick Simon, if it came down to that.

Simon wheezed, "Can you please call this hooligan off me?" Now that there was no more bonedust and no one left for him to threaten, his voice sounded whiny and pleading.

They turned their attention to the slimy assistant professor. "How'd it go?" said Tina.

"We came to an understanding," reported Poet.

It was time to go, to sneak back into the crowded hall between classes, as though nothing had happened. John peeled off his bloody shirt and threw it in the trash. He'd probably have to run shirtless to the boys' locker room to get his gym clothes. But Poet took off his Marlowe shirt and jacket and handed it to John.

John looked at the clothes, then at the shirtless guy in front of him. "What are you gonna wear?" he asked.

"Doesn't matter," said Poet, smiling, "You're one of us now, and LBs look out for their own."

John beamed. He proudly pulled the shirt over his head. It looked like a dress on him, but that didn't matter.

Wendy knew she would have to tell him about what had happened with Peter, but not yet. Besides, somehow, she knew John wouldn't mind. He hadn't admired the LBs because of Peter; that was for sure. John had plenty of heroes, but he'd never been foolish enough for

Peter to be one of them. In that way, Wendy mused with a little sadness, John had always been right. He'd always been right to suspect Peter.

Something told Wendy that the shirt, the acceptance, was all that John was looking for anyway. John bumped fists with both the LBs and strutted out of the attic. Wendy and Tina followed, and they immediately split up in the hallway crowd at the bottom of the stairs, each heading her own way.

When Simon found out that the fourth bone had been stolen, he began to rant and threaten John. But one warning glance from Poet was enough to shut him up. Besides, John didn't care. John knew when he brought the bone into the labyrinth in his gym bag that he was bringing the five pieces of bonedust together. He knew when he stopped at his locker for the bag that before the night was over, one of them would consume that immortal cocktail; he knew they wouldn't be throwing the bones out into the girls' bathroom for Simon to find.

He just didn't realize that the person consuming the dust would be *him*.

But in all that, Peter was nowhere to be found. He had disappeared as quickly as he had appeared. Wendy couldn't say she was sorry to see him go. But somehow, she couldn't say she was sorry to have met him, either. She couldn't say that it didn't make her chest tighten to imagine him all alone again. After all, regardless of how old Peter was, this was still a high-school romance. Even the worst experiences have parts that are really nice to think about. And the other parts, well, Wendy consoled herself, if you've got just a couple of happy thoughts in the end, you've done all right for yourself.

BEHIND THE WINDOWSILL

All nights, except for one, come to an end. That is to say, there's always that one night in every lifetime that stands out as endless—the night when all those nocturnal monsters, the creeping, slithering hazards of the dark, with names like shame and sorrow and guilt, grab ahold of you and won't let you sleep. In Wendy's case, the culprit was sheer humiliation.

She sat on her bed and tried to remember what her father had said. She had been so ashamed to tell him about Peter—to finally say out loud how she felt. Her father had said that he could never imagine a smarter daughter, or a braver or more loyal one. Why would someone as gifted as Wendy Darling ever cry over such things? Why would she waste her time caring about someone like Peter? Then he had recounted all the embarrassing Peter stories from his LB days, in hopes of cheering her up a bit. And so, Wendy had decided that she didn't care anymore about her borrowed house, or her father's crazy streak, or even the fact that her mother had left. She was nothing like her, and tomorrow she would call Connor. Maybe they could be friends again.

She barely remembered now what happened after she left the attic. She could see herself stumbling, confused and disoriented, through the halls, ignoring the spoiled gossipmongers who wanted to know about Peter. She kept thinking the same thought over and over again: *Peter was going to let John die*. Peter had shown himself for what he was, the most selfish boy she had ever met. How could she love him now?

Before leaving the attic, Wendy had taken the *Book of Gates* from Poet. She had run home, tears streaked down her face. She burned it in their fireplace when Professor Darling was still in school.

And now Peter was gone. He hadn't contacted Wendy for days, and she was sure she wouldn't hear from him again. He was off finding some other way to live forever, some other mythical fountain of youth. A part of her hoped that he would find it. But another part of her wished he would be lost in some faraway timeless place—that he'd never get the chance to come back to New York again.

Wendy did try to redeem herself with Tina. When the book went missing, Simon immediately called the police, making a huge spectacle of the robbery and blaming the new RA (the one who had yet to be fired) and the criminals from the boys' dorm. Wendy could see in his face that he wanted revenge. When the police arrested Tina a few hours later, it was Wendy who gave her an alibi, claiming that Tina had been giving her one-on-one advising. As for the Marlowe LBs, they all had their parents' lawyers on retainer. Tina left soon after to find Peter. She just quit her job and disappeared down a lonely alley off Lexington Avenue.

Professor Darling went back to teaching his famous unit on the five legends as if it were all just a story. But everything wasn't the same. Not anymore. John and Wendy knew now that their father was no kook. As for Professor Darling, he walked to school with his head held higher, because suddenly his kids didn't ask him to wait fifteen minutes after they had left the house. And John had finally accepted his father's Facebook friend request. And this morning, John's status update was John Darling is dusting antiquities with the Professor.

Simon went back to the British Museum, but what could he say? All that had been lost was one book, which most of them believed to be a copy anyway. They had already authorized its donation to the New York governor, so nobody really cared. Except for Simon, who lost his job as gubernatorial curator.

Meanwhile, in the basement of the Marlowe School, a statue of Neferat reclined silently next to a pile of discarded exhibit items. A few feet away, a marble that had once been its left eye rolled along the edge of the wall. A dark fog lingered in the basement, casting a layer of soot and filth over the objects in the room. Up above, the school had gone back to the cheerful place it had once been. But here in the basement, the darkness hung and waited, shapeless, motionless, its broken eye hidden from the world. Now, finally, the dark spirit could recover its strength, and it wouldn't have to be cooped up, away from the malleable world of the living that it so craved. Better yet, it wouldn't have to be satisfied with a weak and sickly body. There in the basement, the wicked nurse waited for her chance to haunt Marlowe once more.

That night, as Wendy turned over in her bed, she thought she saw something move—a long shadow in the windowsill. Was that a figure in the window? She looked again, but there was nobody there. She went back to sleep.

For Peter, too, this night had no end. As far as nighttime beasts are concerned, regret is a tough one to beat back. He lingered behind the glass for a few more seconds. Perched under Wendy's windowpane, he stopped and watched her brush her strawberry hair one last time. Then he darted away, a lonely, haunted look coloring his face.

❖❖❖

PETER

A HAPPY THOUGHT

A tin windup sparrow perches on a wooden jewelry box. A tiny handle on the box's side turns, turns, turns. A boy, Peter watches the bird hop across the box, chirping a three-note melody. His mother sits next to him, applying fairy dust to her cheeks. "The sparrow always comes back," Peter says. His mother says, "Mmm-hmm." The clock hands turn again and again. The sparrow sings the same timeless song. Nothing changes. Nothing changes.